I0614702

THE
CONGRUENT
WIZARD

Book Two of the Congruent Mage Series

The Congruent Mage Series

The Congruent Apprentice
The Congruent Wizard
The Congruent Dragon   *June 2018*

www.CongruentMage.com

The Xenotech Support Series

Xenotech Rising
Xenotech Queen's Gambit
Xenotech First Contact Day (novelette)
Xenotech What Happens
Xenotech General Mayhem

www.XenotechSupport.com

Dedication

To everyone who enjoyed
The Congruent Apprentice
for encouraging me to write
more fantasy and not being
too mad about the cliffhanger.

Copyright © 2017 by Paul David Schroeder

All Rights Reserved. This book or any portion thereof may not
be reproduced or used in any manner whatsoever without the
express written permission of the publisher except for the use
of brief quotations in reviews.

Cover and Map designs by Dan Paulson

ISBN-13: 978-0-9978319-3-1

Spiral Arm Press
1725 Carlington Court
Grayson, GA 30017

www.SpiralArmPress.com

What Has Gone Before

The First Ships sailed to the west more than two thousand years ago. Men and women from the White and Green Isles fled across the Ocean to Orluin to escape the invading legions of the Eagle People. They found the new continent empty of people and rich in timber, fish, and furs. With hard work, the forests were cleared and transformed into productive farms and noble estates.

A large river, which the exiles named the Abbenoth, flowed north to south midway along the coast. It became the dividing line between the kingdom of Dâron, established by folk from the southern White Isle, and the kingdom of Tamloch, established by the Green Isle's arrivals. Clans from the rugged north of the White Isle found familiar new homes in the high hills near the source of the Abbenoth and the mountains of southwestern Dâron.

Athican sages had been the first to unlock magestones' potential. They mapped the capabilities of the congruencies found inside the stones and learned how to direct them. Congruencies opened instantaneous connections between different points in space and allowed wizards to command fireballs, lightning strikes, blasts of cold, and tendrils of tight light that transferred force as well as illumination. Manipulating the properties of congruent interfaces allowed talented wizards to produce fields of force known as *solidified sound* for privacy and protection.

Several generations earlier, most Athican wizards had been captured and co-opted by the Roma, as the Eagle People called themselves. A few wizards fled west, away from the empire. They settled among the people of the White and Green Isles, where they taught the art of wizardry to promising pupils. When the Roma invaded, native-born wizards from the Isles helped build the great armada of First Ships so their people could escape Roma's legions and laws.

Wherever they traveled, Athican wizards introduced the royal game of *shah-mat*. Legend said they'd learned it from *magi* with tall hats from the east. Its ultimate source was reputed to be fabled Indja.

Conflicts between Dâron and Tamloch were frequent over the centuries, with armies carrying Tamloch's green-quatrefoil-on-gold banner and Dâron's dark-blue-dragon-passant-on-light-blue standard clashing frequently. Irregular troops from the northern and southern Clan Lands were often hired as mercenaries or simply swooped in to attack battle-weary soldiers from both kingdoms. Five hundred years later, that changed when the Roma pushed even farther west across the Ocean and claimed the fertile valley of the Abbenoth as their new Occidens Province.

The Roma provided both a buffer and a common enemy for Dâron and Tamloch. Over the *next* five hundred years, the three realms fought each other for territory and control of valuable resources, like iron ore deposits and sources of precious metals. Thanks to its superior military skill and discipline, the legions of Occidens Province held their own against the two kingdoms, even with a smaller population. Land might change ownership from one party to another each generation, but a balance, of sorts, was maintained.

Then a new group of settlers, led by King Bjarni the Great, arrived and settled in the far north of Orluin. They were Northmen from the boreal border of the empire and the Isle of Ice and Fire. Their fleet of dragonships and heavy cargo-carrying knarrs claimed largely-unoccupied territory north of Tamloch and named it Bifurland.

The Bifurlanders made their livings farming, fishing, trapping, and raiding—sometimes as far south as Dâron. They claimed vast lands to the north and west, but few of their people lived more than two days walk from the Ocean or the shores of the Hövlána, the Whale River, that runs east from the Inland Seas.

Centuries passed. Dâron expanded farther west, opening up the lands of the Coombe, a broad, protected valley ringed by modest mountains. Coombe-folk were simple farmers, glad to be far away from the intrigues of the kingdom's capital at Brendinas.

A custom arose and spread across rural Dâron. It was strongest in places near the western border, like the Coombe and the Rhuthro valley. When a young man or woman reached the age of sixteen, they would travel the kingdom for a year and a day, having new experiences and meeting potential mates.

Over time, a new equilibrium emerged—one where wars or significant raids occurred every generation, while the four major powers and the two Clan Lands found opportunities to trade as well as fight during the long lulls between battles.

During one such lull, Seren, the crown princess of Dâron, mysteriously disappeared. Ealdamon, the kingdom's master mage, set off to find her and was never seen again—until he returned twenty years later to help the royal armies of Dâron and Tamloch by freezing the Abbenoth so both kingdoms could attack and defeat Occidens Province.

In the two-thousand-and-sixty-seventh year since the First Ships landed in Orluin, Eynon of Haywall, a tall, thin young man of good character and great curiosity from the Coombe, set off on his wander year. At high noon on the day he left home, he found a magical artifact—a blue magestone in a silver setting—in the middle of a crossroads. The artifact belonged to Fercha, a powerful Dâron wizard, who'd lost it while dueling in the sky with Verro, Tamloch's Master Mage, the previous evening.

Eynon then meets Derry, a nearby landowner. He sends Eynon down the Rhuthro river toward Tyford, the second-largest city in Dâron, to find a wizard who can help him with what he's found. Derry also sends his daughter Merry, an experienced river guide, along to show Eynon the way. Merry is almost sixteen and will soon be ready to embark on her own wander year.

While traveling on the river, Eynon and Merry meet Gruffyd, an old friend of Merry's, and Nyssia, his fiancé. Both want to serve as members of the royal guard. They also meet Doethan, a wizard with a tower along the Rhuthro, who has been teaching Merry magic. Later, they meet and defeat four unscrupulous brothers from the Mastlands. Eynon nicknames them Oaf, Dolt, Fox and Fool. With luck and Merry's magic, the brothers are defeated before they can injure the two travelers.

Later, when they stop in a forest clearing to eat, Eynon is adopted by Chee, a raconette. Chee is the size of a kitten, with the paw-hands and markings of a raccoon and a long fluffy tail. He's fond of apples and dried cherries. Merry realizes that Chee is Eynon's familiar. Eynon and the raconette share a special bond.

As they float with the current, Eynon and Merry discover the entire Rhuthro valley is mobilizing for war with Tamloch. King Dârio, the capricious young king of Dâron, has summoned his forces to defend the realm. The two young people, with help from Chee, fend off attacks by a recruitment raiders who want to kidnap them and forcibly enlist them in the army.

On their trip downriver, Eynon demonstrates his cooking skills for Merry and both discuss their shared joy in reading books. They decide to become lovers and spend two nights together. Charms from hedge wizards ensure control over conception.

Then Doethan warns them *not* to go to Tyford, but to head back upriver to the mysterious Blue Spiral Tower they'd passed earlier. Eynon falls through a gate in the base of the tower and materializes in Melyncárreg, a region far to the west marked by tall snow-capped mountains, geysers, mud pots, striking waterfalls, and air that smells like rotten eggs. He is met by Damon, an old man who says he's a student at the master mage's academy, part of a huge castle perched near one of the falls. Eynon also meets Nûd, a big man not much older than he is, who says he's the master mage's personal servant.

Eynon begins to study wizardry with Damon, but he doesn't tell him about finding the artifact at the crossroads. Damon sends Eynon off to a distant basin filled with hot springs, geysers, mud pots and dangerous basilisks to find a magestone for crafting his own artifact. Eynon finds a large *red* magestone, not realizing wizards from Dâron traditionally use only blue magestones. In the process, he escapes a basilisk attack and is rescued by Rocky, a wyvern with an affinity for the taste of spheres of solidified sound.

Next, Eynon is sent to find gold to craft into a setting for his new red stone. It's a task that usually takes several weeks, but Eynon uses his creativity to collect enough gold in hours. He cuts his magestone, designs his setting, and integrates them both into a unique artifact, since no one has ever heard of a wizard with a red magestone.

Damon teaches Eynon the basics of offensive and defensive magic. Eynon, with help from the subtle capabilities of Fercha's blue magestone and the raw power of his own red stone, proves to be a magical prodigy.

Back at the Blue Spiral Tower along the Rhuthro valley, Fercha returns to find Merry distraught over Eynon's disappearance. She agrees to mentor Merry and help teach her magic. Merry assembles an artifact of her own, with a traditional Dâron blue magestone, and becomes particularly adept at working with beams of tight light guided by her fingertips.

Damon, Nûd, Doethan, Fercha, Merry and Eynon learn that Verro had been scouting out a source for green magestones in a quarry west of the Coombe because the sources of such stones in Tamloch are played out. Rumor has it that he's planning a raid to steal green magestones from the quarry.

Fercha, Merry and Doethan fly west from the Blue Spiral Tower to the Coombe before dawn. Damon and Nûd gate-in from Melyncárreg to the Blue Spiral Tower and follow them, leaving Eynon behind. Eynon triggers an alternate gate and reaches the Blue Spiral Tower as well, riding on Rocky. All six converge on the quarry just as Verro and a cohort of Tamloch wizards and soldiers swoop down to attack.

Chapter 1

The Battle of the Quarry

More than a dozen flying disks bearing green-cloaked wizards poured over the hundred-foot rim of the quarry. Most of the attacking wizards had one or two soldiers armed with swords and crossbows crowded around them on their yard-wide disks. Some soldiers carried buckets and shovels. The sun would be up soon, but for now, the only illumination came from a glowing sphere of light cast by Doethan.

Fercha shouted, "Verro!" and launched herself at the tall, dark-haired wizard leading the attack. He was standing alone on his disk and seemed to be directing the other green wizards.

Buckets and shovels? thought Eynon. *Of course,* he realized. *To collect green magestones!*

Merry, Ealdamon, and Doethan angled their flying disks to engage the rest of the attacking wizards directly, but Eynon remembered the strategy the gryffon had used on the old bull wisent and sent his flying disk above all the other combatants so he could evaluate the scene and attack from an unexpected direction. Below, he saw Fercha and a wizard in green robes who must be Verro exchanging lightning bolts that crackled, boomed and echoed off the quarry's walls. Rocky, the black wyvern who had somehow adopted him, was darting in and out of clusters of Tamloch wizards, using his body to disrupt their flight. Eynon's staff was still tucked into the scarf tied on the big beast's back.

Rocky flicked his tail right and left, knocking four attackers off their flying disks when they were close to the ground. Eynon saw them fall ten or twelve feet to the hard floor of the quarry. Only two of them got up.

Chee wasn't fond of the conflict and retreated from Eynon's shoulder to hide inside his jacket, making nervous *chee-chee-chee-chee* sounds while the battle raged below.

Merry and Doethan were following five Tamloch wizards as they dove to the quarry's floor, dropped off their soldiers, and swooped back up to a higher vantage point. The older wizard sent a congruency ahead of two of the five and used it to release torrents of water onto the retreating Tamloch wizards' spherical shields. With a gesture, he sent a gust of chilled air at the water that was so cold the liquid froze around the shields, blinding the wizards and weighing them down. The pair of attackers descended rapidly and broke their ice shells when they made hard landings.

Eynon was impressed by Merry's skill using thin beams of tight light. He hadn't learned that sort of magic, though Damon had used it against him. Apparently, the beams could carry force, not just light and heat. Merry used dozens of beams the width of her little finger to set the other three Tamloch wizards' spherical shields spinning, making the wizards who'd constructed them twist in dizzying circles.

Far below, Nûd was firing his crossbow. At first, he'd been aiming at wizards on flying disks, but now there were enough soldiers on the ground that he'd shifted his focus to them. Unfortunately, some of the soldiers were shooting back, so Nûd had retreated to crouch behind a quarryman's wagon ten yards behind his previous position.

Drawing on the expertise of his borrowed blue magestone and his red magestone's power, Eynon created a curved translucent red wall of solidified sound between the wagon and the Tamloch crossbowmen. Nûd immediately shifted from direct shots to arcing fire, sending his bolts over the wall and down into clumps of soldiers. The blue magestone somehow maintained his construct without continued attention from Eynon.

He turned to look for Damon, expecting to find the old wizard using spectacular magic to stop more than half the attackers at once. Instead, he saw Dâron's Master Mage casting a massive construct of solidified sound in the shape of a giant dome above the quarry, keeping out a third of the attacking wizards—including Verro—and preventing the ones below from escaping into the clouds.

Speaking of clouds, Eynon caught a glimpse of something purple inside a low cloud that was almost a fog bank. He didn't have time to investigate it, because the wizards above Damon's shield had seen him and were headed in his direction, ready to blast him with their own selected forms of wizardry.

Eynon deployed a defensive sphere of solidified sound around him, leaving a small hole in the back of the sphere to work offensive magic. He created a lens to accumulate magical energy, like the one he'd used against Damon during his testing yesterday, and prepared to take whatever the green-garbed wizards decided to throw at him. He pretended to cower in fear of his attackers. It wasn't hard to do, but he hoped they'd be the ones truly worried in a few seconds.

While his opponents were positioning themselves for attacks from all directions, Eynon was subtly moving small bubbles of transparent solidified sound under the edges of the flying disks controlled by the six green-clad wizards arrayed around him. His hands were balled into tight fists, keeping the bubbles tiny. Then he flung his hands open in a fast, fluid motion and all the bubbles rapidly expanded to ten times their original size, catching the green wizards by surprise and tipping their flying disks almost to vertical. Two managed to hang on, but the other four fell like rocks toward the quarry floor.

They didn't fall far, however. Damon's shield was in the way. The attackers from Tamloch hit Damon's construct and slowly slid along it, pulled down the shield's slope by their own weight. Eynon watched them try to slow their descent with their boots and palms pressing against the curved surface. The two remaining attackers were trying to tilt their flying disks back to horizontal by shifting their weight, so he set them rotating with nudges from their enlarged bubbles.

That should slow them down! thought Eynon.

He glanced below to check on Nûd. The big man was out of his own quarrels and was scavenging bolts the Tamloch soldiers had shot at him before Eynon put up his protective shield.

Eynon saw Nûd shoot one more missile from his crossbow, then start waving his arms and shouting. He was too far away to hear what Nûd was saying, but Eynon realized the soldiers with picks and shovels had filled most of their buckets with green stones— green *magestones* Eynon assumed—dug up from just beneath the quarry's floor.

One of the wizards guarding the soldiers holding shovels and buckets launched a fireball over her head. It exploded below Damon's hemispherical shield in a shower of glowing green sparks. Eynon watched Verro push Fercha away from him with a large expanding bubble of solidified sound. The tall green wizard dove toward the protective dome Damon had created. A tight cone of verdant energy shot from the magestone on Verro's cuff and punctured Damon's sphere like so much soap film.

Verro sped toward the floor of the quarry like a hook-beaked aloysius swooping down on a squirrel. The few remaining green-garbed wizards in the air followed close behind him.

Soldiers in green carrying weapons and full buckets joined the wizards on the ground and somehow found room on their flying disks. Stunned wizards and injured soldiers were placed on fallen flying disks slaved to the wizards who were still capable of flight. Before any of the Dâron wizards could react, Verro created a large circular black gate a foot above the ground. The Tamloch wizards and soldiers shot through it as fast as a herd of sprinting prong-horns. Verro was the last to leave. The gate closed with an audible snap behind him.

Below and to Eynon's right, Fercha shouted Verro's name in frustration. Then she added a series of words Eynon hadn't heard since one of his uncles had smashed his thumb with a hammer while trying to mount a wagon wheel back on its axle. Eynon smiled and filed the words away for future reference.

Thirty feet down to his left, Damon was creating a small, circular black gate of his own. He dropped through it like a rabbit down its hole. To Eynon's surprise, Merry followed Damon across the congruency's interface before it closed with its own snap.

Fercha paused her string of frustrated invectives. She had glimpsed the same hint of purple in a cloud above that Eynon had seen earlier. She leaned forward on her flying disk and sped up toward the suspicious cloud with Doethan a few heartbeats behind her.

Eynon watched a wizard in a strange purple robe emerge from the cloud and cast a third congruent gateway. Her dark hair was piled on her head in elaborate braids and her purple magestone pulsed in the center of a rectangular gold plate hanging around her neck. The purple wizard took one last look at the scene below and unhurriedly directed her flying disk through the gate. Fercha and Doethan followed her at high speed—then *that* gate snapped closed.

Nûd was shouting now—probably in frustration. He and Eynon were the only remaining defenders, but all the attackers and observers had left. Before Eynon could descend to reach Nûd, a small bubble of solidified sound under the leading edge of Eynon's flying disk inflated, flipping it from horizontal to vertical. Eynon was able to grab both of the flying disk's foot straps as he slid down and found himself hanging below his disk, which had turned completely over. He lost twenty-five yards of altitude and found his feet kicking below him like a flying frog churning butter.

Eynon felt like he might lose his grip and fall twenty feet onto hard stone if he didn't regain control of his flying disk quickly.

Chee picked that moment to crawl out of Eynon's jacket and sit on his head. The raconette's tail tickled the back of Eynon's neck and made it more difficult for him to concentrate on keeping his grip on his flying disk.

"Stop fooling around and get down here," shouted Nûd from below. "We've got work to do!"

Chapter 2

Nûd and Eynon

Eynon managed to regain control of his flying disk and didn't bother trying to right it. He descended at an angle to land in front of Nûd, taking a few short steps to cancel his forward momentum. Rocky was already on the ground nearby, resting from his exertions. Chee jumped off Eynon's head and scampered around on the ground, picking up fragments of green rocks.

"Sorry," said Eynon. "I didn't expect one of the green wizards to use my own trick against me, especially with a time-delay trigger."

"It pays to figure out how to defend against your own tactics," said Nûd, "because I guarantee they *will* be used against you."

"That's good advice," said Eynon. He lowered his flying disk and put it down, then double-checked to make sure everything in his pack was still secure before strapping his flying disk on top of it.

Nûd nodded.

"What's next?" asked Eynon.

"Help me recover quarrels," said the taller man. "I wish Damon, Doethan, and my mother had stopped to plan, instead of popping out through random gates without thinking. Was the young redhead your girlfriend?"

Eynon wasn't expecting Nûd's question. He flushed and replied in a rush without thinking.

"Uh huh," he said. "Her name is Merry. She's from Applegarth and she's incredibly smart and well-read and wonderful. She taught me my first spells. We were traveling downriver to Tyford together."

Nûd nodded again, then smiled at Eynon's enthusiasm.

"My quarrels have blue and white fletching," said the big man. "Pick up any of those you find and any of the Tamloch quarrels that are close to the same length. Once that's done, *we* can plan."

"Right," said Eynon. He started to search for Nûd's quarrels near where the Tamloch soldiers had been digging. "Found one," he said, after a few seconds. Chee put down the green stones, joined Eynon, and helped recover more quarrels.

"There should be at least a dozen," said Nûd, "I had eighteen, minus the five or six that hit their targets."

Eynon continued to look. He could feel the magical energy of more green magestones emanating from the holes around him.

"Where did everyone go?" asked Eynon as he kept searching.

"I'm not sure," answered Nûd, "but if I had to guess, I'd say that Damon and your *girlfriend* are in Riyas and Doethan and my mother are somewhere in Occidens Province. Nova Eboracum, maybe."

Eynon tried to ignore Nûd's teasing about Merry.

"Why would Damon and Merry take a gate to the capital of Tamloch?" he asked. Then he answered his own question with another question. "To see what that green wizard—*Verro?*—was up to?"

"That's my bet," said Nûd. "Damon has friends—spies, really—in Riyas. He probably wants to check with them in person."

"Why do you think Fercha and Doethan are in Eagle People territory?"

"The purple robes are a giveaway," said Nûd. "The Eagle People are the only ones to wear that shade."

"Her magestone was purple, too."

"That's the color Roma wizards prefer," said Nûd, "though they sometimes use black ones."

"Made from obsidian," said Eynon.

Nûd eyes widened when he looked at Eynon. It seemed like he was surprised at himself for being surprised Eynon knew the word.

"What's Roma?" asked Eynon.

"That's what the Eagle People call themselves."

"Thanks."

Eynon had pretty much figured that out from context, but he appreciated the confirmation. There wasn't much he could do to help Merry, or Damon or Doethan or Fercha, for that matter. He tried not to worry and hoped Merry and Damon would get along well, though he had his doubts about Merry putting up with Damon's teaching methods. He kept picking up quarrels and mused that it was far better than picking quarrels, like he did with his little sister. Braith was probably up now, feeding the chickens. She wasn't far away, and neither were his parents.

"Would you like to stop at my place for breakfast while we plan?" asked Eynon. "My family lives nearby and my parents are great cooks."

"Breakfast sounds great, and I'd *love* to meet your sister," said Nûd. "She has long braided red hair and freckles, right?"

Now it was Eynon's turn to smile. Nûd had been isolated two thousand miles away to the west in Melyncárreg, the site of Master Mage Ealdamon's castle and a major school for Dâron's wizards, for many years. He hadn't had much of a chance to meet young women close to his own age. Braith would certainly appreciate Nûd's attention, even if she was too young for courting.

"Red hair in braids, freckles, a lovely singing voice, and can shoot a plum off a post at a hundred yards with a longbow. Mind your manners around her—she's only fourteen."

"You will find me the epitome of decorum," said Nûd. "But forgive me if I admire her."

"There's a lot to admire," said Eynon.

When he thought about it, Eynon realized he wasn't just saying that because she was his sister. Braith *was* growing up and would soon be on *her* wander year. He hoped she didn't settle too far away from Haywall. Then he realized *he* was likely to end up far from his home village in a wizard's tower somewhere—maybe one he shared with Merry, if they both survived the upcoming conflict with Tamloch. He couldn't see *any* king, let alone one as mercurial as young King Dario, tolerate an invasion and theft of magestones by a foreign power, which would likely escalate and accelerate the next war.

"Here's the last Tamloch quarrel," said Nûd, tugging a green and yellow-fletched bolt from the wooden side of the quarryman's wagon.

"And here's the twelfth one with blue and white fletching," said Eynon, stooping to pick it up.

"That should be all of them. Is it time to leave for breakfast?"

"If Rocky is awake," said Eynon.

The black wyvern opened one eye, then the other, and yawned, showing impressive dentition. Eynon was glad Rocky liked him. The great beast flexed its wings and allowed Nûd and Eynon to board. Chee held on to a pair of protrusions farther up the wyvern's neck where he had a good view. After a glance to confirm everyone was secure, Rocky launched himself into the air and Eynon directed him southeast toward Haywall.

I've got to land away from the milking barn, thought Eynon. *Half the cows would go dry if they saw a wyvern.*

It seemed like less than a minute for Rocky to fly the two-and-a-half leagues from the quarry to Haywall. Eynon used a ball of tasty, magic-infused solidified sound to guide the wyvern down to a stone square just east of his home. Rocky landed to one side of the village well in the center of the square. Several cottages, including Eynon's, screened Rocky from the milking barn. Most people in Haywall were still in the barn or making breakfast, but Braith was near the middle of the square chasing a chicken who seemed determined to drown itself in the well instead of peck at grain.

Chee jumped back on Eynon's shoulder. When Nûd and Eynon stepped down from Rocky's back, Braith was there to meet them, holding the confused chicken upside-down by its feet.

"What are *you* doing back?" she said, smiling at Eynon. "Wander years are supposed to be a *year* and a day, not a *week* and a day. And who's your friend?"

"I'm Nûd," said the big man, trying to stand tall.

"Not you," said Braith. "The wyvern."

Her eyes were dancing and Nûd gave Braith a slight bow to acknowledge her teasing.

"That's Rocky," said Eynon, sweeping his arm to indicate the wyvern.

"Who's your other friend?"

Nûd puffed his chest out, waiting to be introduced.

"This is Chee," said Eynon.

The little raconette puffed his chest out, imitating Nûd. Then Chee bowed and shifted to Braith's shoulder from Eynon's.

The little beast reached down and shook Braith's hand, then offered her a damp dried cherry.

"I wouldn't eat that," said Eynon. "It's probably been in his cheek pouch."

Braith rubbed Chee under his chin and the raconette's body seemed to vibrate in happiness.

Eynon finally took pity on Nûd and introduced him.

"This is my new friend, Nûd."

"Pleased to meet you. I'm Braith." She gave Nûd a slight bow of her own. "And this—" she indicated the chicken, "—is dinner."

"Or maybe breakfast," said Eynon. "Do you think we could talk Mother and Father into making us some?"

"If it will give them a chance to hear what you've been doing since you left home, I think you can count on it," said Braith, "though it might be wiser if Rocky went hunting for deer on top of one of the mountains first. People might talk."

Eynon laughed. He was sure other village dwellers had spotted the big wyvern and tongues would be telling the tale for several decades to come.

"Would you like a nice white-tailed deer for breakfast, Rocky?" he asked.

The wyvern's head bobbed up and down. Eynon still wasn't sure how much the beast understood, but there seemed to be some sort of bond between wizard and familiar. He sent the sphere of solidified sound arcing up towards the mountains to the east and Rocky rose to follow it. Eynon hoped he would find a wild deer, not some farmer's prize ewe to dine on.

Braith motioned to Nûd.

"Our house is this way."

Nûd and Eynon followed his sister and the chicken, the younger man grinning at the older.

Braith turned and took in her brother's red magestone in its intricate gold setting.

"You *have* been busy, haven't you?"

Chapter 3

Damon and Merry

Merry bumped into someone—Ealdamon, she assumed—and they bounced off something—probably a wall. It was hard to tell because she couldn't see. It was as black as Queen Cashelle's cats wherever they were. From the echoes of her footsteps, she could tell the ceiling was low. She smelled cider and beer.

"Where are..." she began to ask. A hand covered her mouth and Merry could feel warm breath near her ear.

"Quiet, girl," whispered a voice she thought was Ealdamon's. "Wait until I see if it's safe to speak."

Merry nodded and the hand moved away from her mouth. She felt Ealdamon shift around her, then heard the distinctive creak of old wooden stairs behind her. A crack of light appeared and Merry turned around. The old wizard had lifted a trap door at the top of the stairs and was peering out into whatever space was above them.

As her eyes adjusted to the low light, Merry could see huge tuns of cider, wine, and beer along one wall of a low-ceilinged cellar. They were nearly as tall as she was. She spotted a loading ramp at the far end of the space where the huge casks could be brought into the cellar and a square platform with ropes and pulleys around it that could serve to raise a tun to the next level. Taffaern's inn had a similar cellar in Tyford.

Merry increased the glow of her new magestone and used its light to read what was burned into the ends of the casks. *Sammadd's Ale,* read one that smelled like beer. *Five Lakes' Grapes' Blood* was the label on a large tun of wine. She ran her finger around the tap. It was a sweet and fruity red. Merry remembered the Five Lakes region was in western Tamloch, at least according to her father's maps. The lakes, which looked like five fingers on a hand, were in territory that had frequently passed from Tamloch to Dâron and back again. She thought they were under Tamloch's control at present.

She nearly stumbled over a smaller barrel stored horizontally on a short X-shaped frame that kept it off the ground. It looked familiar. Merry leaned in to read the logo etched in its lid, then pulled back in a hurry.

Applegarth Select, read the inscription.

How did Applegarth cider end up in a cellar next to Five Lakes Grapes' Blood wine? Merry wondered.

She didn't have long to think on the question. Ealdamon was coming back down the stairs.

"There's no one upstairs in the pantry," said the old wizard. "It's safe to leave. Follow me."

They ascended the stairs together and both pushed the trapdoor up. Merry held it in place for Ealdamon to exit, then he returned the favor and gently lowered the door back into place. The room above was wide and deep. The mechanism for raising tuns of beer and wine was in the back and a strong, iron-banded oak door was at the opposite end.

"You're Ealdamon?" asked Merry.

"Call me Damon," said the gray-haired wizard. "Ealdamon makes me feel old."

"But you *are* old," said Merry.

"Not you, too," said Damon. "It was bad enough to hear that from Eynon."

Merry smiled.

"Sorry, Damon."

"Whatever made you decide to follow me to Riyas?" asked Damon. "I'd planned to make this a solo reconnaissance."

"It seemed like the right thing to do. I'm Merry, by the way."

"Hrrumph," said Damon. "I'm seldom of that disposition—not for two decades, anyway."

"What happened in those ancient times to change your outlook?" asked Merry.

She waggled her eyebrows and one corner of Damon's mouth turned up for an eye blink.

"That's too long a tale for present circumstances, lass," he said.

"For now, I need to see if the kitchen and common room at the *Blue Whale* are occupied."

"On the other side of that door?" asked Merry, indicating the stout oak portal. "Let me."

She went through the words and gestures needed to invoke the listening spell and put her ear to the door.

"There are two people in the kitchen—one large and one small, from their voices and breathing," she whispered. "The common room sounds empty. I can't even hear spoons scraping bowls."

Merry stood up and crossed to move next to Damon.

"Why are we in Riyas, by the way? Are we chasing Verro?"

"I'm trying to find out what he's up to first," said Damon. "Verro plays a long game—but so do I. Once we know, *then* we can act."

"That makes sense," said Merry. Her tone was uncertain, however, as if she wasn't sure anything Damon had said truly made sense. "What's the *Blue Whale?*"

"An inn and tavern near the royal palace," Damon replied. "It's a great place to hear gossip."

"Hmmm..." said Merry, remembering the bench on the street of the jewelers in Tyford where she liked to read—and listen.

Damon moved to open the door. Merry grabbed his elbow.

"Stop," she said. "I told you there were two people in the kitchen."

The older wizard pushed her gently aside and pulled the heavy oak door open on silent, well-oiled hinges.

"Don't worry. They're friends, of a sort."

"Of a sort?" came a deep voice from the kitchen. "And you're a wizard *of a sort,* old man."

The door opened all the way and Merry saw a short man with a fringe of fox-tail colored hair wearing a stained linen shirt, green breeches, and a green apron. His mid-section resembled the sort of cider barrels that would last a farm family for a year. Next to him, in a similar outfit but wearing a long green skirt instead of breeches was a tiny woman whose waist was smaller than one of the short man's upper arms.

"Don't tease him, Tibbo," said the woman. "He'll turn you into a toad."

"Never, dear Tannis," said Damon. "I'd have to change him into the namesake of your inn to use up all of him in the transformation."

"I'd be more of a dolphin than a whale if you tried," said Tibbo. "Good to see you, you old scoundrel." He shook Damon's hand then gave him a crushing hug. Tannis stood on her tiptoes and kissed Damon's cheek when Tibbo had finished.

"Who's the young lady?" asked Tannis, finally noticing Merry.

"Don't tell me you have *another* grandchild," boomed Tibbo.

"To the best of my knowledge I'm no relation," said Merry, stepping forward.

"You're still welcome at the *Blue Whale,* lass," said Tannis. "Would you like some breakfast?"

"That would be lovely. I'm Merry—from Applegarth."

"Are you now," said Tannis with a soft lilt that made it seem like a question.

"Breakfast sounds like a fine idea," said Damon.

"I'm sure you're ready for some good home cooking with the way Damon feeds his apprentices," said Tannis, looking Merry up and down.

"I'm not one of..." began Merry.

"You can see she's perfectly healthy—not wasting away from lack of nourishment," Damon interjected. "You know I love your cooking, dear lady, but I'm in a bit of a rush and need information while we eat."

"I'll bar the front door and set four places at table," said Tibbo.

As he moved out of the kitchen and into the common room, Merry could see the big man was light on his feet. She spotted a heavy cudgel leaning against the back of the bar on the other side of the pass-through from the kitchen and expected Tibbo was quite effective at quelling any sort of disturbance inside the inn. He effortlessly placed the thick length of wood by the front door in a pair of iron brackets, ensuring no one would enter from that direction with anything short of a battering ram.

"How do fried duck eggs, sausage and fresh manchet bread sound to you, dear?" Tannis asked Merry.

"Wonderful," Merry responded.

"It might be worth lifting a knife and fork for," said Damon.

"Feed him gruel and bacon drippings," said Tibbo from the common room. "I'll eat his eggs."

"You'd eat an old shoe if someone put gravy on it," Damon responded.

"But with Tannis as my wife I don't have to," said Tibbo. "She's the best cook in Tamloch, nay, in all of Orluin."

"There's a young man I know I'd put up against her for that honor," said Damon.

Merry put her hand on the old man's shoulder. He turned to her and she smiled. He was talking about her Eynon, she was sure.

"What can I do to help?" asked Merry.

"You can slice the bread," said Tannis. "It's in a box behind the dough trough."

Merry spotted a long, narrow and deep carved piece of wood the size and shape of a child's toboggan leaning against a kitchen counter a few yards down. Her mother had one just like it for kneading the big batches of bread dough a household went through every week. This one had knotwork along its outside edges. Merry was glad her mother's wasn't ornamented. The tiny crevices inside the intertwining designs would be a wolf and a bear to keep clean. She pumped water in the sink across from the hearth and washed her hands. Then she found the bread box, opened it, and took out a round loaf near the front.

"This one?" she asked, holding the bread up for inspection.

"That's it," said Tannis. She'd already put a huge soapstone griddle on the coals, which Damon helped along with a touch of fire magic. A string of a dozen sausages hung from a wrought-iron hook near the griddle and the tiny woman was cracking eggs into a glazed green bowl. "Use the knife on the left side of the block to slice it."

Merry found the knife and a cutting board and proceeded to methodically cut the round loaf into neat, even slices. The manchet bread was white, made from fine, double-sieved flour instead of whole wheat flour with husks included. Her mother only made manchet bread on special occasions. She cleaned off the knife and returned it to its place in a block, then carried the cutting board and sliced bread to Tannis. The tiny woman was pouring eggs on the griddle next to the sizzling sausages.

"Put that bread here beside me," said Tannis, patting a four-legged wooden footstool to her left. Merry did as she was instructed. "Now be a dear and grate me some cheese," said Tannis, pointing at a white block on a plate resting on the edge of the hearth.

Merry removed her dagger from her belt and sliced thin slivers from the block of cheese until she'd collected a sizable stack. "Will this do?" she asked.

"It's perfect," said Tannis. "Add the cheese to the eggs, please."

With the back of her dagger, Merry pushed the cheese onto the cooking eggs. Tannis was scrambling them about with a flat metal turner in one hand and turning sausages with a long, two-tined fork in the other. When all the cheese was distributed, Merry put the plate with the remaining cheese back on the hearth. She noticed the left half of the broad soapstone griddle was empty.

"Should I put the bread on to toast?" asked Merry.

"Ask Damon how he wants his," Tannis replied. "I like toast, but my Tibbo doesn't. He says it makes bread taste like burnt beer."

"That doesn't make any sense," said Merry.

"Neither does Tibbo half the time," said Tannis. "He finds it helpful to be underestimated."

Merry got up and walked across the kitchen to lean over the pass-through to the common room.

"Do you want your bread toasted, old man?" she asked with a smile in her voice.

"Yes, infant," Damon replied, "if you can manage not to burn it."

"I'll try my inexperienced best," said Merry, resolving not to tease Damon quite so much.

She returned to kneel next to Tannis.

"Toast for three," she said.

"That means toast half the loaf," said Tannis. "Tibbo will eat the other half."

"Guard your plate or I'll eat *your* bread, too, toasted or not," said Tibbo.

Merry could hear the smile on his face even though he was out of sight.

"Come out and help carry the food to the table," Tannis commanded. Tibbo joined his wife by the fire, took a pair of thick wool mittens off the wall, and picked up the entire soapstone griddle before carrying it to one of the long trestle tables in the common room. Damon and Tibbo had set places with trenchers and salt for eating, plus pewter goblets filled with strong ale for drinking. The soapstone griddle was placed in the center of the table and where everyone could help themselves.

Merry carried the untoasted manchet bread slices to the table and Tannis followed with a crock of butter marked with a four-leafed clover on top. That made Merry think about the crock of Flying Frog Farm's butter she'd shared with Eynon. She felt her cheeks get red at the memory of that and what had happened after and hoped the others would attribute her flushed face to her work at the hearth.

Once they were all seated, Tannis passed around the turner and sausage fork. When it was Merry's turn, she took a generous portion of eggs, two sausages, and two slices of toast. When she spread butter on the manchet bread, its white surface turned gold.

Damon lifted his glass and so did Tannis and Tibbo. Merry lifted hers a second later.

"To the Blue!" said the old wizard.

"To the Blue!" echoed Tannis and Tibbo, with Merry joining in a beat late with, "The Blue!"

Did they mean the inn? The Blue Whale? Then she understood. *The Blue was the Kingdom of Dâron. She should have realized it. She was in the midst of spies.*

"Well," said Damon, clearing his throat after swallowing a bite of sausage.

"You probably want to know what Verro is up to," said Tibbo.

"Of course I do," said Damon.

"I'm not the one you need to talk to, then," Tibbo continued. "Sal's your man. He's been working in Verro's tower for a fortnight, pouring drinks and cleaning goblets."

"Fine," said Damon. "How soon can I talk to him?"

An odd pattern of raps sounded on the front door. One rap. Another. Then two, close together. Then three. Then five.

Merry recognized the sequence. She hadn't heard it since she was a child. *But it couldn't be...*

"Sal has a good head on his shoulders, but he can be quite melodramatic with his secret knocks," said Tannis. She laughed like a small bird chirping.

Tibbo got up to unbar the door and Merry followed. The short, barrel-chested innkeeper removed the length of wood and a tall, well-proportioned young man with curly red hair, a pointed beard, and a bright smile on his face stepped inside.

His jaw dropped when he saw Merry. Her eyes were wide. After a long second, she spoke.

"Salder? I thought you were dead."

Chapter 4

Fercha and Doethan

The sun was farther up in the sky when Fercha and Doethan emerged from the gate. Ahead of them, the purple-robed wizard was hovering above a cluster of other wizards on flying disks moving in strange patterns and smacking balls of solidified sound with an odd assortment of magical constructs.

There seemed to be four levels of play, if what they were doing was indeed a game, and Doethan became so entranced with the players' motions that he stopped following the purple-robed wizard. Fercha had to circle back to get his attention and redirect his focus back on their quarry.

Doethan's distraction didn't matter, as it turned out, because the purple-robed wizard moved her flying disk to join them.

"Welcome to Nova Eboracum," said the wizard in purple robes. Small wisps of dark hair escaping her beaded braids danced around her face in the wind. The purple magestone on the gold plate resting on her neck glowed with a steady light. "You're Doethan," she said. "We've got quite a lot of information about you."

She smiled at Doethan. He didn't notice.

"And you must be *Fercha*. Perhaps you'll be able to fill in the blanks on our records of your career during your visit with us, *domina*."

Fercha spoke in her usual blunt manner while Doethan had difficulty shifting his attention away from the wizards below.

"Why were you spying on Dâron?"

The Roma wizard laughed. The ease of her voice as she did, made it clear she laughed often.

"A rhetorical question, I'm sure," said the wizard in purple. "Everyone spies on everyone else these days—and always has. If it's any consolation, I wasn't spying on you, I was spying on Verro."

Now Fercha laughed.

"That's much more understandable," she said. "Trouble buzzes around Verro like flies on carrion."

"From that reaction, perhaps my records about your relationship with Prince Verro are incomplete," said the purple-robed wizard.

"He's not a prince," said Fercha quickly. "He gave that up when he chose to learn wizardry. And your records are woefully out of date regarding my feelings about that son of a..."

"What are the rules?" interjected Doethan, joining the conversation at last.

Fercha stared at Doethan like he'd grown a second head.

What was it about serving as the leading mage of Dâron that turned every man filling the role into a complete idiot? she considered.

"For that matter," said Fercha, "since you seem to know so much about *us,* who are *you?*"

The wizard in purple robes first answered Fercha, then Doethan.

"My apologies. My name is Laetícia. I'm the spymaster for the governor of Occidens Province." Laetícia moved closer to Doethan and spoke louder to be sure she got his attention. "The game is *qua-qua, quattuor quadratum,* and the rules are quite complex."

"Ah, so *you're* Laetícia? Your fame proceeds you," said Fercha. "It's called four square?"

"Correct," said Laetícia. "And sometimes the duck game, because *qua-qua* easily becomes *quack-quack.*"

"*That's* the duck game?" asked Doethan. "I've heard about it, but never seen it played. It's supposed to be how the wizards of the Eagle People practice for war."

"Also correct," said Laetícia. "There are four rising square levels: black, green, blue and gold for earth, crops, sky and sun, with a congruency in the center of each. Teams of wizards push balls of solidified sound through lower congruencies and they come out through one a level higher. The team that pushes the most balls through the most congruencies when all sixteen balls have been played is the winner."

"But what about..." began Doethan.

"Please," said Laetícia. "Come to the governor's palace with me to break your fast and I will have one of the master *qua-qua* strategists of the province instruct you in the nuances of the game."

Doethan nodded at Laetícia and returned to following the motions of the players below.

"I take it this is more a command than an invitation," said Fercha.

"One thing our records did say about you was that you were wise—at least in some matters," said Laetícia.

Fercha smiled, letting Laetícia's implied criticism roll off her like water off the back of a goose.

"And if we attempt to gate out?"

"There are more than thirty well-trained wizards just below us, counting players, officials, and spectators," Laetícia replied. "I wouldn't advise it."

Fercha tugged hard on the sleeve of Doethan's robe, tilting his flying disk and getting his attention.

"It's time to go," she said. "We're having breakfast at the palace. You can learn more about *qua-qua* there."

"Very well," said Doethan reluctantly.

"This way," said Laetícia, indicating the stone citadel and city built at the tip of the island below, near where the Abbenoth River emptied into the sea.

"Do you think you'd be able to arrange a meeting with the provincial governor?" asked Fercha, thinking of opportunities to enlist the help of the wizards and legions of the Eagle People in the upcoming war with Tamloch.

"I'm certain we can," said Laetícia.

"How can you be so sure?" asked Fercha.

"He trusts my judgment explicitly," said Laetícia. "And he's my husband."

* * * * *

"I never knew I liked pickled lark's tongues," said Doethan.

"It's the honey, almond milk and saffron reduction that makes the dish," said the governor, Quintillius Marius Africanus, a *very* tall, well-muscled man with tightly-curled graying black hair who looked like he was carved from a block of obsidian.

The provincial governor had a ready smile and a strong voice. He had insisted Fercha and Doethan must call him Quin, and they obliged. Quin and Laetícia had been plying them with wine and delicacies, seated at padded wooden chairs around a mosaic inlaid table, rather than reclining on couches.

Fercha was happy to be sitting up. She'd always thought it was uncomfortable to eat lying on her side. She drank sparingly and kicked Doethan's shins under the table when the governors' servants had filled his goblet a third time. The fundamental rule of diplomacy—and espionage—was to say little and listen more. Doethan was saying a lot, but Fercha was thankful it was only about *qua-qua*.

For her part, she thought the complex game might have a lot to do with why the Roma wizards were more effective in combat than those from Dâron and Tamloch. The two kingdoms' crown wizards were masters of palace intrigue, not battle strategy, and the soldiers who led their armies played drinking games, not *shah-mat*. Fercha had seen a *shah-mat* board and carved onyx pieces in a library they'd passed on the way to the dining chamber. She'd need to keep her wits about her.

"So the young king wants to make a name for himself and create his own legacy," said Quin as he spooned fish sauce on Doethan's salmon fillet with dill and white wine. "I did the same when I was young. Did I tell you about taking Timbuktu for the emperor?"

Laetícia whispered to Fercha. "He tries to work that into every conversation with someone new."

Fercha smiled and nodded, sure that both she and Doethan were being squeezed for information by a pair of masters.

"Is that what earned you a governorship?" asked Doethan, who seemed to have shaken off his fascination with *qua-qua* for the moment.

"Indeed it did," said Quin. "You should have been in Roma to see my triumph."

"He says that to everyone new, too," whispered Laetícia.

"Is that why Quintillius was sent twenty-five hundred miles away to be a governor?" asked Fercha softly.

"Crossing the Ocean *is* a bit more of a logistical challenge than crossing the Rubicon," replied Laetícia. "Why were Verro's soldiers digging rocks from a quarry in Dâron?"

Fercha smiled, but only to herself. Build intimacy, then pump for information. That was what Verro had done to seduce her so many years ago. He'd even married her before she'd slept with him. She smiled to herself again, thinking of Verro pumping away, then trying to worm secrets of Dâron's Conclave of Wizards out of her during pillow talk.

"I don't know," said Fercha. "Perhaps they needed green stones for a mosaic floor in a new palace."

"Perhaps," said Laetícia.

"Do you think Dârio will send his troops up the Brenavon or the Moravon?" asked Quin, trying a similar tactic on Doethan.

"Who can tell?" said Doethan. "He's a fool, and follows only his own counsel."

"An unpredictable enemy can be a challenging one," said Quin.

"For his own people, as well as his opponents," Doethan replied.

All four of them laughed. Laetícia made a subtle gesture with one hand and the servants withdrew from the room.

"Enough fencing," she said. "It's fortunate that two senior members of the Dâron Conclave, including their acting Master Mage, followed me through my gate to Nova Eboracum. I had to keep it open long enough for the two of you to enter, after all."

They all laughed again, Fercha and Doethan nervously. *What was Laetícia up to?* Fercha wondered. The spymaster continued.

"We know that you know Tamloch's source of magestones in the Green Mountains is mined out. Without new magestones, they wouldn't be able to train new wizards, giving Dâron a long-term advantage. We don't know how many usable green magestones they were able to gather from the quarry in the west of Dâron. Certainly fewer than they would have if you and your fellow wizards hadn't been present."

Fercha and Doethan had the presence of mind to nod sagely, as if Laetícia was only telling them things they already knew.

"It is in the best interest of Occidens Province and the emperor to have Dâron and Tamloch evenly matched and at each other's throats instead of one decisively defeating the other," added Quintillius Martius in his deep, powerful voice.

"Therefore..." said Laetícia.

"...the wizards and legions of Occidens Province are prepared to assist Dâron in the coming conflict," Quin continued.

"With a proper enticement," added Laetícia.

"Enticement?" said Fercha. "Bribe, you mean."

"Why do you think Dâron needs your help, not Tamloch?" asked Doethan.

Laetícia raised an eyebrow and lowered her chin the length of an apple seed.

Quin answered Doethan.

"Because, as you say, your king is a fool."

Doethan shrugged, accepting the characterization of his monarch.

"And because King Túathal of Tamloch is a wily old wolf, smart enough to get others to fight his battles for him," Quin added.

Doethan and Fercha both nodded, keeping their faces like stone to avoid revealing anything that might damage Dâron.

The four of them sat like statues for a few moments before Fercha gave in first. She turned up her palms on either side of her plate of sweet *libum* cakes.

"What do you mean?" she asked.

"Túathal has paid the dragonship raiders of Bifurland to attack Brendinas in force," Laetícia replied. "They should be there in days."

"Oh," said Doethan.

"What sort of enticement did you have in mind?" asked Fercha.

Laetícia leaned forward to share her proposal.

Chapter 5
Nûd and Eynon

Eynon's family fell in love with Chee. The raconette charmed Eynon's mother by helping her set the table and assisted Eynon's father with cooking by passing him bowls of chopped herbs to add to the eggs he was scrambling in a large frying pan above hot coals. The small beast had set a place at the table for himself and imitated Eynon's every move as he ate what his father had cooked.

It had been hard for Eynon to keep from laughing when Braith managed to change into her fancy festival-day outfit with its black skirt, white blouse, and intricately embroidered red vest in the brief interval between arriving home and sitting down to eat. During their shared meal, Nûd and Braith exchanged so many glances Eynon lost count. It was entertaining to watch the two compete to see which of them could smile more at the other's stories.

After a quick breakfast, Chee stood up on the table and marched along its length, formally shaking hands with Glenys and Daffyd and Braith in turn. He earned a small bag of dried cherries from Eynon's mother for his courtesy before climbing up to his usual perch on Eynon's shoulder.

All five of the humans—and Chee—left the cottage and stood blinking in the early-morning sun. The two young men were ready to leave Haywall village after only half an hour. Eynon hugged his mother and father while Chee hopped down to chase chickens before returning to his favorite spot.

Nûd bowed to Braith and she curtsied in return. It was clear they wanted to hug each other, but they refrained while Eynon and his parents were looking on. Eynon could see that his parents were having the same problem keeping their laughter inside that he was.

If anything did come of Nûd and Braith's interest in each other, thought Eynon, *that would be fine—if it happened after Braith started her wander year. He wouldn't mind having the big man as a brother-in-law.*

By that time, Nûd would be twenty-four and Eynon's sister would be sixteen, which wasn't an unheard-of age difference among the farm families in the Coombe, especially if a farmer had waited to have his own land before marrying. Still, as far as Eynon was concerned, it was a good thing he and Nûd would be flying off soon.

Eynon's parents had been pleased to meet Nûd and happy to see Eynon. They were particularly surprised to see a red magestone in a gold setting around his neck. It was clear they weren't sure what to make of their son any longer, especially when Braith told them about Eynon and Nûd arriving on wyvern-back. Nothing remotely like this had happened in the Coombe in living memory.

Braith gave Nûd a long dark-wool hooded cloak to replace his wisent-skin coat, which she stored for safekeeping. The cloak had been a hand-me-down to Eynon from an even taller cousin, and not really Braith's to give, but he didn't say anything. At least it fit Nûd well. Eynon gave Braith his wisent-skin coat to store as well. The weather was warmer here and heavy coats were no longer needed, even when flying.

Just before they left, Braith took a small basket from her mother and presented it to Nûd.

"Some food for your trip, kind sir," said his sister.

Eynon didn't laugh, but wanted to. He couldn't remember his sister saying *kind sir* to any man or lad in quite the same way before. His little sister was growing up. Nûd gave Braith one last bow and thanked her and her parents for their hospitality.

Braith stood on tiptoe and stuck a fresh cutting of holly leaves in Eynon's cap, replacing leaves that had lost their color. He inhaled the scent of the new leaves and kissed the tip of her nose the way he had the first time he'd left home to wander. The sun was an hour above the eastern horizon and it was time to leave.

Nûd and Eynon climbed on Eynon's flying disk and headed toward the eastern mountains where Eynon had sent Rocky to look for deer. When they had flown a few miles from Haywall, they landed on an empty field beside a narrow track.

Eynon sent a sphere of solidified sound high in the air, then exploded it in a shower of red and blue streamers. From a nearby hill, Rocky trumpeted the news that he'd seen Eynon's signal. The wyvern launched his body high in the air and glided down to join them in the field. Eynon pretended he didn't see the wool stuck in Rocky's teeth.

Eynon gave Rocky a large ball of tasty solidified sound magic to lick while he and Nûd climbed on the big beast's back. His staff was still tucked in place, secured by the scarf Nûd had given him when he'd set out to find his magestone what seemed like ages ago. He sent the ball off to the east, above the same mountains Eynon had climbed on the first day of his wander year, just over a week ago.

"Where to?" asked Eynon.

"Brendinas, I guess," said Nûd. "We have to tell the King and the Conclave what happened. Head east and I'll fine-tune our course as we go."

"Sounds like a plan," said Eynon. In the back of his head he was thinking about the Conclave of Wizards.

They sat together side by side on Rocky's back for several minutes without speaking, watching the green land flow below them. Nûd broke the silence.

"Your parents are nice," he said. "I've spent most of my life surrounded by wizards, and nice is not the first word that comes to mind to describe *them.*"

"I'm a wizard and I'm nice, I think," said Eynon.

"Yes, but you're the exception that proves the rule."

"Doethan seemed quite nice. So did your mother. And Merry is *very* nice."

"I expect you haven't spent enough time in Doethan's company to tell one way or the other—and you're certainly wrong about Fercha. She's many things, but one thing my mother isn't is *nice.*"

"Doesn't she send you cookies and sweets?"

"Yes. On my birthday and festival days. But I know she buys them in Tyford."

"Oh," said Eynon.

He'd never had cookies baked by a bakery—just his own or ones from friends or relatives. He wondered if they tasted different somehow.

"There's Applegarth," said Eynon, pointing down to his left. "It's just west of the Rhuthro—that's the river heading north."

"I see it," said Nûd. "That's where your *nice* girlfriend is from?"

"Uh huh," said Eynon. "Her father is a baron."

"Right," said Nûd with a tone that said he had more to say but wasn't saying it.

"What?"

"A farmer's son and a baron's daughter in love. It sounds like one of the old tales that doesn't necessarily end well, that's all."

"Some of the old tales have happy endings," Eynon insisted.

"And some don't," said Nûd. "I hope your story is one that does."

"Thank you."

"Your sister is nice, too."

Eynon kept his answer short and clipped.

"Yes. She is."

"Don't be that way," said Nûd. "I'm not going to arrange a rendezvous with her in the hay barn while you're asleep—not that I could if *she* didn't want to. It's just that I haven't seen a young woman who couldn't blast me with a fireball or zap me with a lightning bolt since I've become a man. It's a lonely life looking after Damon at Melyncárreg."

"Why did you stay?" asked Eynon.

"Damon and my mother insisted it was for my own good," said Nûd. "They both said I should stay out of Brendinas."

"Which is why that's where we're going?"

"Exactly," said Nûd.

"Are you sure you're not related to the young king?" asked Eynon. "You're making as much sense."

"I certainly hope not," said Nûd.

They flew on in companionable silence. Nûd and Eynon must have both fallen asleep. It was understandable, since neither had gotten much rest the night before and the rush of excitement from the battle had worn off hours ago. Rocky continued to head east, following the sphere of solidified sound Eynon had set in motion.

The young wizard was the first to wake. Eynon was initially disoriented and might have fallen if not for the long, knitted scarf that tied him to the wyvern's back. He saw a ribbon of blue water dividing the land beneath him.

"Nûd! Wake up! There's a big river ahead. Is it the Brenavon?"

Eynon knew Brendinas was on the Brenavon—the Royal River—not far north of where it met the sea.

Nûd yawned and looked down over the leading edge of Rocky's wing.

"I think that's the Moravon, the Great River," said the big man. "And that city must be Tyford. I think it would be wise if we stopped there. Damon has a knowledgeable friend who runs an inn in Tyford. It would be a good idea to get his advice before we go to the capital."

"Is his name Taffaern?"

"Do *you* know him?" asked Nûd. "He's one of the most trusted members of Damon's network of informants."

"No, but Merry and I were taking four tuns of cider down the Rhuthro to deliver to him," said Eynon. "She said he was Applegarth's best customer."

He was quite pleased at the thought of visiting Tyford and its street of booksellers, then remembered they were in a hurry and needed to inform people in the capital about the Tamloch raid on the quarry west of the Coombe. Rocky stayed high, just under the clouds as they approached the city.

"There's a big square in the center of town," said Eynon. "Should I direct Rocky to land there?"

"It might be smarter *not* to land a wyvern inside the city walls," noted Nûd. "They have archers and he might not be well received. There's an island in the middle of the river that looks uninhabited. It would be better for Rocky to land there."

"Then how will we get from the island to Taffaern's inn?" asked Eynon.

Nûd smiled. "You *are* new at being a wizard, aren't you? You still have a flying disk strapped to the back of your pack."

"So I do," said Eynon. "There's a clearing at the north end of the island that should be fine for Rocky."

"With a plenty of squirrels and few wild shoats grazing on acorns to provide him with entertainment..." added Nûd.

"And a snack," said Eynon.

Minutes later, they were on the ground and Rocky was sticking his long neck into the trees, helping Chee annoy the squirrels. Nûd and Eynon were skimming above the river, heading for Tyford. Soon they could see the docks and buildings lining the Moravon's eastern shore.

"How will we find Taffaern's Inn?" asked Eynon.

"I don't know," said Nûd. "We may have to stop someone on the street and ask the way."

Eynon recognized a design painted on the end of one pier jutting out into the river. It was a wide, wavy blue line between two red apples.

"Wait!" said Eynon. "That's Applegarth's mark. This must be it."

They hovered and inspected the pier. It looked like there was a stone dock farther back underneath it. They went into the shadows and landed on its rough granite surface. Eynon tucked his magestone inside his shirt and strapped his flying disk to his pack, hiding its shape with his bedroll. He didn't want to advertise he was a wizard.

Broad, iron-banded double doors were at the back of the dock. They led into the lowest floor of a sturdy wooden building. Eynon tried to open them, but they were locked.

That makes sense, thought Eynon. *This must be where Merry would unload the cider for the inn. Taffaern's storerooms must be on the other side of those doors. Of course he'd keep them secured.*

Nûd stepped forward, lifted one of the dark metal rings in the middle of a door, and used it to knock three times. The sound echoed underneath the pier, bouncing off wood and stone and water. Nothing happened for a minute, then a small door above the knocker opened and an eye looked out.

"Do you have my cider?" asked a mellow voice behind the door. "If you do, you're late."

"I don't have your cider, but I know where it is," said Eynon.

"I hope the Rhuthro Keep didn't confiscate it," said the voice.

Eynon heard bolts being thrown, then both big doors swung open. A man of middling height with a big nose and a long, elaborately braided gray beard was standing in the doorway. The ends of his bushy mustache were also braided and hung down to his chin. The man was wearing a black conical felt hat, dark-blue canvas pants, and a white apron that stretched from his neck to his knees over a light-blue linen shirt. His boots were thick-soled and made from bright red leather. Eynon wasn't sure what a big city innkeeper was supposed to look like, but he added the man's appearance to his definition of the profession.

"Are you Taffaern, sir?" asked Eynon.

"I am," said the man. "And Taffy to my friends. Tell me who the two of *you* are and we'll see if you'll fit in that category."

"Yes, sir," said Eynon. "I'm Eynon, from Haywall, in the Coombe, and this is my friend Nûd. He's from farther west."

"On your wander year, I see," said the innkeeper, nodding at Eynon. "And you're both big'uns, aren't you?"

"Yes, sir," said Eynon.

Nûd rolled his eyes. He knew it had been a rhetorical question. And he'd seen the innkeeper's eyebrow go up when he'd heard Nûd's name.

"What's this about knowing where my cider is?" said Taffaern, staring at Eynon. "Has something happened to it?"

"Um," said Eynon. "It's been delayed."

"Delayed how? Delayed where? Will I get my shipment? I'll soon have thirsty mouths upstairs. There will be a revolt if they don't get Applegarth cider soon."

"Your shipment is secure," said Eynon. "It's in the Blue Spiral Tower, up the Rhuthro."

"What would Fercha want with my cider, lad?" said Taffaern. "It sounds like you've got a longer tale to tell that would go better with a mug of ale in a private room upstairs than down here on a cold stone pier in the shadows. Come in, young gentleman, and welcome. Mind your heads."

With that, the innkeeper stepped back from the door. Eynon and Nûd followed him into the inn's cellar storeroom, past barrels of potables, and up a well-worn flight of wooden steps that came out next to the kitchen. Ahead of them was the inn's spacious common room and to one side were several side alcoves screened with heavy curtains that reached all the way to the floor.

The common room was deserted at this hour—guests had been fed and serious drinkers didn't start until after noon—but Taffaern indicated they should enter the first alcove. Moments later he joined them with three large mugs of foaming ale. The innkeeper took a deep swallow and so did Nûd, but Taffaern noticed Eynon didn't touch his mug.

"Not much of a drinker?"

"No, sir," said Eynon. "I try to save it for special occasions."

"Nothing wrong with that," said Taffaern. "Give me a moment or two and I'll be back with something to wet *your* whistle."

The innkeeper slipped out of the alcove and returned half a minute later with a mug of something that foamed but didn't smell like beer. When the innkeeper waved it under Eynon's nose it smelled delicious.

"Taste it," said Taffaern. "I make it with boiled water and birch bark. It's safe to drink and you won't have a headache in the morning."

Eynon tilted the mug, getting foam on his upper lip, then sipped the drink. Its flavor was even better than its smell. He'd have to bring *this* idea back to the Coombe. He was sure it would be popular there.

"Mmmm," said Eynon.

Taffaern smiled.

"Now, lads," he said. "Call me Taffy, and tell me about my cider and why you're *really* in my inn."

With his last comment he turned to Nûd and added, "How's that old reprobate Damon doing in Melyncárreg, by the way?"

Nûd and Eynon looked at each other, smiled, and shrugged. Then they told the innkeeper well-edited versions of what had happened, with frequent interruptions for questions.

"Fercha will figure out a way to get me my cargo, I'm sure," said Taffy when Eynon and Nûd had paused to sip from their mugs. "I'll keep my eye out for my cider to arrive in the next few days."

"I hope so," said Eynon.

"Doethan's involved in all this, too, eh?" said the innkeeper. "You say he followed Fercha through a Roma wizard's gate?"

"I think so," said Nûd.

"Her robes *were* purple," confirmed Eynon.

Taffy frowned. "Who knows *what* will come of that?"

The innkeeper wiped his hand on his beard. He'd poured the contents of Eynon's mug of ale into his own mug and Nûd's when their mugs were halfway down.

"And Damon and Derry's daughter—she's a wizard now, you say—went through *another* gate?"

"She's a very good wizard," said Eynon. His foam mustache made it hard to take him seriously, but Taffy didn't smile. He remembered what it was like to be sixteen.

"They left before Doethan and Fercha," said Nûd. "We rushed here on wyvern-back from the Coombe." He drank a large swallow of ale. "We need to tell King Dârio and the Conclave of Wizards in Brendinas about the Tamloch raid, but I don't know who to contact in the capital so we're taken seriously. Damon's primary connection there of late was Doethan and he's gone. I know he has other agents in place, but I don't know who they are."

"No need to worry," said Taffy. "I'll get word to the Conclave and one of the king's advisers, if he hasn't banished them all in the last twenty-four hours for not kissing his arse with enough enthusiasm."

Eynon laughed and foam went up his nose. He brushed it away with the back of his hand.

"What do you recommend we do?" asked Nûd. "Just sit here and drink your beer?"

"That would be my advice," said the innkeeper. "The last thing you want to do is go to the capital. Word from the north is that King Túathal of Tamloch has paid King Bjarni and the dragonship raiders of Bifurland ten pounds of gold to send five hundred ships to sack Brendinas. They should arrive up the Brenavon in a few days."

Eynon looked at Nûd. Nûd looked back. They nodded.

"There's still time," said Eynon.

"We have to go," said Nûd. "Your gate to Melyncárreg should be big enough."

So that's how Nûd and Damon got their supplies, thought Eynon.

"For what?" asked Eynon.

"For Rocky," said Nûd.

"It's a big gate—as big as the double doors on the pier," said Taffy. "It has to be, to get your tuns of wine and beer through. How big is your wyvern?"

"He might fit," said Nûd.

"Let's find out," said Eynon.

They left the alcove and made their way down the stairs to the cellar storeroom without waiting to see if Taffy was behind them.

Chapter 6

Damon and Merry

Merry punched the man in the door with both her fists, pounding his abdomen until Salder blocked her swings and her arms moved around his neck. Merry held him like she was afraid he might evaporate.

"You're not dead, you're not dead, you're not dead, you're not *dead!*" she repeated while crying tears of joy.

After a few minutes, Merry pulled herself together, stopped her litany, and took three deep breaths. Salder kept his arms around Merry until the third breath, then he held her at arms length and took her in from foot to head.

"It's great to see you too, little sister. What are *you* doing here? You're not so little now."

"I came with Damon," Merry replied. "And you still look like you did the day you left on your wander year,."

"A bit more mature than that, I hope," said Salder. He wore a big smile and his eyes were wet and bright.

"You were twenty-five at sixteen," said Merry. The corners of her mouth turned up as she felt herself fill with joy at her brother's unexpected return to life. "You must be thirty-five by now."

"Only twenty-two," said Salder. "Don't make me old before my time."

Merry rubbed her wet cheeks. Tannis handed Merry a linen napkin and the younger woman dried her tears.

"Excuse me," said Damon, inserting himself into their reunion. "I need information, and we shouldn't be standing in an open doorway where anyone passing by can hear."

"I'll take care of that," said Tibbo.

Tannis escorted Salder and Merry to the trestle table while Tibbo shut the door and reset the thick length of wood that kept it closed.

"We told you I was dead because you were too young to keep that big a secret," said Salder. "You were only ten and our parents didn't want to risk it."

Merry affectionately punched Salder below his ribcage.

"You should have told me," she said.

"If it makes a difference, I thought we should," said her brother. "I knew you could keep a secret. You never told on me when I went to visit..."

"They said you'd been killed by a raiding party from the southern Clan Lands on your way home," said Merry.

She was leaning against Salder's shoulder and holding her brother's hands in hers like she was afraid to let them go in case he disappeared again.

"That was the story Da and Damon and Doethan came up with," said Salder. "I needed to disappear from Dâron to come here."

"Wait! You already know Damon?" asked Merry.

"Of course," said her brother. "He's been working with Da and Doethan for decades."

"Did the three of them talk you into being a spy?" asked Merry. Her head was spinning as she considered the implications of what she heard and what it meant for her understanding of her father and Doethan and Damon.

"I volunteered for the job," said Salder. "They needed someone to keep an eye on what's happening inside the royal palace in Riyas."

"And what *is* happening?" asked Damon. "How many magestones did Verro's men collect and what does he plan to do with them?"

Salder kissed Merry's hands and gave them a squeeze, then turned to face Damon.

"Verro doesn't say much, but some of his wizards do, especially when they've had a few glasses of wine," said Merry's brother. "Tamloch's magestone mines in the Green Mountains have played out, I hear. A dozen wizards are out searching for more sources of green magestones in Tamloch territory, but so far they've been unsuccessful."

"Without more green magestones," said Tibbo as he joined them at the table, "there would be no more green wizards in a generation. There were also rumors they needed lots of green magestones of any quality for one of Verro's special projects."

Damon nodded. "I hadn't realized the shortage was that severe," he said. "How did Verro discover green magestones at the quarry west of the Coombe?"

"Completely by accident," said Salder.

Tannis shook her head in frustration, then filled a plate with eggs and sausage and toast for Merry's brother. Merry gestured and warmed them up for Salder with a touch of heat magic. Salder stared at her for a moment with a look that said *we'll discuss* this *later.* He shifted to face Damon and enjoyed his now-hot breakfast while he talked.

"From what I heard, Verro was flying to the southern Clan Lands. He hoped to recruit them to attack Dâron territory," Salder continued. "You know about the dragonship raiders, right?"

Damon nodded and waved a slice of toast to indicate Salder should keep talking.

"He felt something when he flew over the quarry on his way to a meeting with the southern clan chiefs, then decided to check out what he'd sensed when he returned."

"That must be when he ran into Fercha," said Merry. "She told me about losing her magestone. It must have been during their duel."

"Verro came back without his flying disk," said Salder. "The other wizards teased him, and he told them to shut up and hope *they* never ran into a wizard as powerful."

"I wonder..." said Damon, rubbing his chin.

Merry distracted the older mage before he realized Eynon was the one who found Fercha's lost magestone. She wasn't sure the old wizard had heard Eynon tell Fercha he had her artifact back at the quarry a few hours ago.

"Did Verro's team collect a lot of magestones?" she asked. "Can they train up a lot of new wizards now?"

"I don't know," said Salder. "No one said anything about *how many* magestones they'd found. They were grumbling about how Verro had told them the quarry would be undefended and complaining about being attacked by two dozen Dâron wizards, a crazy giant with a crossbow, and a wyvern."

"There were only five Dâron wizards," said Merry. "I hope the others aren't hurt—the ones who fought the Tamloch wizards and soldiers, I mean," she told her brother.

Fercha and Doethan and the tall crossbowman, thought Merry. *But mostly Eynon. Her Eynon.*

"I've heard something from one of the palace chambermaids," said Tannis. "King Túathal wasn't sure his younger brother Verro would be able to find a new source of green magestones. He wanted to hit Dâron hard now, while Tamloch still has more crown wizards."

"Tamloch has more wizards than Dâron?" asked Merry.

"More *crown* wizards, certainly," said Damon. "Many crown wizards left the capital when the old king died. Some, like Doethan, were forced out earlier. There's been a boom in tower-building on the edges of the kingdom over the past two years. The Dâron Conclave has fewer crown wizards now than it did when the old king, Dâroth XXIV, ruled."

"Here in Riyas, King Túathal treats *his* crown wizards well," said Salder. "I should know—I serve them enough wine. He trusts his brother to keep them in line and they fight less amongst themselves than I've heard is true of the wizards of the Dâron Conclave."

"Verro was always a skilled manipulator," said Damon, looking like he'd just bitten into a sour persimmon. "He knows how to herd the cats and tigers in his Conclave. And you're right about Dâron. Our crown wizards would rather score points on each other than work together in the best interests of the kingdom."

"That's why you left, eh, old man?" said Tibbo with a grin to soften his words.

"No," said Damon. "I had other reasons to leave court. But it's one factor in why I never returned."

"If Verro's raid gained him high quality green magestones, could he train new wizards fast enough to make a difference in the battles ahead?" asked Merry.

"He could if he used modern training approaches," said Salder. "My da said Dâron mages trained thirty new wizards in thirty days during the last war with Tamloch."

Damon snorted.

"What?" asked Tannis.

"Half of those thirty died in a fortnight," said the old mage.

"But how many Dâron soldiers didn't die thanks to their sacrifice?" asked Tibbo.

Merry noticed a long scar on the barrel-shaped man's forearm and realized he might have been one of those soldiers.

Dâron's Master Mage put his elbows on the table, interlaced his fingers, and cradled his chin on the backs of his hands.

"There *are* other uses for magestones and magestone fragments," said Damon cryptically. "Even so, the pieces are in play. Dragonship raiders, southern Clan Land forces..."

"And the northern Clan Lands as well," said Salder.

"Barbarians from both Clan Lands," Damon continued, "plus Tamloch's royal army and navy, all arrayed against Dâron."

"Sounds bleak," said Merry.

"But you've left off our greatest disadvantage, old man," said Tibbo.

"King Dârio," said all five of them in unison.

"If I were King Túathal, I'd want to defeat Dâron decisively, depose young king Dârio, and unite the kingdoms," said Damon.

"You think rule by a competent Tamloch king would be better than Dâron led by our own incompetent monarch?" asked Tannis.

"Not historically," said Merry. "Quite a few monarchs in Dâron lacked wisdom, at least according to what I've read. Somehow the kingdom survived."

"She's right," said Damon. "Though quite a few of those unwise monarchs ended up dead before their time."

Tibbo spoke. "Perhaps that can be arranged for Dârio?"

"Without an heir?" said Tannis. "There'd be chaos."

"Making Túathal and Verro's plans to conquer the kingdom even easier," said Salder with a sigh.

Merry stopped leaning against her brother's shoulder and sat up straight.

"There's got to be a better answer," she said.

"There is," said Damon. "And it's in Occidens Province. I've got to get to Nova Eboracum."

Before Merry could fully process Damon's words there were three loud knocks on the *Blue Whale's* front door.

"Open up!" said a gruff voice. "City guard."

"We should be going," said Damon.

He stood quickly and so did Merry. Tibbo rose slowly.

"Don't worry," said the barrel-shaped man. "It's collection day and the sargeant is making his rounds."

Tibbo casually walked to the front door while Merry gave Salder a quick hug.

"Don't get yourself killed before we have a chance to talk," she told him, then followed Damon into the kitchen.

"Give me a minute, Podhri," shouted Tibbo as he lifted the length of wood barring the door. "I need some time to hide the bodies."

Chapter 7

Fercha and Doethan

"...control of the Five Lakes region, congruent gate access to the black rock mines west of the upper reaches of the Brenavon, and King Dârio's firstborn son," said Laetícia, reading the words written on the sheet of fine vellum like she was reciting a list of things to buy on market day.

"What?" asked Doethan.

"She's joking," said Fercha. "She just wanted to make sure you were paying attention."

The two women exchanged glances. Fercha was glad Laetícia *had* been joking.

Everything else she and her husband had asked for, including an exchange of dignitaries—a polite term for hostages—was a small price to pay for two Roma legions and sixty purple wizards on Dâron's side against Tamloch. Ten thousand well-trained and disciplined foot soldiers' swords, shields and spears would be worth twice their numbers in Dâron or Tamloch levies. Dâron had plenty of archers and a core of heavy cavalry that would complement the Eagle People's forces nicely. It would be enough to tip the scales against Tamloch if they could march to Brendinas fast enough to counter the approaching Bifurlander dragonships.

"Agreed," said Fercha.

"Quite reasonable," said Doethan.

"I've always found it more expedient to offer reasonable people reasonable terms at the beginning, instead of after prolonged negotiations," said Quin. "You end up in the same place and it takes much less time."

"Without sitting through as many banquets," added Laetícia.

"Do you think you can convince the young king to sign?" asked Quin.

"He'll sign if I have to put the quill in his hand and threaten to boil his brain if he doesn't," said Fercha.

Doethan laughed.

"She'd do it, too, and the Conclave would back her," he said. "I could pay off half the kingdom's debt by charging a fee for nobles to watch."

"I'll send the legions south immediately," said Quin. "With wizards to transport their gear and supplies, they should be in Brendinas by midday on the day after tomorrow.

Or maybe faster, thought Fercha.

"Excellent," said Doethan. "The promise of a second hostile force on his doorstep if he *doesn't* sign should make Fercha's task to convince Dârio that much easier."

"Where's your gate to Brendinas?" asked Fercha.

"Nearby," said Laetícia. "We'll have to take you through blindfolded, of course."

"Of course," echoed Fercha.

"Take these tokens," said Laetícia, handing the two Dâron wizards small silver disks with three short arms like a caltrop cut through them. "Use them to gain entry into the palace if you take your own gates back to Nova Eboracum. Quin used caltrops to stop a cavalry charge when he took Timbuktu, so he puts them on everything."

"Thank you," said Doethan.

He and Fercha tucked the tokens away. Quin stood up, revealing every inch of his imposing height, and clapped his hands. A servant approached carrying two thick canvas bags with handles. Quin took them.

"Before you leave, I have gifts for both of you," he said.

He grinned and gave the first bag to Doethan.

"There are two books inside," said the governor. "The thicker one has the rules of *quattuor quadratum,* the thinner is a commentary on *qua-qua* strategy by the empire's best player. I hope you find them both enlightening."

"Thank you, governor," said Doethan. "I'm honored."

"And I'm in a hurry," said Fercha. "Can we speed this up? If it matters, I didn't bring you anything."

Laetícia laughed. So did her husband. He handed Fercha the second bag.

"I have two books for you as well, *domina,*" said Quin. "They're brief histories of the royal houses of Dâron and Tamloch, with genealogical charts. I hope they prove useful."

"You're too kind," said Fercha. "We'll have to come back for them later. For now, bring on the blindfolds. I want to get to King Dârio before he's had too much to drink."

Chapter 8

Nûd and Eynon

"Can wyverns swim?" asked Nûd.

"We may find out," said Eynon.

Nûd and Eynon had returned for Rocky on Eynon's flying disk. The wyvern was following a glowing red ball of solidified sound down the Moravon from the island to Taffaern's dock. He was skimming so close to the river's surface that his wingtips touched the water on down strokes, leaving circular ripples in the liquid. People along the eastern shore were staring at the great black beast and its riders as they made their way south. Soon they were near their intermediate destination.

Eynon sent the red ball under Taffaern's wooden pier and along the solid stone dock below it. The double doors were open. Rocky tucked in his wings and went through them, skidding his claws along the floor of the storeroom. Eynon used the commands Taffy had told him to trigger the gate at the far end of the storeroom and moments later the three of them were in the largest pantry off the kitchen in the Melyncárreg castle.

Rocky fell forward on his belly and scraped his way along the rough stone to let friction absorb some of his velocity. The wyvern stopped inches from the wide door to the kitchen, but Nûd and Eynon didn't. They somersaulted over Rocky's body on either side of his long neck and flopped against the wall ahead of them. Rocky bellowed his displeasure. Chee had managed to retain his hold on Rocky's neck. The raconette was chittering at them both in what Eynon was sure was his way of laughing.

"We made it," said Nûd. "I finally managed to get out of Melyncárreg and now I'm here again voluntarily."

The big man stood and extended his hand to help Eynon up. Eynon was on his back like a turtle, rocking on the slightly concave flying disk strapped to his pack. He needed Nûd's assistance.

"It's for a good cause and we won't have to be here long," said Eynon.

"I know," said Nûd. "I just wished my sense of duty wasn't so well developed. I really liked what we saw of Tyford."

"So did I," said Eynon. "And we'll get to see Brendinas soon, too." He stepped into the kitchen and looked in vain for any sort of large exit to the outside world. Wyverns couldn't fit through normal-sized doorways, at least not without being coated in lard first. He turned to Nûd. "How do we get Rocky out of the kitchen?"

"Through the banquet hall, of course."

"There's a banquet hall?"

"Certainly. It's for festival-day feasts and meetings of the Conclave. The kitchen and hall are connected."

"I worked in this kitchen for three days and never saw any kind of door to a banquet hall," said Eynon.

"You're not thinking like a wizard," said Nûd. "It's not a door—it's a congruent gate wide enough for ten servants to pass side by side leading to the banquet hall one level up."

"And where is this gate to be found?" asked Eynon. "I didn't think there was enough empty wall space in the kitchen to put one."

"Behind the work tables where you set up your distilled water system," said Nûd. "When Damon is hosting the Conclave, we move those work tables into the center of the kitchen to provide extra prep space."

"But there was a sink next to the one I was using," protested Eynon. "They'd have to relocate the plumbing."

"You're still thinking like a farm boy," said Nûd with a smile. "Water *and* drains are provided by congruencies as well."

Eynon shook his head, both to clear it after his tumble and to help recalibrate his brain for the many ramifications of magic for everyday life. He walked back to Rocky and rubbed the wyvern's jaw. The beast's head and neck extended into the corridor outside the pantry.

"Are you doing well, boy?" he asked. "No harm done from that landing?"

The wyvern tilted his head and stuck out his tongue, licking Eynon's face before he could put up a shield. It felt like sandpaper and smelled like a doused campfire, but wasn't as unpleasant as it might have been. Eynon rubbed Rocky's eye ridges as the wyvern leaned down further and the big beast made contented rumbles deep in its throat.

"I guess that question's answered," said Eynon.

"Help me move tables," said Nûd. "It will go faster with two of us."

They entered the kitchen proper and crossed to a wall filled with work tables, near where Eynon's solidified sound distilling apparatus was still dripping out sulphur-free water. Together, Nûd and Eynon moved tables until they'd cleared a sixteen-foot section of bare wall.

"You have to say *Agor-y-droos*," said Nûd.

Eynon reached out to connect with both his magestones and repeated the phrase Nûd had given him. A thin blue rectangle that looked like a painted fresco briefly sparkled and outlined a wide opening. Then the wall shimmered away and a hall large enough to seat two hundred guests appeared in front of him. It was mostly empty, with disassembled trestle tables and benches neatly stacked against one wall. A tall pair of doors were at the opposite end. Eynon assumed they led out into the castle's courtyard.

The hall's ceiling was framed with huge wooden beams, carved and painted, and the floor was some sort of polished white stone veined with blue. It looked like a place to hold royal balls. Eynon had read about them in Robin Goodfellow's *Peregrinations*.

Do wizards dance? Eynon wondered. *It would be fun to dance with Merry if they do.* He resolved to contact Merry with his ring tonight to make sure she was safe, which she probably was. She was with Damon, after all. But he missed her and wanted to hear her voice.

"Eynon?" asked Nûd. "Are you still in Melyncárreg? Or are you back on the river with that baron's daughter?"

"Tease me all you want," said Eynon as he put his reverie on hold. "You're the one enraptured by a *farmer's* daughter."

"With cute freckles," said Nûd.

"And a temper. You haven't seen that yet."

"Perhaps I'll have a chance to," said Nûd. "You help Rocky turn the corner and enter the banquet hall. I'll go upstairs and get some sacks for the gold."

Eynon watched the big man take the stairs two at a time, then went back to join Rocky in the largest pantry. The wyvern was happily watching Chee dance in the short hall in front of him. The raconette was nibbling on a giant bulb of garlic almost bigger than his mouth. Eynon noticed Chee had added a bag labeled as dried plums from another pantry to go with the dried cherries he'd been given in Haywall. He resolved not to sleep anywhere near the little scamp that night.

"Come along, Rocky, let's get you out to the kitchen," said Eynon. He used treats made from solidified sound and encouraging words to convince the wyvern to contort his large body around the angle required to move from pantry to kitchen, then led Rocky over to stand in front of the congruent gate to the banquet hall. He heard Nûd's feet on the stairs.

"I've got the bags," said the big man when he reached the bottom.

"Those are pillowcases," said Eynon.

"They're bags for gold now," said Nûd. "Ready to go?"

"Almost," said Eynon. "Is there any parchment and a pen, or slate and chalk, or wax and a stylus close at hand?"

"All of that is back upstairs in Damon's study," said Nûd. "You want to leave a message?"

"In case Damon comes back or Fercha and Doethan show up."

"There's no chance of my mother appearing, and nothing to write with, so we'd best be on our way."

"Just a minute," said Eynon.

He found the flour bin and scattered a thick layer across one of the tables used for preparing meals. Eynon used his finger to write a note.

Getting gold to bribe raiders not to attack.

"Short and sweet," said Nûd, "and it gets your point across."

"Short, maybe," said Eynon. "But not sweet. If that's what I'd wanted, I would have written the message with honey."

Nûd shook his head and laughed.

"Mount up and lead Rocky across the hall," said the big man. "I'll open the doors at the far end."

"Get away from that flour, Chee!" said Eynon.

The raconette climbed up to Rocky's neck. Nûd walked through the gate ahead of them and opened the doors to the courtyard. Eynon found his seat on the wyvern's back and guided the big beast through the banquet hall and outside. Nûd closed the doors, clambered up and got himself secured. Rocky pranced around the castle's courtyard, flexing his wings and stretching after squeezing through the narrow storeroom and hall earlier.

Eynon created a ball of tasty solidified sound magic for the wyvern, but his mind kept drifting back to Merry. Maybe he'd contact her in an hour or two instead of waiting until tonight. There'd be plenty of time for a call while they were waiting for the gold dust to accumulate in his collection cylinders.

Merry must really be in my head, thought Eynon as he directed Rocky upward after the ball of solidified sound. *I almost thought I saw her waving from one of the castle windows.*

Chapter 9

Damon and Merry

"It stinks!" said Merry. "And it's cold."

"Welcome to Melyncárreg and the Academy," said Damon.

"Do you *live* here?" asked Merry. "How do you stand it?"

"I stand it quite well, child. It's been my home for forty-five years." Damon's tone was prickly at first, then it softened.

"You'll get used to the smell."

"I doubt that," said Merry.

She turned around and saw a tall archway painted on the wall behind her. Hundreds of green vines and acanthus leaves were twining around arched, faux-granite stones. It seemed a fitting representation for a congruent gateway to somewhere in Tamloch. Merry watched as the dark cellar at the *Blue Whale* faded out, replaced by a painted scene of a cascading, ribbon-like waterfall next to colorful cliffs. The gate had closed.

Merry started to shiver. It was almost freezing in the narrow room, which didn't have a carpet or rushes on the floor. Damon was standing beside an open door leading out to some sort of corridor.

"Come along," said the old wizard. "We're headed for my study and I'll light a fire if Nûd has brought up any firewood."

"Fercha's son lives here?" asked Merry as she followed Damon down a dim hallway.

"He does," said Damon.

They went down a winding staircase and along another hall before Damon opened a door and entered a room. He held the door for Merry then closed it against the chill. They were in a much warmer room—in furnishings, if not yet in temperature.

A fireplace sat between two tall windows overlooking a courtyard. In the center of the room was a large desk overflowing with inkpots and leaves of parchment. Several quills were arrayed haphazardly next to a penknife with a blue stone handle. An oval two-sided mirror in a rotating gold stand was in one corner of the desk. She was pleased to see that firewood had been set in the fireplace.

"Light the fire," said Damon. "I've got to learn the latest news from Nova Eboracum before I gate there."

Merry focused her will and her magestone to heat the tinder under the logs in the fireplace until it burst into flame. Tongues of fire reached up to lick at the logs. The study got warmer immediately. Damon pulled the mirror closer to him and muttered something too low for Merry to hear. Then he spoke louder.

"Also scout ahead before you use a congruent gate if you can," said Damon. "It's unwise to jump into an unknown situation."

"Is that an epigram for your next book?"

Damon found a small piece of blank parchment in the chaos on his desk, dipped a quill in an inkpot, and jotted down a few words.

"It is now," he said.

An image was forming in the mirror—a hooded woman who could only be seen in shades of gray.

"Is that you, Tempora?" asked Damon.

"Who else would it be on our private connection, old man?" asked the woman. "Though for all you know I could be Laetícia."

Merry listened closely, without allowing any part of her person to show in the mirror. She smiled at the code name—a gray lady in Nova Eboracum named Tempora was more than a bit melodramatic.

"Laetícia would be more honey and less vinegar, dear lady," said Damon. "Speaking of the provincial spymaster—and her husband—do you have any news from the palace? Is there anything I should know before I gate in to reconnoiter?"

"First Fercha and Doethan, then you?" asked Tempora. "Nova Eboracum will need to open an inn just for visiting senior Dâron wizards."

"The two of *them* are in the city?"

"Not any more," said Tempora. "They just left. My contact is one of the governor's servants and he said they were just sent through a gate to Brendinas after having breakfast with Quintillius and

Laetícia. He also overheard something about getting King Dârio to agree to terms for help from Occidens Province or having his brains boiled."

"I can imagine Fercha saying that very thing," said Damon. "It sounds like they're a step ahead of me and I won't need to go to Nova Eboracum after all."

"If the young king gets mulish, it might be wiser for you to head for Brendinas as well," said the shadowed woman. "My man also heard talk of two legions and sixty wizards marching and flying there, trying to arrive ahead of the dragonship raiders."

"Dârio doesn't listen to the Conclave or his privy council," said Damon. "Why would he listen to me?"

"There is a certain mystique that goes along with being the near-mythical Master Mage of the kingdom," said Tempora. "You could be a subtle voice of reason appealing to his ego to counterbalance Fercha's more direct approach."

"From what I've heard, Dârio and reason parted ways when he took the throne," said Damon. "I'm more inclined to hold him down while Fercha fries him—if I could stand to be within a furlong of the woman."

"Will you ever tell me what your feud with Fercha is about?" asked Tempora.

"No," said Damon. "It's personal."

"You didn't sleep with her, did you?"

Merry watched Damon's face turn red and saw a vein throbbing in his neck. Then he caught himself and controlled his response.

"No. That's ridiculous."

"I'm not that much older than Fercha and *I'd* sleep with you," said Tempora.

"You just want to count me on your tally board," said Damon. "Have you slept with more than half the men in the provincial senate yet?"

"What makes you think I'd restrict myself to the men?" asked Tempora.

"My mistake," said Damon.

Merry smiled and made sure not to lean too close to see more of Tempora's face in the mirror. She knew the woman would use her presence as an excuse to tease Damon further.

"Thank you for your kind offer," Damon continued. "If my heart had room for another, I'd be glad to take you up on it."

"Your loss," said Tempora. "My offer remains open if you ever change your mind."

Damon smiled and nodded and shook his head the same way her father did when Merry asked Derry about his years in court after the previous war between Dâron and Tamloch.

What good was having a life if there were large parts of it you wanted to forget? thought Merry. After a few seconds to reflect, she considered how she'd feel if anything happened to Eynon and felt more charitable toward Damon and her da.

"Thanks again for the information," said Damon. "It will keep me from making an unnecessary trip to Nova Eboracum."

"Glad to assist," said Tempora, "Though if you changed your mind about my offer, you might find frequent trips here necessary."

"Has anyone ever told you you're incorrigible?" asked Damon.

"I can't remember a day when someone hasn't," said Tempora.

"Let me know if you ever add Quintillius Martius Africanus to your tally sheet."

Merry was pleased to hear a smile back in the old wizard's voice after his earlier melancholy.

"I'm adventurous, not suicidal," said Tempora. "Laetícia would cover my naked corpse in plaster and set it up on a plinth near the palace baths to remind her husband of his folly if I tried."

"I didn't think Laetícia was the jealous type," said Damon.

"She's not," said Tempora. "The plaster statue option is only if I tried to sleep with him behind her back. As spymaster for the province she has certain professional standards to uphold."

"Good to know," said Damon, chuckling under his breath. "You never fail to amuse me, dear lady."

"I'd do more than that if you'd..."

"I've got to go. Best regards to your family."

"Goodbye, you old…"

Damon cut contact with a gesture and Tempora's shadowy image vanished from the mirror. He looked over at Merry and saw her grinning.

"What?" he said.

"I always forget that old people have sex, too."

"Every new generation thinks it's invented the concept without thinking through the reason for their own existence," said the old mage.

He found the same piece of parchment he'd scribbled on earlier and wrote a sentence.

"There. Now that will be in my next book, too."

"When do we leave for Brendinas?" asked Merry.

"We don't," said Damon. "I do. You can stay here and keep out of trouble."

"That's unlikely."

Damon frowned at her then realized her statement was true.

"You can come to Brendinas if you'll do what Nûd usually does for me."

"And what's that?" asked Merry.

"He tends to all my needs, so I can focus on important matters of wizardry."

"He's your servant, you mean?"

"That's one way to put it."

"You *do* seem to need looking after," said Merry. "If that's what it takes to get away from this cold, foul-smelling place, I'll be your servant until Fercha's son reclaims the position."

"Fine," said Damon.

"Fine," Merry repeated.

She walked over to the tall windows on either side of the fireplace. It felt liberating to move freely around Damon's study now that he wasn't connected to Tempora in Nova Eboracum. Morning sun was streaming in and she raised her hand to interpose it between her eyes and the light, but was too late. She looked directly into the sun for half a breath. Dozens of black spots danced in front of her eyes, temporarily blinding her.

Merry lowered her hand and raised it again to see if she could get a better angle for protection, but the damage had been done. She thought she might have seen movement out of the corner of her eye in the courtyard below, but when her vision cleared, the cobblestone-covered space was empty.

No matter, she thought. *There can't be anyone else here—the castle is clearly deserted. It hasn't been properly cleaned in months. She couldn't get to Brendinas soon enough.*

Chapter 10

Fercha and Doethan

"When can I take off this stupid blindfold," grumbled Fercha as carriage wheels bumped over cobblestones.

"Practice patience," said Doethan. "I can't see either, but I *can* smell flowers—and horse manure. We're between the royal gardens and the royal stables. I expect they'll be letting us out soon."

"Or we could be next to an undertaker's wagon," said Fercha.

"It won't be long now," said a young woman's soft voice—one of Laetícia's agents in Brendinas, most likely.

Outside the carriage they could hear the bustling noise of thousands of people in the capital going about their daily lives. Drovers shouted at their horses, wagon wheels squeaked, and merchants cried their wares. They were familiar sounds to Fercha, but less so to Doethan, who'd only recently returned to court.

After another minute of the cacophony of urban life, their driver called to his horses and the carriage stopped. Doethan and Fercha heard the door to their carriage open and its stairs drop down.

Gentle hands removed their blindfolds. They belonged to a slim woman in a blue gown with white trim, wearing a hat with a narrow circular brim and an almost opaque white veil. Her face was completely hidden.

"It's time for you to leave," she said. "The gentleman was correct. You're not far from the palace. Get the King's signature as soon as possible. Laetícia told me to tell you that the legions can march back to Nova Eboracum as easily as they can march to Brendinas if Dârio doesn't agree."

"Tell Roma's mistress of spies her message is received," said Fercha over her shoulder as she carefully stepped down.

"Have a good day," said Doethan when he made his exit.

"And you," said the woman. Doethan suspected she was laughing behind her veil.

The woman pulled the carriage's folding stairs up and its door down. The conveyance creaked its way along Garden Street and turned onto Royal Boulevard, joining a dozen of others exactly like it on the busy thoroughfare.

"Well," said Fercha, smoothing her robes. "I'm glad *that* piece of spy-craft theater is over."

The palace was only a block away, its ornate yet indefensible form standing out, but somehow less than the imposing stone walls of Dâron Castle on the heights above it. *That* was a fortress.

"So am I," said Doethan, blinking in the bright sunlight while he got his bearings. "I was right. We're next to the royal gardens."

"But not on the side near the royal stables," said Fercha. "It's an understandable error. There's so much horse manure in the gutters *every* street smells like a stable's dung pile."

"That's one of King Dârio's new economies," said Doethan. "It was instituted a few weeks ago, just after you left for points west. Streets are cleaned once a week instead of every day."

"But the smell," said Fercha. "And the flies. It will make half the city sick."

"The savings are supposed to be substantial, according to the new exchequer…"

"I'll fry *his* brain, too, when I get to the palace."

"*Her* brain," said Doethan. "The old exchequer stepped down in protest. This one knows better, but when Dârio said he needed more revenue, she had to get it from somewhere."

"Quite a few somewheres, it seems," said Fercha, taking in the rundown state of the gardens. The plants inside the gardens' waist-high walls looked like they hadn't been pruned or weeded.

Doethan was surprised by Fercha's expression. It wasn't the disgusted look he expected and seemed more like pride. He resolved to talk to her about it later.

"If it's a choice between gardeners and guardsmen, I'll take guardsmen," he said. Doethan leaned over the garden's low wall and pulled a red flower on a thorny vine close enough to inhale its perfume.

"No time to stop and smell the roses, old friend," said Fercha. "We can use the South Gate. It's time for me to knock some heads."

"I thought you were boiling brains," said Doethan.

"I may do *both*."

* * * * *

"Go away," said King Dârio to an approaching servant. "I told you, no interruptions."

His shaved head glistened with sweat as he tried to concentrate on three games of *shah-mat* simultaneously. Some said the young king kept his scalp shaved because his hair was dark, not red like his father's or grandfather's or the old king's before it went white. Others said Dârio wanted to set his own style and make that as different from the old king's reign as possible.

The sweat on the young king's scalp may have also had something to do with the revealing gowns worn by his three young opponents—comely daughters of noble Dâron families all hoping to be the kingdom's next queen. Dârio had selected them for their skill at *shah-mat,* not their looks, but at eighteen he did have a young man's appreciation for the female form. One of the young women in a wine-colored dress was giving him a good game. He needed to focus on squares and pieces, not curves.

The servant hadn't left.

"What?" said Dario.

"It's Fercha," she said. "And Doethan. From the Conclave. They said their matter was urgent."

The woman in the wine-colored dress advanced her royal adviser. Dârio would be in check in three moves. Reluctantly, he turned up his palms.

"I'm sorry ladies, but we will have to continue our games after I meet with a pair of dreary old wizards."

The three women withdrew. The one who'd just moved her royal adviser looked over her shoulder as she left the young king's study to be sure he knew he was in trouble.

Dârio gave her a small smile. She'd earned it by her play.

Once the women were gone he instructed the servant to show his new guests in. Fercha entered with a quick stride, her blue robes swirling. She held the parchment she'd received in Nova Eboracum. Doethan made a more sedate entrance. They stood on the far side of the game boards, next to the chairs the *shah-mat* players had previously occupied.

The door to Dârio's study remained open. Fercha was sure more than one servant would be listening to everything that was said.

"What does the Conclave want this time?" asked Dario, waving a hand holding a previously captured castle. "Money for rope to lasso the Moon to bring it down on our enemies?"

"Nothing so dramatic," said Fercha.

"More pragmatic," said Doethan.

"Something that might keep you on your throne past the summer solstice," said Fercha.

Dârio slammed the *shah-mat* piece he was holding down on the nearest table and jumped to his feet. His face was red and so was his scalp. Doethan thought he might kick over the game boards at any second.

"What are you talking about? Who wants to take my throne?"

"Tamloch," said Doethan quietly.

Dârio shook his head and turned from Doethan to Fercha. He gestured to the parchment she held.

"Is that what's supposed to keep me on my throne," he said, seeming to spit the words.

"The Eagle People have offered their support in our war against Tamloch," said Fercha quietly. "These are their terms. I've heard them and they're quite reasonable. You should sign this document and accept them."

"Why should I?" asked Dârio. "What could the provincial legions give me that my own armies and wizards could not?"

"Victory," said Fercha.

"Hah!" said Dârio. "I'm sure it's a plot by Occidens Province to have us give up territory without a fight. Dâron will defeat Tamloch the way it always has—on the field of battle."

"That's not precisely true, Your Majesty," said Doethan. "In the times before the old king's reign Dâron often lost clashes with Tamloch, like at the Battle of..."

"You're not helping," said Fercha, tapping Doethan's heel with the side of her foot.

"Two legions and sixty wizards are already on their way to Brendinas from Nova Eboracum," said Doethan.

Fercha tapped Doethan's heel again and muttered under her breath.

"Still not helping."

"The Eagle People are invading?" shouted Dârio. "Why didn't you tell me that in the first place?"

"Because they're *not* invading," said Fercha. "They're coming to help. At least they will be if you sign the agreement."

"Get out!" said Dârio, louder than before. "You wizards and the whole Conclave are useless."

"At least read the agreement before discounting it," said Doethan.

Fercha extended the document and Dârio leaned across the gaming tables and snatched it.

"Fine," he said, showing less anger. "I'll take it under advisement and let you know my decision in a week or two."

"But the legions will be here the day after tomorrow," said Doethan.

"And Dâron's forces will counter them if they try to invade our territory," said Dârio.

He pointed at Doethan.

"You're not worth my time. What part of *get out* don't you understand?"

Doethan turned toward the door.

"You can stay," said the young king to Fercha. "I need your help with a love charm."

"Yes, Your Majesty," said Fercha.

"What happened to boiling his brains?" muttered Doethan under his breath as he left.

"And shut the door!" Dârio shouted to Doethan.

The kingdom's Senior Crown Wizard and acting Master Mage shut the door and was glad there wasn't a dog to kick on the way out to release his anger. Rowsch, his canine familiar, would never forgive him.

Fercha crossed to the door and bolted it. Dârio walked around the *shah-mat* boards and joined her. They stood a few feet apart on a circular carpet woven with thousands of tiny flowers in shades of blue. Fercha created an opaque bubble of solidified sound around them and nodded at Dârio. Only then did the two embrace, hugging each other like friends who'd been apart for too long. When the embrace ended, they stepped back and smiled.

"How did I do?" asked Dârio. "Was I a suitable monster?"

"You played your part well," said Fercha. "Tamloch is acting before they're completely ready, and we got everything we wanted out of Quintillius and Laetícia."

"Excellent," said Dârio, carrying the parchment to his desk and dipping a quill in an inkpot. "Where do I sign?"

Chapter 11

Nûd and Eynon

"Do you remember how to get to the right spot on the river?" asked Nûd as they flew west from the castle.

"Even if I didn't it appears that Rocky knows the way," Eynon replied.

The wyvern was confidently flying high above a broad grassy plain covered with thousands of dark splotches. The splotches seemed to be moving.

"Are those wisents?" asked Eynon.

"One of the bigger herds," said Nûd. "There are seven of them in the area."

"That's a lot of wisents," said Eynon. "Are they dangerous?"

"Only if something spooks them and they stampede," Nûd replied. "I'm glad we're high enough up not to cause problems."

"Me too," said Eynon, though part of him thought a wisent stampede would be something worth seeing.

Rocky started to descend. Soon, he was circling a familiar stretch of the Melyncárreg River marked by a beach of smooth, rounded stones and weathered driftwood. The big black beast landed and settled into a spot in the sun that already had a circular depression in the scattered stones from the last time he'd napped there a few days ago. That's when Eynon's creative wizardry with solidified sound constructs had allowed him to collect a pound of gold in a few hours. He'd needed the precious metal to cast the setting for his magestone.

"I've got the bags for the gold dust," said Nûd as he climbed down from Rocky's back.

"I've got the basket of food Braith gave us this morning," said Eynon. Chee had climbed farther up Rocky's neck and was sprawled between two protruding neck scales soaking up spring sun. He'd perked up when Eynon had mentioned food, but the raconette closed his eyes when Eynon didn't take anything out of the basket.

They were all lucky the weather had changed and the morning was warm, since the humans had left their heavy coats back in Haywall.

"Lazy bones," said Eynon, addressing his familiar.

The raconette waved one of his front paws, but didn't open his eyes.

Nûd stuck his tongue out at Chee but the raconette was oblivious.

"Looks like everything is up to us," said Eynon.

"Up to you, you mean," said Nûd. "You're the wizard. I'll fend off any attacking gryffons."

Nûd took off his backpack, detached his crossbow, and placed half a dozen quarrels in easy reach on a larger rock.

Eynon took off his own pack and put it on top of a second big rock where his flying disk tipped back and forth on the dome in its center. He stretched his physical muscles, then his magical capabilities by crafting one of the grooved cylinders of solidified sound he'd previously used to collect gold dust. The structure formed easily, as if his blue magestone remembered what it had made before.

Using both his red and blue magestones, Eynon duplicated the construct over and over again. Soon he had five rows of ten rotating cylinders crossing the river from one bank to the other, each row a dozen yards apart. Nûd nodded his approval.

"That was faster than last time," he said.

"It's easier when you know what you're doing," Eynon replied.

"That's true for lots of things," said Nûd.

"How much gold do you think we'll need to bribe the Bifurlanders?" asked Eynon.

"Taffaern said King Túathal gave them ten pounds to attack," Nûd replied.

"Fifty should be enough then," said Eynon.

Nûd smiled when Eynon turned away to watch the cylinders turn in the river.

"More than enough," he said. "It's a good thing you're giving this gold to Bifurlanders."

"Why?" asked Eynon. "Wouldn't it be helpful to give King Dârio gold to help the war effort?"

"I don't think so," said Nûd. "If we give the gold to King Bjarni's people, they'll mostly make ornaments and jewelry out of it—rings and torques and earrings and such. Most of the gold won't be used to buy things."

"Why would it be a problem if people bought things with gold?" asked Eynon. He tweaked the locations of two of the cylinders to make sure they were getting enough rich sediments.

"What happens when you have a great harvest?" asked Nûd. "If there's lots of wheat, the price of wheat goes down, right?"

"What's that got to do with gold?" asked Eynon. "Back in Haywall, if there's lots of wheat in one year, we store it in case of a bad harvest in a future year."

"My example might not work as well in places like the Coombe," said Nûd. "Let's try something else, like books in Tyford or Brendinas."

"I like books!" said Eynon. "Merry told me there's a whole street of booksellers in Tyford. I wish I could have stopped there when we were in town."

"Some other time, I'm sure," said Nûd. "If someone brings ten pounds of gold to a city and starts to spend it, the price of books and almost everything else will go up."

"Why?" asked Eynon.

"Because the person with the gold can outbid anyone else for whatever they want."

"If they buy a lot of books, maybe I could convince them to loan some to me, so I could read them," said Eynon.

"This isn't working the way I'd hoped," said Nûd. He rubbed his forehead. "Let me try again. What if you wanted to buy books and every time you offered to buy one, a person with lots of gold bought it for twice the price you could pay?"

"Then the bookseller would have more money to get more books."

"That you couldn't afford to buy," said Nûd.

"Oh," said Eynon.

"And what if it was bread instead of books?"

"I'd eat oatmeal," Eynon answered.

"But the oatmeal is more expensive, too."

"Then I'd trap rabbits and squirrels and forage for tubers."

"Not if you lived in a city like Tyford or Brendinas," said Nûd. "With a lot more gold around, city people couldn't afford to feed themselves."

"So they'd have to move to the country," said Eynon. "I don't know if I'd like a lot of city people moving to the Coombe."

"If we don't give King Dârio any gold," said Nûd, "you can avoid that problem."

"I think I understand now," said Eynon. "Though if the city people were willing to move farther west and settle in the Border-lands, that would work, too. They'd just have to build stockades to protect themselves from raids from the southern Clan Lands."

Nûd rubbed a spot above his eyes.

"I think my head hurts."

"Mine, too," said Eynon.

He checked the fifty gold-dust collection cylinders again. They were all concentrating gold effectively and doing so much faster than before. Perhaps there was something about having them in rows that churned up more flecks of the precious metal from the mud of the riverbed. The two young men stood quietly, watching the water flow and the cylinders turn for a few minutes. Already, a sizable collection of gold dust had settled into each cylinder. Eynon shaded his eyes against the early morning sun and spoke. His words came out as puffs of warmth in the cold air.

"Why do you stay in Melyncárreg working for Damon? It must be boring without anyone close to your own age around. And Damon's not exactly cheerful company."

"I've asked myself that question more times than there are stars in the sky," said Nûd. "The simple answer is Damon and my mother both said it wasn't safe for me to leave."

Eynon nodded. "Is there a complicated answer?"

"All the rest of my answers are complicated," Nûd replied. "I feel like I'm standing on top of one of the cliffs by the falls near the castle, waiting to grow wings so I can jump."

"Have you ever considered learning how to be a wizard?" asked Eynon. "Your mother is very talented that way."

"The one thing I *know* is that I *don't* want to be a wizard," said Nûd. His voice had grown louder and he began to pace up to the edge of the river and back, his crossbow swinging in his left hand.

"Is there something wrong with being a wizard?" Eynon asked.

"Of course not," said Nûd. "But I don't want to be one. I don't want to turn out like Damon and my mother."

"Grumpy?"

"Cynical. More concerned with political machinations than helping people."

"That makes sense," said Eynon. "I'd rather help people than worry about politics myself."

He gave Nûd a sympathetic look when the big man's pacing brought him back toward Eynon. Nûd didn't seem happy, so Eynon tried to distract him.

"I understand that your servant act was partly put on for my benefit, but what do you do with your time in Melyncárreg when you're not waiting on Damon's every whim?"

"He's not so bad," said Nûd. "I spend a lot of time in the library."

"If I were stuck in Melyncárreg I'd do the same. What do you like to read?"

"Histories. Philosophy. Law books. Travelers' tales. Poems. Story collections. Even books of wise sayings, like Ealdamon's *Epigrams*," said Nûd. "And most of the atlases in the Map Room."

"I envy you the opportunity," said Eynon. "It sounds to me like you're not so much waiting as preparing for *something*."

"Maybe," said Nûd. "But I wish I knew what. Turn around slowly."

"Huh?" said Eynon.

He saw the concerned look on Nûd's face and carefully rotated his body. A dozen wisents, including two calves and a massive shaggy bull, were making their way toward the section of riverbank where Eynon and Nûd were standing.

Wisents had notoriously bad eyesight, so they hadn't noticed Rocky. They probably thought the wyvern was a large black rock.

Humans were small and inconsequential. They could get out of the wisents' way of their own accord or be pushed aside and trampled like so much sage grass.

There was still a gap of three spear-lengths between them and the tiny herd. Nûd raised his crossbow, then lowered it and put his hand on Eynon's shoulder.

"Does the wizard have any ideas?" Nûd asked.

"Scream loud enough to wake Rocky?" offered Eynon.

"That might make them stampede."

"Fly above them?" asked Eynon.

"Good answer," said Nûd. He put on his own pack, attached the crossbow with a strap, and tossed the extra quarrels into his hood. Then he removed Eynon's flying disk from the back of the young wizard's pack and handed it over.

"I'll put that on," said Eynon, indicating his pack. Nûd held the pack up and Eynon slipped his arms into the straps. He put the flying disk on the ground, stepped on it, and beckoned Nûd to stand behind him. Eynon directed the disk to rise, keeping his movements slow and controlled so they didn't frighten the wisents. They soon had enough altitude for the shaggy horned bovines to pass below them.

"I may have forgotten to tell you that this stretch of bank is also a ford," said Nûd. "The river is shallow here, which makes it a good place to pan for gold and for wildlife to get across."

"That's a major oversight," said Eynon.

The cows and calves had reached the water. Their quiet grunts and snorts as they drank didn't disturb the peaceful riverbank. Then the bull came up and drank while two of the cows watched for predators. Eynon realized the entire herd was about to cross the river at the exact spot where he'd positioned all his gold-collection cylinders. He could move the cylinders, but that would set his schedule back.

It was time to try something creative. One of the cows was about to step into the river and begin to cross. Eynon used the subtle control of the blue magestone around his neck to form a wide, stiff sheet of transparent solidified sound beneath the cow's feet. He added power from his red magestone and extended the sheet until it covered the entire river, gently arching a few feet over the tops of the cylinders.

The wisents proceed across without further incident. Eynon watched them amble up the far bank and enter the forest, unperturbed by their encounter with wizardry. He dispelled the sheet of solidified sound.

"Nicely done," said Nûd.

Eynon smiled and gave a small bow, which caused his flying disk to tip precariously. He'd have to remember not to do that again.

When they got back to Chee and Rocky, the raconette opened one eye and nodded at Eynon before going back to sleep. Rocky had napped through it all.

Nûd and Eynon watched as a family of mule deer stopped to drink from the river. They didn't try to cross and left quickly, with nervous glances at the humans and the large black rock sleeping in the sunlight, making rumbling noises. A fox nosed its head around a boulder, inspected the scene, and left without getting a drink.

Eynon was growing hungry, so he opened the basket to see what his family had packed for them to eat. He hoped most of the contents had been prepared by his mother and father rather than his sister. Braith had many talents, but cooking wasn't one of them. If Nûd had lived on his own cooking for years, Braith might still be a good match for his friend in a few years. Maybe Eynon could teach Nûd what he'd never been able to teach his sister about the culinary arts.

As soon as he pulled back the cloth covering the basket, Chee was chittering on his shoulder.

"You got a whole bag of dried cherries from my mother and took a bag of dried plums from the castle's kitchen," said Eynon. "Wait your turn and let the humans eat first."

Nûd and Eynon leaned against the rock supporting the basket and ate the smoked sausage and cheese and small loaves of dark bread Eynon's family had provided. It was simple fare, but filling. Chee managed to beg morsels from both of them.

"How long have the cylinders been running?" Nûd asked when they had finished their snack.

"Only half an hour," said Eynon. "It's probably time to check them again. I'll need to bring one ashore to confirm it's really as full of gold as it looks."

"Damon creates lenses from solidified sound so things farther away look closer and little things look larger," said Nûd. "That might save you time."

Eynon loved making lenses. He experimented for a few minutes but couldn't make them augment his vision.

"I think Damon might have created them in pairs," added Nûd. "Two for each eye."

"That might help," said Eynon.

When he tried that option he felt his blue magestone pulse in approval. Instead of two lenses, he got four, as Nûd had specified. Now he could see wisents nibbling on new green grass near the forest on the far side of the river. Fercha must have saved a lot of valuable magic in her magestone. He lifted one of the cylinders in the middle of the river and zoomed in on its collection chamber. It was indeed full of gold dust.

"What do you see?" asked Nûd.

Eynon reached out to the blue magestone and generated another pair of double lenses for Nûd.

"Look for yourself," said Eynon.

"Thank you, I love it," said the big man. "Damon never shared his far-eyes spell with me. Time to bring the cylinders in?"

"I think so," said Eynon.

He heard stones clattering behind him and turned to see a huge animal that looked like a cross between a deer and a wisent making its way down to drink from the river.

"What. Is. *That?*" Eynon whispered.

"A flathorn," said Nûd. "Don't startle it. They can be worse than wisents when they're frightened."

Eynon saw that the big animal's antlers were indeed flat, not round and pointed like the deer back in the Coombe or the local pronghorns. They made its great head look even bigger.

"They're antlers, not horns," Eynon protested.

"Don't blame me," said Nûd. "Damon and his wife named the animals and plants near Melyncárreg before I was born."

"Damon was married?"

"Was married, is married, I don't know. He doesn't like to talk about it."

"It's certainly hard to get information out of him when he doesn't want to give it," agreed Eynon.

Nûd stood up when he finished eating. He removed two of the pillowcases from Rocky's back and put one inside the other. Eynon tilted his head while his companion was at work.

"I'm making the bags double-strong," said Nûd. "Gold dust is heavy—and I don't want any to escape when we fly back to the castle to melt it."

"Why do we have to fly back to the castle for that?" asked Eynon. "I can melt and form it with magic."

"I guess you can at that," said Nûd. "I still haven't cleaned the gold off the ceiling and floor of the artifact studio."

"I'll help you with that," said Eynon.

"Don't bother," said Nûd. "Once we leave, I don't think I'm coming back here again."

"Oh," said Eynon. He knew *he* would—there were so many books he wanted to read in the library.

"Does that mean I won't need these pillowcases?" asked Nûd.

"It does. I can dump gold dust from the cylinders directly into spheres of solidified sound for heating."

"Why can't you just transform the cylinders into spheres?"

"Maybe I can," said Eynon.

He lifted one cylinder out of the water and brought it over to float in the air in front of them. Then Eynon made the cylinder shorter, closed its ends, and spun it into a large sphere, adding heat as he did. He moved his hands together like he was squeezing a ball and the sphere got smaller and even hotter. The gold dust inside melted together and puddled in the bottom of the sphere. Eynon spun the sphere around and pushed one of his palms toward the other. The upper and lower parts of the sphere met in the center, turning it into a small ring.

Eynon inhaled and his magestones' wizardry chilled and solidified the molten metal. He dispelled the solidified sound construct and caught the gold ring before it could fall. It was about three fingers across and as wide as an arrow shaft in cross section. Eynon hefted it and tossed it to Nûd.

"What do you think it weighs?" asked Eynon.

"A bit over a pound," replied Nûd.

"Perfect. I think I can have my magestones do the work to repeat the process."

Eynon instructed his magestones to make forty-nine more rings from the gold dust in the remaining cylinders. While they were heating, spinning and cooling, Chee made the same gestures Eynon had made. The raconette was pretending that *he* was a wizard. Eynon and Nûd didn't laugh, but they did grin at each other when Chee couldn't see them.

As the rings formed, Nûd suggested putting them in the pillowcases and tying them to various bony protrusions on Rocky's back.

"At least they'll be good for something," he said.

"And we don't want to advertise we're carrying fifty pounds of gold," noted Eynon. "Though lumpy pillowcases might make people wonder what's in them."

"We're two humans—one a young wizard with a *red* magestone— riding on a wyvern," said Nûd. "Anyone seeing us won't be wondering about lumpy pillowcases."

"Right," said Eynon. "At least it hasn't taken us long."

When the last few rings were finished and bagged, Eynon and Nûd approached Rocky. Chee clambered up the wyvern's neck and began to dance on his scaly head. Rocky stretched, raising Chee four or five feet higher, then yawned, revealing an impressive collection of long, sharp teeth.

Eynon made Rocky a tasty ball of solidified sound to lick while Nûd anchored pillowcases filled with gold rings around the wyvern's back. He tried to make sure the extra weight was balanced.

A minute later, they were all flying back to the castle.

"Where's the gate to Brendinas?" asked Eynon.

"There are two of them," Nûd replied. "One on the second floor of the castle and one in Damon's tower, but they won't do us any good."

"Why not?"

"I don't know how to open them," said Nûd.

"And I'm not interested in trying to cram Rocky back into the pantry to use the gate to Taffaern's inn," said Eynon. "It looks like we're going back to Fercha's tower."

"Do we have to?" asked Nûd. "She has an animated broom and dustpan that frightened me when I was small."

"I'll protect you," said Eynon. "I think they're cute—and useful."

"If you insist," said Nûd.

Eynon brought Rocky in for a landing near the four blue-and-white striped pillars outside the castle marking the gate to the Blue Spiral Tower.

"Blast!" said Eynon as he was about to trigger the gate. "I forgot to contact Merry!"

Chapter 12

Damon and Merry

Merry couldn't breathe after she entered a gate from the second floor of the castle in Melyncárreg to Brendinas. She'd been standing next to Damon somewhere in the castle, leaning against an Athican-style fresco of cavorting nymphs and small winged-horses. A moment later, a cloud of heavy fog enveloped her head. She couldn't see and started waving her arms. After a few seconds of asphixiation, Damon noticed her gyrations.

"Stop that," the old wizard commanded. "Up!"

The fog-cloud thing rotated once around Merry, mussing her hair before it rose to float just below the whitewashed ceiling covered in hundreds of multicolored arcane symbols. The young woman inhaled deeply several times, glaring at Damon when she had more confidence she'd survive.

"What was *that?*" asked Merry once she could speak again.

"A servant to keep my rooms tidy," said Damon. "It's not alive but it has a tiny fleck of magestone to animate it and is very protective."

"It caught me by surprise or I would have blasted it with a fireball."

"A transparent sphere of solidified sound around your head might be more effective," said Damon.

"Only if you'd warned me so I could put it in place before I stepped through your gate," protested Merry.

"Sorry. I forgot the little thing even existed. It's so good at dusting with blasts of air that I didn't remember how it reacted to strangers. And it's been two decades. Usually I'm the only one here."

"Right," said Merry, feeling—rightly—that Damon wasn't too pleased to have her tagging along. She thought about tying the old mage up in the bottom of a coracle and stranding him in the marshes along the Rhuthro when the midges were swarming. Merry smiled at Damon and the old mage turned away, as if he could sense what she was thinking. Then he changed the subject.

"I used to have an animated broom and a congruency dustpan, but had to replace them with the fog-cloud."

"I think I saw them in Fercha's tower," said Merry.

"No, those weren't mine," said Damon. "At least the broom wasn't. She kept the dustpan and made a new broom for herself. I sold mine to a farmer who needed help with irrigation."

"Why did you get rid of yours?" asked Merry.

"I gave it arms and taught it how to carry water for my bath," said Damon. "But things got out of hand."

Merry laughed, imagining an overflowing tub and a broom that wouldn't stop dumping buckets. Then she thought about it more.

"Why didn't you just open a congruency to a hot spring to get warm water?"

"I was trying to impress a woman," said Damon.

Merry put a hand over her mouth to hide a grin.

"What?" asked Damon. "I was young and foolish. Not much older than you are."

"Did it work?" asked Merry. "You must have been close to her if you were bathing together."

"Oh no, it wasn't like *that*," said Damon. "She was a wizard, too, and I wanted to show off. I was teaching her in secret and wanted to demonstrate how to animate objects. We didn't fall in love until later."

"I see," said Merry.

Wheels were spinning in her head. She tried to imagine Damon at Eynon's age and was only partly successful, but she resolved to draw the old mage out over time and learn more of the story. For now, she looked around the place they'd gated into.

It was a large suite with white walls and dark oak wainscoting. A desk like the one she'd seen in Damon's study was in the center of the room, with several low bookcases and cabinets in easy reach. She could see a wooden tub through an open door to one side—the location of the overly zealous broom's labors, she assumed—plus a bedchamber through another open door. A tall leaded-glass window let in sunlight and stood across from what was probably the door to the suite. That door was barred. Merry could sense strong wards on it as well.

Three tall, narrow tapestries were hanging on the wall behind her. One showed a high waterfall descending past cliffs marked with bands of red and brown and gold. Its colors reminded her of Melyncárreg. The second showed a night sky with hundreds of tiny stars formed from crossed silver threads and one large star made from thousands of crystals sewn in a five-pointed pattern. The big star twinkled in the light streaming in the window. The third tapestry was more domestic. It showed a small family sharing a meal at a table by a fireplace. A boy on the edge of manhood was reading a book while the rest of the family ate dinner. The mother in the tapestry was trying to slide a plate of meat and bread toward her son.

Merry smiled, wondering if the third tapestry depicted a happy time in Damon's own life, or if he'd just seen it and decided to buy it. From her position, she and Damon must have stepped through the first tapestry, which made sense. She'd have to ask Damon about a waterfall at Melyncárreg when she got the chance, which wouldn't be soon.

"Come along," said Damon as he removed the bar on the suite's door and busied himself removing wards. Merry stood behind him, far enough away so she wouldn't distract him from his work. The animated fog-cloud moved along the ceiling to hover over her head. When Merry looked up at it, the cloud turned dark and triggered small, silent cracks of lightning along its lower surface.

While Damon's attention was elsewhere, Merry extended the fingers on her right hand and used five rods of tight light to move the cloud back to the far side of the ceiling. She didn't want to risk another attack. She also didn't understand why Damon would use a cloud to dust—wind would just move the dust from one place to another, not permanently remove it like a dust cloth. *Perhaps he'd created the cloud when he was young and foolish as well?* she mused. *I wonder who he was in love with?*

Soon, the door opened and Damon led Merry out into a wide deserted corridor.

"We're in the royal palace in Brendinas," he said. "There will be guards in the halls—more as we approach the King's rooms—so stay close to me and don't say anything. I didn't want you along, but you're here and your father will hold me responsible for your safety."

"Are you and my father friends?"

"Yes," said Damon.

The man's curt answers could be infuriating. Merry realized how uncharacteristic it had been of Damon for him to talk about himself earlier. *Perhaps she could encourage him to talk more over the next few days by asking leading questions?*

When they turned the corner in a corridor they saw a pair of guards in royal livery. They wore helmets, carried swords and snapped into a defensive posture when they saw Damon and Merry.

One of them looked familiar—it was Gruffyd. He stood stiffly at attention and didn't give any indication he'd recognized Merry, even though she knew he must have.

"What business do you have before the king?" asked the guard who looked marginally more experienced—a tall woman with brown hair to her shoulders.

"That's no concern of yours," said Damon. "I am the master mage of the kingdom and I wish to speak to the king on matters of state."

The guard who'd challenged them muttered something that sounded like *this is above my pay grade* and bowed.

"I will need to consult my superiors," she said.

Gruffyd remained on duty while the other guard opened the door, went in, and closed it behind her.

Merry winked at Gruffyd and stuck her tongue out at him, but he didn't react, though she thought she saw a twinkle in his eyes. She invoked her listening spell, so she could follow what the absent guard said to her superior.

"An old man and a girl are outside," she heard the guard say. "He says he's the master mage and didn't give her name. I thought that Doethan fellow was Master Mage."

"No, he's Senior Mage and only Acting Master Mage. Wizards can be sticklers about getting their titles right."

One corner of Merry's mouth turned up. So were guardsman and nobles—most especially nobles. She remembered once before his wander year when Salder addressed an earl the way you'd address a baron. It took him more than a year to live it down.

"Let me get a look at him," said the guard's superior. "There's a portrait of Master Mage Ealdamon in one of the upper halls. I'll see if this man looks anything like him."

"He just showed up at our door," said the guard. "We didn't have any word from other guards about him entering the palace. Maybe it is him? Isn't there supposed to be a suite for the Master Mage not far from here?"

"There is, but I've never seen it. The door to it is always barred," said the senior guard. "Return to your post. I'll handle things now."

"Yes, sir."

Merry put a serious look on her face as the first guard and her superior stepped out. The tall woman resumed her post while her superior—who turned out to be a somewhat older, medium-sized man with big shoulders—examined Damon. The old mage evidently resembled his portrait, because Damon and Merry were escorted into the next room, which Damon whispered was an antechamber to the royal study.

Half a dozen guards, some with swords, some with polearms, were arrayed around the room's inner door. There were several straight-backed wooden chairs against the walls, along with several more-comfortable-looking chairs with arms and cushions in a corner.

"Wait for me here," said Damon, waving toward the comfortable chairs. After that gesture he made a circular motion with his right hand and the door to the king's study flew open. The guards in the antechamber froze. A dozen trumpets blared a fanfare and Damon strode into the king's study like a victorious general with small bolts of lightning sparking around his head. The door slammed shut behind him. A bar fell and a lock turned.

Merry was impressed. The trumpets were a variation on the warding spell with barking dogs and crossbow bolts Doethan had taught her as one of her first spells. Transparent constructs of solidified sound sufficed for opening and closing the door and surprise was all that was needed to freeze the guards long enough for Damon to act. It was good stagecraft, but only basic wizardry.

"Don't bother trying to open the door," she told the guards. "It's barred, locked and warded."

The guard with big shoulders opened his mouth, but decided she wasn't someone who could help. Another guard looked at Merry, her eyes obviously asking what had just happened.

"Don't worry," said Merry. "He really is the Master Mage of Dâron. Be glad he didn't decide to turn you all into frogs."

She didn't think that sort of transformation spell was possible, even with the most advanced wizardry, but it was an effective threat. The guards milled around near the door to the corridor and whispered. Merry could hear what they were saying—it was the usual *covering your butt* nonsense her father kept trying to stop his tenants from practicing. When her da had caught Merry doing something she shouldn't, she made a point of being straightforward about admitting it, at least after that first dressing down she'd received for lying when she was six.

Merry picked the padded chair facing out from the corner and sat to wait for Damon. There was no telling how long he'd be with the young king. Perhaps he'd knock some sense into King Dârio. From everything she'd heard, Dârio needed it. *I wonder if there's such a thing as a wisdom potion,* she considered. *Perhaps that's more along the lines of what a hedge wizard could whip up?*

There was a knock at the outer door. Gruffyd stuck his head inside and gestured to the broad-shouldered guard, who Merry heard say, "Send her in." A tall woman dressed in dark-blue robes with her face concealed in a dark-blue hood entered and slowly walked over to stand in front of Merry. She seemed sad somehow, as if carrying a secret sorrow. Merry sensed something of wizardry about her.

"The queen would like to speak to you," came the woman's voice from inside her dark hood.

There was only one queen in Dâron. Carys, the Old Queen, King Dâroth the XXIV's wife. Some said she'd been the true ruler of the kingdom at the end of her husband's reign, before he died of a broken heart two years ago when Crown Prince Dâri, his grandson and heir, had died.

Young King Dârio, the Old King's great-grandson, was next in line and had been crowned at sixteen.

"I'm sorry, I can't," said Merry. "My friend asked me to wait for him here."

"The guards will tell Ealdamon where to find you," said the woman in dark-blue robes, "and the queen was most insistent."

Merry stood and followed the old woman out of the antechamber. If it was a matter of disobeying Damon or the queen, she knew which course was wiser.

Chapter 13

Merry

Queen Carys didn't have a formal audience chamber. Instead, she had a warm, well-lit sitting room filled with comfortable furniture. Its walls were painted a soothing Dâron blue and covered with stenciled silver stars. Three well-padded chairs were positioned in a bay formed by a trio of tall windows. Dark-blue velvet curtains flocked with more silver stars marked off an area to one side—a servant's alcove, perhaps. The Queen sat with her back to the center window, a beam of sunlight turning the white hair wreathing her face into a nimbus of soft gold.

As Merry was escorted into the old queen's presence, it was clear that she wasn't as tall as she'd been in the royal portrait Merry had seen on a tour of Tyford's smaller royal palace. The queen no longer had her commanding stature, but she wasn't less for it. She seemed concentrated somehow, distilled down to her essence, rather than reduced in any way. When the old queen smiled, Merry curtsied and bowed.

"One or the other would be fine, dear," said Queen Carys. "Though I understand that you might be nervous. I don't bite—or at least not my friends."

"Your Majesty," said Merry, bowing again and giving a second quick curtsy with a twinkle in her eye.

"I think I'm going to like you, Meredith," said the queen. "You have your father's sense of humor. Please sit down."

The woman in dark-blue robes and hood guided Merry to a chair across from Carys. Merry looked at the queen, received a confirming nod, and sat down. Her chair was *very* soft, almost like being hugged. The other woman sat in the remaining chair, a few inches to the right and behind Queen Carys. The three of them were alone in the room.

The woman gestured and Merry felt a transparent sphere of solidified sound form around them, preventing eavesdropping.

I knew she was a wizard, thought Merry.

"Why do you think you're here?" asked the queen once the sphere was in place.

Merry liked her directness. It reminded her of Fercha. She considered for a moment, then answered.

"To tell you what Damon has been doing."

The queen looked over at the woman in dark-blue robes.

"I told you she'd be quick."

The woman in dark-blue robes nodded and the queen turned back to Merry.

"Astrí says little..." said Queen Carys.

"...but hears much," the woman in dark robes completed with a bored tone. "Forgive me, Your Majesty, but there's no need to feed Merry phrases that make me seem strange and ominous, much as you like to play up your personal wizard's mystique. It's bad enough you make me wear these hot robes."

"You know why they're necessary," said the queen. "Go ahead, take them off for the present. I don't see Meredith as the sort to gossip."

"But that's exactly what you're asking me to do about Damon," said Merry, laughing. "I'm glad to tell you what I can. You *are* the queen, after all and must have the kingdom's best interests at heart."

Merry stood to help Astrí remove her robes and hood. The other woman was wearing a soft, pale-blue linen shirt that reached her knees beneath them. Astrí's mouth silently moved to say, "Thank you." Merry nodded.

Astrí was older than Merry had assumed—a grandmother, rather than someone her mother's age. Her hair was short and gray with only a few hints of red. She had a wise, wrinkled face that fit well with her voice and manner. A rich blue light radiated from what must be her magestone, hidden just below the collar of her shirt.

Merry smiled at Astrí. The other woman looked familiar, but Merry couldn't figure out why. *It will come to me,* she thought.

The two returned to their seats and the queen resumed their conversation.

"Don't be so trusting and assume anyone royal has the kingdom's best interests at heart—especially if you ever speak with Princess Gwýnnett."

"King Dârio's mother, you mean?"

"Correct," said Astrí. "She's been trying to kill Carys for half a decade."

Merry's raised an eyebrow, glad her father had decided to leave court before she'd been born if casual attempts at murder were commonplace.

"I'm glad she hasn't been successful, Your Majesty," said Merry.

"So am I," said the queen, who grinned at Merry, showing a sparkle in her aged eyes. "Try to keep the use of my title to once every ten minutes, my dear—when we're alone, that is. You have permission to call me Carys in such circumstances."

"Yes, Your Majesty."

The queen laughed like someone used to laughing.

"I sense Doethan's influence as well as Derry's, don't you?" said Astrí, leaning close to Carys and smiling.

"Clearly," said the queen. "She will pick up even more bad habits from Fercha."

"That's a certainty," said Astrí.

"By the way," said Queen Carys, "don't taste any food brought to my chamber until Astrí has inspected it magically. At least one meal a day contains some poison that has to be neutralized."

"That's terrible!" said Merry. *Who would want to poison Carys, the beloved old queen? Princess Gwýnnett, apparently.*

"Things are different in the capital than they are in the Rhuthro valley," said Astrí. "Princess Gwýnnett has little interest in the well-being of the kingdom and quite a lot in the well-being of Princess Gwýnnett."

"I've known a few like her," said Merry.

"The late crown prince, my grandson and Dârio's father, was wrapped around Gwýnnett's finger," said Queen Carys. "So long as she gave him plenty of time for hunting and practicing skill at arms, he was happy. She was even good at making sure he kept to his schedule of royal duties, reviewing troops, inspecting fortifications, dedicating bridges, and such."

"Don't tell me she tried to poison *him?*"

"I won't," said the queen. "Because as far as Astrí and I can tell, she didn't. He was too useful to her, since she could pull his strings and rule in all but name, once my husband died."

"The crown prince died of a clot formed by a blow from a wooden practice sword just above his right knee," said Astrí. "Doethan and I examined his body and confirmed it. It flowed to his lungs and killed him. That's not the sort of thing Gwýnnett could have arranged."

"I see," said Merry, though she was taking in so much new information she wasn't sure that she did.

Doethan's ring for contacting Eynon began to vibrate on her finger but she didn't do anything about it. It would be inappropriate during a royal audience. She'd reach out to Eynon as soon as she was free. She put the hand with the ring in her lap and covered it with her other hand.

"Enough about Gwýnnett," said Queen Carys. "Back to Ealdamon."

"He asked me to call him Damon," Merry noted.

"That's just so he can see the look of surprise on people's faces when they realize he's the Master Mage of Dâron," said Astrí, shaking her head, but smiling.

"I don't know him well, and not for very long," said Merry. "I first met him early this morning when Fercha and I flew to the Coombe to stop Verro and wizards from Tamloch trying to steal green magestones from a quarry."

"We know about that," said the queen.

"Then we gated to an inn in Riyas and met people in Damon's network who are spying on King Túathal and Verro."

"Verro is Túathal's younger brother, if Fercha hasn't told you that already," said Astrí. "How's Salder?"

"Doing well," said Merry before she realized what she'd said. The other women smiled at her, so she kept talking. "He seems to be a natural spy."

"Of course," said the queen. "And he'll make a good baron."

Merry realized another major plus to having her older brother alive—and now understood why her father was willing to introduce her to Doethan and let her study wizardry instead of insisting she *had* to take over the barony in the future.

"We learned that King Túathal paid King Bjarni of Bifurland to send five hundred dragonships up the Brenavon to sack Brendinas. They should be here in a couple of days."

Astrí nodded. "We know about that, too—and they're more like a day away, maybe less."

Merry could feel her face get warmer as Queen Carys and Astrí's interrogation continued.

"Do you know about the treaty with the Eagle People and the legions marching here from Nova Eboracum?"

"Two of them, I believe," said the queen.

"And sixty purple wizards," added Astrí.

Merry stood up and paced. She was feeling like the conversation was making her brain turn upside down and sideways. She wished she could talk to Eynon. He'd help her get her thoughts in order with an innocent question.

"Is there anything you *don't* know?" asked Merry, nearly losing her temper.

"Yes," said the queen. "Why is Ealdamon in the palace?"

"He hasn't set foot here in over forty years," said Astrí.

"That's news to me," said Merry. "I have no idea. Why don't you ask him yourselves?"

Chapter 14

Damon

"Are you the young fool who's put the kingdom into such a precarious position?" asked Damon as trumpets continued to sound and the door slammed behind him.

King Dârio leaned back unperturbed in a chair by his desk a few yards from the door. His long muscular legs were extended out over one corner of its surface with his dark-blue boots crossed. He held a quill in one hand.

"Are you the old fool who left the kingdom without its Master Mage for two generations?" asked Dârio without raising his voice.

"Your great-grandfather was twice the man you are," shouted Damon.

"My great-grandfather's mind was as lost as a fool on his wander year for three years before he died," said Dârio. "You might have done something to help, but you chose a self-imposed exile over service to Dâron."

"Who are you to judge me?" asked Damon.

"Your rightful king," Dârio replied.

"No," Damon began. Then he closed his jaw and intentionally cut off what he'd been about to say, squeezing his hands into fists and relaxing them. The trumpet fanfares stopped and tiny flashes of lightning that had been dancing around the wizard's head ceased, leaving a faint smell of ozone in the king's study.

"Your Majesty, forgive an old man's impertinence," said Damon, approaching the king's desk deferentially. When he was close enough, Damon abruptly tugged the young king's legs off the desk, stepped close, and leaned over the young ruler. He tried to grab the king by his collar but Dârio was fast enough to block Damon and hold the wizard's wrists. The two were locked together, their faces nearly touching.

"We're days away from utter ruin, you fool," said Damon. "Fercha and Doethan are bringing you an agreement from Nova Eboracum to enlist their support. Don't behave like the idiot I've heard you are and ignore them. Sign the agreement and we may yet save the kingdom and your throne."

Dârio released Damon and pushed the old wizard back to arm's length. The king tickled the end of Damon's nose with a nearby quill and picked up a sheet of parchment from his desk. It was only half the size of a typical parchment and one side was cut in a zigzag pattern.

"You mean *this* agreement, old man?" said Dârio, waving it in front of Damon. "The one I signed half an hour ago? The governor's copy should already be in his hands and his legions will be here later today, thanks to wide gates Fercha is building."

"What?" said Damon, clutching the edge of the desk for support. "She's figured out how to build wide gates? And she's showing the Roma? What is she thinking?"

"She's thinking she's saving the kingdom," said Dârio. "Fercha said she's lined up wizards here for our end of the gate and is headed to Nova Eboracum to help the Roma wizards with their end."

Damon shook his head and took the parchment from Dârio's desk. He read the agreement and saw the fresh-cut indentations where the copy for Occidens Province had been separated from Dâron's. Damon looked like a warrior who'd just caught a solid blow across the helm from a heavy wooden practice sword. King Dârio moved a chair behind him and helped the old wizard sit down. He poured Damon a goblet of watered wine from a sideboard and watched the older man drink it down.

"Is that better?" asked the young king.

"A bit," said Damon. "So you're not a fool, then?"

"No more than we all are," said Dârio, "though not to hear my mother tell it. She thinks I'm a great fool and tells me so at every opportunity."

"Princess Gwýnnett truly *is* a fool, then, to treat you that way," said Damon.

"What does that make you, barging in to frighten and over-awe me into authorizing an alliance with the Eagle People that I'd already signed as soon as it arrived?"

Damon shook his head slowly, as if making sure it was still attached to his neck.

"There's no fool like an old fool," he said.

"Especially an old fool who quotes from his own book of epigrams," said Dârio with a smile.

A small nod marked Damon's response, accepting the teasing.

"It's disconcerting for me to meet you like this," added the young king.

"Disconcerting for you, perhaps, but embarrassing for me. I'd been told you were utterly unsuited to be king."

"And I've wanted to meet you for half my life—Master Mage Ealdamon, the wizard who froze the Abbenoth and brought our armies to the gates of Nova Eboracum. You're one of my heroes."

Damon rested his chin on his palm, supporting his arm with his elbow on the desk. He smiled at the younger man and shrugged his shoulders.

"I'm no hero, Your Majesty. Just an old man with a habit of running away from trouble."

"But you didn't run," said Dârio. "You came when my grandfather called. I've read all the stories about you in the histories and must have all your epigrams committed to memory."

"What comes after, *'There's no fool like an old fool?'*" asked Damon.

"One of my favorites," said Dârio. *"Justice is a sword. Mercy, a healing potion."*

"I think that's right," said Damon. "When you get to be my age, it's easy to forget small details."

Dârio waved at a bookshelf a few feet away.

"There's a copy over there if you'd like me to check."

"No need, Sire. I'm sure you're correct. I'm honored you've read my book."

"I've got three copies—one here, one tucked into a cushion in the throne room, and one on a stand by my bed."

"I'm unworthy," said Damon without a hint of humility.

He grinned at Dârio and began to feel better. The old wizard sat up straight and sipped at his goblet. Dârio refilled it and poured watered wine for himself.

"I've wanted to ask you something for years," said the young king. "Did you ever discover any clues in your search for my great-aunt Seren?"

"That's a *long* story, my liege," said Damon. "One best told when we don't have half a thousand dragonships heading upriver in our direction."

"And when we've something stronger to fortify us than watered wine?"

"That, too," said Damon. "When will the Bifurland fleet arrive?"

"About the same time the legions get here," said Dârio. "It will be a close thing, but the Roma should be on the east bank of the Brenavon ten miles south of the city later today. The dragonship raiders will get to that point first thing tomorrow morning. The royal army is marching down the west bank, and with luck—and help from you—we can smash the Bifurlanders between the hammer of Dâron and the anvil of the Roma. Which brings me to a very important question."

"What is it?" asked Damon. He suspected he knew what Dârio was about to ask.

"Do you think you're up to freezing the Brenavon instead of the Abbenoth?"

Chapter 15

Fercha and Doethan

"Why do I have to carry the bag of magestone dust while you carry the agreement?" asked Doethan.

"Fine," said Fercha, taking the bag from Doethan and slinging it over her shoulder while continuing to hold the cut parchment with the copy of the agreement for Occidens Province. She doubled her pace and Doethan had to speed up to stay with her as they walked from a secret gate in a townhouse in Nova Eboracum toward the governor's palace. They saw soldiers and supply wagons gathering along the paved broad way from the northern wall defending the city to the palace.

Doethan was a few inches shorter than Fercha, so he had to lengthen his stride as well as move faster.

"Do you have your token for the gate guards at the palace?" he asked.

"Do you?" Fercha replied in a serious tone.

Both laughed. They'd fallen back into the teasing banter they'd developed as neighbors along the Rhuthro and allies on the Conclave.

"Why are we carrying a bag full of blue magestone dust?" asked Doethan.

"What do you mean, *we?*"

"Why are *you* carrying it then?"

"Because I know how to get the Roma legions to Brendinas faster," Fercha replied. "I'd intended to use the dust on a demonstration for Dârio on speeding up troop movements, but hadn't had a chance to show him yet."

"I was wondering why you had a twenty-five-pound bag of magestone dust in your rooms in Brendinas," said Doethan. "You finally figured out how Damon made the extra-wide gate from the kitchen to the banquet hall in the castle at Melyncárreg?"

"Sort of," said Fercha. "I had some help."

"And not from Damon, I assume."

"You assume correctly. I'm hoping all this blue magestone dust will help power a gate big enough for a legion to use."

The street around them was crowded and bustling with soldiers and ordinary city residents. Oxcart wheels in need of grease squeaked like thousand-pound mice and the pair of wizards were jostled more than once by passersby as they headed south along the street's rough cobblestones. Doethan wished he had his familiar Rowsch with him. The big dog would have helped clear them a path.

"Did you get it from Carreg Glas?" asked Doethan after dodging a woman carrying buckets of beer on a yoke across her back. He knew proper Roma citizens preferred wine, but the legions of Quintillius Marius Africanus, from the lands south of Egypt, had a taste for beer brewed from sorghum.

Fercha used a quick sidestep to protect the agreement from the sharp elbows of a centurion striding past her in the opposite direction.

"Of course—it pays to use the best when you can get it," she said.

"I have a table in my library with a top made from Carreg Glas blue marble," Doethan replied.

"That no one can appreciate because you keep it covered with books and documents," teased Fercha.

"But I know it's there, and that's enough," said Doethan. "Did the quarrymaster charge you an arm and a leg for the dust?"

"No, he gave it to me for free," said Fercha. "But I had to promise him a week of work around the quarry in return for two particularly fine magestones his men found while cutting blue marble. My new magestone is one of them."

"And Merry's is the other?"

"Yes."

"Have her help you work off your debt," said Doethan. "It will be good training for her."

"The thought had never crossed my mind," said Fercha, her tone making it clear that doing so had been part of her plan since she'd taken on her new apprentice.

"Sorry," said Doethan, in a tone that indicated he wasn't. "It's not like we don't have other, more important priorities at the moment."

"Do you think?" asked Fercha.

They were almost at the north gate to the governor's palace. The street was still crowded with people. There were many tall, long-limbed men and women from Roma's African provinces and a smaller number in the garb of the empire who could have otherwise been at home in the markets of Brendinas.

They must be connected to the legions from Sarmatia, realized Fercha. The settlers from the White and Green Isles who had populated Dâron and Tamloch had originally come from lands to the north and east of Roma.

Everyone avoided walking on the paving stones nearest to the gate, however. None of the passersby wanted to get too close to the squad of guards in brightly polished *loricas* holding unsheathed short swords and barring entry. Doethan removed his token from his pouch and took the bag of blue magestone dust from Fercha. She got out her own token and the two wizards crossed the empty space to present themselves.

"Please tell Laetícia her guests have returned," said Doethan to the senior gate guard, extending his token.

He smiled at the woman and knew the sack of dust on his back made him look like a peddler.

"Go away, old man," said a young guard to one side wearing a helm that was slightly too big for him. "Deliveries are at the west gate, near the kitchens."

"Stultio—report to barracks and have them send us a replacement, then do ten laps around the city in full kit, on the double," said the senior guard.

The dark face of the young guard got darker as blood rushed to his cheeks once he'd realized what he'd done. He bowed to the senior guard, then to Doethan and Fercha, and withdrew into the palace.

"My apologies, good gentles," said the senior guard, smiling at the wizards. "He's a new recruit. I'll put him on night soil collection duties for a few weeks and I'm sure he will learn from the experience."

"No doubt," said Fercha.

"That's the way you handle an apprentice," said Doethan, leaning close to Fercha.

"As if Merry didn't have you dancing to *her* tune more than half the time, I'm sure," Fercha replied, handing her token to the senior guard. The guard shook her head at the wizards' byplay.

"Enforcing discipline is a constant struggle," she said. "Laetícia told me to keep an eye out for you and escort you to her as soon as you arrived. Follow me."

* * * * *

"I got resin on my robes," grumbled Doethan.

"Adjust your spell to banish water from them so it works on tree sap," said Fercha. "It's mostly water, anyway."

"There's no point in bothering with it until the job is done."

"We've finished laying pieces of obsidian between the trees," said a short, stout older wizard in purple robes with a graying dome of dark hair and intricate facial tattoos. She hadn't found it easy to bend down and place black volcanic glass in the fresh plaster now hardening in a trench between two massive maples, but had worked diligently.

"Thank you, Mafuta," said Fercha as she helped Doethan finish sprinkling blue magestone dust on the resin they'd spread up and down the trunk of the left-hand tree. Fercha had already completed preparations for the tree on the right.

"I have the obsidian-crusted rope tied off," said a second purple-robed wizard. He was floating on a flying disk and leaning against the left-hand tree. This one was young, tall, male, and thin enough to almost disappear in profile. Fercha thought he looked like a version of Merry's lover carved from coal instead of ivory.

"Excellent," said Doethan. "Don't tip over, Felix."

"He won't have any problems," said Mafuta. "I'm the one who taught him to fly."

Doethan and Fercha walked back fifty feet to the right-hand tree to double-check their work and have a few moments to talk. Doethan leaned close to Fercha's ear and whispered, "Are you sure it's wise to teach these two how to make an extra-wide gate?"

"It can't be helped," snapped Fercha. "And the gate will only be stable until something breaks the lines."

"We'll have to make sure the legions and their supply wagons don't damage the obsidian," said Mafuta from the left-hand tree. "I didn't need a spell to overhear you, by the way. I could see your lips moving."

Doethan laughed and Fercha frowned. Doethan should have put up a privacy sphere, but he hadn't taken the time.

The short Roma wizard moved out of the way as her younger colleague brought his flying disk down to the base of the left-hand tree.

"We've got boards to cover the obsidian on the ground," said Felix, "and we'll send the wagons through *after* the soldiers, just in case."

"Are they ready to march?" asked Fercha. She was glad Inthíra and other members of the Old Queen's faction in the Conclave were handling the Dâron side of the wide gate.

Mafuta stepped on her flying disk and rose above the tops of the great maples. Felix and two other Roma wizards joined her to assist with the gate's top, bottom, and sides.

"They're ready," Mafuta replied.

Fercha drew on the power of her new magestone. It wasn't as smooth as it had been with her original stone and setting, but it was enough. A curtain of interlaced blue and black magic appeared, framed by the magestone dust on the tree trucks and the imported obsidian pieces above and below. The magical interface flickered, showing a broad, grassy meadow on the other side. The Brenavon's blue water flowed beyond the meadow, and off to the right on the other side of the river they could see the highest pennants above the far-off walls of Brendinas.

"Send them through," said Doethan.

"Why not connect the gate on the other side of the river, closer to the city?" asked Felix.

"Think about it," said Mafuta. "We can fight dragonship raiders from this side, before they reach Dâron's capital."

"Oh," said Felix. "But we're less of a threat ourselves because we'd still need to cross the river to attack Brendinas."

"Precisely," said Mafuta.

Doethan and Fercha nodded at her. They all smiled at Felix.

"How are we going to engage the dragonship raiders without ships of our own or siege engines?" Felix asked. "Can't they just sail past us?"

"Yes," said Mafuta. "How *are* we going to force engagement?"

"We have that in hand," said Doethan, glancing over at Fercha to ensure that they did.

"Yes," said Fercha. "Well in hand."

She hoped Damon's skill with freezing-magic hadn't diminished in the past quarter-century.

No, Fercha considered. *He's still the coldest man I know—with the possible exception of Verro.*

Chapter 16

Nûd and Eynon

"She's not answering," said Eynon as they flew east from the Blue Spiral Tower on the Rhuthro. He almost said *Gwal-o-e-a-den* for the fifth time, but decided against it. Merry had to have a good reason not to respond.

"Your girlfriend must be busy," said Nûd. "Damon has a knack for causing trouble and they're probably both in the middle of it. I hope she can head off his worst impulses."

"Thanks," said Eynon. "That's *so* reassuring." He consciously copied the tone Braith used to mock his attempts to be optimistic.

"You don't understand," said Nûd. "You've only been around Damon for a few days. I've been living with him in Melyncárreg for more than a decade. When he's not running away from problems, he's creating them."

"I'll take your word for it."

Eynon's brain was still whirling with worry, but at least the weather didn't match the storms of concern roiling in his head. The skies were filled with fluffy clouds—and not the sort that could quickly turn into thunderheads. Rocky seemed to enjoy a chance to stretch his wings for a long flight and happily followed the red ball of solidified sound Eynon projected in front of him. Chee had resumed hanging on to the big wyvern's neck after finding one of the pillowcases filled with gold rings uncomfortable napping. The raconette had wrapped his tail around one of Rocky's bony projections, leaned back into the angle of the wyvern's cervical vertebrae, and fallen asleep.

Nûd and Eynon didn't speak for a quarter of an hour, watching western Dâron flow below them, before Eynon turned to face Nûd.

"Where are we headed?" Eynon asked.

"Brendinas, of course," said Nûd. "I thought we'd fly to the capital, then follow the Brenavon south to locate the Bifurlanders."

Eynon thought about his lessons from Euclid's *Elements*. Nûd had described taking two sides of a right triangle.

"Wouldn't it be faster to follow the hypotenuse?"

"What?" asked Nûd.

"You know," said Eynon, sketching something vaguely triangular in the air with one hand. "Why can't we cut off the corner?"

"Oh," said Nûd. "That's easy. That won't help, because we don't know exactly where the dragonship armada is on the river."

"But..."

"And I don't know how to get to the lower Brenavon from here."

"That makes more sense," said Eynon.

"If we don't fly east to Tyford, then a bit southeast to Brendinas, I'm not sure I can find the Brenavon."

"Isn't it a big river? Almost as big as the Moravon?"

"It's not *that* big, but it gets wide south of the capital, according to the maps I've seen back in Melyncárreg," said Nûd.

"That's what I remember, too," said Eynon. "Even though I was only in the Map Room once. Why can't we start flying southeast now, cross the Moravon south of Tyford and its crossbowmen, avoid the capital, and come up on the Bifurlanders from the rear, where they won't expect us?"

"Not a bad thought, but we don't know how far the dragonship raiders have traveled up the river. What if they're too far ahead of us?"

"Then we'll spot the smoke from them burning estates downriver from Brendinas," said Eynon.

"I expect the people living on those estates would be happier if we could bribe the Bifurlanders to turn around *before* their homes and barns were torched."

"You have a point," said Eynon. "I know I would."

"Good," said Nûd. "For a minute there I thought you were being as callous as a Clan Lander."

Eynon shook his head slowly. People in the Coombe had been dealing with Clan Land attacks and skirmishes for generations. They weren't something to joke about.

"Maybe we can angle just a little bit southeast," Eynon suggested. "We could still bypass Brendinas, but hit the Brenavon not far below the capital."

Nûd smiled over at Eynon.

"I understand now," he said. "You overheard Damon telling me about the Conclave testing you and want to avoid them."

"Uh huh," said Eynon. "At least until I know more about what the testing involves—and we've paid off the Bifurlanders."

"I can't fault your logic there," said Nûd. "Bifurlanders first, then the Conclave. It's a matter of priorities. Start Rocky heading slightly southeast now, and we'll see where we hit the Brenavon."

"I like that plan better," said Eynon. Something that had been tight in his chest relaxed a few degrees. The thought of dealing with the Conclave—especially without Damon's guidance—had been weighing on his mind, along with Merry's unresponsiveness.

"It's too bad we couldn't have detoured back to the Coombe," said Nûd. "I would have appreciated a more substantial snack."

"You just wanted to see my sister again."

"That too," said Nûd.

"I'm not hungry enough to turn around," said Eynon. "And there are estates south of us depending on our speedy arrival."

"Along with the entire population of the capital," added Nûd.

He smiled at Eynon hanging on beside him.

"Prepare for double-time," said Eynon, accelerating the ball of solidified sound Rocky was chasing. "Let's see how fast Rocky can fly."

Wind streamed past them, ruffling their hair and making their cloaks and jackets rattle. Eynon created small lenses of solidified sound over their eyes to serve as goggles. He even made a tiny pair for Chee. It wasn't long before they saw a broad river threading between newly-planted fields like a blue ribbon. Nûd pointed.

"Is that the Moravon?" asked Eynon. "I think I can see the walls of Tyford off to the north."

"It must be," said Nûd. "We're on course, I think. Turn a bit to the south so we'll miss the capital."

"Turning," said Eynon as he moved the ball of solidified sound to the right. Rocky tracked it with a jaunty tilt of his rapidly beating wings.

The fields below them were changing from long, narrow strips that hugged the undulating ground west of the Moravon to large squares and rectangles on the comparatively flat lands east of it. Some fields were green with sprouting wheat, oats, or barley. Others showed rich, newly turned dark earth waiting to be sown with flax and peas and beans.

"I guess farms are larger closer to Brendinas," said Eynon.

Nûd nodded. "Some of that is the Duke of Tyford's land," said the big man. "The Duchess of Whitrose has her holdings up ahead and the Duke of Blûddau's estates are south of hers, according to a book full of maps I studied in Damon's library. They need big estates to support all the knights they owe the crown."

His baron back in Caercadel in the southern part of the Coombe only had a dozen knights, Eynon considered, *though they did drink a lot. It probably took quite a bit of barley to keep them in beer.*

"How many dukes and duchesses are there?" Eynon asked.

"Twelve," answered Nûd. "Plus twenty-four earls or countesses—and who knows how many barons."

"That's a lot of nobles," said Eynon.

"Dâron is a big kingdom," Nûd replied.

"We hardly ever see nobles in the Coombe."

"From what Damon's told me, you should count yourself lucky on that score. The greater the noble, the greater the ego, he says."

"Is that going to be in his next volume of epigrams?" asked Eynon.

"If I remind him to write it down," said Nûd. "But I don't plan to continue being Master Mage Ealdamon's servant any longer."

Eynon was pleased to hear the certainty in Nûd's voice.

Nûd should have had his wander year five or six years ago, Eynon guessed. *Maybe his friend would take time to travel before deciding what he wanted to do next?*

Eynon calculated that Rocky was flying high enough to look more like a large hawk from the ground than a wyvern. He could barely make out men and women below him as tiny figures herding cattle and tending fields. Very few looked up.

There were more people in the lands they were flying over than back in the Coombe, however. They must have flown over a hundred villages and a dozen fortified manor houses. Eynon had seen three sizable castles along their path and thought he'd seen another off to the northeast. They seemed at least as big as the earl's fortress at Rhuthro Keep.

The weather was changing, too. The sun was still shining, but additional clouds were clustering in the sky around them, more densely packed above like the villages below. Rocky descended slightly to stay beneath them, following Eynon's tasty ball of solidified sound.

"Do you think it's much farther to the Brenavon?" asked Eynon, straining to look ahead.

"Not much farther at all," said Nûd. "I can see it in the distance. We're almost there."

"Where?" asked Eynon. He remembered the far-seeing spell he'd used when they were collecting gold earlier and called on his blue magestone to generate the appropriate lenses.

"There," said Nûd, pointing to the right. "There are hundreds of dragonships on the water. I can see their sails."

Eynon guided Rocky in a slow turn to the right so he could see what Nûd had seen. Ships with colorful square sails and pointed prows and sterns filled the Brenavon from bank to bank. With his magically aided vision, Eynon could see round shields along the sides of the ships and oars moving rhythmically, moving the vessels upriver. The largest dragonship was three ranks back. It had a white sail with a wide gold stripe down the center and some sort of animal—a beaver, Eynon realized—painted in black on the stripe. A crown was outlined in black above the beaver.

That must be King Bjarni's ship, thought Eynon.

He yawned—which made sense given how little sleep he'd had the previous night—and tried to put thoughts of Merry and the Conclave aside while he focused on the negotiations ahead, hoping

Nûd would take the lead in dealing with the king of the Bifurlanders. Then any hope of gaining focus shattered like ice sliding off a slate roof onto cobblestones.

A dozen gold blurs descended from the clouds above them, some slapping at Rocky, Nûd, and Eynon with pointed tails. Others were snapping at them with heads filled with sharp teeth on the ends of long necks. Chee leaped down and landed on Eynon's head, distracting him and slowing his response to the attack. The raconette crawled around so his belly was in Eynon's face and held on to Eynon's ears with his tiny claws digging into unprotected flesh.

Rocky twisted and turned, trying to escape his tormentors, without success. There were too many of them and they wheeled about in intricate attack patterns, bumping the wyvern's head, neck and wings with their bodies. Eynon and Nûd had to concentrate on hanging on to the scarf tied to bony protrusions on Rocky's upper back. They were hanging upside down more than once, a thousand feet in the air, before the wyvern rotated back to his usual orientation for flight.

There were lots of screams causing pain for the inside of Eynon's ears like Chee's claws were hurting their exteriors. Eynon knew *he* wasn't screaming. Chee's belly fur covered his nose and mouth so he could barely breathe. Rocky was trumpeting his distress with a deep *basso* bugle, but the screams were high-pitched—like a horde of children playing tag on the village square in Haywall.

Eynon could feel more bumps as something or a group of somethings smacked against Rocky's sides behind him. Rocky rose, suddenly lighter, and Eynon managed to push Chee around so the raconette was clutching the *back* of his head, not the front. Thus liberated, Eynon leaned up and tried to determine exactly who or what was attacking him.

He saw a dozen small, gold-scaled dragons, each the size of a wisent, wheeling up and away back into the clouds above him. They were carrying riders with long yellow braids who seemed to be children, not fully grown. *That explains the high-pitched screaming,* thought Eynon. *And they had the pillowcases filled with gold. Blast!*

Eynon turned to his friend to see why the big man had been uncharacteristically quiet during the attack, but didn't see him.

Nûd was gone.

Chapter 17

Merry

"Why don't we ask him ourselves?" asked Queen Carys. She frowned and looked at the ceiling for a moment. Her tone had shifted from comfortable great-grandmother to unhappy sovereign.

Astrí said nothing and seemed to retreat into a hood she was no longer wearing.

"Damon left Brendinas forty years ago and hasn't returned," continued the queen. "He won't even talk to Fercha and she's..."

"...his favorite student," said Astrí, finding her voice. "They can't stand to be in the same room together and haven't spoken in two decades."

"What happened?" asked Merry.

"Fercha made choices Damon disagreed with," said Queen Carys. "She followed her own path and stumbled on the way. Damon never let her forget it."

"Aren't apprentices supposed to become masters and seek their own course?" asked Merry. "They make their own mistakes and learn from them. That is the natural order of things, isn't it?"

"Their particular situation was more complex," said Astrí. "And they could both teach stubborn to a bull wisent."

Merry smiled.

"I've only been Fercha's apprentice for a short while, but that was obvious from the start. Damon seems to be cut from the same cloth."

"They were like two flathorns clashing antlers," said Astrí. Her eyes were unfocused, staring at a distant corner of the room, like her thoughts were drifting back to somewhere long ago and far away.

"Flathorns?" asked Merry.

"Big deer from Melyncárreg," said Astrí. "Like stags as big as oxen, with huge, flat antlers."

"That helps explain something about the gate in the pool at the bottom of Fercha's tower," said Merry. "I remember her saying, 'I'm not going back through that gate if the legions of the Eagle People *and* the royal army of Tamloch are on my doorstep.'"

"I can imagine Fercha saying those very words," said Queen Carys.

"I've *heard* her say them," said Astrí. "She set up that gate outside the castle so she could send things to her son."

"Without Damon interfering," whispered the queen.

"The tall, dark-haired man with the crossbow?" asked Merry.

"I expect so. Nûd favors that weapon," said Astrí. "Where did you see him?"

"He was with Damon at the quarry when we fought the Tamloch wizards and soldiers. The last I saw him, he was behind a quarryman's wagon shooting back at Tamloch archers."

"That sounds like Nûd," said the queen.

"He gave it away when he called Fercha *Mother*," said Merry.

"And rightly so," said Astrí, "since she *is* his mother."

"He was one of Fercha's *stumbles* that Damon was afraid might happen," said the queen, leaning forward in her chair.

"Nûd seems like quite a nice man, whatever his origins," said Merry. "He was very brave at the quarry."

"That's good to hear," said Astrí. "He *is* a nice young man, even if he has spent too much of his life in Melyncárreg."

Merry was concerned for Eynon. He'd tried to contact her four times using Doethan's magic ring. She wanted to end this interrogation by two old women who seemed to know when every squirrel dropped a nut in the royal forests along the Rhuthro. Enough was enough, even if one of the inquisitors was the dowager queen of Dâron. Merry had conducted enough subtle questioning sessions of her own to know when one had reached a point of diminishing returns. She hadn't spent enough time traveling with Damon to have more information to give Carys and Astrí.

"It's been a pleasure to meet you both," said Merry, "but I really need to be getting back to the antechamber outside the king's study, so I can wait for Damon. Perhaps I'll learn more from him—something the two of you don't know already."

Merry stood, smiled, and performed another bow and curtsy.

"I told you she was her father's daughter," said Queen Carys.

Astrí stood as well. "Help me on with my robes and hood before you leave, please?"

Merry assisted the older wizard and adjusted the folds of her robes so they draped properly. Astrí's face disappeared under her hood again.

Someone rapped sharply on the door to the chamber.

"Did you summon a servant?" Astrí asked Carys.

"No," said the queen. "I thought you'd show Merry back."

Astrí fashioned a thick protective bubble of solidified sound around Queen Carys by adjusting and strengthening the privacy bubble she'd put in place earlier. Once that defensive measure was complete, Astrí stepped past Merry to the door.

"Who's there?" she asked.

"Open up or I'll have it knocked down," said a voice that might have been pretty if it didn't honk out each syllable like an irritated goose.

"Oh, her," said Queen Carys.

"I'm afraid so," said Astrí.

"Guard your tongue, dear," said the queen to Merry, "and count your fingers if you shake her hand. Don't eat or drink anything she offers you."

"Yes, Your Majesty," said Merry.

"Go ahead, open it," said Carys.

Astrí removed the wards and pulled the door open. A woman of medium height with raven hair done up in a tower above her head and wrapped with strings of pearls was standing in the doorway. She wore a low-cut sky-blue satin gown with white vertical stripes under a dark-blue, ermine-trimmed velvet surcoat adorned with pearl buttons. A silver coronet made from twisted wire in knotwork patterns with sparkling diamonds perched above her forehead at the base of the tower of hair. Her nose was sharp, and her face was powdered and rouged to such a degree that she looked like a garish child's doll, not the mother of a king.

The woman's face darkened like a thundercloud until she glanced beyond Astrí and spotted Merry.

"There you are," said the woman. "I'm Princess Gwýnnett, King Dârio's mother. You may have heard of me."

Merry nodded, impressed by the ensemble if not by the princess.

"Of course you have," said Princess Gwýnnett. "Leave these old women to their naps and join me in my apartments. We have *so* much to talk about."

That said, the princess took Merry's arm and bustled her out the door.

Chapter 18

Damon

"Freezing the Brenavon?"

Damon sat back in his chair, stroked his chin, and stared at the young king.

"How did you manage to fool so many people into thinking you were an idiot?"

"It wasn't hard."

Damon laughed, spraying a mouthful of watered wine. He wiped his mouth with the back of his hand.

"My mother helped," Dârio continued. He leaned against the corner of his writing desk closest to Damon, sighed, and crossed his long legs.

"She's in on your subterfuge?"

"Not at all," said Dârio. "My vain, venal, and manipulative mother has been telling everyone in court she's the real ruler of Dâron ever since my father and great-grandfather died two years ago."

He refilled Damon's goblet from the pitcher on his sideboard.

"She's the one spreading stories about my capricious moods and poor judgment. I just decided to play the part she chose for me. I'd hoped it would entice Tamloch into attacking us sooner rather than later, since they can't train new wizards easily."

"Since the mines in the Green Mountains played out," said Damon, half to himself. "I sense the delicate touch of Queen Carys at work."

Dârio smiled back, revealing nothing—and everything.

"Your hope was well-founded, it seems," said Damon. "Tamloch *does* appear ready to attack us."

"If sending five-hundred dragonships to sack Brendinas counts as an attack," said Dârio.

"It would for most kings," said Damon.

The two men grinned.

"I'll need a map of the river," said Damon.

"Which I happen to have on my desk," said Dârio, retrieving a parchment from behind him.

The young king and the master mage held the map in front of them, considering options for stopping the Bifurlanders like two old friends deciding where to travel for a holiday.

Chapter 19

Fercha and Doethan

"Now what?" asked Doethan as he and Fercha stood to one side of the legions and watched the first ranks of soldiers march through the gate to Dâron. A privacy sphere shimmered around them.

Fercha was lost in thought, half-hypnotized by the rhythm of the legionnaires measured paces. Doethan touched her arm.

"Is it time to go back to Brendinas? I'm concerned the Conclave's in-fighting will get out of hand without adult supervision."

"You're taking your role as nominal head of the Conclave far too seriously," said Fercha, pulling herself away from wherever her mind had wandered. "Remember, you're not herding house cats—you're trying to keep a squawk of angry gryffons from following their nature."

"So I shouldn't try to lead the Conclave?"

"I didn't say that. Someone has to keep them in line, and you're elected. But you shouldn't get your hopes up for civilized behavior."

"I harbor no illusions," said Doethan. "The members of the Conclave often elect the person to lead them that most of them think they can browbeat."

"Though not in your case. You were selected because the various factions saw you as a potentially fair referee."

"Won't *they* be surprised," said Doethan. His face looked like he'd bitten into a particularly sour persimmon.

"Maybe it *is* best if you return directly to the capital," said Fercha.

"And where will *you* be going?"

"Riyas."

"You can't leave me to cope with the machinations of the Conclave on my own," protested Doethan. "I need you to hold them down while I beat them with a club."

"I'm sure you'll manage without me," said Fercha.

"Or *be* managed," said Doethan. "I was counting on your vote—and your unique approach to diplomatic persuasion."

"Threaten a fellow wizard with immolation once and you never live it down."

"It was hardly just a threat. You burned off half his beard."

"The randy goat deserved it," said Fercha. "He's lucky I didn't burn off the hair somewhere else."

"As I said—your unique approach."

"Taxing hedge wizards for healings, charms, and potions was one of the most ludicrous ideas I'd ever heard."

"Most of our colleagues agreed with you," said Doethan. "And now many of them fear you—or fear crossing you, anyway."

"I like to think I command their respect."

"You do," said Doethan. "And that makes us a good team. I'll need your help when it comes to getting the others to follow their assignments in the war effort."

"I understand," said Fercha. "I'll try to get back as fast as I can. Princess Gwýnnett's faction will be hard to handle even with me around to knock heads—metaphorically, of course."

"Of course," said Doethan. "Say hello to Verro for me."

"What makes you think I'm going to Riyas to see..."

Doethan smiled at her.

"Right. I *am* that transparent," said Fercha. "Maybe if I can talk to him I can defuse tensions and get this war called off before the first blows are struck."

"Hah," said Doethan. "It's more likely you'll be taken prisoner, leaving me at the mercy of Gwýnnett's faction."

"The princess is not one of your favorite people," said Fercha. It was a statement, with no hint of a question. "Has she done something particular to earn your ire of late?"

"Other than trying to slip potions of compliance into Dârio's meals, you mean?"

"Hasn't she been doing that for the past two years?"

"Yes, but now she's trying to get him to marry her sister's daughter."

"His first cousin? Just to keep power in her family?"

Doethan nodded, then slowly shook his head from side to side.

"There's more?" asked Fercha. "I don't think anything that woman does would surprise me. She's capable of anything."

"True," said Doethan. "Since you're going north to talk to Verro, I should tell you the rest of it."

Fercha glanced around and saw Mafuta and Felix near the gate ensuring its integrity. She made the sphere of solidified sound protecting their privacy opaque as well as soundproof.

"Tell me," said Fercha. "It might give me some leverage."

Doethan laughed. "It will at that," he said. "Do you remember when Derry had to move from his estates in the east to the Rhuthro valley?"

"Of course. That was the same time you came west as well and built your tower. Eighteen or nineteen years ago."

"Did you ever wonder *why* we left Brendinas?"

"The story for public consumption at the time was that you wanted to get away from court and Conclave politics," said Fercha. "Though the gossip around the palace was that the two of you had royally ticked off Princess Gwýnnett for some unknown reason. I was young and naïve enough at the time to believe the first version."

"The gossip was more accurate," said Doethan. "As a soldier, Derry had ceremonial duties in the palace along with tending his estates. By chance, he was assigned to guard the princess while her husband, Prince Dâri, was on a hunting trip to the mountains."

Doethan paused.

"Go on," urged Fercha, glad they couldn't be seen by anyone around them.

"Derry heard *interesting* sounds from inside the royal chambers and contacted me using a ring I'd given him. I was close at hand in the palace library and came immediately."

"Who was her lover?" asked Fercha. "A groom? A noble?"

"A prince," Doethan answered. "Derry wanted to make sure the princess wasn't being taken against her will, though I told him it certainly didn't sound like it. We made our way to the servant's entrance to her chambers by side corridors. I unlocked the service door with magic. We entered, stood behind a curtain, and peered around it. Derry and I saw enough to identify the man."

Fercha had a pained expression.

"Tell me," she said. "Was it Verro?"

"No," said Doethan. "Verro wasn't in court."

"Then who?" Fercha demanded.

"King Túathal, then *Prince* Túathal. You were there when the royal delegations from Tamloch first came to Brendinas."

"I was," said Fercha. "I have a permanent reminder of that visit."

"This was their second, after Dâri had married Gwýnnett. Don't you remember how the princess flirted with Túathal?"

"I'd left court by then, shortly after the *first* visit from Tamloch royalty, if you'll recall," said Fercha. "I was in Melyncárreg coping with an energetic three-year-old by the time of their second visit. I only heard about Gwýnnett flirting with Túathal second hand."

"That's right," said Doethan. "I forgot. You left and got as far away from Brendinas as you could manage."

"With good reason," said Fercha. "Court is no place to raise a child."

"As young Dârio knows all too well," said Doethan. "Have you told Verro about Nûd?"

"No, and I don't plan to," said Fercha. "It's bad enough *you* know. I shouldn't have told you all those years ago..."

"My lips are sealed," said Doethan, cutting her off.

"Thank you," said Fercha, clasping her hands in front of her chest and bowing slightly. "What happened afterward? All I know is you and Derry were my new neighbors shortly after I moved from Melyncárreg to the Rhuthro valley. My friends at court and Conclave didn't have much to tell me, and the two of you weren't talking."

"What do you *think* happened? We told Queen Carys and she advised us it was best to get as far away from Brendinas as we could manage. She arranged for a new barony for Derry and funds to help me build my tower close by upriver."

"Now it all makes sense," said Fercha. "And Prince Dârio arrived on the scene..."

"...nine months later. Exactly," said Doethan. "I confirmed it with a consanguinity spell when he was born."

"You always were interested in hedge-wizard magic."

"It helped me play the part while in exile."

"Why did you come back to Brendinas and take such a public role on the Conclave, then?" asked Fercha. "Wouldn't it be wiser to stay out of sight in the west?"

"That was the old queen's idea," said Doethan. "Having me around reminds Gwýnnett that Carys has something on her."

"Thank goodness Queen Carys is keeping her hand in," said Fercha. "I'm much happier being part of *her* faction than the alternative."

"Supporting the princess isn't an option," said Doethan. "I'd go into permanent exile before serving Gwýnnett."

"Now you're sounding like Damon."

"He was motivated by love—my motivation would be the opposite."

Fercha inclined her chin and brought it back up. She returned to the same unfocused, half-hypnotized look she'd had earlier. After a few seconds her face changed, and her eyes lit up with newfound knowledge.

"Dârio's not the rightful king," she said.

"You *have* been paying attention."

"And that means..." Fercha began.

"That can wait until later," Doethan interrupted. "Go to Riyas. Find Verro. See if you can talk him and King Túathal out of this war—which I doubt—and get back here as soon as you can."

"Right," said Fercha.

The opaque bubble around them faded like dew on a summer day. Fercha confirmed her flying disk was still on her back. She inserted herself into a space between ranks of legionnaires marching through the gate and was on the other side in a heartbeat. Doethan waved at her, but she was already on her disk flying north toward a gate to Riyas somewhere in Brendinas.

He fiddled with a ring on his left little finger and had a brief, but productive conversation with a friend and ally. Inthíra would get the word out to Dâron's crown and free wizards to assemble.

Reluctantly, after waving to Mafuta and Felix, Doethan waited for a gap between cohorts and trudged through the gate's interface. It was time to return to the capital and cope with the Conclave.

Chapter 20

Nûd and Eynon

"Nûd?" said Eynon, then repeated it louder, *"Nûd!"*

There was no response. Nûd's end of the extra-long scarf they'd used to anchor themselves to Rocky's broad back was flapping in the wind. Eynon hoped his friend hadn't been trying to get out his crossbow to fight off their attackers and untied the scarf around himself in the process. He leaned to the right—Nûd's side—as far as he could without untying his own end of the scarf, but couldn't see anything except a long way down to a stretch of brown fields. There wasn't even a convenient lake, river or stream Nûd might have landed in, though Eynon realized, after a moment, that any such body of water would have been at least a mile behind them.

Chee was only a step away from pure panic. The raconette was still on top of Eynon's head, using Eynon's ears like the handles on a heavy cast-iron pan. Rocky was flying straight and level, continuing their previous course, even without the tasty ball of solidified sound Eynon used to guide him. The wyvern's head was moving back and forth like a batsnake considering a mouse, scanning the fluffy white clouds above for signs of the small gold dragons who'd attacked them.

Chortles of high-pitched laughter came from inside the nearest cloud. *Those murdering dragon-riding thieves were still close by,* thought Eynon. His red magestone pulsed and glowed. Eynon felt blood rush to his face and sensed his heart pounding in anger now, not fear.

They killed my friend and stole the gold we'd collected to save Dâron from the Bifurland invaders. It's time to teach them the folly of attacking a wizard!

Eynon reached up and slowly removed Chee's claws from his ears. He stroked Chee's fur to calm him, then lifted the little beast over his head and tucked him into a hollow at the base of Rocky's neck. The raconette wrapped both his small arms around the nearest bony projection and held on, reflexively stuttering out a nervous *chi-chi-chi-chee*.

Eynon rubbed Chee's velvet-like fur, then reached over his head again and felt the reassuring smoothness of his flying disk on top of his pack. He tugged at it and the disk came free. Eynon held it tight in one hand while untying the knot in the scarf holding him in place with the other. When he was no longer tethered to Rocky's back, he generated a plane of solidified sound above him the same color as the wyvern's hide to disguise his movements, shifted his chest until it rested on top of his flying disk, and ascended to enter the clouds.

It wasn't easy to see inside the nearest cloud. Drops of water coated his body and ran down the back of his neck. Eynon took a deep breath to help him think and realized he didn't have to put up with that sort of annoyance—he was a wizard. He generated a thin wall of solidified sound close to his skin to keep the moisture away and used a tiny fraction of the heat his red magestone could channel to dry himself off.

Now if I can only figure out how to see, Eynon considered. He remembered the lenses that helped him get a closer view of things far away and called on the stored wisdom of his blue magestone to craft a set of them. They didn't help—vision inside the cloud was so constrained that far away and close at hand were much the same.

Eynon wondered what it would take to see inside a cloud and suddenly he could. Everything around him was indistinct and had a red tinge, but he could make out twelve dragons flying ahead of him with twelve small human forms on their backs.

Eynon said a silent *thank you* inside his head to both his magestones. He didn't know which one had responded to his thoughts, but he was pleased with the results. Now he could *do* something. Eynon moved a few feet up and got closer to the dragons. He could hear their riders talking and laughing.

"Did you see that boy's head, Sigrun?" asked one. "Was that a baby raccoon?"

"Or some other strange southern animal," replied a voice Eynon assumed belonged to Sigrun.

"Maybe it was a monkey?" said a third rider. "My uncle saw one when he went across the Ocean."

"No one cares about your uncle and a monkey on the other side of the world, Rannveigr," said a slightly deeper voice.

"Hah hah, hah, Holgir—*you're* a monkey!" said Rannveigr.

"Am not!" said the slightly deeper voice that must be Holgir.

"The dark-haired one was cute," said another girl.

"Good thing you caught him," said Sigrun.

"It's a long way down," said the first voice.

Nûd was alive? Where was he?

The new lenses somehow showed living creatures fairly clearly. They glowed, even through the hats and furs the riders were wearing. Nûd's large body wasn't on the back of any of the dragons. *Where was his friend?*

Eynon's anger began to grow again, then he realized the dragon riders were girls and boys younger than his little sister. He reined in his emotions, given that Nûd hadn't fallen to his death. He didn't know if the attack had been serious or sport, but either way he wanted to find his friend, recover the gold, and be on his way. If he could teach the young dragon riders a lesson in the process, so much the better.

Drawing on the power of his red magestone, Eynon warmed the air around him, like a small sun burning inside a whitewashed room. Seconds later, the cloud surrounding him—and the dragon riders—had evaporated. His special lenses, no longer needed, were gone as well. The dragon riders—most with long blonde braids and conical leather hats—turned their mounts to see what had vaporized their hiding place.

Eynon stood tall on his flying disk and expanded the protective shell around his body a few inches, turning its color red-gold. He used more energy from his red magestone to generate crackling flames around him and shaped a transparent cone of solidified sound in front of his mouth to amplify his voice.

"LAND AT ONCE OR BE IMMOLATED!" he said, trying to make his voice sound deep and menacing. It cracked twice and only ended up being deep, but he'd gained the dragon riders' attention. He made the flames around him burn brighter to reinforce his message.

"Thunder and lightning!" one rider exclaimed.

"What does *immolated* mean?" asked another.

"Burned alive," said Sigrun. "We'd better do what that *thing* says."

One of the riders on the far side of the wing of dragons tried to run for it, but Eynon stopped her with a small fireball a few feet ahead of her mount's nose. He pointed to a broad limestone outcrop near a square of well-tended woodlands on the edge of an estate below. The riders descended.

Eynon saw Rocky hovering close by and created a red sphere of particularly tasty solidified sound to guide the wyvern down as well. He saw that Rocky carried something in his claws—it was Nûd. *Thank goodness!* thought Eynon.

Rocky landed on one side of the flat expanse of rock, gently placing Nûd on a bed of green moss. All twelve of the dragon riders touched down on the other side, their eyes tracking Eynon floating a few feet above them.

"DISMOUNT!" Eynon commanded.

The riders reluctantly climbed down from their dragons and stood by their arrowhead-shaped heads, helping them stay calm. Their dragons' gold scales flashed in the afternoon sunlight and shimmered red where they reflected Eynon's fiery, designed-to-intimidate form. He noticed that the riders—ten girls and two boys, from what he could tell—all carried knives and axes on their belts. A short boy had a one-handed crossbow and a tall girl had a short sword with twin gold dragon heads as its hilt.

"DISARM!"

Eynon burned a circle the diameter of his flying disk into the rock twenty paces in front of riders. Each one in turn stepped forward, removed their weapons, and put them in the dark circle. The tall girl with the short sword was the last to approach. She tossed her knife and hand-axe into the circle but didn't move to unbuckle her sword belt.

"Do what he says, Sigrun!" urged one of the girls. "You don't want him to burn you."

"My parents gave me this sword," said Sigrun over her shoulder. She looked at Eynon defiantly. "Turn me to ash if you want, but you can't have it."

"YOUR SWORD IS OF NO IMPORTANCE!"

Eynon was making things up as he went along, but was used to dealing with stubborn people.

Sigrun continued to stand her ground.

"YOU CAN RECLAIM IT WHEN YOU'VE RETURNED MY GOLD!"

"There's *gold* in those bags?" asked a girl.

"We're rich!" said another.

"We're dead if we try to keep it," said Holgir, the boy with the crossbow.

Sigrun was still standing in front of the circle burnt into the rock. She stared up at Eynon. He saw she wore two large gold broaches pinning an embroidered apron of fine white fabric to her bright yellow shirt.

"Those bags are ours by right of plunder," said Sigrun. "Any gold they have belongs to us now."

Eynon admired the girl's courage, if not her wisdom. He thought about telling her he was plundering it back, but tried another approach.

"THAT GOLD IS MEANT FOR THE KING OF THE BIFURLANDERS, NOT FOR YOU!"

His statement didn't prompt the reaction he expected. Instead of showing fear, Sigrun laughed. So did the other dragon riders behind her. Even their dragons snorted.

"WHAT?" said Eynon, too surprised to continue his act.

"King Bjarni is my father," said Sigrun. "If you're taking it to him we'll help you load it back on your wyvern and see to your companion. We'll even escort you to the fleet."

"He's the *cute* one," said the girl with the longest braids.

"UM..." said Eynon, his flying disk slowly descending without him consciously directing it to do so. The cone in front of his lips faded away.

"Come on, team," said Sigrun, waving to her companions. "Grab your weapons and start carrying bags."

Eynon touched down and dropped his flaming façade. He was eager to check on Nûd.

"The skinny one isn't much older than *we* are," said a girl.

"He's still a wizard," said Sigrun. "Treat him with respect even if he did try to scare us to death."

"I can still throw fireballs," said Eynon, but any hint of menace had left his voice. "Can you help me see to my friend?"

"Bring your healer's kit, Rannveigr," said Sigrun. She'd retrieved her knife and axe and looked Eynon up and down like a judge trying to tell if he was lying about who owned a pig. Rannveigr and Sigrun walked past Eynon, heading for the bed of moss near Rocky where Nûd had been placed. Eynon followed them, wondering who was being taught a lesson. He saw Chee sitting on the moss near Nûd's head, stroking his hair.

"When we finish moving the gold, can we have lunch?" asked the boy who wasn't Holgir.

"Lunch would be good," said Nûd, leaning up on one elbow. "I don't know where I am, but I'm hungry enough to eat a wisent."

Chapter 21

Merry

"You look *so* much like your father," said Princess Gwýnnett when she and Merry were seated in a not-so-cozy corner in the princess's suite. Gwýnnett had contrived to have her chair look like a throne, six inches taller than the ones around it. Merry's chair had wide arms and a broad seat. It was so thickly padded that Merry felt like she'd rolled into the center of an old feather bed and faded into its folds. She perched on the edge of her seat to avoid disappearing entirely.

Merry smiled and nodded. She expected she'd be doing a lot of that during her conversation with the princess.

"I had a crush on him when I first came to the palace," said Gwýnnett. "He was a dashing young man then. One of the heroes of the battle at the gates of Nova Eboracum. My late husband, Prince Dâri, was a hero, too, you know, but he wasn't skilled at polite conversation."

Smile and nod. Don't eat or drink anything. Count your fingers.

"Your father was more than just a soldier," the princess continued. "He read books and was friends with that wizard. What was his name?"

"Doethan," said Merry.

"Yes, that's it," said the princess. "Though he went by Llandoethan then. A nosy fellow. Always getting into other people's business. Would you like some tea, dear?" She gestured toward a pot on the table in front of them with two finely made cups beside it.

"No thank you," said Merry.

"As you wish," sniffed Gwýnnett, "but you're missing out on a treat. It's delicious."

Smile and nod.

"Anyway, I don't see why he had to come back to Brendinas after all this time. It's rude, that's what it is. He should have stayed away far to the west and kept making fertility potions and healing farmers' broken legs."

*Keep my mask up. Don't let her see how much I want to respond.
She knows much more about Doethan than she wants me to think.*

"He should have stayed along the Rhuthro, like your father," said Gwýnnett. "Salderwen is a wise man—smart enough to leave court when it was sensible to do so, and wiser still to stay away."

Merry turned up her palms, smiled, and nodded.

"You'll tell him that, won't you? Next time you see him?"

Nod, then smile.

"Good," said Gwýnnett. "I knew you'd understand. And if you see Llandoethan, give him the same message. I understand the two of you are quite close. What's he like, dear? You know... is it true what they say about wizards."

Merry knew Princess Gwýnnett was trying to provoke a reaction from her. The princess must have spies that told her Merry spent time in Doethan's tower when she made trips down the river to Tyford. It didn't matter if Gwýnnett *believed* Merry was sleeping with Doethan, so long as the insinuation prompted Merry to say more than she should.

"I don't understand, Your Highness," Merry replied haltingly, like she was ten, not almost sixteen. "What do you mean? People say lots of things about wizards."

"There are rumors about what they can do with solidified sound," said the princess.

"Oh yes," said Merry, pitching her voice to sound younger. "I've seen Doethan walk across the Rhuthro without getting his feet wet using circles of solidified sound."

Gwýnnett smiled and nodded. Merry could sense the older woman's brain calculating more points to anchor her webs as she sought another approach for her interrogation.

The princess lifted a plate off the table and presented it to Merry. "Try one of the currant cakes, dear," she said. "They're quite tasty."

"No thank you," said Merry. "My brother used to tell me the currants were midges from the local marches."

Blast! thought Merry. *I should have stopped at "No thank you."*

"And how *is* Salder doing in the north these days?"

Caught, thought Merry. She couldn't prevent her mask from slipping for a moment and took an extra beat to say, "How is my brother doing? He's not doing anything—he's dead."

"Oh dear. I'd forgotten. My condolences on your loss."

The princess looked as sorry as a fox in a hen house with feathers caught in its fur.

Merry lowered her head as if she was about to cry, but really to hide her face. She considered the fact that Gwýnnett knew Salder was alive and probably knew he was in Riyas.

Blast!, she thought. *Damon had a mole in his spy network, and that put her brother at risk.*

"Were you there when the Tamloch wizards invaded the western marches this morning?"

Everyone else seemed to know about the battle, so Merry didn't see any need to dissemble.

"Yes. I was at the quarry near the Coombe where the Tamloch wizards came to dig for magestones."

"And were they successful?" asked Gwýnnett.

"Who?" asked Merry. "The invaders or the defenders."

"The invaders, as you call them," said Gwýnnett. "I'd have thought that was obvious from context."

"Forgive me, Your Highness, I was up early, and it's been a long day."

"Take your time, then," said Gwýnnett. "Do have some tea—it will wake you up."

Merry shook her head and went on.

"We drove the Tamloch forces away, but they did manage to collect several buckets of green magestones."

"Did they?" asked Gwýnnett. "That's fascinating. Verro pulled it off."

The princess licked her lips and made Merry think of a cat who'd finished a bowl of cream.

Merry tried to analyze Gwýnnett's words. It seemed like she was less interested in Dâron's success than Tamloch's. That made no sense. Her son was king of Dâron. She'd have to share what she'd heard with Queen Carys and Astrí and Damon to see if they could figure it out. It was time to leave and find them.

The princess had continued to speak and Merry's mind only now caught up to what her ears had heard.

"It's too dangerous for you to return to Applegarth or Upper Rhuthro Keep," Gwýnnett had said. "You should stay here in the palace with me, where you'll be safe."

Did Gwýnnett really intend to hold her prisoner?

"I appreciate your generous offer, Your Highness, but Damon expects me back in the antechamber to the king's study. He's probably wondering where I am already."

"Nonsense, young lady. You'll be much better off nearby, where I can ensure your continued good health. I'm confident whoever Damon is, he'll understand. I can send word so he won't worry."

"Thank you, Your Highness, but..."

"No, no, it's settled," said Princess Gwýnnett. "I've got a very cozy room for you just down the hall. It's quite private."

Merry smiled and nodded. If she was going to be imprisoned, she'd go gracefully, then do her best to escape as soon as possible. She was a wizard, after all, if rather new at the profession.

"Guards!" called the princess.

A man and a woman in sky-blue royal Dâron livery, gold-plated armor, and tall helms topped with blue feathers entered and bowed to the princess. The man lumbered, but the woman had the grace of a dancer, or a well-trained swordswoman.

"You know where to take her," said Gwýnnett.

The guards bowed again and helped Merry to her feet. With a hand on each elbow, they steered her out the door and down the corridor.

"The princess is *so* kind to give me my own room," said Merry. "I thought I'd have to find an inn nearby, but she's saved me the expense."

The guards didn't react, even though Merry added a thick layer of sarcasm to her tone, like mortar between stones in a castle's curtain wall. After more steps than expected, Merry was standing in front of a door more appropriate for a treasure room than guest accommodations. It was banded with iron reinforcing stripes and looked like it would take hours for an axe to chop through. The door had a small viewing panel protected by vertical iron bars and a hinged section at the bottom that opened from the outside.

For delivering the prisoner's meals, thought Merry.

The man took a key from his belt and opened the door. Merry tried to examine its details so she could fashion a duplicate from solidified sound, but the man blocked her gaze with his body. The door swung wide, its hinges making a terrible squeak.

It makes sense not *to oil cell doors,* though Merry, distracting herself from her current situation. *I'd better get away now, before I'm inside.*

She called on her magestone's power and sent four blasts of tight light against the back of the lumbering guard's head. The man fell forward onto the cell's hard stone floor and moaned. He wouldn't be getting up soon. Merry turned to deal with the other guard when she saw the woman had removed her helmet. It was Nyssia, Gruffyd's fiancé, the woman from Brendinas she and Eynon had met on their first day down the river.

"It's a pleasure to see you again," said Nyssia, tossing her long blonde braid.

"The pleasure is all mine," said Merry.

"Under present circumstances, I'm sure that it is," said Nyssia. "I hadn't realized you were a *wizard*. Nice work dealing with my colleague before I had to. He's not one of my favorite people. Neither is Princess Gwýnnett."

Merry smiled and gave a small bow. "Good to know we're on the same side."

Nyssia looked left and right down the hall. "We are if you support Queen Carys," she said. "Now we've got to get you out of the palace. Follow me."

Chapter 22

Damon

"Where's the girl who was with me?" Damon asked a stocky young man in royal guards' livery. "I told her to wait."

Gruffyd, the stocky young man, was standing inside the antechamber to the king's study along with several other men and women in armor. Unlike his fellow guardsmen, Gruffyd was smiling.

"Merry was never very good at following orders."

"You know her?" asked Damon.

"We're childhood friends," said Gruffyd.

"Huh," said Damon. "Where did she go?"

"Astrí came to take her to the queen," Gruffyd replied.

"Who is Astrí?"

"The old queen's personal wizard, of course."

"Carys has a personal wizard now, does she," said Damon, mostly to himself.

"One of the older guards told me she's been serving the queen for decades."

"Really?" Damon rubbed his chin. "Decades..." he said softly.

The old wizard studied Gruffyd for a few seconds, taking in the young man's stocky form and heavy broadsword.

"I didn't know," said Damon in a more conversational tone. "I've been away from court for a long time."

"I just got here," said Gruffyd. "This is my first assignment."

"I see, young man, uh..."

"Gruffyd."

"Yes. Guardsman Gruffyd. I'm going to borrow you."

"I can't leave my post," said Gruffyd.

"I'll take care of that," said Damon.

He returned to the door leading to the king's study and pounded on it. The other guardsmen in the antechamber saw Damon's wizard robes and wisely decided to do nothing.

"Dârio!" he shouted. "I need one of your guardsmen for a few hours."

The king opened the door and stuck his head out.

"This one?" said Dârio. "Gruffyd, isn't it? Do what Damon asks of you until I tell you otherwise."

"Yes, Your Majesty," said Gruffyd, bowing.

"You don't have to bow when you're on duty," said the king.

"Sorry, Sire."

"Don't worry, you'll get the hang of it after a few more weeks," said Dârio.

The king stepped into the antechamber and turned to Damon.

"See that you return him in one piece."

"I'll try my best, but no guarantees," said Damon, smiling.

"Consider it a royal command."

"I said I'd try," said Damon.

"You'd better do more than try, old man. It's important you succeed."

Damon nodded to Dârio.

Gruffyd shifted his weight from foot to foot, sensing that the young king and the old wizard weren't really talking about his health.

"You there! Henddyn," said the king to an older guard.

"Sire?"

"Find that young lady in the wine-colored dress, the good *shah-mat* player, and send her in," said the king. "We have unfinished business."

Dârio winked at the older guard.

"Then see that we're not disturbed."

"Yes, Your Majesty."

Dârio smiled at Henddyn and returned to his study. The door closed gently behind him.

"Find Jenet and tell her the king wants to see her immediately," said Henddyn to a young woman in his squad. The woman left the room with the soft chiming of jangling mail trailing behind her.

"Are the queen's rooms still in the south wing?" asked Damon.

"They're in the west wing now, your wizardness, ever since King Dârio took the throne," said Gruffyd.

Henddyn winced. "Call him 'Good wizard,' lad, unless he has a title."

"Sorry," said Gruffyd, trying to apologize to Henddyn and Damon simultaneously.

"I've got a title, but it hasn't had much use in decades," said Damon. He opened the door to the corridor. "Lead on, Gruffyd. That's what I borrowed you for, after all."

* * * * *

Someone was tapping on the door to the queen's sitting room.

"What is it?" asked Queen Carys. She was doing a piece of intricate embroidery while discussing matters of state—mostly Princess Gwýnnett's latest plotting—with Astrí. The other woman was weaving thin rods of tight light into colorful patterns. Her dark-blue hood and robes were on the arm of her chair.

"A wizard and a guardsman are at the door with urgent business," came a servant's muffled words through the thick door to the sitting room's antechamber.

Astrí was surprised. "Fercha's returned from Nova Eboracum already?"

"Tell the queen I'm back, but still haven't found her daughter," came a loud male voice from the other side of the door.

"It's Damon!" said Carys. Her embroidery fell to her lap and her heart nearly skipped a beat. "You have to..."

Astrí was already moving. Her tight-light pattern had exploded into a full spectrum of colored sparks before disappearing. She'd picked up her robes and hood and was running to a dark-blue curtained alcove on the far side of the room where servants could wait until the queen required them. It had its own door to an outside hallway.

"You can't enter the queen's presence without being announced," came a protesting servant's voice from the antechamber.

Damon opened the door and stepped into the sitting room with Gruffyd behind him.

"The years have treated you well, Carys."

"You always did know how to give a lady a compliment—and make an entrance," said the queen, steepling her fingers in her lap.

Damon strode purposefully across the room and sat in the same chair Merry had occupied earlier. Gruffyd stood behind Damon, trying his best to become part of the furniture.

"Have a seat," said the queen. "Make yourself comfortable."

"Thank you, I will," said Damon, settling himself deeper into the padded upholstery.

Gruffyd, his face impassive, felt like he was watching the first crossing of blades in a fencing match.

"I'm looking for a girl," said the old wizard.

"Weren't you supposed to be doing that more than forty years ago when my daughter disappeared?"

Damon nodded. The queen had scored the first touch.

"I suppose I deserve that," he said.

This time the queen nodded.

"I'm looking for a younger girl this time. She's only fifteen. The guards said your personal wizard came to fetch her."

"What makes you think you'll be any more successful finding Merry of Applegarth than you were finding Princess Seren of Dâron?"

Damon saw an opening and took it.

"So she *was* here?"

"Yes," said Carys. "Just like Princess Seren was in the palace for eighteen years."

"Stop trying to confuse me with ancient history," said Damon. "And before you can say it, I know I'm easily confused."

Queen and wizard exchanged smiles.

"Merry was here and talked to us—talked to *me,* I mean—for almost an hour," said the queen.

"Us?" asked Damon. "You and your personal wizard, you mean? Who did you rope into *that* job?"

"Her name is Astrí," Carys answered. "She came to court long after you left."

"Decades ago, I hear."

"About that long," said the queen.

"I'd like to meet her," said Damon. "I'm sure we'd have a lot to talk about."

"No doubt," said Carys. "I'll let her know when she returns."

"Off on one of your errands, then?" Damon crossed his legs and sat farther back in his chair. "Did she go to Riyas? Nova Eboracum? Bjarniston? Or perhaps the southern Clan Lands?"

Queen Carys laughed.

"I sent her to the Conclave's library to do some research."

Gruffyd couldn't understand all the levels of their conversation, but he could tell the queen was ahead on touches, though neither one had yet drawn first blood.

"Researching *what?*"

"Freezing spells, if you must know."

Damon's face lit up with a grin. Gruffyd could see it reflected in the window panes behind the queen and in the queen's amused reaction.

"You have a devious mind, Your Majesty."

"Thank you," said Carys. "You didn't think you were our only hope of stopping the Bifurlanders, did you?"

"I knew you always think eight moves ahead," said Damon. "You're the one who taught Seren *shah-mat,* after all."

"And she was an excellent player," said the queen. "Before she disappeared."

"Before she disappeared, aye," said Damon. "This Astrí must be a powerful wizard."

"She's skilled."

"Strong enough to freeze the Brenavon?" asked Damon.

"Perhaps, if it comes to that."

"If Astrí is that strong, the two of us should work together to make it happen."

"Now that I know you've agreed to help, I'll suggest that to her."

"Good," said Damon.

"Fine," said Carys.

Gruffyd was confused. It seemed like the match was over. *What about Merry?*

"What happened to the girl?" asked Damon.

Tight muscles in Gruffyd's neck relaxed.

"Derry's daughter?" asked the queen. "She left with Princess Gwýnnett nearly an hour ago."

"Why didn't you stop her?" asked Damon.

"Merry? Or the princess?"

"Either," said Damon. "Both."

"She's a resourceful young woman," said the queen. "I thought she might learn something."

"Or Princess Gwýnnett might," said Damon, shaking his head.

The wizard looked up and over his shoulder at Gruffyd.

"Do you know the way to the spider's lair?"

"I can take you to Princess Gwýnnett's apartments," said Gruffyd after he loosened his jaw. His teeth had been clenched ever since he'd heard who Merry had left with.

"Let's get moving," said Damon as he rose and started to follow Gruffyd to the door. "It's been a pleasure chatting with you, Your Majesty."

"It certainly has, Master Mage," said the queen. "We'll have to do it more often."

Chapter 23

Fercha

Fercha flew into an open upper window in her townhouse in Brendinas. Her bedchamber was much the way she'd left it. She tossed her flying disk on the bed and traded her blue wizard's robes for green ones before reclaiming her disk and strapping it to her back. A thin sleeve of yellow beryl turned her new blue magestone green, completing her transformation.

She rolled up a tapestry of a mage and a unicorn to the left of the fireplace across from her bed and tied it in place with leather thongs. A fresco of a faux stone archway framing an emerald green landscape was revealed. Fercha knew a second fresco remained hidden behind a similar tapestry on the right, but the left side was where her heart was. She stood in front of the fresco. With a word and a gesture, the gate opened and Fercha stepped through into the highest room in a tower anchoring one corner of the royal palace in Riyas.

* * * * *

A dark-haired, powerfully built man dressed in sumptuous green fabric trimmed with white fur sat on a straight-backed chair beside a wide bed. He was a few years older than Fercha and had an air of command about him, as if he was used to his word being obeyed.

"Your Majesty," said Fercha.

King Túathal of Tamloch tilted his head and regarded her for a few moments.

"You were expecting to find my brother?" he said.

"I was expecting to find an empty bedchamber."

"And instead you found me," said the king. "Verro's out seeing to various preparations for the upcoming battle. I like to sit in his rooms from time to time. It helps me feel close to him when he's away."

"How touching," said Fercha. "Brotherly love. I'm *glad* you were waiting for me. You're the real decision-maker."

"That's the burden of being a first child," said Túathal.

He gestured to another chair at a nearby writing table. Fercha sat.

"It's a shame, really," said the king. "Verro would have been a better ruler, but he was second in line and took himself out of the succession by becoming a wizard."

"You've done well as king," said Fercha, "except for restarting the war with Dâron."

"Except for that," said Túathal, a corner of his mouth turning up. "I take pleasure in knowing this will be the *last* war between our kingdoms."

"Oh?"

"After this conflict, Tamloch and Dâron will be one realm, under one king."

"And that king would be you?"

"Perhaps. Perhaps not," said Túathal. He smiled, showing his teeth.

"You never married and don't have an heir," said Fercha. "Won't that be a problem?"

"Less than you'd think," said Túathal.

Fercha thought his expression was far too close to that of a cat who'd just lapped up a bowl of cream.

"Why did you never marry?" she asked.

"Don't you know?" asked Túathal. "It's heartbreaking when the one you love only has eyes for another."

The king of Tamloch stared at her long enough to make Fercha feel uncomfortable. He frowned at her, then smiled.

"At least my brother has good taste."

Fercha nodded slightly and tried to keep her face impassive. Verro had told her Túathal knew about them, but could the king be hiding feelings for his own brother? Stranger things had happened in the royal families of both kingdoms.

"Very well," said Túathal. "Let me save you time. I'm *not* calling off the war. Verro and I have been planning it for far too long to stop now. Tamloch and Dâron *will* be united. Together we'll push the Eagle People into the Ocean and put an end to the Clan Lands, north *and* south."

Túathal likes to hear the sound of his own voice, thought Fercha. *Verro said little, except for pillow talk after...* She stopped that line of thought, even though they were in Verro's bedchamber with all its reminders of the times they'd spent making love on the mattress not five feet away.

Fercha considered what Doethan had told her about then *Prince* Túathal and Princess Gwýnnett—and what their affair implied about King Dârio. *Perhaps Túathal was still figuring out his preferences when he was younger,* she considered. *Or perhaps he didn't consider gender as an essential qualification for selecting a bed partner? Many didn't.*

"You're going to marry Princess Gwýnnett and step aside to install King Dârio as the sole monarch for the combined kingdoms."

"Bravo," said Túathal. "You're every bit as clever as Verro said you were. It would be a marriage of convenience, of course. Gwýnnett has assured me Dârio is tightly under her thumb."

"Right," said Fercha, keeping all traces of irony out of her voice. "And your younger sister Rúth will conveniently die of the wasting disease while the war is in progress, leaving the succession even more clear."

King Túathal smiled.

"Is Rúth even sick or will it all be Gwýnnett's poisons?"

"Whatever could you mean?" said Túathal, flicking imaginary dust from the cuffs of his shirt.

"You and Gwýnnett weren't married when Dârio was born. She was officially married to Prince Dâri."

"There's the beauty of our plan," said Túathal. "Dâron's nobles and wizards will gladly accept my compromise—after our battles or perhaps before. The king of Dâron will rule the combined kingdoms, while I pull his strings with help from Princess Gwýnnett."

"And a little thing like a formal marriage has never mattered in the Tamloch succession," said Fercha.

"You've been reading our history books," said Túathal.

"I've found it pays to know my enemy."

"We don't *have* to be enemies, dear lady," said Túathal. "Wouldn't you love to openly share Verro's bed when the kingdoms are united?"

Fercha leaned against the tall back of her chair and glanced over at Verro's bed. *Would Túathal's plan be all that bad? Especially if it ended the conflict between Dâron and Tamloch? Dârio was far more than Túathal knew, Fercha considered, and Princess Gwýnnett could be dealt with. She could be locked in the Blue Spiral Tower along the Rhuthro, for that matter. Her horned-owl familiar, Tuto, could keep watch. The Blue Spiral Tower in Melyncárreg was also an option. King Túathal would be more of a problem, however.*

"I'm tempted, Your Majesty."

"That's the idea," said the king.

"What could *I* do to support your plan?"

"You could smooth our way with the Conclave and advise the old queen that uniting the kingdoms would be the wisest course."

"I could," said Fercha. "But no promises. Dâron's Conclave is unpredictable and Carys follows her own counsel."

"Understood," said Túathal, "but your thumb on the scale couldn't hurt."

"As you say, Your Majesty," said Fercha. "I may want to discuss this with Verro. Where might I find him?"

"Where he can cause the most trouble for Dâron, of course."

"I see," said Fercha. "You've been most helpful."

"A good king wants to help his subjects—and his *future* subjects," said King Túathal.

He stood when Fercha rose from her chair. They froze in place for a moment, their eyes locked. Neither one gave ground.

Fercha was the first to turn away. She reopened the gate with a word and a gesture and stepped through into her townhouse in Brendinas.

Too bad you're not a good king, she thought, not looking back.

Chapter 24

Doethan

Every time Doethan saw the Conclave's octagonal hall from the air he wanted to reverse course and return to the reassuring rooms of his comfortable tower. The walls of the hall were made from blocks of blue-veined gray marble and the bright-blue glazed terracotta tiles on its high-pitched roof sparkled in the afternoon sun. A long rectangular wing with a flat roof extended from one of the octagon's sides. It provided a safe spot for Doethan to land. He reluctantly touched down, slung his flying disk on his back, and steeled himself for the confrontations to come. He didn't have long to wait.

"It's about time you got here," said a muscular wizard a foot taller and ten years younger than Doethan. He had dark, short-clipped hair and was blocking the entrance to the stairway leading down to the eight-sided assembly hall. "Where have you been?"

"You'll know in a few minutes when I brief the Conclave, Hibblig."

The big wizard was wearing a short blue-on-blue striped robe that marked him as a member of Princess Gwýnnett's faction. Its length allowed him to show off his muscular calves. He looked as ready to throw Doethan off the roof as let him pass.

"You're keeping us in the dark about Tamloch's plans, aren't you?"

Hibblig wasn't just a member of Gwýnnett's faction, he led it. Doethan would have been glad to postpone their discussion, but Hibblig wasn't giving him a choice.

"Tell me, old man," said Hibblig, reaching out to put one of his large hands on Doethan's shoulders. Doethan generated a small disk of solidified sound that pushed Hibblig's hand aside.

"You're as charming and courteous as ever, I see," said Doethan. "I've returned to brief everyone on the Conclave's role in the kingdom's defense. You'll hear what I have to say along with everyone else."

"That's not good enough," said Hibblig. He stuck out his jaw. "I deserve to know before the others."

"People don't always get what they deserve," said Doethan. "Now step aside. Time is of the essence. I'd have given the briefing half an hour ago, if I could have managed it."

A small woman slid past Hibblig from the stairwell like an otter gliding around a rock on a river. She joined the men on the roof.

"You'll have to settle for ten minutes from now," said Inthíra. She was a comfortable-looking wizard a few years younger than Doethan. Inthíra had with curly brown hair and wore a solid sky-blue robe marking her as part of the faction of crown wizards supporting Queen Carys. Doethan was glad to turn away from Hibblig and lean down to hug her.

"So good to see you," he said, raising his voice so it echoed in the stairwell behind them.

"The princess wants to replace you," Inthíra whispered, her lips brushing Doethan's ear. "She wants him as Senior Mage."

Doethan nodded into Inthíra's shoulder. Princess Gwýnnett's ambitions for Hibblig weren't exactly new news. They broke their embrace and Doethan spoke.

"Everyone's waiting in the assembly hall, I assume?"

"Every crown and free wizard in Brendinas," Hibblig replied, sounding smug. More of his faction lived in the city.

"I've notified the wizards outside the capital," said Inthíra. "They should gate in momentarily."

"Excellent," said Doethan. With luck, Gwýnnett's faction wouldn't have a disproportionate presence.

"Let's get on with it, old man," said Hibblig, his voice sounding like it was only a matter of time until he was in charge.

The three wizards descended the stairs with Doethan and Hibblig walking side by side, each trying to take the lead.

* * * * *

It was noisy in the assembly hall. Wizards liked to talk, especially to other wizards.

Doethan stood between Hibblig and Inthíra on a rectangular raised platform along one of the octagonal sides defining the hall's broad open space. Above and behind the platform was a carved wooden balcony. More than a hundred wizards filled the octagonal floor. They stood or sat on constructs of solidified sound, catching up with each other while waiting for Doethan to speak. Some seemed hostile, some friendly, some just curious.

Many wizards wore their flying disks slung over their backs. Quite a few younger wizards painted theirs with heraldic beasts, landscapes, abstract designs or sky-blue camouflage. *As fads went,* Doethan considered, *painted flying disks were at least clever.*

The free wizards gathered in small clumps apart from the crown wizards. They kept their conversations to themselves. It was easy to tell them apart from the wizards employed by the kingdom, not due to any clues from their physical appearance, but more from their general attitude. They tried too hard to show they were every bit as skilled and powerful as their crown wizard counterparts. For some, it came off as confidence. Others seemed like they were trying too hard.

The crown wizards were close to evenly divided between those in striped robes supporting the princess and those in solid-colored robes supporting the queen. The free wizards controlled the balance of power on the Conclave, but were such opinionated individualists that they could never be persuaded to vote as a block for one side or the other.

Doethan had been cultivating free wizards in the past weeks, hoping to swing them one by one to the queen's side, with limited success. Even free wizards sympathetic to the queen were reluctant to say so and eliminate a potential bargaining chip.

He narrowed his eyes and scanned the remote corners of the hall. Astrí and her dark-blue robes were nowhere to be seen.

"Good wizards," Doethan began. "We thought there'd be more time for us to prepare to fight Tamloch on the northern borders of the kingdom, but trouble is coming straight up the Brenavon to our doorsteps as I speak. An armada of Bifurland dragonships is on the river and could reach the city's docks tomorrow if they're not stopped."

The assembled members of the Conclave buzzed like a nest of angry wolf-hornets.

"The king has formed an alliance with Occidens Province. Two legions and sixty Roma wizards are already gating in south of the capital to aid us."

The buzzing grew louder, bordering on panic. Occidens Province was second only to Tamloch on the list of Dâron's traditional enemies. The thought of purple-robed Roma wizards in Dâron was especially galling, since the Conclave was particularly zealous about guarding its territory from magical incursions.

A meaty hand grabbed Doethan's shoulder and spun him around. Hibblig was leaning over him and shouting.

"Traitor!"

Conversations in the assembly hall ceased as all eyes and ears focused on the confrontation on the platform.

"Let me go," said Doethan, trying unsuccessfully to step back and break Hibblig's grip. "We don't have time for this. We have to stop the dragonships."

"We don't have time for *you* leading the Conclave any longer, old man," said Hibblig. A large vein pulsed red on his neck. He shook Doethan before the older wizard could push him away with a construct of solidified sound. The wizards closest to the platform gasped when Hibblig threw Doethan to the floor.

"I challenge you for the right to be Senior Mage of Dâron," said Hibblig. "Get up and fight or slink away like the traitorous worm you are."

Inthíra laughed at Hibblig's melodramatic statement. She helped Doethan to his feet while others echoed her laughter and wizards in striped robes began to chant, "Hib-blig, Hib-blig, Hib-blig!"

"We *don't* have time for this, but if you insist," said Doethan. "Let's get on with it."

"Clear the center of the hall," said Inthíra, using a megaphone of solidified sound to amplify her voice.

The wizards in the audience moved to stand by the walls. Hibblig jumped to the floor and strode across the hall to the end opposite the platform. Doethan walked down the steps on one side and took a position a few feet in front of the platform, opposite Hibblig, leaving fifty feet of empty space between them.

Why did he allow Queen Carys to talk him into returning to court? he mused. *And why did I allow myself to be nominated to head the Conclave anyway?* He spared a few moments to mentally kick himself, even if he'd been the compromise candidate most acceptable to the free wizards.

Doethan hoped he'd acquit himself well, but knew Hibblig must have been practicing for months for this. If the excuse of the alliance with the Roma hadn't been the reason for their fight, something else would have been.

The wizards lining the walls and standing in front of the platform cast more than a hundred individual shields to form a protective barrier between themselves and the combatants. They wouldn't be dropped until either Hibblig or Doethan was unconscious or surrendered.

The wizards in striped robes continued to chant, "Hib-blig, Hib-blig, Hib-blig!" Wizards in solid blue robes countered with, "Doe-than, Doe-than, Doe-than!" Most were stamping their feet.

"Ready?" asked Inthíra.

"Aye," said Hibblig, his big voice carrying over the chanting and stamping.

Doethan turned to face Inthíra on the platform above him. He rolled his eyes and nodded. She would keep Fercha and Queen Carys informed if he was incapacitated, or worse. He knew Hibblig would be trying to kill him, not just knock him out. He shifted to face his opponent.

"Lay on!" shouted Inthíra.

Hibblig gestured with one hand and spoke a trigger word, generating a suit of solidified-sound armor around his body that made his considerable bulk seem even larger. Then he charged.

Chapter 25

Nûd and Eynon

Nûd was in good spirits after spending time visiting with the young dragon riders and sharing a meal. Eynon wasn't quite sure he liked the taste of the small pickled fish they'd fed him—but he didn't have much experience eating things with fins. The flatbread they'd shared was quite good, though, and the tart blue jam that went with it was delicious. Eynon and Nûd contributed what was left of the bread and cheese and smoked sausage from the basket Braith had given them early that morning. The Bifurlander youths thought as highly of Eynon's parents' skills in the kitchen as he did.

Chee liked everything the dragon riders fed him. He scurried from rider to rider, begging morsels from each of them. The raconette's belly was soon full and he returned to his favorite spot on Rocky's back to nap. The wyvern was relaxing, soaking up sunlight and admiring glances from dragon riders. He even let Holgir rub him under his jaw with the back of his axe, which apparently did a lot to boost the lad's reputation for bravery.

Sigrun was clearly the leader of the wing of dragon riders, with Rannveigr her second in command. *She's a princess, so that only makes sense,* thought Eynon. *Do Bifurlanders even have princesses?* he considered. *They have kings and queens, so they must have them.* Rannveigr was also some sort of noble—and Sigrun's first cousin, if Eynon had heard things correctly over lunch. Trying to follow twelve fast high-pitched interweaving conversational threads, most of which were about people he didn't know, hadn't been easy.

Several of the girls were flirting with Nûd and some tried doing the same with Eynon, making him uncomfortable, until Nûd told them about Eynon's *girlfriend.* The boys were boasting about their skill as hunters and accepting good-natured teasing from the girls. Eynon shifted to sit next to Sigrun.

"What's your father like?" Eynon asked. "I've never talked to a king before."

"He's a giant," said Sigrun, "over seven feet tall and as strong as a grizzly bear with a black eye patch and scar from an axe blade running from his jaw to his ear."

"I see," said Eynon, hoping she was pulling his leg. "Sounds like one of my uncles."

"You're no fun," said Sigrun, laughing. "My father and mother can be intimidating, but not *that* intimidating."

"Do you resemble your mother?" asked Eynon.

"No, her father," teased Rannveigr. "Especially when she wears *her* eye patch."

Sigrun playfully punched her friend in the shoulder and accepted a similar punch in return.

"King Bjarni and Queen Signý are good rulers," said Rannveigr. "They listen, and they're fair."

"Do you think fifty pounds of gold would be enough to convince them to stop their invasion?" Eynon asked Sigrun.

"I don't know," said Sigrun. "My father gave his word to King Túathal."

"For fifty pounds of gold, he'll do it," said Rannveigr after she swallowed a bite of smoked sausage. "For that much, he'd even attack Riyas instead."

"You don't know that," said Sigrun. Then she smiled and shrugged in a *what-can-I-say* gesture. Eynon felt optimistic.

"So long as they don't decide to take *us* along with the gold," said Nûd. "I'm not fond of cold weather."

Eynon was about to say, "But you live in Melyncárreg," then he thought better of it.

"We'd better get back to the fleet," said Sigrun. "This was just supposed to be a scouting expedition, after all."

"And we don't want your father to be worried," said Rannveigr.

"I'm more concerned about my mother," said Sigrun.

"And rightly so, I expect," said Rannveigr as she stood. "Mount up, everyone. Time to get airborne." She walked toward the small gold dragons.

"We'll fly in formation around your wyvern," said Sigrun.

"Can't we just follow you?" asked Eynon.

"You don't want to give the wrong impression when we get to the fleet," said Sigrun. "If you're behind us, our wizards *and* warriors might think you're in pursuit and try to attack."

Eynon nodded. "That makes sense."

"Eynon," said Sigrun.

"Yes?"

"When you have an audience with my parents, don't say the gold is a bribe. Tell them it's a gift from Dâron to Bifurland—and a sign of Dâron's respect for our people's prowess in battle."

"I can do that," said Eynon.

"Maybe I should do the talking," said Nûd. He'd stood and crossed to join Eynon and Sigrun when the circle of girls around him had left.

"Would you?" asked Eynon. "That would be great! You don't learn how to talk to kings and queens growing up on a farm."

"And you don't learn growing up with only a cranky old man for company either," said Nûd, "though I've read enough history books to know the customs of the court."

"The court of Dâron, maybe," said Sigrun. "I've read history books too, and you'd be surprised how different things are in Bifurland."

All three of them laughed. Sigrun turned to Eynon.

"You may be better at talking to my father than Nûd," she said. "Ruling is a part-time job in Bifurland. My father has a large dairy farm outside Bjarniston and sits on the stool beside me for the morning milking when he's not in town being king."

"How large is your herd?" asked Eynon.

"Twenty dozen," said Sigrun proudly.

"That's more than we have in my entire village," said Eynon. "I've done my share of morning—and afternoon—milking. Do you make any interesting cheeses?"

"Everyone loves our sharp cheese," said Sigrun. "We age it for two years and..."

"...the two of you could talk about cows and milk and butter and cheese for twice that long, I'm sure," said Nûd. "We'll both speak, and you can give us a signal if we're getting off track."

"I'll rub my chin if you're doing well, and put my hand on my cheek if you're not," said Sigrun. "That's the best I can do."

Nûd extended a hand to Eynon and helped him to his feet. Eynon did the same for Sigrun in turn. He remembered seeing a funny-looking carved *shah-mat* piece owned by one of his neighbors back in Haywall that showed a queen with her hand on her cheek and smiled.

"What?" asked Sigrun.

Eynon explained.

"Oh, those," she said. "We have three sets. They *are* funny, aren't they—especially the queen. She always looks so worried."

"Like your mother?" teased Eynon.

"I'm the one who's worried," said Sigrun, "not her."

Sigrun started to walk to her companions who were already mounted, then she turned around to rejoin Nûd and Eynon.

"I almost forgot. Space is tight, even on the flagship. I'll land first and make sure they clear room in front of the mast for your wyvern."

"And don't shoot us with quarrels," said Nûd.

"Or blast us with fireballs," added Eynon.

"Our wizards are more fond of lightning bolts," said Sigrun, "but yes, I'll tell them not to attack you. I'll wave when it's safe for you to land."

"Thank you," said Eynon.

Nûd nodded and smiled. "Yes, thanks," he said.

"We can talk about cows later," said Sigrun.

Her long blonde braids bounced as she ran to her dragon. Eynon and Nûd climbed on Rocky's back, pleased that the pillowcases filled with gold rings had been returned. Soon they were in the middle of the wing of dragons with the sun at their backs, heading for the Bifurland fleet.

"Be sure to stay strapped in this time," said Eynon.

"Don't worry," said Nûd. "I will."

Chapter 26

Merry

Merry stayed even with Nyssia as she guided them through the maze of dusty corridors on the lower levels of the palace. She counted turns and paces, but wasn't completely sure what direction they were heading or how far they'd traveled. They'd moved quickly along the empty, echoing stone halls for ten minutes without encountering another human being. Then Merry saw a hooded figure waiting in the corridor ahead of them, standing in the shadows. When Merry and Nyssia got closer, they saw the figure was standing next to an archway that opened to a narrow flight of stairs ascending into darkness. Nyssia didn't seem concerned, so Merry let out the breath she hadn't realized she'd been holding. The figure threw back her hood.

"I'll take her from here," said Astrí. "We have to get to the Conclave. All the wizards in the kingdom have been summoned."

"The closest exit to the Conclave's hall is up those stairs," said Nyssia, giving Astrí a small bow.

"I know," said Astrí. "And we have to hurry."

Astrí put her hand on Merry's arm and tugged her gently toward the stairs.

"Thank you," said Merry, breaking away and giving Nyssia a quick hug. "Give my best to Gruffyd."

"I will," said the young woman in guard's armor. "I'd tell you to stay out of trouble..."

"...but where's the fun in that?" completed Merry. "I hope this doesn't get *you* in trouble."

"If it does, I'll talk my way out of it," said Nyssia. "I have an easy excuse since Princess Gwýnnett forgot to tell us you were a wizard. How can a brand-new guard be expected to cope with magic?"

"How indeed?" asked Merry with a smile. "I don't think she knew." Merry took Astrí's sleeve and followed the older woman up the stairs.

As they climbed, Astrí whispered, "Llachar," and a small globe of light appeared, floating above her head. It helped the two of them see where they were going.

There was a landing at the top, with a solid wooden door in front of them. The door had an ornate cast-iron box big enough to hold a pair of ladies' shoes where a lock should have been. There wasn't a latch or a doorknob, and Merry couldn't see any place to fit a key.

Astrí pulled her hood back up.

"It's a wizard's lock," she said. "This is the door that wizards use to get back and forth from the palace to the Conclave's hall without being seen. You need a construct of solidified sound to open it."

Merry nodded. Her earlier exuberance was muted by the prospect of her first visit to the Conclave's octagonal center. She'd seen a woodcut of the building in one of the books in her father's library.

"Create a rod of solidified sound about an inch in diameter," said Astrí.

The older wizard pointed to the lower left side of the lock.

"Insert it here, then extend it like a three-tined cooking fork to the right until you hear three clicks."

Merry followed Astrí's instructions. It was a very simple construct and she soon heard three clicks bounce off the walls on either side of the landing.

"Good," said Astrí. "Pull out your magestone and wear it so it can be seen. It will serve as your pass for entering the assembly hall."

Her gold-and-silver electrum setting was warm from resting against her skin when Merry moved it to hang outside her shirt. The circular blue magestone in its center pulsed with inner light.

Astrí took her setting out from under her robes. It was an elegant silver openwork filigree, holding a large oval stone. Astrí's stone pulsed as well.

It looks like the artifact Eynon found, thought Merry.

"Come," said Astrí, pushing the door open. It led to another long stone corridor, much like the ones in the palace, but less dusty. Merry half-expected to find an animated broom and dustpan hard at work around a corner.

"What should I expect when we get there?" asked Merry as they walked.

"Chaos and conflict," said Astrí. "Princess Gwýnnett and her faction will be trying to take over leadership of the Conclave. Take extra care if you speak to any wizard wearing striped robes."

"I will," said Merry, "but I don't understand. I assumed Queen Carys had been the one truly running the kingdom for the last few years. How did Princess Gwýnnett's faction grow so powerful? And who was leading the Conclave?"

"Fercha led the Conclave, with help from Inthíra," said Astrí. "You haven't met her yet, but you'll like her. I help where I'm needed, though I'm just the queen's personal wizard."

And I'm just a Mastlands' pig in a wallow, thought Merry. *With wings.* She held back a smile.

"That means you must have dragooned Doethan to come back and lead the Conclave once Gwýnnett's faction got more power," said Merry.

"We did," said Astrí. She held back a smile of her own. Merry had real talent for political analysis, even at fifteen. She reminded Astrí of another young woman, many years ago.

"How did you and Carys lose your grip?" asked Merry. "How could you give Gwýnnett and her faction the time and opportunity she needed to challenge you?"

Astrí didn't reply for several paces. They turned a corner and had to sidestep to avoid an animated broom and round black gate on the floor playing dustpan. Merry was pleased she'd predicted their existence.

"The answer is grief," said Astrí. "Losing her husband *and* grandson in the space of a week took a toll on Carys—and on me. We lost our focus and shut ourselves off to be alone with our pain. Our allies didn't know when or *if* we'd resume our former roles."

"And Gwýnnett and her people filled the void."

"Like they'd been expecting it," said Astrí. "I think Gwýnnett must have slipped something into our food when I was less vigilant about inspections after the state funerals. My mind stopped being fogged when I decided to fast more than a year later. I made sure Queen Carys didn't eat anything adulterated immediately afterward, and she was soon her earlier self, if sadder and maybe wiser."

"That explains it," said Merry. "Is King Dârio kept drugged as well?"

She could see sunlight entering the corridor up ahead.

"No," said Astrí. "That's one of the bright spots of the situation. Young Dârio is an ally. He has no fondness for his mother, but feigns being under her thumb to avoid Gwýnnett's more extensive manipulations."

"Thank goodness for *that*," said Merry.

They'd reached the sunlit spot. A spiral staircase led up a level. They ascended into a massive assembly hall. A pair of wizards— one in striped robes, one in solid-colored robes, noted their magestones and let them pass. Merry heard shouts from the other side of a wall near the spiral stairs.

"Blast!" said Astrí. "It's already started. Let's get inside."

Chapter 27

Damon

"Blast," said Damon when they'd left the queen's apartments. His magestone had just glowed with three quick flashes of blue light. "The Conclave has been summoned. I thought I might have at least another hour."

"This way, your wizardness," said Gruffyd, starting down the hall toward a staircase.

"Where are *you* going?" asked Damon.

"To the wizard's door to the Conclave's headquarters," said Gruffyd. The big guard looked from side to side uneasily. "It's three levels below us."

"I *know* where it is," said Damon, "I had the wizard's door built myself, so my comings and goings wouldn't be advertised to every busybody in the kingdom. But I can't attend a meeting of the Conclave looking like *this*."

Damon moved his hands from his shoulders to his waist. Gruffyd took in his well-worn robes and scruffy wisent-skin jacket.

"I can see that," said Gruffyd.

"Take me back to my quarters," said Damon. "I should have something more impressive to wear there."

"Where *are* your quarters, your wizardness? Somewhere in Brendinas?"

"They're on the second floor, not far from King Dârio's study. Get me there and I can find my suite myself. And don't call me *your wizardness*. My name is Damon—Ealdamon if you're being formal. If you *must* use a title, call me Master Mage."

Gruffyd's eyes grew large. "Yes, Master Mage Ealdamon."

"Gruffyd, is it?" asked the wizard. "There's no need to be formal when it's just the two of us. *Master Mage Ealdamon* takes too long say and makes me feel old. Just call me Damon."

"But you *are* old, Damon," said Gruffyd with a grin. It was what Merry would have said, he was sure.

"Get moving," said Damon, smiling back, "or I'll turn you into a frog."

"Can wizards even do that?" asked Gruffyd as he started walking away from the staircase.

"Now you're thinking," said Damon as he lengthened his stride to keep up with the clanking armored youth. *Perhaps the lad wasn't as much of a blockhead as he seemed.*

* * * * *

Damon kept his overly-protective dusting cloud away from Gruffyd's head with a stern look. The old wizard tossed four robes down on the white goose-down comforter covering his bed. All were cut from sumptuous fabric that Gruffyd was sure would drape well, even if Damon's thin form made him look like he'd been on short rations for years.

You'd think the kingdom's Master Mage would be able to afford a decent cook, thought Gruffyd.

"Which one do *you* think looks more impressive?" asked Damon. "The solid blue? The blue-on-blue stripes?"

Gruffyd bit his lower lip and looked uncomfortable. Nyssia had asked him similar questions about her ensembles in the past and he never managed to come up with an acceptable answer. He glanced around the room, buying time. A tapestry to one side of the fireplace showed a young male figure in dark-blue robes standing in the middle of a carved wooden balcony above a crowd of wizards. Gruffyd pulled his eyes away. Damon was still talking.

"What about the particolor in different shades of blue? Or the one that sparkles?"

The old wizard was staring at him, expecting an answer, so Gruffyd went with the obvious.

"They're all a bit old-fashioned, sir."

"Of *course* they're old-fashioned. They're forty years old, for goodness sake. If I hadn't protected them from moths they'd be full of holes by now."

"Yes, your wizard—" Gruffyd stop. Damon looked frustrated. "Yes, Damon. On you, old-fashioned would look good."

Frustration turned to exasperation.

"Yes, but which one should I wear if I want to disrupt the meeting of the Conclave and make their jaws drop."

"I think having Dâron's near-mythical master mage show up would get everyone's attention, even if you showed up naked," said Gruffyd. "Maybe especially if you showed up naked."

"That's not my style, lad. Try again. Which robe?"

"You support King Dârio?"

"Of course I do. He's the king."

"But not his mother, I think," said Gruffyd. "I remember you called her the *Spider*."

"Correct," said Damon, carefully enunciating each syllable. "She's a conniving poisonous..."

"Then I wouldn't wear the striped robe," said Gruffyd, cutting off Damon's tirade.

"Blast! That's right. It slipped my mind," said Damon. "Princess Gwýnnett's supporters are using striped robes now. It's a shame I won't be able to wear this one any more." He folded the striped robe and put it carefully away in the large chest at the foot of his bed.

"If you support the old queen, the solid-colored robe would work," said Gruffyd.

"I do, but it won't," said Damon.

Gruffyd's eyes followed Damon, waiting for details.

"If I'm going to reassume my place as the leader of the Conclave, I want the wizards to see me as *above* their petty factions—here to rescue the kingdom in its time of need."

"I wouldn't put it to *them* that way," said Gruffyd. "Nyssia says they're proud and stubborn."

"Nyssia?" asked Damon.

"My fiancé," said Gruffyd.

"Takes one to know one. I'll win them over—but I still need to decide between particolor and sparkly."

"I've seen free wizards in the taverns and shops near the palace," said Gruffyd. "They tend to dress in particolor."

"Good point," said Damon. "And since they control the balance of power on the Conclave, it might not be bad to look like one."

Gruffyd nodded, attempting to seem sage and not managing to.

"Still," said Damon, stroking his chin. "It wouldn't do for the Master Mage of the kingdom to put himself forward as a free wizard. I may have been gone for forty years, but I'm still Dâron's most senior *crown* wizard."

"Uh huh," said Gruffyd. He didn't know what else to say.

"The sparkly robe it is," said Damon, a broad smile animating his lined face. "Observe!"

Damon held up the sparkling dark-blue robe he'd selected by its shoulders, so it caught the sunlight. Couched threads of silver and gold on the sleeves and body interlocked in intricate patterns of reflecting knotwork. Its tall, stiff, loose-fitting collar was covered with pearls and silver piping.

The collar makes the robe look old-fashioned, thought Gruffyd. *But it's still impressive.*

"Go-li-â-char!" said the wizard, giving the fabric a shake.

Luminous spiral fractal patterns were shining with a blue light resembling the glow of Damon's magestone. Sparkling sapphire patterns pulsed across the robe, looking like a glorious summer sky full of stars.

Gruffyd swiftly inhaled, then let his breath out slowly.

"That's the one to wear, your wizardness," he said. "It's spectacular."

"Thank you. It was a gift from Princess Seren."

"You knew Princess Seren?" asked Gruffyd, his eyes going wide.

"Of course," said Damon. "She hadn't disappeared yet when I came to court. That was probably before your *father* was born."

"It was," said Gruffyd. People, even barons, married young in the Rhuthro valley.

"Seren put the powdered magestone dust on herself," said Damon. "It took her a week to get it off her fingers. She looked like a woad-painted Clan Lands' barbarian."

"If you're the old Master Mage, weren't you the one who was supposed to *find* Princess Seren? How did that go?"

"That's a long story, lad. A tale for another time," said Damon. He stroked his chin again, as if deep in thought, and his eyes seemed to lose focus.

Gruffyd watched Damon's expression with concern. It seemed like the old wizard was miles—or years—away.

"Ahem," said Gruffyd, clearing his throat loud enough for the sound to echo around Damon's bedchamber.

"What?" said Damon. "Oh, yes. The Conclave. Turn around, young man, while I change."

Gruffyd executed a crisp *about face* maneuver. He heard rustling sounds as Damon slid his flying disk off his back, took off the plain robe he'd been wearing, and pulled the sparkly robe over his head. A soft *thump* marked the old wizard mounting his flying disk. Gruffyd felt a rush of air and turned back. The tapestry next to the fireplace seemed to shimmer for a heartbeat.

Damon was gone.

Chapter 28
Fercha

Back in her townhouse, Fercha threw herself on her bed, then rolled over to face the ceiling and laced her fingers behind her head. She needed to think, and her current configuration of limbs was her favorite thinking position.

What was wrong with Dârio being king of both Dâron and Tamloch? He was young, but he had promise, despite his mother.

Fercha chuckled.

What was wrong was Túathal and Gwýnnett treating Dârio as a catspaw, she considered. *No one, even a king, could be protected completely. Dârio deserved to mature into the fine ruler Fercha thought he could be without the pressure of a manipulative mother and secret father trying to use him.*

She stretched her legs under her robes and tried to pull her toes toward her head while keeping her legs straight. Fercha could feel her calf muscles relax, but the tendons in her neck still felt like tightened steel wires.

Of course, the same problem of constant night and day protection applied to Túathal and Gwýnnett. Queen Carys and Astrí wouldn't go along with having either of that charming pair killed, but imprisoning them both in a tower on a rocky island somewhere in the Ocean east of Riyas would serve. Those two of deserved decades with only each other for company. Unfortunately, imprisoning them wouldn't work.

Fercha took a deep breath and flexed her elbows up and down like wings.

It wouldn't work because Verro would find a way to rescue them. She couldn't understand why, but Verro loved Túathal, though not in the way Túathal wanted to love Verro.

She chuckled again. The laugh made her neck less tense.

Verro could be so insightful, she thought, *but couldn't see something the size of a Bifurland mammoth under his nose.*

Fercha smiled, considering some of the things Verro was very, very good at. The tension behind her eyes decreased and her breathing slowed, then started to speed up when she moved her hands the way Verro moved his when they were alone together. She knew she shouldn't pause to rest—there was too much yet to do—but release might keep her centered, better able to handle the stress of the Conclave meeting. Her magestone flashed three times in close succession.

Blast! she thought. *Can't I have a moment's peace? Can't I have a moment's happiness? Would it be so bad if Verro and I could share a bed every night?*

She pulled her shoulders back and sat up, putting both feet on the floor.

It can't be helped—and I've got to get to the Conclave.

Fercha was straightening her robes, preparing to gate out to the assembly hall, when four solid knocks landed on the front door three floors down. She crossed to a window with a view of the street, opened it, and leaned out. Five royal guardsmen with striped gambesons were below. One rapped on her door again with the hilt of his unsheathed sword held like a hammer.

"What?" asked Fercha, her tone suggesting she'd gladly dump the contents of a chamberpot on their heads if she had one at hand.

"Come to the palace immediately," said the guard in front with the unsheathed sword. "Princess Gwýnnett requires your presence."

"Tell the princess I have other plans."

"She said that's what you'd say," said the guard. He held up a letter with a dark-blue wax seal. "She told me to give you this."

Fercha send down a bubble of solidified sound and took the letter, lifting it up to her window. She opened it and saw seven words written in Princess Gwýnnett's overly precise handwriting.

"I need your help," it read. "Dârio is missing."

Chapter 29

Nûd and Eynon

Eynon saw a large river ahead. It was every bit as broad as the Moravon near Tyford and far greater than the Rhuthro. From their current altitude, he could also see hundreds of dragonships with their billowing square sails catching the wind, tacking north.

"Is that the Brenavon?" asked Eynon.

"If it's not, there are two Bifurland fleets attacking Dâron," said Nûd. "At least there's no trouble figuring out which one is their flagship."

Eynon looked closer. The lead dragonship was more than twice as large as the others, except for some wider vessels near the rear of the armada.

"What are those ships in the back?" Eynon asked. "They look like *fat* dragonships."

"I'm not an expert, but I think they're called *knarrs*. At least that's what they were labeled on the woodcut in a book about Bifurland I read in Ealdamon's library. They're merchant ships and are probably along to haul back plunder."

"Uh-oh," said Eynon. "I think we may have overlooked something by only bringing fifty pounds of gold."

Nûd realized it only a second later. "The value of the treasure the Bifurlanders would get when they sacked Brendinas. That would be a lot more than fifty pounds of gold."

"Maybe we can talk them into sacking Riyas instead?"

"Why would they do that?" asked Nûd. "They're almost to the city."

"I wonder if that's why the dragon riders were laughing at us?" Eynon considered.

"Probably," said Nûd. "Want to change your mind about meeting Sigrun's parents?"

"I don't know if we've got much choice about it now," said Eynon, looking up. The girls and boys on dragon-back were crowding Rocky, forcing the big black wyvern down toward the flagship.

"Can't you use some sort of wizardry to stop them?" asked Nûd.

"I could," said Eynon, "but I don't want to hurt them. And maybe King Bjarni and Queen Signý would rather have gold without needing to fight?"

"You haven't read any of the Bifurlanders' sagas, have you?"

Eynon shook his head. There weren't a lot of books in the Coombe.

"They glory in battle. I wouldn't suggest that they'd prefer *not* to fight."

"Right," said Eynon. "I guess we might as well talk to them. We'll muddle through *somehow*." Eynon called on his magestones to make distance viewing lenses and gave the fleet a closer inspection. *"Hey!"* he said.

"What?"

"The pictures of dragonships in Robin Goodfellow's *Peregrinations* all showed them with dragon heads fore and aft. The flagship and the lead ships around it don't have them, just flat boards above pointed prows and sterns."

"Make me some lenses—let me see for myself," said Nûd. Eynon did and Nûd used them. "You're right. I don't understand it," said Nûd.

A few minutes later they *did* understand. The gold dragons had guided Rocky down to the flagship. Room had been cleared for him in front of the ship's mast. Sigrun and Rannveigr's dragons landed at the front and back of the vessel, then climbed up and rested on the flat boards with their long necks sticking out beyond the prow and stern, forming living figureheads. The rest of the gold dragons took up similar posts on the other lead ships.

"Now they look like the pictures," said Eynon. Nûd moved his chin up and down in agreement.

Chee jumped down from Rocky's neck, stole an apple from a basket on deck, and climbed the single mast like a squirrel. When the little raconette reached the top Eynon could hear one long triumphant, "Cheeee!" from above. He wondered if Chee would try to hit someone with the core when he'd finished eating. Eynon would have chastised him for his theft but he was too far above him to hear any reprimand and Eynon had more important things to do.

Nûd and Eynon saw an imposing couple in their late thirties standing near the mainmast. The woman had golden-blonde braids and the man had a long red-gold beard and massive arms the size of most people's legs.

"That must be King Bjarni and Queen Signý," said Eynon. "She resembles the worried queen in my neighbor's *shah-mat* set."

The royal couple wore fur vests and sparkled with gold torcs, bracelets, rings, earrings, and necklaces—the king every bit as much as the queen. Behind them were three women in gold robes wearing thick amber necklaces.

Sigrun and Rannveigr weaved through warrior-sailors milling about on the ship until they got to Rocky's side. They helped Nûd and Eynon unload the pillowcases filled with gold rings and piled them by the mast. Sigrun's parents watched without speaking until their daughter, her friend, and the two young men stood before them.

"Welcome," said King Bjarni. He had a warm, welcoming smile. His huge, bushy red-blonde beard was like Eynon's cousin Euwen's. Euwen was twenty years older than Eynon and fairly famous in the family for his pigheadedness. He'd made a pact with himself that he wouldn't cut his beard until the young woman he'd met and fallen for on his wander year married him. The young woman had married someone else and now had two children, so Euwen's beard had become quite impressive.

Queen Signý moved her hand from her cheek and smiled. "Who are your friends?" she asked Sigrun. The gold-robed figures remained in the background.

"This is Nûd, and the skinny one is..."

"Eynon, Your Majesties. Our wyvern's name is Rocky."

Signý motioned to one of her soldiers who returned half a minute later with a goat for the wyvern. Rocky curled his tail around the flagship's mast and began to consume the caprine offering.

"Join us toward the stern," said Queen Signý.

"This way," said Sigrun. She tugged on Nûd and Eynon's sleeves simultaneously.

There were two folding thrones set up a few dozen feet behind the mast. Bjarni and Signý sat and benches were brought for Nûd, Eynon and the girls. The gold-robed figures with amber necklaces—Bifurland wizards, Eynon assumed—stood behind the thrones. Warriors with iron helmets, round shields, and long-handled axes or spears kept guard to either side. It reminded Eynon of the court of the king and queen of flowers at the spring festival back in the Coombe—but with more edged weapons. The king motioned for them to sit.

"Who are *you?*" asked King Bjarni, once everyone was situated.

"They're bringing you *gold*," said Sigrun.

"Let them speak for themselves," said Bjarni, smiling at his daughter. "Anyone arriving on wyvern-back deserves that, at least."

"Gold?" asked Signý.

"Yes, Your Majesty," said Nûd to the queen. "The first of many gifts of gold if you'll turn your warriors' wrath away from Dâron and seek glory elsewhere."

"How *much* gold?" asked the king.

"Fifty pounds," said Sigrun.

"Shush," said Rannveigr, putting her hand over Sigrun's mouth. She removed it in a hurry when Sigrun bit it. "Ouch!"

"Serves you right, sister-daughter," said Signý. "She needs to learn to control her tongue on her own without your help." The queen put her hand back on her cheek and gave both girls a look that said she was shocked, *shocked* by their behavior. She laughed and so did both girls.

"That's quite a lot of gold," said Bjarni.

"Five times what Túathal gave us," said Signý, rubbing a hand on her chin in one of Damon's familiar mannerisms. Nûd took that as a good sign. She was thinking about it.

"It's in those bags by the mast," said Sigrun.

"Fetch them here, both of you," said King Bjarni. "It will help you work off some of your youthful energy and I'd like to see their gift."

Sigrun and Rannveigr stood, acknowledged Sigrun's parents, and rushed back to the mast chattering to each other like songbirds.

"Children are wonderful," said the king.

"I agree, Your Majesty," said Nûd. "Your daughter is charming."

"I wouldn't go quite *that* far," said Bjarni, a smile showing through his copious beard. "Especially when she's with all the other dragon riders."

Nûd nodded and smiled in return. One of the gold-robed women leaned forward and whispered in Queen Signý's ear.

"Who might *you* be?" the queen asked Eynon. "A wizard, I assume, but with a *red* magestone. Are you from a distant land across the Ocean?"

"No, Your Majesty," said Eynon. "I'm from the Coombe, good farmland in the west of Dâron. My village keeps dairy cattle, just like you do. I found my magestone far away."

Queen Signý stroked her chin again and said, "Hmm..."

King Bjarni looked over at his wife and then turned over his shoulder to see the gold-robed figures with amber necklaces. One nodded at him.

"It sounds like my daughter has been talking more than listening," said the king.

"I was not," said Sigrun, skipping up with her blonde braids bouncing and Rannveigr close behind. She dropped her bag in front of her father and Rannveigr handed hers to the queen. Bjarni reached down to pick up his bag while Signý was already removing a gold ring from hers. She held it up to the light while the girls ran back to get more.

"Very high quality," said Signý.

"Beautiful shine," said the king, turning a ring back and forth to catch the sun.

"The first of *many* such gifts?" the queen asked.

"Yes, Your Majesty. The first of many," said Nûd.

"*How* many?" asked King Bjarni.

"How many would it take for you to seek glory by sacking Riyas instead of Brendinas?" asked Nûd.

"What kind of king would I be if I turned on a fellow monarch like that?" asked Bjarni.

"A richer one," said Eynon, smiling.

Nûd glanced over at Eynon and smiled back. He'd said just the right thing.

King Bjarni turned to his wife. She nodded.

"We will take the matter under advisement," he said. "How long would it take you to gather a larger gift?"

"That depends on how much larger the gift would need to be," said Nûd.

"Five hundred pounds," said Queen Signý.

"In total, counting the fifty we've given you already?" asked Nûd.

"Five hundred pounds *more*," Signý confirmed. "That would balance out what we could expect to extract from Brendinas."

"As you say, Your Majesty," said Nûd. "It will take us several days to collect such an additional gift. You could anchor your fleet on the east bank just to the north while you wait. There's a royal hunting preserve for the crown of Dâron there, with plenty of deer and wild boar for the taking."

"Hmm..." said King Bjarni, tugging his beard instead of rubbing his chin. One of the gold-robed figures nudged his shoulder and he dropped his hand. "Before anything is decided," said the king, "give us a demonstration of your red magestone wizardry."

"Of course," said Eynon. He stood and bowed to Bjarni and Signý. "What would you like to see?"

"Something big and showy," said Sigrun, returning along with Rannveigr carrying more bags of gold rings. The rings made muffled clunks.

Eynon looked at the king and queen. They nodded. So did the gold-robed women behind them.

It will have to be a fireball, thought Eynon. *That fireball I threw at the lake back in Melyncárreg was impressive.*

He looked at the river off to port. Nûd shook his head slightly and held up one finger, pointing toward the clouds.

Right, thought Eynon. *It wouldn't be smart to vaporize too much of the river. People might be hurt and ships might be damaged.*

"I'd like to have my staff for the spell I've got in mind," said Eynon. "It's back with my wyvern. Do I have your leave to get it?"

"Sigrun," King Bjarni shouted, "bring back the young wizard's staff with the next bag of gold."

"Yes, father!" came Sigrun's reply. A few seconds later she was back with more gold and Eynon's staff.

He took it and twirled it a few times, trying to look impressive, then realized he'd need a lot more practice before he could. He held his staff aloft and concentrated, calling on his red magestone for just the right level of power and his blue magestone for control plus a few extra fillips to make the explosion more colorful. He closed his eyes for a moment, then opened them and released a concentrated ball of energy skyward from the tip of his staff.

Then Eynon was bowled over by three tight-light force blasts from the gold-robed Bifurland wizards. Energies erupted from their amber magestones and would have caved in his chest if he hadn't reflexively thrown up a shield in time. As it was, the blasts pushed back his spherical shield and tumbled him over and over until he came to rest against the mast. Nûd was reaching for his crossbow before he realized it was still strapped to Rocky's back.

Seconds later, everyone was tossed to the deck by a tremendous explosion overhead. King Bjarni and Queen Signý were knocked backward on their folding thrones into the three gold-robed wizards who stopped their attack and landed in a heap. Nûd was tossed over his bench and had to close his eyes to prevent himself from being blinded by Eynon's fireball.

Concentric rings of blue fire surrounded the glowing red ball. They turned purple where they were touched by its crimson flames. A massive boom like the loudest peal of thunder ever heard assaulted their ears. Waves of heat beat down on the flagship, but luckily not enough to set the sails alight. The guards were on their knees or had the nasals on their helms pressed to the deck. Chee slid most of the way down the big square sail, digging three sets of claws into the canvas while a paw-hand still clutched his half-eaten apple.

Eynon recovered first, when Rocky nudged his protective sphere of solidified sound upright. The wyvern licked the sphere enthusiastically and had seemed to enjoy the light, heat and noise. After creating a new sphere for Rocky to lick, Eynon dispelled the sphere that had saved his life and stepped over to help Nûd to his feet. They both helped Sigrun and Rannveigr up. The girls were unharmed, if a little dazed. They brushed each other off while Eynon and Nûd extended hands to King Bjarni and Queen Signý. Guards helped the other wizards stand.

"What was *that* about?" demanded Eynon as he confronted the king and queen and the gold-robed wizards. "I thought we were your guests?"

"It was just a test of your shields," said one of the Bifurland wizards.

"A test that would have killed me if I hadn't been fast enough to raise them," said Eynon. His red magestone was pulsing angrily and the trio of gold-robed wizards took a step back. King Bjarni, now standing, held up his hand.

"You're right," he said. "You *are* our guests. I will see that these three are disciplined for their actions."

Eynon nodded. The pulses from his red magestone slowed and became less bright.

"We accept your offer of a gift of five hundred pounds of gold to direct our warriors elsewhere," said the king.

"That offer is no longer on the table," said Nûd. "The new offer is the fifty pounds we've already given you and my friend not burning your fleet to the waterline."

"We'll take that under..." began Bjarni.

"We accept," said Queen Signý. The three gold-robed wizards, now gathered close behind her, were nodding vigorously.

Around the flagship, other dragonships were recovering from Eynon's fireball. Warrior-sailors were picking themselves up and moving barrels, crates and ship's supplies back where they belonged after being tossed about. Some ships had holes in their sails and one had tipped enough that it had taken on water. Nearby ships were helping it offload food, armor and weapons so it could be bailed out more easily.

Rocky leaned his head around the flagship's mainmast and looked at Rannveigr, Sigrun, and Sigrun's parents. Sigrun approached the wyvern and rubbed the bottom of his chin with the hilt of her sword. Rocky made a rumbling noise deep in his chest and Bjarni signaled to his guards to toss the big beast another goat, which disappeared almost as fast as the first.

"Do you have any stones?" asked Eynon, holding his cupped hands to indicate a certain size. "He needs rocks to help his digestion."

Queen Signý sent a team of guards below and they quickly returned with baskets full of ballast stones. Rocky crunched and swallowed some of the stones *and* a basket. Soon a different sort of rumbling came from the wyvern's belly.

"I like Rocky," said Sigrun.

"He likes you, too," said Eynon. He was impressed that his familiar had allowed Sigrun's familiarity.

Eynon turned to Nûd and mouthed, "Now what?" Nûd smiled.

"What next, Your Majesties?" Nûd asked.

"How soon will you be leaving?" asked King Bjarni.

"There's nothing keeping us," said Nûd.

"Except giving Rocky a few minutes to digest his food," said Eynon.

Everyone's attention was distracted by shouts from forward and starboard. Sigrun and Rannveigr ran up and quickly returned.

"One of the scout boats is returning," said Sigrun.

"They have news from upriver," said Rannveigr.

"Bring the scout-captain here as soon as he's on-board," said Bjarni.

A few minutes later, a clean-shaven Bifurlander dressed like a prosperous Dâron farmer stepped in front of the king and queen where they'd resumed their seats on their folding thrones.

"Welcome back, Skavendr," said the king.

"Good to *be* back, Bjarni. You won't believe what we saw."

Skavendr sat on one of the benches the girls had vacated.

"Cut the dramatics," said Signý. "What did you see?"

"Two Occidens Province legions and their wizards are marching down the east bank of the Brenavon."

The king and queen both raised their eyebrows.

"Do you have anything to say about this information?" Queen Signý asked Nûd.

"It's news to me, Your Majesty."

"Really," said the queen. "Yet you wanted us to attack Riyas instead of an understrength Nova Eboracum garrison."

"The quarrel between Dâron and Tamloch is a lot older than our disagreement with the Roma," said Nûd.

"True," said the queen. "And our warriors have always wanted to test their mettle against Roma legions..." Her voice trailed off.

"There's more, now that I can get a word in," said Skavendr.

"What?" asked Signý, her hand back on her cheek.

Skavendr grinned, showing a predatory smile that marked him as anything but a farmer.

"I've got a present for you," he said.

"A present?" asked Queen Signý. "What kind of present?"

"One I'm sure you'll appreciate," said the scout-captain. "We've captured a spy!"

Chapter 30

Dârio

Henddyn knocked on the door to the king's study.

"Jenet is here, My Liege."

"About time," came Dârio's voice through the door's thick timber.

The door opened, and the young king stuck his shaved head out.

"There you are," he said, looking at the young woman in the wine-colored dress and leering. "I've got *plans* for you."

Dârio took Jenet's hand and pulled her inside.

"See that we're not disturbed," he said, with a wink for Henddyn and the other guards.

The door was pulled closed with a loud *thunk* and everyone in the antechamber could hear a heavy bolt being thrown. Henddyn and the members of his squad grinned at each other. The young king was the *young* king, after all.

On the other side of the door, Dârio gave Jenet a hug, then stepped back, keeping his hands on her shoulders.

"You know what to do?" he asked.

"Stall as long as possible," Jenet replied.

"It won't be a problem for you?"

"I can pretend to sigh and moan and say, 'Oh, Dârio!' for several hours, if that's what you mean."

"Great," said Dârio. "I'd appreciate as long a head start as you can give me."

"Trust me, I'll be convincing," said Jenet. "But I'd rather come with you."

"And I'd rather have your company, but I need you for your skills at misdirection."

"You could summon my sister, too. She could provide misdirection and I could watch your back."

"Imagine how the guards would gossip if I was alone with *both* of you for several hours," said Dârio.

"Especially with constant cries of, 'Oh Dârio,' coming through the door," said Jenet with a grin. "My sister is quite good at imitating my voice, by the way."

"I'm sure she is," said the young king, rolling his eyes and making Jenet laugh.

"Stop it," she said. "Why do you have to pretend to be such a pig in public?"

"You know why."

"I do," said Jenet, frowning. "It's so your mother won't drug you into compliance. Far better for her to think you're a fool caught up in his passions."

"You won't give me away, will you?" asked Dârio, smiling and raising his eyebrows.

"Not if you kiss me," said Jenet. Dârio did, enthusiastically. Reluctantly, Jenet moved a few inches back after two dozen rapid heartbeats. She smiled at Dârio. "And if you take me with you..."

"Next time," said the young king. "I need to leave *now* so I'm not gone too long. I don't want mother to get suspicious."

"If you're not back in a few hours, I'll tell her that you wore me out and I fell asleep. When I woke up, you were gone," said Jenet. She fluttered her eyelashes and gave a convincing imitation of a noble's crown-chasing daughter, new to court and in awe of the queen.

"Let's hope I'm back soon enough that you won't need to lie to my mother."

"If you're back soon enough, you can wear me out before you unbolt the door."

Jenet shrugged and her wine-colored dress fell to the floor revealing only Jenet beneath.

"That's sufficient incentive to encourage an early return," said Dârio. "Maybe I won't need to ask your sister to join us with *that* inspiration."

Jenet moved close to Dârio again. He could feel her soft skin in his arms and warm breath on his neck.

"Blast!" he said, stepping back. "You don't play fair."

"Knight takes Queen's Advisor," said Jenet as she bent to pick up her dress and pull it over her head. "Check."

Dârio took off his clothes while Jenet admired his well-muscled form. He crossed to his desk and removed traveling clothes more suitable to a poor merchant than a rich monarch from the bottom drawer of his desk.

"Let me help you put those on," said Jenet.

"I don't think so," said Dârio. "I can only handle so much temptation at one time."

Jenet bared a shoulder, revealing her breast momentarily, and laughed.

"I promise to behave," she said. "And it will go faster if I assist."

"Go ahead, then," said Dârio.

Between the two of them, Dârio was promptly dressed in loose-fitting breeches, a patched linen shirt, a quilted jacket, hose and well-worn boots.

"Don't forget this," said Jenet, putting a dark-haired wig on Dârio's head and topping it with a floppy blue hat.

"Do I look anything like a king?" he asked.

"Not a bit," Jenet answered. "Should I put a sprig of holly in your cap, so you'll look like a farm lad on his wander year?"

"Do you have one?"

"No, but I'll try to remember for next time."

"Please do," said Dârio. "No one expects much from hayseeds on their wander years."

"Don't be an ass," said Jenet.

"Just staying in practice," said Dârio. As if remembering something he'd almost forgotten, he returned a book that had been open on his desk to an empty spot on a bookshelf. That accomplished, he gave Jenet a hug and a peck on the cheek, then passed through the curtain hiding the servants' alcove and out of the royal suite.

Jenet picked up the fine clothes Dârio had been wearing and arranged them artfully on the floor around the huge overstuffed couch pressed against one wall of the king's study. With luck, their placement would support the king's deception. *They'd served that purpose well many times before,* thought Jenet.

She walked halfway around the room to a wall holding built-in floor-to-ceiling bookshelves. Jenet examined Dârio's extensive collection and noted the title of the book he'd just returned. Its subject didn't appeal to her, so she selected a thick volume on the Roma invasion up the Abbenoth.

Taking a seat on a comfortable chair next to the *shah-mat* boards with the book on her lap, Jenet considered Dârio's likely move to escape check so she could properly counter it. Every so often she'd touch herself for inspiration and say, "Oh, Dârio!" loud enough for the guards to hear her. She hoped the king had a productive trip and made a speedy return. He was always so *energized* when he came back from his excursions outside the palace.

* * * * *

Dârio left the palace through the merchants' gate carrying four flat empty wicker baskets arrayed in tiers and slung from a leather harness behind him. They were the sort of baskets used for fresh strawberries—berries that were only available this early in spring in the southern reaches of Dâron. He made his way through the city, admiring the vibrant life of Brendinas and the colorful language of its inhabitants.

That language—and its vocabulary—grew even more colorful as he reached the docks. Dârio filed away a few new insults to use for his private musing about his mother and found the narrow courier boat he was looking for along a short pier far from the royal docks. He nodded to the woman wearing mail and carrying a spear who'd been guarding the vessel and claimed a soft blue velvet pouch that he'd left with her for safekeeping.

After first removing the wicker baskets and harness and placing them amidships, Dârio carefully climbed into the boat near the prow and positioned himself on a thwart. He found a sturdy wooden pole at his feet and inserted it into a slot designed to hold it. Then he opened the velvet bag, removed the pull-stone and cord within, and hung it from the pole.

He leaned back, triggered the pull-stone with a phrase, and reached below the thwart for an oar to help guide the vessel's course as it sped down the Brenavon.

This was no ordinary pull-stone. It was a royal courier pull-stone Dârio had *borrowed* to assist with his surreptitious explorations of his kingdom. Dârio felt like he was skimming along the river as fast as a wizard zooming by above on a flying disk.

The Bifurlanders' fleet couldn't be far. Dârio needed to see its strength for himself if he was going to make good decisions as a battlefield commander. He sped south until he saw hundreds of square-sailed ships filling the river ahead. His attention was completely focused on the Bifurland armada, so he didn't notice another, larger boat hiding behind the roots of a downed tree hung up on a sandbar near his course.

Grappling hooks bit into the stern of Dârio's courier boat and its speed didn't do him any good when the other boat hauled his in.

"What do we have here?" asked one of the sailors from the larger boat, a woman with gold hoop earrings.

"A present for the queen," said Skavendr. the larger boat's scout-captain. His look reminded Dârio of one of the feral wolf-dogs in the royal menagerie.

"And a *very* fast pull-stone," said Hoop Earrings.

"Aye," said Skavendr. "Too fast for a merchant, but perfect for another profession I can think of."

Hoop Earrings and the other crew members laughed.

I should have stayed in Brendinas with Jenet, thought Dârio. *Blast!*

His captors trussed him up with anchor rope and dumped him in the bilge water at the bottom of their vessel while they tied his courier boat to its side and floated with the current, south to the Bifurland fleet.

Chapter 31

Merry

Astrí and Merry entered the assembly hall through a side door and found themselves trapped in a crowd of wizards, stuck between their shields and the walls. Doethan was standing in front of a platform on the left and a big wizard in striped robes was opposite him on the right.

"Hibblig always was a bully," said Astrí.

"Doethan! Look out!" shouted Merry, clutching Astrí's arm. She wanted to help her friend and mentor, but was stuck on the outside looking in.

Hibblig shot a dozen cubes of solidified sound ahead of him as he leaned forward and lumbered toward Doethan on the far side of the Conclave's assembly hall. The big man looked more like a knight's charger than a knight in his bulky magically-generated armor. His fists were similar cubes, ready to deliver massive blows to his opponent.

Doethan pulled his flying disk off his back and didn't take time to mount it. He held it in both hands and flew above Hibblig's cubical missiles, floating near the domed ceiling of the hall. The inertia of Hibblig's forward motion slammed him into the bottom of the platform and stood him up. He shook his head to clear it and turned to search for Doethan, scanning the floor of the hall—but Doethan was overhead, not on the floor. He'd managed to stand on his flying disk during the brief interval when Hibblig was disoriented.

Doethan banked a heavy ball of solidified sound off the shields above the platform so it hit Hibblig in the back of the head and knocked him down and forward. The big man was as awkward as a tortoise for a moment, his bulky magical armor making it hard for him to get back on his feet. Force-beams of tight light pulsed from Doethan's hands toward Hibblig's neck, rocking Hibblig's head against the fitted-stone floor a dozen times before he could strengthen his shields.

"You'll be sorry for that!" shouted Hibblig as he stood and glared up at Doethan.

"I'm *already* sorry we're wasting time on this," Doethan replied softly. The hall was quiet enough that all the assembled wizards had no trouble hearing him.

Hibblig shocked Merry by immediately launching a fireball at Doethan. The older wizard dodged, but the fireball hit the shielded ceiling above him and exploded. The shock wave it generated flipped Doethan upside down. His boots stuck through leather straps were the only things connecting him to his disk. Pressure from the wave also pushed Doethan down into Hibblig's reach.

The big man rushed forward from his position in front of the platform and hit Doethan's dangling head with an oversized fist of solidified sound bigger than a maul. The older wizard interposed a shield before the blow hit, but its impact still spun him around six times and sent him hurtling against the shields of the observing wizards opposite the platform. Doethan bounced off their hard surface and continued to hang, suspended upside down. He was stunned and shook his head to clear it as his flying disk slowly descended. Several nearby crown wizards in solid-colored robes wanted to help, and so did many of the free wizards, but longstanding custom prevented them from taking action.

If Hibblig tries to kill Doethan, I won't care about custom, thought Merry. Her hands clenched into fists, but she tried to stay calm. She'd never thought her introduction to the Conclave would include a literal battle for leadership.

Hibblig hadn't paused in his attack. It wasn't in his nature to give Doethan time to recover. The big wizard in bigger magical armor rushed across the assembly hall like a stampeding wisent and bashed Doethan against the wall of shields. Doethan's flying disk was nine or ten feet above the floor, which meant his head was hanging at exactly the right level for Hibblig to hit it with his augmented fists.

The leader of Princess Gwýnnett's faction threw the first of what was intended to be a series of punches, but Doethan's head was no longer there. Instead, the older wizard, still dangling upside down below his flying disk, was back near the ornate domed ceiling. Hibblig made quick modifications to the legs of his magical armor and leapt like a giant locust toward his foe.

Merry was pleased to see that tactic must have been just what Doethan had been waiting for. Force-beams of tight light sped from his fingertips and struck Hibblig's left hip and shoulder. The big wizard began to spin as he ascended. Doethan continued to use force-beams to accelerate Hibblig's rotation. Hibblig extended his arms to slow his motion, but Doethan—still inverted—targeted his wrists and hands, using them as levers to make Hibblig spin even faster.

"Yes!" Merry shouted as the big wizard's motion became a blur. *That's got to make him dizzy!*

Astrí put a cautionary hand on Merry's arm. *I get it,* thought Merry. *The duel isn't over.* And it wasn't.

Hibblig dispelled his massive armor and pulled himself into a tight ball inside a protective sphere of solidified sound, negating much of his rotation. As the big wizard fell to the floor, Doethan righted himself on his flying disk and circled the hall, seeking a spot far from where his opponent would land. Hibblig rolled his sphere half a dozen times to soak up momentum, then stood facing Doethan.

"Nice trick," said the big wizard. "Too bad you won't live long enough to benefit from it."

Merry heard several wizards near her inhale sharply. Some wore striped robes, not just solid-colored ones.

Astrí whispered, "Hibblig's crossed the line now. Duels for leadership aren't supposed to be to the death—they're tests of skill."

"Let's get this over with," said Doethan.

Merry thought he seemed tired. *Wouldn't you be?* she considered.

Hibblig balled his hands into fists, bent his elbows, held his arms in front of him and moved one of his forearms around the other as if winding rope on a torsion catapult. Merry didn't know what Hibblig intended, but she hoped Doethan didn't give him time to find out.

"Watch," whispered Astrí.

Doethan used his wizardry to open a tiny congruency near Hibblig. It was so small hardly anyone saw it, but Merry did. She remembered her friend and first mentor had an entertaining way of keeping unwanted guests away from his tower. Then she smiled as a deafening chorus of barking hounds, supplemented by the clanks of cocking crossbows, filled the room. Merry knew what came next. The hounds were just a distraction.

"Call off your dogs—they won't save you," said Hibblig. Merry thought his voice sounded more like a mountain cat's snarl than human speech.

Hibblig stopped moving his forearms and slapped at the side of his head.

"As you wish," said Doethan.

The baying hounds and soldiers with crossbows went silent. Thanks to the excellent acoustics in the hall, every wizard assembled there could hear the annoying whine of a single midge flitting around Hibblig's left ear.

Merry's laugh joined the midge's whine. *He's put the congruency in Hibblig's ear canal!*

Eyes turned to stare at her and Merry moved behind Astrí's dark-blue robes to be less visible.

Hibblig was slapping at both ears now.

Doethan generated a second congruency!

One midge was joined by ten more, then a hundred, then a thousand, then ten thousand gathered in a dark cloud around Hibblig's head. More wizards around the assembly hall started to laugh. Hibblig's face turned red and Merry could see he considered opening his mouth but thought better of it, deciding he didn't want to inhale midges. The tiny fliers' wing-beats changed from a thin whine to a loud hum, reminding Merry of an unhappy hive of bees.

Hibblig made a gesture then reluctantly lowered his jaw and spoke a trigger word. His suit of solidified-sound armor formed around him—but it didn't help. The congruencies linked to marshes filled with midges were *inside* his ears, not outside his armor.

I wonder how far south Doethan had to reach to get midges? wondered Merry. *It will be another month until they're a problem on the Rhuthro.*

In the middle of the assembly hall, Hibblig was looking more and more frantic. His face under his transparent solidified-sound helmet was speckled with black dots. He was crouching in the center of the hall and tossing small fireballs at his own head, trying—ineffectually—to eliminate the midges. Doethan descended and stood in his original position on the platform with his flying disk strapped to his back. Still more wizards were laughing at Hibblig and others were applauding Doethan's cleverness.

Thank goodness the duel's over, thought Merry. But it wasn't.

Hibblig bellowed Doethan's name and erupted from his crouch, charging toward the older wizard on the raised platform. Ten quick steps and a small jump put Hibblig beside his opponent. He locked Doethan in a bear hug and used a much bigger jump to carry them both to the center of the hall. Doethan had gotten his own body shield up in time, but Hibblig still held him by the neck in his left hand while he pummeled him with hammer-like blows with his right. Doethan's shield started to waver from transmitted impacts and Hibblig added a long triangular blade to the armor on his right fist.

"No!" shouted Merry. She didn't know how to get around the other wizards' shields, but she had to do *something* to save her friend. Astrí held Merry's shoulders and they both watched in horror as Hibblig's arm moved back, ready to administer a killing blow. All eyes were on Doethan and Hibblig. No one was breathing. Then everyone went blind.

Merry blinked, trying to see again after a flash of golden light brighter than the sun at noon splashed out above the platform, filling the hall. She felt a chill and heard a familiar voice.

"WHAT IN THE NAME OF THE FIRST SHIPS IS GOING ON HERE?"

Merry shook her head and rubbed her ears. She could make out a gleaming figure in sparkling blue robes descending on a flying disk toward Doethan and Hibblig. Something about the two combatants was different. They were literally frozen in place, held in tableau by a thick coating of ice.

Without conscious agreement, the dozens of shields surrounding the assembly hall came down. Clumps of wizards buzzed with conversation like clouds of midges.

"I go away for forty years and everything goes to pieces..." muttered Damon as he landed and adjusted the drape of his robe's beautifully decorated fabric.

Inthíra stepped forward.

"Greetings, good wizard," she said. "Who *are* you, if you don't mind me asking?"

"I don't mind a bit. I'm Ealdamon, Master Mage of Dâron, and I'm here to get things back on track."

Merry turned to see her companion's reaction, but Astrí was gone.

All eyes were on Damon, wondering what sage pronouncement the semi-mythical Master Mage of Dâron would utter.

Damon slapped at his ear and waved his hands in front of his face, looking annoyed. Then he spoke.

"How did all these blasted *midges* get in here?"

Chapter 32

Fercha

"Where did he go?" asked Fercha.

Princess Gwýnnett was looking uncharacteristically like a mother, rather than a cold-blooded spider, but Fercha wasn't convinced.

"If I knew that, I wouldn't need *you*," said Gwýnnett.

They were alone in a private chamber somewhere in Princess Gwýnnett's apartments. Gwýnnett was seated. Fercha had chosen to remain standing. Given the other woman's penchant for poisons, she was afraid to touch anything and certainly wouldn't accept any offers of refreshments. She wasn't even sure about breathing, but didn't have much choice about that. She created a transparent bubble of solidified sound around her head just to play it safe.

"Yes, but why me?" asked Fercha. "Why not one of your own tame wizards, like Hibblig?"

"Hibblig is more of a blunt object," said the princess. "This calls for someone with more creativity and finesse."

And Hibblig is at the gathering of the Conclave, thought Fercha. *Causing trouble, no doubt. I should be there helping Doethan, not here verbally fencing with a traitor to the realm.*

"When was the last time anyone saw the king?"

"Early this afternoon. He was talking to a deluded old man with the nonsensical claim of being the master mage of Dâron, then summoned a young woman to be his *shah-mat* partner."

"From your tone of voice, I assume chess wasn't the only form of entertainment Dârio expected?"

"That's quite likely," said Gwýnnett. "My son has a way with women."

Fercha nodded, but her face revealed nothing. Gwýnnett *thought* Dârio's female companions were effective tools for her to use to control her son and keep track of his actions.

"Which one was it this time?" asked Fercha.

"Jenet. Duke Háiddon's eldest daughter."

"I'm not sure I know her," said Fercha, trying to make the lie convincing. "A redhead?"

"She has dark brown hair," said Gwýnnett. "Slim. Small bust. Wears dresses in jewel tones."

"That describes a third of the young women in court," said Fercha.

"The guards tell me they found her naked under a blanket on a couch in Dârio's study."

"*The* couch?" asked Fercha. "The infamous couch of King Dârio? The one where every noble's daughter who wants to be queen has to audition?"

"Whatever do you mean?" asked Gwýnnett. She raised an eyebrow to make sure Fercha knew that she was quite familiar with the rumors. She'd probably helped to spread them to ensure her son's popularity did not become so great that he'd think he could defy his mother. Fercha knew a good many more would-be queens had claimed they'd spent time on *the* couch than actually had.

"What did this *Jenet* say?"

"That she fell asleep after she defeated Dârio at a game of *shah-mat* and the two of them decided to take a nap."

"Naked?" asked Fercha.

"How do *you* sleep?" asked Gwýnnett.

Fercha inclined her head and let half a smile flit over her face.

"Let me guess," said Fercha. "When she woke up hours later, Dârio was gone."

"Correct," said Princess Gwýnnett. "His clothes were on the floor next to the couch, but Dârio had disappeared."

"Did any servants see him leave the royal apartments?"

"No, but all the retainers in the alcove behind the curtain in the king's study had been dismissed. That was standard practice when Dârio played *shah-mat*."

"I understand," said Fercha. "Young men value their privacy."

"So do young kings," said Gwýnnett. "The guards started to worry when they didn't hear anything inside the study for several hours. They found one of Dârio's personal servants relaxing in the kitchens after eating lunch and had him open the servants' entrance. He said he had the only key to the door and he'd left it locked."

"Curious," said Fercha. She knew that particular servant well, and might have to talk with him one-on-one. His loyalty was to Dârio, not Gwýnnett, though. He might or might not tell her the truth. Fercha was sure Gwýnnett *also* had a key to the servants' door, in addition to the main entrance to her son's study. Gwýnnett was too controlling *not* to have keys. "Was there any blood?" Fercha asked.

"You mean was Jenet a virgin? I doubt it. She's played *shah-mat* with Dârio in private before."

"No," said Fercha. "I was asking whether or not there were signs Dârio might have been injured when he was abducted."

"Oh," said Gwýnnett without a hint of emotion.

So much for maternal concern, thought Fercha.

"Do you think he *might* have been kidnapped?" asked Gwýnnett. "I hope that's not the case. I need him back—as quickly and discreetly as possible."

For your treacherous spider-plot with Túathal, thought Fercha.

"What would you like me to do?"

"Talk to Jenet. Talk to the servant. Talk to the guards," said Gwýnnett. "Do whatever you have to do, but *find the king.*"

Fercha considered it telling that the princess had not said, "… *find my son.*" *Then again,* thought Fercha, *I'm hardly a model of maternal concern myself. I wonder where Nûd and Merry's lover from the Coombe went after the battle at the quarry early this morning. Maybe the skinny boy with the dried holly leaves in his cap took Nûd to his home and they're both safely out of harm's way weeding fields and milking cows?*

"Is something wrong?" asked Gwýnnett.

Fercha realized she'd been silent for several seconds. She'd just remembered that Merry's lover—Eynon, his name was—had her original magestone. That was yet another problem to address.

"No, I'm fine," said Fercha. "I'm thinking about questions for Jenet."

"Don't just think—get moving," said Princess Gwýnnett. "Lost kings don't find themselves."

You may be wrong about that, thought Fercha.

"Where's Jenet now?" she asked.

"Still in Dârio's study under guard," said Gwýnnett.

"I'll keep you informed," said Fercha as she walked to the door.

"See that you do," said the princess.

* * * * *

Fercha had ordered the guards to leave the king's study and finished expanding a privacy sphere to include Jenet and herself.

"We can't be overheard now. Where did he go?"

"I have no idea," said Jenet. "When I woke up, he was gone."

"You're going to make this difficult, aren't you?"

"What do you mean?"

"I know about the act," said Fercha. "I helped Dârio design and refine it."

"The guards said Princess Gwýnnett sent you."

"I am no more a pawn of Gwýnnett's than a sparrow is a gryffon," said Fercha. "I think she asked me to help find Dârio as much to keep me away from the Conclave as to find your *shah-mat* partner."

"You're part of the old queen's faction, aren't you?" asked Jenet. "You were coming in to Dârio's study when I was leaving this morning."

"That's right," said Fercha. "But I'm not just *part* of the queen's faction. I help *lead* it—along with a few others."

"I thought so," said Jenet. "In that case..." she continued, her voice still uncertain.

"My only interest is in helping Dârio," said Fercha. "Where did he say he was going?"

Jenet gave Fercha a wary glance.

"Of course," said Fercha. "He wouldn't tell you. He'd want you to be able to say you didn't know where he'd gone without needing to lie."

A smile played over Jenet's face.

"Did you teach him that?" she asked.

"I didn't have to," said Fercha. "He figured that out on his own."

"Well," said Jenet, crossing to the bookshelves. "He was reading *this* just before he left." She removed a slim volume and placed it face up in Fercha's outstretched hand.

Fercha noted the title. *Bifurland Naval Tactics and Strategy*.

She nodded, remembering a gate she'd built for an innkeeper in Brendinas who'd inherited a second establishment in Arthábben, a small town on the west bank of the Brenavon, twenty miles downriver. With luck, she'd catch up to Dârio before he reached the Bifurland fleet.

As she moved to leave the king's study, Fercha glanced at the *shah-mat* board next to where Jenet had been sitting.

"Nice game," she said. "Checkmate in four moves."

"Three," said Jenet. But Fercha was already gone.

Chapter 33

Nûd and Eynon

Nûd and Eynon stepped away from the Bifurland royals' folding thrones and put their backs to the mainmast. A young man a little older than Eynon and a little younger than Nûd was on the deck, trussed like a goose on a spit. His head was shaved. Eynon thought he looked familiar, but wasn't sure why.

"Where did you find him?" asked Queen Signý. "And what makes you think he's a spy, not a merchant with head lice?"

"He had a pull-stone as good as a royal courier's," said the scout-captain, holding the stone in question by its thong and letting it swing. "We found him just north of the fleet. What else could he be but a spy?"

The scout-captain slipped the pull-stone over his head, so it rested on his breastbone. He then pulled a floppy blue hat and a dark wig from his belt. Both were damp.

"He was wearing a disguise," added the scout-captain, waving the wig and hat in disgust. "And not a very good one."

King Bjarni stood and shoved the prisoner across the deck a few feet with the sole of his boot.

"What do you have to say for yourself?" he asked.

The prisoner shifted his bound body as best he could until he faced the king and queen.

"I sell strawberries from the southern provinces," he said. "That pull-stone helps us get them to market in Brendinas faster. It's been in our family for generations."

"Next thing you'll be telling me is that it was enchanted by the legendary Master Mage Ealdamon himself," sneered the scout-captain before kicking the prisoner in the ribs.

"Skavendr," said the queen, holding up her hand as a note of caution.

The prisoner glared at the scout-captain and spit out his reply.

"Our pull-stone was made for my grandfather's grandfather. It's far older than the wizard who couldn't find Princess Seren."

"Perhaps we'll chain you to an oar instead of kill you then," said Queen Signý.

Sigrun and Rannveigr had moved to stand beside Signý.

"Please don't *kill* him," pleaded Sigrun. "I like the way his head looks like an egg."

"I think he's cute," said Rannveigr. Both girls giggled.

"Cute or not," said Queen Signý, smiling at the girls indulgently, "he rows, or he dies."

Sigrun and Rannveigr gave the queen a look that Eynon knew how to translate. He'd seen the same look from his sister plenty of times, usually accompanied by, "Awww, *Mom!*" The stakes weren't usually as high as a man's life, however.

Nûd and Eynon exchanged glances. Eynon put his hand on his red magestone. Nûd nodded and stepped forward.

"He will be coming with us, Your Majesties. We'll see that he's returned to his family."

"Along with my pull-stone," said the prisoner.

"Don't push your luck," said King Bjarni. "It's Skavendr's now."

"He's a thief," said the prisoner.

"And you're a spy," said the scout-captain.

Eynon turned to Nûd, his expression asking, W*ho does this fool think he is?*

Queen Signý laughed. So did King Bjarni.

"You've got spirit, lad," said the king. "I like that. Care to fight him for the stone, Skavendr?"

To Eynon's eye, the scout-captain appeared to be ten years older, fifty pounds heavier, and a much more experienced warrior than the prisoner. Tattoos on Skavendr's arms wove in and out of long white lines from old sword or axe wounds. A scar ran down his left cheek, ending at the corner of his mouth and giving him a menacing appearance. The only thing remotely menacing or intimidating about the prisoner was his shaved head.

"Why don't we up the stakes, Sire?" asked the scout-captain. "If he wins, the young wizard and his friend get the spy *and* his pull-stone. If I win, I keep the stone and you can give me the spy as my thrall?"

King Bjarni turned to Queen Signý. The queen nodded.

"Very well," said Bjarni. "Cut him free and give him a chance to stretch his muscles. I don't want it said that a trial in my court isn't fair."

"A trial, Your Majesty?" asked Nûd.

"By combat, lad," said the king. "Don't you have trial by combat in Dâron?"

"Not officially," said Eynon, thinking about how people would get into fights in the seven taverns down in Caercadel.

Skavendr cut the prisoner free and the young man with the shaved head rose to his feet.

"How does this work?" asked Nûd.

"Yes," said the prisoner, looking at Nûd and Eynon, then turning to address the king and queen. "Do I have my choice of weapons?"

"Weapons increase your odds of dying," said Queen Signý sternly. "Wouldn't you rather live as a thrall than be cut down by an experienced warrior's blade?"

The prisoner paced and rubbed his chin. "Decisions, decisions," he said, smiling.

"You find your situation amusing?" asked the queen.

"Victory and freedom," said the prisoner, holding up one hand. "Defeat and slavery—or death," he continued, holding up the other.

"Maybe he's a poet, not a spy," said Skavendr. "He sounds like a skald."

The scout-captain stepped over to the prisoner and put a hand on his shoulder.

"Don't worry, lad. I won't *try* to kill you. I don't want to reduce your value as a slave."

The prisoner shifted out from under Skavendr's hand and took two steps away from the older man until he stood between the king and queen. He moved his hands up and down, as if weighing his options, then spread his arms wide.

"The choice before me is clear," he said. "I'll just have to win."

Skavendr laughed. King Bjarni tried to keep his face neutral but failed and broke into a smile.

"You can try," said the king. "What will it be, lad? Swords? Axes? Knives? Bare hands?"

Eynon took a close look at Skavendr. The muscles in his right arm were larger than those in his left, like his cousin who'd served as an axeman in the levies. His cousin trained with a long-handled double-bladed axe, which gave him asymmetrical muscles.

"I'm not clear on the rules for your trials," said Nûd. "Must both parties use the same weapon?"

"Not if individual choices of weapons are otherwise acceptable," said the queen.

"You won't have my preferred weapon, anyway," said the prisoner.

"Daggers in the back?" teased Skavendr.

The prisoner grimaced. "Would that be *your* choice?"

Skavendr caught Bjarni's eye. "You're right, Sire. He *does* have spirit."

"What *is* your preferred weapon?" asked the king.

"You won't have one."

"Try me," said the king.

"It has a long, straight, narrow v-shaped blade with a single edge and a bell guard."

"A toadsticker!" said Skavendr. He laughed from his diaphragm.

"A weapon for those who lack the strength to wield a broadsword," said Bjarni.

"I'm sure there are some below," said the queen. "We've taken them from slaves captured on raids. I'll have a few brought on deck for you to choose from."

"Thank you, Your Majesty," said the prisoner.

"Fetch my axe," Skavendr ordered one of his boat mates.

The prisoner went through a series of stretching exercises and calisthenics that included knee bends and lunges while they waited for their weapons. Skavendr's warm-up wasn't nearly as strenuous. He shrugged his shoulders several times and pretended to swing a heavy double-bladed axe. Eynon used the break to whisper with Nûd.

"I'm not going to let Skavendr kill him," said Eynon quietly. "He's just a strawberry merchant, and he's not much older than I am."

"If we have to leave in a hurry, we'll need a distraction," said Nûd.

Eynon touched his red magestone.

"*Not* another fireball," Nûd whispered. "If we have to go in a hurry, please try for something more subtle."

"I'll think about it," said Eynon. *Bifurlanders don't favor subtlety,* he thought. *They're more direct.*

"Will Rocky be ready to fly?" asked Nûd.

"I hope so," said Eynon. He leaned back and looked for Chee in the rigging. The raconette had returned to his former position sitting on the horizontal pole that held the sail aloft with his back to the mainmast. Eynon magically augmented his distance vision and saw that Chee was nibbling the last of his apple and watching the proceedings below with interest.

Sigrun and Rannveigr followed Eynon's gaze and waved to Chee. The raconette waved back and held up his mostly-consumed apple like a trophy.

The sailor returning with Skavendr's axe came back first. The weapon was as tall as the scout-captain, with a double-bladed steel head like two crescent moons and steel strips reinforcing the thick length of ironwood forming its shaft. Skavendr hefted it and swung it back and forth with the ease of a child waving a twig. The scout-captain showed off his skill with heavy strokes at imaginary targets, trying to intimidate the prisoner. The younger man watched with interest. Beads of perspiration formed on his shaved skull, despite the light wind on the river.

Most of a minute passed before another sailor appeared, holding what Queen Signý had asked her to retrieve.

"I could only find three," she said, standing in front of the queen holding the blades across her outstretched arms like lengths of firewood.

"Ooo, *pretty!*" said Sigrun, taking a blade from the sailor. Rannveigr took one, too, and the two blonde-braided girls crossed them and danced across the deck, shouting with exuberant glee and enjoying the clangs as their swords crossed.

"Girls!" said Queen Signý, her voice cutting through the clamor. "Don't make me send the two of *you* to take a turn on the oars."

"Yes, *mother*," said Sigrun.

"Yes, Aunt Signý," said Rannveigr.

The girls crossed their blades one last time and delivered them to the prisoner for inspection before the ringing faded. The sailor holding the third blade raised her eyebrows and smiled at the queen, then did likewise. She stuck the point of the sword she held into the deck, with its bell-guard swinging back and forth with the ship's motion. The prisoner stuck the swords he'd been given by the girls into the deck and tested the strength and flexibility of each blade by leaning down on them.

One blade was very flexible, but it didn't spring back straight. Another wouldn't bend much at all when tested. The third blade, however, met with the prisoner's approval. He inserted his right hand into the bell-guard and put his left hand over the rounded metal, gripping the light blade like a broadsword. He lifted the weapon above his head and brought it arcing down several times, like he was swinging an axe to cut a tree.

Skavendr and King Bjarni exchanged a knowing look. *Spirit* on the part of the prisoner wouldn't be enough to give the scout-captain much of a fight.

"Clear the deck," the king commanded.

Warrior-sailors moved the benches that had been put in place for Nûd and Eynon. The king and queen stood and moved their own folding thrones back a spear-length, opening a square space about fifteen feet from side to side and mast to thrones. Skavendr moved to port and indicated to the prisoner that he should move to starboard. Bjarni and Signý sat comfortably on the repositioned thrones with Sigrun and Rannveigr close together at their feet like a pair of playful puppies. The three wizards in gold robes stood directly behind the thrones. Eynon and Nûd stood next to the mainmast, with Rocky farther toward the prow behind them. Members of the crew who weren't required for safe sailing gathered wherever they could find a good spot to watch.

"What are the rules of the trial?" asked Nûd, addressing the king and queen.

"They're simple," said Skavendr before either monarch could answer. "When the egg-head is dead or surrenders, it's over." The scout-captain grinned across the deck at his opponent, who was holding his blade down and shifting from foot to foot uncomfortably.

"So the only rule is that there aren't rules?" asked Nûd, locking eyes with Bjarni, then shifting his gaze to the queen, then back to the king.

"The trial is over when *I* say it's over," said Bjarni. "Anyone jumping over the side will get a crossbow bolt through their chest. Any use of wizardry to aid either party is forbidden."

The king glanced at Eynon, who nodded. The three women in gold robes with amber necklaces stared at Eynon in a way that made it plain they'd enforce their sovereign's prohibition on magic.

"Are we ready to begin?" asked Queen Signý.

"Aye," said Skavendr.

"As I'll ever be," said the prisoner.

The queen turned in her seat and nodded to the women in gold robes. Before she could turn back, a yellow-tinted wall of solidified sound ten feet high materialized in front of the thrones, protecting the king and queen. The woman in the middle of the gold-robed trio extended her hand toward Eynon, who created a similar wall on his side with a pink tinge. A breeze from the river moving from port to starboard swirled dust on the deck inside their makeshift arena.

"Lay on," said King Bjarni to both combatants. "And don't play with your food," he added as an aside for his scout-captain.

"I'll make it quick," said Skavendr, moving the head of his axe in front of him in a mesmerizing figure-eight pattern. "I've got more to tell you about the Roma legions."

The scout-captain and the prisoner approached each other and circled just outside the maximum reach of Skavendr's axe. The prisoner held his sword at waist height close to his body with the blade reaching up in front of his face. Skavendr stamped his boot on the deck and lunged, letting his hands slide down to the last foot of the haft of his axe. He aimed for the prisoner's stomach, hoping to push him off balance.

The prisoner's eyes went wide and he flailed at the axe-head with his bell-guard, pushing it down and to the side.

"You *do* know that toadsticker has a blade, don't you," said Skavendr. He'd pulled his axe back and resumed circling the prisoner. "Then again, you wouldn't get much experience using blades just taking strawberries to Brendinas."

The prisoner shifted from holding his blade straight up, close to his chest, and extended his arm, the tip of his sword wavering uncertainly. He didn't speak, though his face looked like a mouse cornered by a cat.

"If you're a spy, you probably *do* have experience with blades," Skavendr continued, as he tested the prisoner by batting at the other man's outstretched sword. "Just shorter ones."

"I told you not to play with your food," said King Bjarni with a smile in his voice. "Finish this."

The prisoner took advantage of the distraction provided by the king's words and rushed the scout captain, swinging his blade wildly. Skavendr parried the blows easily, blocking them with the reinforcing strips on the haft of his axe. He swung the head around, twisting it to hit with the flat, not the blade, aiming for the side of the prisoner's skull. Unfortunately, his target was no longer where it had been. The prisoner's head was a foot lower as he cowered from the scout-captain's attack.

Nûd whispered to Eynon. "Are you going to *do* something before baldy is killed?"

"Wait," said Eynon.

Something about the prisoner's movements reminded him of the way his quarterstaff instructor back in the Coombe—a distant cousin—used to play with new students at weekly levy drills.

Skavendr took one hand off his axe and beckoned to the prisoner. "Come here, Strawberry," he said. "You'll look good with a thrall's torc around your neck." As he spoke the last word, Skavendr tossed his axe in the air, grabbed the last foot of the haft, and repeated his original attack aimed at the prisoner's stomach.

The prisoner beat the axe-head down with his bell-guard, forced it to the deck with a booted foot, and walked up the haft toward

Skavendr. The scout-captain didn't have good control of his weapon since he'd only been holding it in one hand. He was staring down at the deck, ready to retrieve his axe, when the prisoner's bell-guard caught him under the chin, snapping his jaw shut and knocking him backward. Skavendr's head hit the deck and he lay still.

"You talk too much," said the prisoner.

He gave the scout-captain a gentle shove with his boot and only got a small moan for his effort. Bending down, he lifted the pull-stone on its thong around Skavendr's neck and placed it around his own neck.

Sigrun and Rannveigr were clapping until Queen Signý gestured to them and they stopped. Nûd gave Eynon a *what-did-you-know-that-I-didn't-know* look, then stared at the prisoner.

The bald young man faced the thrones. "I assume I'm free to go?"

Behind him, an apple core fell from the top of the mainmast and bounced off Skavendr's nose.

Chapter 34

Damon

Damon waved his hands in front of his face a few more times, then opened a congruency to a high, cold mountain. The resulting difference in air pressure sucked most of the midges out of the Conclave's assembly hall.

"Who's in charge of this madhouse?" he said, amplifying his voice with a transparent solidified-sound megaphone.

"That's what those two were trying to determine," answered Inthíra.

"Of all the foolish nonsense to be wasting time doing..." Damon began. He stopped abruptly when he realized his subconscious grumbling was loud enough to fill the hall. He took a deep breath and pointed at the two wizards coated in ice. "Someone thaw them out before they get frostbite."

Three young wizards with painted flying disks strapped to their backs stepped forward. One opened a link to the far south and directed warm sunlight on the combatants. Another connected to a desert's hot winds. The third opened a temporary circular hole below the once-dueling mages to ensure the melting water didn't pool on the tile floor of the assembly hall.

"Why aren't you already formed into fighting units and joining the royal army?" Damon asked Inthíra. "There's a Bifurland dragonship fleet heading up river and the army's already marching down the west bank of the Brenavon to stop them."

"We know," shouted a solid-robed wizard with long brown hair and a deep contralto to Damon's left. "That's what Doethan was trying to tell Hibblig, but Hibblig wanted to fight for leadership of the Conclave."

"Doethan was one of the people fighting?" asked Damon. "I didn't see *who* was fighting, I just saw a duel in the middle of the assembly hall and sent a blast of cold to stop them." Damon muttered softly, still not realizing his solidified-sound megaphone amplified *everything*. "I would have expected more sense from Doethan."

"He didn't want to fight," said Inthíra.

"Hibblig forced the issue," said the wizard with long brown hair.

Unamplified muttering hummed around the hall as the gathered wizards talked about the duel and Ealdamon's arrival. In the center of the hall, the ice around Doethan was almost completely melted. The young wizard who'd created the temporary hole to drain water rose on his flying disk and pried Hibblig's fingers off the older wizard's neck. The two descended to the floor and Doethan held the younger wizard's arm to stay upright with one hand and rubbed his neck with the other.

"I'm glad you're not dead," said Damon, smiling.

"So am I," said Doethan. "There was nothing to worry about. I had him right where I wanted him." Doethan grinned and a wave of laughter sped around the hall. Even some wizards in striped robes joined in.

"Sorry I had to freeze you," said Damon.

"Think nothing of it, Master Mage," said Doethan, releasing the young wizard's arm and stepping toward Damon on the platform. "A mug of hot cider will warm me up. I'm glad you're here to lead the Conclave and get us organized. I didn't really want the job."

"No one with any sense *would*," said Damon.

"Uhhh-uhh-oof!" said Hibblig as the last of the ice around him melted and he tumbled to the hard tile floor. The two young wizards melting his cold coating had tried to slow his fall, but Hibblig was too big and had too much inertia for them to be successful.

I wonder if either one of them tried very hard, thought Damon.

More laughter—at Hibblig's expense—filled the hall. The big man got to his knees and shook himself like a dog. Nearby wizards put up shields to save themselves from flying droplets. A few seconds later, Hibblig stood and glared up at Damon on the platform.

"I'm the kingdom's master mage," said Damon. "Leading the Conclave has always been a prerogative of that role. Do you want to challenge my right to lead?"

Hibblig stood up straight and squared his shoulders. "You've been gone for forty years, Old Man. What do *you* know about the kingdom?"

"More than you might think," said Damon. "And I've probably trained half of the wizards in this hall at my Academy."

From the tone of the murmurs around the hall, Damon was right. Hibblig had not been one of the wizards accepted for study in Melyncárreg, however. Few wizards now wearing striped robes had.

"A wizard's duel isn't the only way leadership in the Conclave is determined," Hibblig said. His chin stuck out in challenge. "And it shows your character for you to suggest it when you stopped me from earning my rightful position. It's unfair for you to suggest a duel after I'm already tired from defeating Doethan."

"Hah!" Doethan exclaimed from near the platform.

"There is another way to determine who will lead us," Hibblig continued. "I call for a vote of all wizards present."

Damon shook his head. "Are you always this stubborn and opportunistic?"

"Afraid you won't win, Old Man? Afraid the kingdom's wizards want younger and more *vigorous* leadership?"

"I'm confident the Conclave will prefer someone who hasn't been swilling potions to increase his strength and aggression," said Damon.

"How did—I mean—how *dare* you level such baseless accusations?"

"What did she tell you they'd do?" said Damon softly. Everyone heard what he'd said.

"Enough of this foolishness," said Hibblig. He raised his arms to encourage his followers. "I've called for a vote. Do I have a second?"

"I second!" came from a wizard with a long white forked beard in striped robes.

"I second," said a short free wizard wearing shoes with three-inch wooden soles.

"I second," said Doethan. "The sooner we finish with the vote, the sooner we can join the royal army."

"The motion to vote has been made and seconded," said Inthíra. "Does anyone other than Ealdamon and Hibblig wish to stand for leadership?" She scanned the hall. "Very well. Vote for Damon by projecting a circle of tight light on the ceiling to the left of the platform, or for Hibblig by projecting a square to the right."

Wizards made their choices and sent their votes up to the domed ceiling to be counted. Damon added his glowing blue circle and Hibblig his square. The vote was far closer than Damon expected. *Princess Gwýnnett must have offered substantial inducements to a great many free wizards,* he thought.

"Have you all made your choices?" asked Inthíra. She glanced around the room and saw every wizard's arm raised and many nodding heads. "Very well. Let's see who's won."

After first nodding to Damon and Hibblig, Inthíra commanded the voters to take the next step. "Pair up!" she shouted.

Damon and Hibblig matched theirs first. Circles and squares blurred across the ceiling until each square had a circle inside it. One circle remained unbound by a square. It was Merry's vote.

"Who *is* this?" complained Hibblig. "She's not a member of the Conclave. She hasn't been tested."

"Fercha trained me," said Merry, amplifying her voice. "Let me demonstrate my skill."

She pulled her circle-vote down from the ceiling and made it grow until it was a dozen feet across. Moving her fingers faster than Damon's eyes could follow, she filled the circle with a knotwork net of glowing blue force. Taking a deep breath, Merry shot the net forward, wrapping Hibblig up in its interlaced azure strands and lifting him to the ceiling where more iridescent-blue cables of tight light held him fast.

"Would anyone care to dispute my membership in the Conclave?" asked Merry in her sweetest voice.

The hall was silent except for Hibblig's protests from overhead.

"Ealdamon wins," said Inthíra. "What next, Master Mage?"

"We head for a certain inn near the palace," said Damon. "It has a gate to the village of Arthábben, on the west bank. We can link up with the royal army there."

Half the wizards cheered—the ones in solid-colored robes and a good fraction of the free wizards. The ones in striped robes and the remaining free wizards didn't look happy, but most of them seemed willing to comply.

Damon told Inthíra the name of the inn and she led a procession of wizards out of the assembly hall to walk the few blocks to their interim destination. Soon, Merry, Damon, Doethan and Hibblig were the only ones left.

"That was a nice piece of tight-light work," said Damon.

"Thank you, Master Mage," said Merry, making a small bow.

Damon shook his head and smiled at her.

"You learned a lot from Fercha in a short time," said Doethan.

"You gave me a good start," said Merry. "And Fercha worked me hard."

Hibblig continued to complain above them. Damon, Doethan and Merry looked up.

"An excellent spell," said Damon, admiring how Merry's net of light grew tighter around Hibblig the more he struggled.

"Are you going to release him?" asked Doethan.

"You've made your point," said Damon.

"Neither one of you is any fun," said Merry. "But don't worry. I've put the tight-light net on a time delay."

Soon, the construct disappeared and Hibblig had to scramble to craft a solidified-sound sphere to break his fall.

He was the only witness to his downfall, however. Damon, Doethan and Merry were already gone.

Chapter 35

Túathal and Verro

"You're sure this will work?" asked King Túathal. "We're going to win?"

"We're talking about war, brother," said Verro. "There aren't any guarantees, but I'm confident."

King and wizard stood on a low hill above a broad marshaling field west of Tamloch's capital. With his palace and the walls of the city behind him, Túathal reviewed the royal Tamloch army filling nearly every acre of the wide, flat plain below. Pipers wailed as new forces marched in to ensure the empty spots were filled.

There were thousands of foot soldiers with swords, pikes, spears and axes. Ranks of archers, separated into crossbow and longbow corps, were interspersed between squares of infantry. Units of heavy cavalry—barded horses carrying armored knights—were smaller in number but took up a disproportionate amount of space. Fast scouts on horseback, mounted infantry, and horse archers were in the van. Green banners snapped in the strong breeze off the cool water of Fadacaolo Bay. They signified the warriors' duchy, county, or barony.

Túathal turned to look at his capital. Riyas was located at the north end of the bay. It was the best harbor in the kingdom and was usually a forest of masts, but now the docks were almost empty. Every ship that could carry supplies had sailed south days ago. A young man with curly red hair and a pointed beard, carrying a silver tray, two goblets, and a large, green-glass bottle approached.

"Would you care for refreshment, Your Majesty? Master Mage?" asked the young man.

"Yes, thank you, Sal," said Verro. "I could use some wine. Herding unit commanders is thirsty work."

"Just half a cup for me, boy," said Túathal. "And for him," the king added, indicating Verro. "I want him to have a clear head."

Sal filled a goblet halfway with red wine from the bottle and handed it to the king with a small bow, keeping the tray perfectly level as he did. Turning to Verro, Sal filled the second goblet three-quarters of the way to the top and gave it to Verro with a sly wink. The wizard nodded his appreciation. Sal bowed again and backed a dozen feet away downhill—close enough to hear what was said, thanks to the listening charm Doethan had made for him.

Túathal's gaze shifted back to the marshaling field where his forces were mustering, then focused in on the pair of tall poles at the south end. A rope was strung between the poles—it sparkled green in the sunlight, as did the sides of the poles and fresh white plaster in a shallow ditch between them.

"Did you get enough green magestones and magestone powder for the gates we need on your raid?" asked Túathal.

"I did," said Verro. "Plus enough to pull off that not-so-little surprise I told you about. We even found some high quality magestones suitable for new wizards in what we collected."

"Excellent," said Túathal. "That's great news. Tamloch and Dâron will soon be united with my son on the throne."

"With you and your new bride, Princess Gwýnnett, pulling his strings."

"As you say," said King Túathal, putting his hand on Verro's arm. "It would only be a marriage of convenience."

Verro pulled his arm away gently and smiled at his older brother. He loved Túathal, but not the way his brother wanted to be loved.

"Whose convenience?" Verro asked. "Yours or hers?"

"Mine, of course," answered Túathal. "Once I solidify my influence over young Dârio, she'll meet with a *convenient* accident."

"Just be sure you're not the one dying prematurely," said Verro. "I've got my best young wizard testing your food and drink now, and will add another once Gwýnnett comes to Riyas. I hope that will be enough."

Verro smiled down the hill at the short wizard in green-on-green robes standing not far from Sal, near a field table topped with wine bottles, cubes of cheese and rectangles of seed-covered flatbread.

"At least with small, permanent gates between Riyas and Brendinas it will be easier to rule the united realm," said Túathal.

"And with Gwýnnett's faction added to my loyal Tamloch wizards, there will be no question that I'll lead the combined Conclaves," added Verro.

"I think I'm looking forward to you being the master mage of Tamloch and Dâron *almost* as much I am to seeing Dârio 'lead' both kingdoms," said Túathal.

"Almost," said Verro with a grin. "For myself, I'm looking forward to the intercourse between the halves of the united realm increasing."

"You mean growing trade between Tamloch and Dâron? Or were you thinking about something more personal?" teased Túathal.

"What do *you* think?" asked Verro.

"Perhaps I'll appoint you as Minister of Trade as well as Master Mage, then," said his brother.

"You'll need me as your *de facto* Minister of War until we push the Roma back into the Ocean," said Verro. "They will be our final obstacle to controlling all of Orluin."

"True enough," said Túathal, "but Duke Néillen will hold that title in name if not fact. He can be your deputy as well as my own until Dâron is defeated and Occidens Province is erased from the map of Orluin."

One corner of Verro's mouth turned up. "The duke is competent enough," he said, "and I may have a way to get Quintillius and Laetícia to leave without a battle. They're both ambitious, and the Ocean is just a wider Rubicon."

"I like it," said Túathal. "You're almost as crafty as I am."

"Almost," said Verro.

The tall wizard made a half-turn to face south.

"You're sure you've got King Bjarni's loyalty?" Verro asked. "He's still on track to hit Dâron's forces from the river while the royal army attacks by land?"

"I'm sure he is," said Túathal. "Ten pounds of gold was sufficient inducement. Once our army is between him and Brendinas, we won't allow the Bifurlanders to sack my soon-to-be southern capital, of course. They'll have to settle for what riches they can strip from the bodies of the fallen Dâron soldiers."

"Especially Dâron's heavy cavalry, eh, brother?" asked Verro. "The more of them who die, the more estates in the south you'll have to give your noble supporters in Tamloch."

Túathal looked up at the clouds, afraid he'd laugh if Verro caught his eye.

"That thought had never occurred to me," said Túathal.

Both brothers laughed. Túathal hugged Verro and Verro allowed it, but only for a moment.

"I've got to go and see to my surprise," said the tall green-robed wizard. "My team will be able to handle moving the royal army without my direct supervision."

"I know how to reach you if there are any problems," said Túathal, tapping a gold ring on his little finger.

"Just don't use it unless there's an emergency," said Verro. "Pulling off my surprise will require my full attention."

"Best of luck then," said Túathal. He waved as his brother mounted his flying disk.

Verro waved back, spun around, and flew off to the east, toward the walls of Riyas.

Túathal returned his attention to the marshaling field and smiled. The first units of the royal army were passing through the new wide gate to Dâron.

Chapter 36

Nûd, Eynon, and Dârio

"Who *are* you? How did you tame a wyvern? Why do you have a *red* magestone? And *what* is *that* creature?"

Eynon, Nûd and the young man with the shaved head were flying north to Brendinas, away from the fleet of Bifurland dragonships. Sigrun and Rannveigr had given them leather straps and buckles to make proper harnesses to ride on Rocky safely—adapted from equipment the girls used to ride their small gold dragons. The man with the shaved head and extraordinary skill with a sword rode between Eynon on the left and Nûd on the right on the wyvern's back. Shaved-head man rested on a thickly padded saddle of sorts that prevented the knobs of bone on Rocky's back from making his position miserable. Chee was wearing a long strap around his waist that allowed him to scamper up and down Rocky's neck. At the moment, he was seated on an unpadded knob of bone, facing the man and rubbing both of his tiny hand-paws on the stranger's smooth head.

"Cut that out," said the man. He tried to push Chee's hand-paws away, but the raconette just climbed over his head to lodge between his shoulder blades where he was harder to reach and kept rubbing.

Nûd and Eynon tried not to laugh—and mostly succeeded. A few seconds later, the stranger sighed.

"Go ahead, little fellow," he said. "Keep rubbing. It's starting to feel good."

Chee rubbed more vigorously.

"I'm Eynon and this is Nûd," said Eynon. "I didn't tame Rocky—he tamed himself. He's my familiar—one of them, actually. I have a red magestone because it called to me and I didn't know better. And the little beast on your back is a raconette. His name is Chee."

"Thanks," said the man with the shaved head. He paused for a moment, then spoke. "Call me Río."

"Pleased to meet you," said Eynon. "Are you from Brendinas? I'm from the Coombe, that's in the far west of the kingdom, just east of the Bordermarches."

"I know where the Coombe is," said Río. "And yes, I'm from Brendinas."

"That's great," said Eynon. "I can't imagine many people in the capital knowing or caring about the Coombe."

"Merchants have to stay informed on trading possibilities everywhere in the kingdom," said Río.

"Uh huh," said Nûd. "What do you trade during the winter?"

Río leaned back into Chee's fingers and let out a long breath. After a few more heartbeats he said, "Sometimes I take letters back and forth to the southern reaches for people who can't afford help from a wizard, but most of the time I study."

"Swordplay?" asked Nûd.

"Among other things," said Río. He quickly changed the subject. "Did you see that huge fireball? It was spectacular. It nearly swamped Skavendr's scout boat. I know, because I was flat on my back looking up at the sky when it exploded. I'm surprised it didn't blind me."

"Sorry about that," said Eynon.

"*You* threw that fireball?" asked Río. "I'm impressed. I've never seen a wizard create one so big at exercises with the royal army—or at the Midsummer festival."

"I wasn't trying to throw such a big one," said Eynon. "It's just that I saw the three Bifurlander wizards in gold robes about to attack me and had to shift part of my attention to defense instead of concentrating completely on keeping my fireball a reasonable size."

"Did you often attend exercises with the royal army?" asked Nûd.

"No," said Río. "But my friends and I liked to watch the king's troops maneuver when the wizards were practicing with them. Fireballs! Tight light beams! Lightning bolts! Freeze blasts!"

"Uh huh," said Nûd. "Didn't they send you and your friends away so you wouldn't get hurt if a fireball went off course?"

"They tried," said Río. He turned his head to face Nûd and smiled, causing Chee to scramble to his left to keep rubbing.

"Right," said Nûd.

"We have to get word to the king and the Conclave that we've paid off the Bifurlanders," said Eynon. "There's no need for Dâron to attack them."

"It may be too late for that," said Río. "Too much is already in motion."

"Who *are* you?" asked Nûd. He stared at Río with eyes as intense as twin beams of tight light.

"I'm not what I seem," Río admitted.

Eynon turned to stared as well. "You mean you don't sell strawberries?" he asked.

"No," Río replied. "I don't sell anything, except selling my mother on an act that I'm an easy-to-control pig-boy."

"You're not dirty enough to be a pig-boy," said Eynon. He sniffed. "And you don't smell as bad as one—though your clothes *are* damp and have a bit of fish-stink. Maybe you washed recently, or had a dip in the river?"

"I spent twenty minutes in the bilge water in the bottom of Skavendr's scout boat!" Río complained.

He shook Chee off the back of his head. The raconette climbed up Rocky's neck and scolded him with a loud, "Chee-chee-chee-CHEE!"

Eynon thought Río would have been close to pulling his hair out if he'd had any.

"Sorry," said Eynon.

"You still haven't told us who you *really* are," said Nûd.

"I'm getting there," said Río.

Before he could say more, a blue fireball exploded in front of them and Rocky dove rapidly so he wouldn't collide with its flames.

"Turn around!" shouted Nûd.

Rocky spun his body in a tight turn with his wings furled until he faced in the opposite direction. A few hundred feet below him on a flying disk was a wizard wearing blue robes. She had short auburn hair that stood out from her head like a dandelion in seed. The wyvern shot toward her.

"Mother!" Nûd exclaimed when he recognized Fercha.

"Nûd?" asked Fercha. "What are *you* doing here?"

"Heading for Brendinas to tell the king and Conclave that Eynon and I have paid the Bifurlanders not to attack after all," said Nûd.

"Seems like you've already told the king," said Fercha as Rocky hovered beside her flying disk.

"What?" asked Eynon.

"Hello, Dârio," said Fercha. "I've been searching for you for hours. Your mother's worried about you."

"Hah," said Dârio. "My mother is concerned when I'm out of her clutches for longer than it takes to visit the garderobe."

"You're the king of Dâron?" asked Eynon.

"King Dâroth the Twenty-fifth, but my friends call me Dârio."

"Your Majesty," said Eynon.

The king gave him a stern royal look.

Eynon tried again.

"Pleased to meet you, Dârio."

"That's better," said the king. He looked over at the woman on the flying disk. "Why are you here?"

"I told you," Fercha replied. "Your mother is worried. She sent me to look for you."

"Are you going to take me back to the palace?" asked Dârio.

"Of course not," she said. "We should go to an inn a few miles north of here where we can talk on the ground with a mug of ale in our hands."

"The Dormant Dragon?" asked Dârio. "In Arthábben, near the blue marble quarry?"

"You've been there?" asked Fercha, raising her eyebrows.

"Once," said Dârio. He turned to Eynon, then to Nûd. "Does stopping at an inn to talk meet with your approval?"

Nûd leaned up so he could see Eynon over Dârio's shoulders and saw his friend nodding.

"Great," said Nûd. "Rocky—follow Fercha!"

The wyvern waited until Fercha directed her flying disk to the north then tracked her from ten yards behind where the turbulence of his wing strokes wouldn't disturb her flight. Eynon considered how Rocky had protected Nûd during and after the attack by the gold dragon riders and how he seemed to be glad to follow Nûd's commands, even without Eynon creating spheres of magically tasty solidified sound to reward him.

"Rocky really likes you," said Eynon.

"And I really like him," said Nûd. "Who's a good boy!"

The big black wyvern made a pleasant rumbling sound low in his throat.

"*You're* a good boy," Eynon added.

He was happy to hear Rocky's rumbling grow louder.

A mug of ale sounds good, thought Eynon as they sped upriver. *And maybe if I have a minute to myself I can contact Merry?*

Eynon fingered the gold communicator-ring on his finger. Doethan had given it to Eynon so he could stay in touch, then given his matching ring to Merry. Eynon had seen her at the quarry this morning. The sight of her had been like a ray of sunshine heralding the dawn, but then she'd gated out with Damon to who knows where. If they could talk, maybe they could figure out a way to be in the same place at the same time. He *missed* her, and hoped she missed him, too.

Sensing Eynon's mood, Chee climbed down from Rocky's neck and cuddled into Eynon's shoulder. Soon the raconette was asleep, breathing rhythmically. A few minutes later, so was Eynon.

Chapter 37

Outside the Dormant Dragon

Eynon woke in mid-flight with his gold ring pulsing. Chee reluctantly climbed back up Rocky's neck and Eynon acknowledged the ring's connection. The gold band expanded until it was the size of a barrel hoop. Merry's face smiled at him from inside its circumference.

"Did I wake you?" she asked.

"Yes, but I'm glad you did," said Eynon.

He was glad for the new harness fastening him securely to Rocky's back. It made it easier for him to hold the enlarged ring.

"I was planning to contact you in a few minutes, but you beat me to it," Eynon continued.

"I finally had time to myself," said Merry. "The other wizards from the Conclave are off to the north joining the army. I'm here with Doethan and Damon, catching my breath. I have *so* much to tell you."

"And I have so much to tell you, too," said Eynon. "Fercha and Nûd are with me, too, but you'll never guess who *else* is with me."

"I don't want to try," said Merry. "I just want to hear your voice and be with you *soon*. Where *are* you?"

"We're almost there," said Nûd over Dârio's back.

Eynon looked down and saw a quarry cut into a high hill west of the Brenavon. It had tall, blue-veined walls and held a deep-blue lake. A narrow gravel track followed the stream flowing from the lake to the river and led to a two-story inn with a blue-slate roof that sat in a corner where the track intersected the main north-south road.

"We're about to land at an inn called the Dormant Dragon in a village downriver from Brendinas named Arthábben."

Eynon heard Merry shout from two directions. One came through the ring, the other rose up from the inn's blue-slate courtyard. He leaned forward. Merry was waving at him from below.

"See you soon!" he shouted and closed the ring. Seconds later, Rocky touched down. Eynon unstrapped and slid off the wyvern's side.

"Eynon," said Merry, hugging her friend and lover fiercely.

"It's *so* good to hold you," said Eynon as he leaned down so Merry could rest her head on his shoulder.

The two of them were oblivious to their surroundings and might have stayed that way for an hour if Chee hadn't decided he wanted to be part of the reunion as well. The raconette jumped up to Eynon's shoulder, then squirmed down to insert himself between Eynon and Merry's bodies—creating a gap where none was to be found—and emitting a low, contented hum, punctuated by the occasional *chee*.

Eynon and Merry took a step apart, but continued to support Chee with their forearms.

Behind him, Eynon heard familiar voices. Dârio was talking to Nûd.

"Fercha is your *mother?*"

"I claim that honor," said Fercha.

"She is," said Nûd in a flat voice.

"Oh," said Dârio. "It's like that, is it? I hope you get along with *your* mother better than I do with mine."

"So do I," said Fercha. "Leaving him in Melyncárreg while I was off helping Queen Carys hardly puts me in the same league as Princess Gwýnnett. It's not like I was trying to rule the kingdom through him and threatening him with compliance potions."

"At least not yet," said Nûd. "There's still time left in the day."

"Not much of it," said Dârio, looking west at the sun approaching the horizon. "It will be full dark in a couple of hours."

"I'm trying to remember," said Fercha. "Do Bifurlanders attack at night?"

"If they do, it's not very often," said Dârio. "At least not according to..."

"Bifurland Naval Tactics and Strategy," completed Fercha.

"I thought I'd put that back on the shelf?"

"You did, Your Majesty—but Jenet has sharp eyes," said Fercha.

"And a keen mind," said Dârio.

"She said she had you in *shah-mat* with mate in three," Fercha added with a smile.

"Perhaps *too* keen," said Dârio.

"Who's Jenet?" asked Nûd.

"A woman—a Duke's daughter—I play *shah-mat* with," said Dârio. His cheeks and forehead turned pink.

Fercha waved a hand toward Eynon and Merry.

"And those two are just good friends," said Fercha.

Nûd raised his voice. "Eynon! Introduce me to your *girlfriend*."

Eynon turned around, still managing to hold Merry's hand. The tops of his ears were as pink as Dârio's cheeks. Chee, dislodged from his spot, slid down Eynon's leg and scurried over to Dârio. He climbed up to the young king's shoulders and resumed rubbing his shaved head. Dârio thought better of trying to remove the raconette and tried to appreciate the scalp massage.

"Nûd, Dârio—this is Merry. Her father is the baron of the Upper Rhuthro."

Merry gave a cursory bow to Dârio and turned to Nûd.

"Pleased to meet you, Nûd," said Merry. "We saw each other at the quarry west of the Coombe this morning, but were never properly introduced."

"Small things like attacks from Tamloch wizards and soldiers tend to get in the way," said Nûd, giving Merry a nod and a grin.

"I have a great deal of respect for your patience," Merry answered with a nod and a grin of her own. "I only had to put up with Damon for a few hours and I was ready to strangle him more than once. I understand you were you in Damon's service?"

"Not exactly," said Nûd. "It's complicated."

"Did someone mention my name?" asked Damon. He and Doethan had just stepped out of the inn and were standing in the courtyard a few paces away.

Chee looked over at Damon with his colorful robes and his mostly-bald head. He started to slide down Dârio's torso to switch to Damon until the raconette saw the old wizard glaring at him and changed his destination to the padded saddle on Rocky's back.

Nûd raised an eyebrow at Damon's sparkling ensemble.

"Auditioning for court jester?" Nûd asked.

The old wizard ignored him.

"Hello, Damon," said Eynon. "Or should I say *Master Mage Ealdamon?*"

Eynon gave a polite bow to the older wizard. He'd wondered why the Master Mage had never shown himself at the castle back in Melyncárreg and was still less than pleased with Nûd and Damon for their subterfuge. He vowed to be less trusting in the future. *Yet another aspect of my education,* he considered.

"This is my *good friend* Merry," said Eynon. "Though I expect the two of you are already acquainted, since you gated out from the battle at the quarry together."

"True enough," said Damon. He smiled at the two young wizards indulgently. "You're a well-matched pair—and you should have time to spend alone together tonight. It will be dark soon, and I expect we won't see the Bifurlander's fleet, the royal army, and the Roma legions meet until first light tomorrow."

"The Bifurlanders won't be attacking Dâron," said Nûd. "Eynon and I bought them off with fifty pounds of gold."

"You went back to Melyncárreg to collect more gold the way Eynon got some for his setting," said Damon. It was definitely a statement, not a question.

"Correct," Nûd confirmed. "King Bjarni and Queen Signý agreed not to attack us, though they did talk about testing their warriors' valor against the legions of Occidens Province."

Dârio spoke up, addressing the older wizards. "Could one of you get word to the legions and tell them to hang back and avoid engagement? I don't want to see lives lost due to any unfortunate miscommunication."

"I can see to that," said Fercha. "And spoken like a responsible monarch. I'll let Mafuta and Felix know. They're with Quintillius and the legions."

"Be sure to inform Laetícia," said Damon.

"Wouldn't it be more fun to keep her in the dark?" teased Fercha. "As if anyone could."

"There is that," said Damon. "She will probably get the message just seconds after you send it."

"Efficient intelligence networks are something to be admired," said Doethan. "And speaking of networks, Damon, shouldn't you check in on your contacts in Riyas in case they've got more to report?"

"I was in Riyas!" said Merry. Her face lit up. "My big brother is there. He's not dead."

"I didn't know you *had* a big brother," said Eynon, "but I'm glad he's not dead."

Dârio caught Merry's eye and put his finger to his lips. Then he squeezed his thumb and index finger together in front of his mouth.

"Sorry, Your Majesty," said Merry. "I should know better than to discuss things in the open air that are best kept secret."

"We're all friends here," said Dârio, "so no harm done, Merry. I just wanted to give you a friendly warning."

"Like when a sailor bragging in a tavern in Bjarniston gave away the Bifurlanders' surprise attack on Riyas back during the reign of the Old King's grandfather, Dâroth XXII," said Nûd.

"Loose lips sink ships!" said Merry, Eynon and Dârio simultaneously.

Everyone laughed. The phrase, adopted by Bifurland, Tamloch, Dâron and Occidens Province, had become a familiar saying across Orluin, thanks to a bard from Riyas making it part of the chorus of a popular ballad. The Bifurlanders, in particular, had taken it to heart. It took them more than a generation to rebuild their fleet.

Braith knows that song word for word and note for note, mused Eynon. He could picture his sister singing it while she milked.

"Let's go inside and get some dinner," said Damon. "Ice magic makes me hungry and I missed lunch."

"Ice magic?" asked Eynon.

"At the Conclave meeting," said Merry. Her eyes were wide as she remembered.

"Like when you froze the Abbenoth river?" Eynon asked.

"On a much smaller scale," said Damon. "But I have to keep my strength up."

"Sure you do," said Nûd. "And if the cook at the inn can't prepare a decent meal, we'll send Eynon to the kitchen."

"I'd be glad to assist, if that would be helpful," said Eynon.

"He's teasing you," said Merry.

She cuddled in under Eynon's arm and put her own around his waist, then began to guide him toward the inn's main door. Eynon resisted.

"What about Rocky?" he said. "Do you think the innkeeper can spare a sheep for him?"

"He just had two goats on the Bifurlander's flagship," said Nûd. "How hungry can he be?"

"I don't know," said Eynon, "but I don't like *us* having dinner without making sure Rocky is fed as well. If we were back in Melyncárreg, he could just grab a wisent. There are tens of thousands of them there."

"I suggest you encourage Rocky to check out the river," said Doethan. "It's teaming with hundred-pound sturgeons."

"I never thought about him eating fish," said Eynon.

"You're from the Coombe," teased Merry. *"You've* just learned to eat fish."

"There is that," said Eynon with a smile.

"Maybe I can help," said Doethan. He boarded his flying disk and floated up and across until he was a dozen feet above the swift-flowing waters of the Brenavon. Two minutes later, he returned with a huge, pointed-nosed fish inside a sphere of solidified sound. The fish was still writhing when Doethan dispelled the sphere and the fish dropped in front of Rocky's snout.

Eynon whispered to Merry. "Is that a sturgeon?"

"Yes," she replied. "Let's see if he likes it."

The wyvern sniffed the fish, then bent his long neck to grasp it in his teeth and toss the sturgeon high in the air. In a well-practiced motion, Rocky opened his jaw wide and intercepted the fish as it descended, head first, down his throat.

"I think he likes fish," said Merry.

"Evidently," said Eynon.

Chee had been thrown off the saddle when Rocky moved. Eynon caught him with a bowl of solidified sound and floated the raconette gently down to Dârio's shoulders.

"Thanks a lot," said the young king. His initial tone suggested annoyance, but when Dârio pulled Chee off his back and held him cradled in front of him, rubbing his belly fur and saying, "Aren't you the cutest thing," Eynon knew it wasn't really a problem.

Rocky found large chunks of gravel by the side of the road to the quarry and added several of them on top of the sturgeon. Then he curled up on the warm stones of the slate courtyard and closed his eyes.

Fercha held the inn door open for Damon.

"As suggested, I've got to reach out to my network," the old wizard said. He moved his thumb and forefinger together and winked at Merry, but she was talking softly to Eynon and oblivious once again. He smiled at Fercha and entered the inn. Doethan followed him.

"I think I'll listen in," said Doethan, indicating Damon's back with a shift of his chin. "Give my best to Mafuta and Felix."

Dârio and Chee approached the door and Fercha gave a small bow.

"Your Majesty," she said, looking at Chee. The raconette waved at her. "You too, Dârio."

"If my great-grandmother didn't like you so much..." said Dârio.

"Yes, Your Majesty," said Fercha.

Nûd was next. He gave Fercha a restrained hug.

"It *is* good to see you," he said quietly. "Will we have time to talk tonight? We *need* to talk."

"I hope so," she said. "I'll tell you what you've been waiting to hear."

"Who my father is?" said Nûd.

"Yes," said Fercha. "That—and more."

"More?" asked Nûd. His eyebrows rose.

"Later," said Fercha. She gently pushed Nûd inside and started to close the door. She looked behind her and saw Eynon and Merry kissing near one of Rocky's outstretched wings. Fercha smiled, took a step, and let the door shut behind her.

"Eynon," said Merry a few minutes later. "Damon said something about the two of us having time to spend alone together tonight."

"Uh huh," said Eynon, still reveling in the joy of holding and kissing Merry.

"I'd appreciate it if you'd do me a favor," said Merry.

"Anything," said Eynon. He smiled at Merry with the innocent enthusiasm of Chee contemplating an Applegarth apple.

"Don't eat too much tonight," she said. "I've got plans for you and don't want you falling asleep before they're put into action."

"Yes, dear lady," said Eynon. His eyes grew brighter. "Those sound like very good plans indeed."

"I wonder if Rocky would mind if we crawled in *under* his wing?" asked Merry.

"Probably not," said Eynon. "He seems to be asleep. Is *this* one of your plans?"

"No," said Merry. "This is something unplanned and spontaneous."

"I like spontaneous," said Eynon as he took off his padded jacket and opened it up on the cobblestones under Rocky's wing.

"Stop talking and kiss me," said Merry.

Chapter 38

Inside the Dormant Dragon

"Well, well," said Dârio with a bit of a sneer as Eynon and Merry entered the common room of the Dormant Dragon. "So glad you could join us."

"Your Majesty," said Fercha. "Don't be an ass."

"Sorry," said Dârio. "It's hard to drop the role when I'm among friends."

"Not to mention you're so *good* at it," said Nûd.

"Hey," said Dârio.

"Nûd," said Fercha. "Behave. It isn't easy being king of Dâron."

Nûd shook his head. "Sorry, Mother. *That's* a job I'd never want."

Fercha sighed and glanced at Damon. The old wizard was studiously looking down at the bowl on the trestle table in front of him. He was focused on a honey-and-raisin baked apple wrapped in a sweet pastry crust.

The common room of the inn was large—larger than needed by a town as small as Arthábben, thought Eynon, *unless there was something about the place he wasn't aware of.* It held six long trestle tables with benches on either side. A sizable stone fireplace filled the left-hand wall, while a wide, well-worked tapestry depicting a sleeping blue dragon hung on the wall to the right, next to the stairs. *That explains the name of the place,* Eynon considered. *I'd rather deal with a sleeping dragon than one wide awake and angry.* A polished wooden bar with a pass-through to the kitchen behind it occupied the side of the room across from the entrance.

"Innkeeper," said Dârio. "Two mugs of cider for my friends. They must be thirsty."

A solid-looking middle-aged woman in pants, not skirts, nodded at Dârio and drew mugs of rich brown liquid from a barrel. She put them on a tray and collected a platter of bread and cheese from a slender woman about the same age on the other side of the pass-through. *She must be the cook,* thought Eynon. The cook touched the innkeeper's hand after putting the platter on the tray and gave the innkeeper a loving smile. *This must be a family business,* Eynon realized. He knew what a happy couple looked like from observing the way his parents treated each other.

At the far end of the bar, Eynon saw two small unwashed faces under wild, straw-colored hair peek out to look at him and Merry, then disappear in a chorus of giggles. *The cook and innkeeper's children?* Eynon wondered.

Merry turned to Eynon and raised an eyebrow. Dârio noticed her look and explained.

"A few minutes ago, the children raced in from the courtyard telling their parents about the strange noises the sleeping wyvern was making," said the young king. "When one of their mothers asked what they meant, the children did an exceptional job of repeating what they'd heard."

High-pitched imitations of sounds of love-making came from behind the bar.

"That's enough of *that* nonsense," said the innkeeper as she rounded the end of the bar where the children were hiding. She brought the mugs and platter out to Eynon and Merry, not bothering to hide a grin at Eynon's evident embarrassment. Merry's face was also red, but she was smiling and nudged Eynon in the ribs.

"We'll have to add *amusing the children* to *frightening the deer,*" she said, remembering a time they'd stopped in a clearing to make love on their trip down the Rhuthro.

"Let's not," said Eynon. Then he laughed and sighed. "It was worth it, though."

"Mmmm..." said Merry. "Yes it was. I'm looking forward to sharing a feather bed with you tonight."

That comment prompted another chorus of giggles from the children and scattered laughter from the rest of the adults in the common room.

"Get on with you," said the innkeeper to the children. "Go feed the chickens."

"Yes, Mother," said the two little ones simultaneously. Eynon could hear, but not see them leave through the kitchen, receiving smiles from their second mother as they went.

When the children were gone, the innkeeper apologized.

"Sorry about that," she said. "Children are interested in everything."

"And a wyvern sleeping in the courtyard..." said Eynon.

"Would be irresistible," said Merry. "We should be the ones apologizing to your children."

"It's not something they haven't heard already," said the cook. She smiled at her wife by the bar.

"Your room is at the top of the stairs on the right," said the inn-keeper. "A bed might be more comfortable—and private—than the courtyard."

"Yes, ma'am," said Eynon.

Merry smiled at the innkeeper, then winked.

"To change the subject," said Damon, "You won't need to help out in the kitchen, Eynon. The food is excellent!" He waved to the cook and the slender woman behind the pass-through gave him a small bow to acknowledge the compliment.

"That's good," said Eynon, "because I'm hungry enough to eat..."

"Chicken pie," said Nûd. "We saved slices for you and Merry."

"It's got eggs and mushrooms and sliced leeks and spring onions and doesn't have a top crust," said Dârio. "I want her to teach the cooks at the palace how to make it."

"That's high praise," said Merry.

She sat at the trestle table across from Damon and pulled her eat-ing knife from her belt. Eynon sat beside her, close enough so their knees touched. Doethan and Fercha were across from him. Nûd and Dârio were on opposite sides of the table beyond Fercha and Eynon. Chee was reclining in the middle of the table beyond Dârio, allowing the young king to feed him morsels of bread, cheese, and sliced apple like a Roma noble leaning back on a couch at a dinner party.

Eynon and Merry began to eat the nutty dark bread and firm white cheese on the platter while the rest of the table was working on dessert. A few minutes later, two steaming slices of chicken pie were placed in front of them by the helpful innkeeper. After a few bites, Merry was sure she wanted to get the recipe to take back to Applegarth and Eynon vowed to spend time in the kitchen, so he could learn how to make it himself.

Doethan caught Damon's eye and saw the older wizard tilt his chin up and down a few degrees. Raising both his arms, Doethan cast a translucent sphere of solidified sound around the table, ensuring their privacy.

Eynon was surprised by Doethan's spellcasting. *What if I want dessert?* he thought, as he cut off another morsel of chicken pie and brought it to his mouth.

Damon asked Eynon a question just as the young wizard began to chew.

"Are you sure the Bifurlanders won't attack Dâron?" he asked.

While Eynon tried to swallow, Nûd replied.

"Fifty pounds of gold wasn't enough to dissuade them from sacking Brendinas, but a demonstration of Eynon's fire magic convinced them it wouldn't be a good idea."

"What did you *do,* Eynon?" asked Damon.

"He launched a fireball that was brighter than the sun," said Fercha. "I was in the air, flying south from Brendinas to find Dârio and was nearly blinded and blown off my flying disk from five leagues distant."

"It was even more impressive closer up," said Nûd. "Half the Bifurlanders' ships nearly capsized or lost their sails."

"I see," said Damon. "What did I tell you about *control,* lad? You can't let that red magestone of yours release *all* its power. You have to moderate its exuberance."

"I tried," said Eynon. "I used the power of my red magestone, of course, but counted on the blue magestone I found to keep it in check. It's just that a trio of Bifurlander wizards was about to attack me, so I had to switch the focus of the blue magestone from control to defense at the last minute, and my fireball got a little too big."

"I'll say!" Dârio interjected. "I was tied up in the bottom of a scout boat and felt like I was almost baked alive."

"Sounds like *you've* got a story to tell, Dârio," said Doethan.

"Later," said Damon. "You're sure about the Bifurlanders?"

"Pretty sure," said Nûd, "but remember—they found out about the legions from Occidens Province coming south on the east bank and spoke about testing their warriors against *them*. It sounded like they wanted to do it for *fun*, not profit."

"Bifurlanders," said Damon, shaking his head. "They're almost as bad as the hordes from the Clan Lands."

"But the Bifurlanders are more disciplined," said Dârio.

"Don't believe everything you read in books, Your Majesty," said Damon.

"I got word to Mafuta and Felix while you two were otherwise occupied," said Fercha, indicating Eynon and Merry. "They'll get the legions to hang back and will try to avoid engaging."

Dârio handed Chee a cube of cheese and rubbed the raconette's belly while he ate it. "I don't want anyone hurt if we can avoid it," he said.

Merry turned her head and stared at the young king. She was still getting used to this version of Dârio. He wasn't the arrogant fool he was reputed to be.

Eynon's eyes widened, as if from a sudden memory. He reached under his shirt and lifted an oval blue magestone in a silver filigree setting from his neck.

"This is yours," he said, offering the magestone to Fercha. "I'm sorry I didn't have a chance to give it back this morning."

Fercha nodded and smiled at Eynon. "That was perfectly understandable given the circumstances," she said. Fercha reached out to take the offered magestone, but Damon's hand on her arm stopped her.

"Wait," said the Master Mage of Dâron. "Are you saying you're attuned with two magestones at the same time? The blue stone is helping you control the red?"

"Uh huh," said Eynon, not sure if he'd done something wrong. He held his head high, but looked left and right nervously.

"If you hadn't been distracted by the three Bifurlander wizards' imminent attack, you would have been able to control your fireball?"

"I think so," said Eynon. "And the blue magestone is *smart,* somehow. It knows how to do lots of things already, so I can just *do* them without thinking about it and put the power of my red magestone behind them when I need to."

Damon turned his head to face Fercha.

"Can you live without your old stone, do you think?" he asked. "I don't want the lad to blow himself up and us along with him if he uses his red stone without something to constrain its power."

Fercha sat silently for a few seconds, then nodded.

"I've lasted this long without it," she said. "And my new stone is well on its way to being trained—but if not having my original stone gets me killed, I'll never forgive you."

"I'll never forgive my*self,*" said Damon.

"Here, take it!" said Eynon. He shoved the blue stone and silver setting across the table toward Fercha. She didn't move to accept it.

"Damon's right, Eynon," said Fercha. "There's never been a wizard with a red magestone in the history of Dâron. I think we'd all feel better if you have all the help you can get to control it."

Fercha pushed the chain and setting back across the table with the tip of her eating dagger.

"Put it back around your neck," she said. "We can discuss it later, after the war is won."

Eynon slowly reached out and took the chain, lowering it around his neck and positioning the blue magestone under his shirt, against his skin. He let out a deep breath, surprised at how glad he was to have his rapport with both stones reestablished.

"Thank you, good wizard," he said, bowing his head to Fercha.

Merry caught Fercha's eye and raised one brow, then silently mouthed a *thank you* of her own.

Fercha nodded back to Eynon and Merry, then turned to Damon.

"Do you have news from Riyas?" she asked. "Is the threat to Dâron over, now that the Bifurlanders won't attack Brendinas?"

"What do *you* think?" asked Damon.

"I think that Verro is creatively devious," said Fercha, "and King Túathal can be trusted to be untrustworthy."

"Right on both counts," said Damon. "I just learned Verro has mastered making wide gates and Tamloch's army is coming though one now. They'll be between our army and Brendinas."

"And plan to crush the royal army of Dâron between them and the Bifurlanders," said Dârio. "I've got to join up with the army immediately. They need to see their king."

"I'll fly you north with me in a few minutes," said Damon. "It will do more for morale to have you appear alongside the master mage of the kingdom."

"It will at that," said Dârio. "Thank you." He gave Damon a sly sideways smile. "And if you're able to work that wizardry we discussed, the legions can cross the Brenavon and we can crush Tamloch's army between *our* forces."

"Provided Bifurland's fleet doesn't decide to attack the Roma," said Doethan.

"Damon's magic should handle that as well," said Dârio.

"There's more," said Damon. "My source..." —he paused to smile at Merry— "...says Verro has a surprise up his sleeve. It may involve the southern Clan Lands."

"What could it be?" asked Dârio.

"An attack from our rear, I expect," said Fercha. "Whatever it is, we're not going to like it."

"We'll have to stay flexible and be ready to cope with the unexpected," said Damon.

"Like in any battle," said the young king.

"You say that as if it's easy, Your Majesty," said Doethan. "I can assure you, when you're actually *in* a battle, a surprise attack can be devastating."

"I'll have to count on your network of spies to assure we're not caught off guard then," said Dârio.

"Maybe we should be thinking about a few surprises of our own?" suggested Nûd.

Damon nodded, then leaned down and spooned up the last of his dessert, licking honey off his upper lip. He took a deep breath and let it out in a long, low sigh.

Damon thinks he's getting too old for this, thought Eynon. *My great-grandfather used to do the same thing before he stopped farming. I wonder who could ever replace Damon as Master Mage of Dâron?*

"Will the rest of you be heading north with us now?" asked Dârio. "Battle is sure to be joined in the morning."

"Nûd and I have to talk," said Fercha. "We'll meet up with you at first light tomorrow."

"Those two deserve a night alone together," said Doethan, indicating Merry and Eynon. "They can do the same."

"If they get any rest," teased Dârio.

"I plan to get some rest," said Doethan. "And I'd much rather sleep here in a real bed than on the ground or a cot in a military camp."

"You and me, both, my friend," said Damon. "But we don't all get a choice in the matter. Come along, Your Majesty."

"See you at dawn," said Doethan. He dispelled the sphere of solidified sound protecting their privacy.

"See you at dawn," said Damon and Dârio.

Chee waved goodbye and climbed up a post into the rafters to sleep where the air was warmer.

He may actually get some rest, thought Eynon. It was getting harder to keep his eyes open.

Eynon yawned. Merry poked him in the ribs with her elbow.

"See you at dawn," said Eynon.

Merry helped Eynon up from the table and guided him toward the stairs.

Chapter 39

Nûd and Fercha

Damon and Dârio left a few minutes later. The innkeeper gave each of them a small canvas sack with chicken and cheese between slices of the nutty dark bread prepared by her wife. Dârio wore a long blue wool cloak over a white linen shirt and dark-blue canvas pants, all loaned to him by the innkeeper before dinner. The pant-legs barely came to his knees, but the ensemble was a major improvement over his earlier, bilge-water-soaked outfit.

"Goodnight, Fercha. Goodnight Nûd," said Doethan as he got up and moved to the stairs. "See you in the morning."

"Goodnight," Fercha and Nûd echoed. They listened as his footsteps squeaked their way up the treads to the second floor.

The innkeeper called to them from behind the bar.

"We have to put the children to bed," she said. "Can I get you anything before I leave?"

"Two mugs of applejack, if you have it," said Fercha.

"Better make it three," said Nûd, slowly shaking his head.

"I'll bring you a pitcher," said the innkeeper. A moment later, she was as good as her word, putting a tray with two full mugs and a pitcher on the table between Nûd and Fercha. The rich aroma of fermented apples filled the air.

The innkeeper and cook opened a door at the back of the kitchen and Nûd and Fercha heard their children's high-pitched voices as they scattered grain for the chickens and pretended to be flying on wyvern-back. Then the door closed and the common room was dark and silent.

Fercha cast a sphere of solidified sound so their conversation would stay private.

"Mother," said Nûd.

"Nûd," Fercha replied. "You don't know how much I wish I could hear you say that word with even a hint of affection."

"Huh," said Nûd. It was more an exhalation than a word. "I do love you, Mother. I just don't *like* you very much."

"I suppose I deserve that. I did leave you alone with your grandfather in Melyncárreg for far too long. But I had my reasons."

"Do you know what it's like to live with that old curmudgeon?" asked Nûd. Then he laughed and rubbed his forehead. *Of course she did.*

Nûd and Fercha each drank from their mugs.

"He wasn't so cranky when your grandmother was still with him."

"That's one of the things I wanted to ask you," said Nûd. "Where's my grandmother's grave? I want to show my respects."

One corner of Fercha's mouth turned up. "What makes you think she's dead?"

"You mean she's *not?*" asked Nûd. "Damon always *acts* like she's dead."

"He's never forgiven her for leaving."

"Why did she leave? Where did she go?"

"She left to watch my back," said Fercha. "And *her* mother asked her to come home."

"My grandmother is in Brendinas?" asked Nûd.

"Do you even remember her?" asked Fercha. "You were just a small child when she left Melyncárreg."

"I remember a kind face and auburn hair," said Nûd. "She had a wonderful smile."

"That's Seren," said Fercha. She smiled and Nûd saw echoes of his childhood memories.

"Is that why you keep your hair so short? You don't want anyone seeing her in you?"

"Yes," said Fercha. "They're so busy comparing me to a dandelion that they overlook the resemblance—not that there are that many people left in court now who remember my mother."

"What about all the statues?"

"They *never* resemble their subjects," said Fercha. "And they're also twice life-size and plated with gold."

"That makes sense," said Nûd. "Though you were always larger than life to me."

He smiled at Fercha and she smiled back. They touched mugs and drank.

"Keep that up and you might make me think you like me," said Fercha.

Nûd shook his head. "Don't get your hopes up. We still haven't talked about the Bifurland mammoth in the room."

"Your father."

"Who was he, Mother? Is it Doethan?"

Fercha laughed long enough for Nûd to feel uncomfortable. She drank twice from her mug, then wiped her lips with the back of her hand.

"No, Nûd. Doethan's not your father—though it might have made things easier for both of us if he was. He's been carrying a torch for Princess Rúth of Tamloch for longer than you've been alive."

"Huh," said Nûd again. "How did Doethan meet a Tamloch princess?"

"After the battle at the walls of Nova Eboracum..." began Fercha.

"When Damon froze the Abbenoth..."

Fercha nodded. "Correct. Prince Dâri and Prince Túathal became good friends after standing side by side to defeat the commander of the city and his guards. For many years, Tamloch and Dâron were at peace. Prince Túathal and his brother and sister visited Brendinas several times. Prince Dâri and Princess Gwýnnett traveled to Riyas for state visits as well."

"They weren't exchanges of hostages?" asked Nûd.

"No, they were friendly visits," said Fercha. "Too friendly, really." She seemed lost in thought for a few heartbeats.

"Poor Doethan," Nûd mused. "In love with someone unattainable."

"Tell me about it," said Fercha, her lower lip trembling.

"Mother?"

Fercha held her head in her hands. She seemed close to crying.

Nûd stood and walked around the table. He sat next to Fercha and hugged her. Her body shook, but her eyes stayed dry. Nûd waited for her to stop shaking. Fercha took deep breaths until she regained her equilibrium.

Nûd filled her mug with more applejack from the pitcher and Fercha drank it down. She took another deep breath and squared her shoulders.

"I'm sorry," she said.

"For what? Being human?"

"For keeping secrets," said Fercha.

"What can be a bigger secret than me being the rightful king of Dâron?" asked Nûd. "We both know I don't want *that* job."

"Now you know why my parents encouraged me to learn wizardry," said Fercha. "It took *me* out of the succession as Princess Seren's only child."

"Too bad being a wizard doesn't take an entire family line out of the succession," said Nûd.

"You know as well as I do that any heir who *isn't* a wizard is still eligible for the crown," said Fercha. "That's part of the problem."

"What problem is that?" asked Nûd with a soft-voiced intensity. "The problem that you won't share my father's name?"

"Why couldn't *you* be a wizard?" asked Fercha. "That would have taken you out of the running and you wouldn't need to live in secret."

"You and Damon showed me why I didn't want to be one."

"Were we that bad?"

"No," said Nûd. "But you both are so caught up in spies and plotting that you've forgotten about the people of the kingdom. Eynon's the only wizard I know who still seems to remember the farmers and cooks and innkeepers, the people who *aren't* kings, or nobles or other wizards."

"You always did prefer the kitchen and library at Melyncárreg to the classrooms and workshops for wizardry," said Fercha.

"Wizardry is about power. I'm more interested in wisdom."

"From cooks and books..." said Fercha, looking at Nûd tenderly, but with a touch of pity.

"I'm sorry I've disappointed you," said Nûd. "I'm not a powerful wizard. I'm not a wizard at all."

"Given your parents," said Fercha, "perhaps that's for the best."

"Who *is* my father?" asked Nûd. "Tell me!"

"Verro," said Fercha. She seemed almost defiant as she said it, then her shoulders slumped and she deflated.

"King Túathal's younger brother?" asked Nûd. "The Master Mage of Tamloch? *He's* my father?" Nûd slapped his forehead, stood up, and paced along the length of the table behind Fercha.

"Don't tell me I'm the rightful heir to Dâron *and* Tamloch?"

"No," said Fercha. "You're not. Dârio is the rightful heir to Tamloch."

"What?"

"It's a long story."

"Start talking," said Nûd.

"About Verro, or Dârio?" asked Fercha.

"Start with my father, then the king."

"Twenty-three years ago, Verro came to Brendinas while I was at court. He swept me off my feet and we were married in secret. He was back in Riyas by the time you were born."

"Does he know about me?" asked Nûd.

"No," said Fercha. "I left court for Melyncárreg as soon as I knew I was pregnant. I returned four years later, without you."

"You never told him about me?"

"I did it to protect you. Verro might have pulled you into intrigues in Tamloch."

"Just like you kept me in Melyncárreg to keep me out of intrigues in Dâron. I had to live in exile—for my own protection."

"Yes," said Fercha. "I'm sorry."

"Why is Dârio the rightful heir to *Tamloch?*"

"Verro and I weren't the only ones forming interkingdom relationships..." said Fercha.

"You mean Túathal seduced Princess Gwýnnett?"

"It was more of a connection of mutual convenience," said Fercha. "Gwýnnett had been trying to give Dâri an heir for years, without success. Her motivation was obvious. Túathal was playing a much longer game."

"That's playing out now?" asked Nûd. "Dârio is king of Dâron, so let me guess. Túathal will *lose* to him so Dârio can be king of Dâron *and* Tamloch—and then be the power behind both thrones."

"I always knew you were intelligent," said Fercha.

"Maybe so," said Nûd. "It remains to be seen if I'm wise."

Nûd stopped pacing and returned to sit across from Fercha again. He refilled his own mug and drank it down.

"Why didn't you tell the others about all this?" asked Nûd.

"I don't *want* them to know about Verro," she said. "Or the fact that we still meet from time to time."

Nûd leaned back and stared at Fercha.

"Are you a traitor, Mother?"

"We never discuss matters of state," she said. "And he *is* my husband."

Nûd shook his head. "It's not right. I can't handle this."

"Now you know why I've kept it from you for so many years."

"And I had to press you for it."

"That's on you," said Fercha. "Would it really be so bad to have the kingdoms united?"

"It would be if Túathal—and Gwýnnett, I assume—are controlling Dârio."

"True," said Fercha. She sighed again. "Are you going to tell Damon?"

"That depends," said Nûd. "Did you teach Verro the wide gate spell?"

"Of course not," said Fercha. "He must have figured it out on his own. Verro's very smart. You two have that in common."

"That's cold comfort—*Mother*," said Nûd. "And it's convenient you waited to share all this until *after* Damon and Dârio departed."

Fercha smiled at Nûd. "That wasn't my plan."

"Do you have any idea what Verro's *surprise* might be?"

"I don't," said Fercha, "but he was flying from the southwest when I found him scouting the quarry near the Coombe."

"The southern Clan Lands are southwest of the Coombe."

"Yes," said Fercha. "They are."

"You'll take me to Damon and Dârio and the royal army in the morning?"

"I will."

"Good night, Mother."

"Good night, Nûd."

Chee, in the rafters above, began to snore.

Chapter 40

Eynon and Merry

"Llachar!" said Merry when she'd helped Eynon into their room. The light was bright and she softened its harsh glow until the room had the illumination of a pair of oil lamps.

"I didn't get much sleep last night," said Eynon. He yawned again.

"I'll assume that's because you're tired, not because I bore you," said Merry with a mischievous smile.

Eynon kissed her on the tip of her nose.

"You must not be *that* tired," she said.

"You inspire me, dear lady."

"Let me continue to do so by helping you out of your clothes," said Merry.

When she got to the point where she removed his shirt, she stopped and stared.

"You really do have a *red* magestone," said Merry. "It's beautiful! May I see it up close?"

"I'll show you mine, if you show me yours," teased Eynon. He leaned forward so his red magestone dangled close to Merry's eye level. She stared at it, wide-eyed.

"It's so *big!*"

"Oh," said Eynon. "You mean my red magestone?"

Merry brought both hands around to tickle Eynon's ribs with her fingers until he could capture the offending digits and bring them up to his lips to be kissed. She let out a low moan and freed her fingers, pulling Eynon's head down so she could kiss him. The results were more than satisfactory and their faces were bathed in pulsing red and blue glows from three magestones.

"I seem to be ahead of you," said Eynon after they broke their kiss. "Let me help you catch up."

He removed Merry's jacket and shirt. Her new magestone and setting rested between her small, firm breasts.

"My eyes are up here," said Merry.

"I was looking at your setting," said Eynon.

"Sure you were," said Merry, squeezing his hand.

"What's it made from?" he asked. "Electrum?"

"Exactly," said Merry. "An alloy of gold and silver. Maybe you *are* looking at my setting."

"They're very beautiful," said Eynon.

"My magestone and setting?"

"Those, too," Eynon teased.

Merry's voice grew serious. "We have a problem," she said.

"We do?" asked Eynon.

"Yes," said Merry, her eyes changing to look as merry as her name. "We're both wearing too many clothes!"

* * * * *

"Mmmm..." said Merry, cuddled naked against Eynon's body under a thick quilt. "That was lovely. Do you think you can sleep now?"

"There was never any question of me being able to sleep, dear lady," said Eynon. "It's just that now I'll fall asleep with a smile on my face."

"Me too," said Merry. "Not only am I in your arms, but today I learned my brother is still alive."

"Tell me about him," said Eynon. "Tell me all about your day, for that matter."

Merry leaned up on one elbow and told Eynon about her travels to Riyas with Damon and their stop in Melyncárreg.

"That *was* you I saw in the window," said Eynon. "You waved to me."

"No I didn't," said Merry. "If I'd seen you, I would have tried to find you."

"It doesn't matter," said Eynon. "We're together now."

"Yes we are," said Merry. She kissed two of her fingers and transferred the kiss to Eynon's lips.

"Knowing your brother Salder is alive helps me understand why Derry didn't object to you learning wizardry."

"What do you mean?" asked Merry.

"As far as you knew, you were his sole heir," said Eynon. "I know you said nobody cares about wizards inheriting noble titles out in the borderlands, but that never made sense to me. Wizards can't rule."

"You're probably right," said Merry. "I was so interested in learning from Doethan I convinced myself it wasn't a problem."

"You don't mind not inheriting Applegarth and your father's lands?"

"No," said Merry. "Especially not if my brother is still alive and can return once he's finished his work in Riyas. Learning wizardry is far more rewarding."

"Good," said Eynon. "I wanted to make sure you were comfortable with not succeeding your father."

"I think my father understood me better than I knew myself," said Merry. "He saw how I was fascinated by Doethan's magic whenever we stopped at his tower on the way to Tyford."

"Your father is a wise man," said Eynon. "I wonder..." His voice trailed off and his hands moved, sliding along her body under the quilt.

"What do you wonder?" asked Merry, beginning to react to his touch.

"What it would be like to have wizards for parents?"

"That *is* an interesting question," said Merry, "and one I'm glad we won't have to face first hand until we both remove our fertility-control charms."

"I didn't mean *that*," said Eynon.

Merry moved her body closer to Eynon's as his hand reached the center of her back and pressed before shifting down her spine in small, circular motions.

"What *did* you mean?" asked Merry.

"I was thinking about Nûd," said Eynon.

"Nûd?" teased Merry. Her own hands reached out for Eynon. "Not me?"

"In addition to you, dear lady. Nûd's mother is a wizard."

"Right," said Merry. "He doesn't get along well with Fercha."

"And vice versa, from what I can tell," said Eynon. "But I was remembering something Nûd said in the common room."

"About you single-handedly intimidating the Bifurlanders into calling off their attack on Brendinas?"

"No," said Eynon, "about us coming up with a few surprises of our own."

"Like what?" asked Merry. Eynon's hands were rubbing her lower back and she was breathing faster.

"Like going back to Melyncárreg to set one up."

"Hmmmm?" asked Merry.

Eynon whispered in her ear.

"Really?" she said. "Do you think it could work?"

"I do," said Eynon. "We'd need help from Fercha and Doethan and Nûd, too, for that matter. Plus a few more wizards."

"Doethan can ask Inthíra," said Merry. "And maybe Astrí could assist."

"Astrí?"

"The old queen's private wizard. Wears blue robes so dark they're almost black."

"Sure," said Eynon. "We can leave that part up to Doethan. Shall we go down and tell them?"

"In a few minutes," said Merry.

She pushed Eynon on his back and straddled his hips. Merry's palms were on his shoulders and the weight of her upper body held them in place. The two of them sank deeper into the featherbed.

"You're not going anywhere right now," she said, smiling down at Eynon. "I've got *plans* for you."

Chapter 41

Laetícia and Quintillius

Laetícia stared into the hoop that had been a ring on her finger moments ago. The sun was two fingers above the western horizon, the time she'd scheduled to contact her husband.

"I've got an update for you, dear," she said.

"Is it anything serious, my love?" asked Quintillius from his tent with the legions and the contingent of Roma wizards on the eastern shore of the Brenavon.

"Just the small matter of barbarians from the northern Clan Lands raiding down the Abbenoth valley," said Laetícia. The purple beads in her dark braided hair clicked as she turned her head to accept a message from a servant. "And every ship in Tamloch is sailing down the coast toward Nova Eboracum."

"I see," said Quintillius. "That sounds like quite an inconvenience. Do you need me to return?"

"Not immediately," said Laetícia. "How much longer do you expect to be in the south?"

"My scouts inform me that we're likely to have a decisive battle in the morning. I'll return as soon as we win."

"I love your confidence, darling," said Laetícia. "Come home to me safely."

"With my shield or on it," said Quintillius.

"See that it's *with* your shield, dear. State funerals are expensive and depressing."

"I love you, too, sweetheart. Try to hold the barbarians north of the Long Lake."

"I'm more worried about the fleet from Tamloch than the barbarians," said Laetícia. "Especially if *our* ships are transporting troops up the river."

"I have some ideas about how to supplement our navy," said Quintillius. "I'll keep you informed."

"See that you do, dear," said Laetícia. "The right information is worth a legion."

"Or two," said Quintillius. "How are the children?"

"Terrorizing their nurses, as usual," said Laetícia. "Primus did ask me when you'd be emperor this morning, though."

"I hope you cautioned him about that sort of talk when others could hear him."

"I did," said Laetícia. "He's only seven, but I think he understands. He told me he wants to command your Praetorians."

"I'll encourage him to aim higher," said Quintillius. "A consulship, at least."

"At least," Laetícia repeated affectionately. "I'll ring you with a status report in the morning."

"Thank you, my love. And see what your sources can learn about a bright light in the sky a few hours ago. It looked like one of Mafuta's fireballs, but ten times as large and a hundred times as bright."

"Curious," said Laetícia. "I'll look into it."

"Sálve," said Quintillius.

"And you, my love," said Laetícia. "Be well."

She ended their connection and collapsed her hoop down to a ring, slipping it on her finger.

Back with the legions in the south, Quintillius summoned a servant—a girl of nine or ten in a loose purple chiton and sandals laced up to her knees.

"How may I serve you, Governor-General?" she asked.

"Please find Mafuta and Felix and ask them to come to my tent at their earliest convenience."

"Yes, Uncle," said the girl. She opened the tent flap and ran off in search of the two wizards.

Quintillius didn't have the heart to stop her and insist that his sister's youngest daughter follow proper military protocol. He'd have a quiet talk with her once they were back in Nova Eboracum.

A few minutes later the wizards entered. Quintillius offered them high stools and took a low stool for himself so their eyes would be close to the same height. He chuckled to himself when he realized that Felix had gone through a growth spurt and was nearly as tall has he was.

"Do you think you could get a private message from me to King Bjarni and Queen Signý?" asked the provincial governor.

"I don't see why not," said Mafuta. "Flying scouts have located the Bifurland fleet. They're less than a dozen miles away."

"How do you proposed to deliver the message?" asked Quintillius.

"Like this," said Felix. The tall, thin young mage in flowing purple robes rotated his hands in front of him like a potter working clay on a wheel. A construct of solidified sound began to form and soon a simulacrum of a golden dragon with outstretched wings hovered before him.

Quintillius smiled and Mafuta extended her right arm and gave her colleague a thumbs up.

"Do you have the message?" asked Felix.

"I will in a moment," said Quintillius. He found a pen and parchment and dashed off three quick lines, then folded the parchment. "Mafuta?" he asked.

The older wizard picked up a stick of sealing wax from the governor-general's camp desk and channeled heat from her purple magestone into its substance until a blob of wax sealed the message. Quintillius pressed his ring of office into the hot wax, then waved the parchment back and forth to help it cool. When the wax solidified, he handed the message to Felix.

"Can you spare a ring-pair?" Quintillius asked Mafuta. "That would speed up our negotiations."

"I have a pair in my tent," said Mafuta. "I'll give one ring to Felix and deliver one to you."

"Excellent," said Quintillius. "How long will it take you to get to the Bifurland flagship?"

"Less than an hour," said the tall young wizard.

"Before nightfall, then?"

"Well before," said Felix.

"Off with you then," said Quintillius. "Safe flying."

Mafuta and Felix stood and gave small bows.

"Governor-General," they said in unison, then took their leave.

Quintillius leaned over a map spread out on a table beside his camp desk. In the morning, his legions would march south along the course of the Brenavon until they were opposite a large island in the middle of the river. They would wait there until they got word from Fercha and Doethan and would do what they could to avoid engaging the Bifurlanders. Part of Quintillius was curious how his legionnaires would fare against the northerners. Roma's legions had the discipline to take on any foe, and the Bifurlanders were only one step removed from the chaotic fighting styles of the northern and southern Clan Land barbarians.

With Fortune's favor, thought Quintillius, *it won't come to that.*

"May I enter?" asked Mafuta from the entrance to the Governor-General's tent. Her right hand was closed.

"Come in please, Mafuta," said Quintillius. "Is Felix on his way?"

"He is, Quin. You can count on him to deliver your message," said Mafuta. "Here's your ring," she said, extending her closed fist.

Quintillius opened his palm and Mafuta dropped a small gold band into it. The governor-general slid the ring on his little finger.

"Now we wait," said Quintillius.

"Now we wait," said Mafuta. "Care for a game of *shah-mat* to pass the time?"

"Set up the board," said Quintillius. "And don't expect me to go easy on you."

"Hah," said Mafuta. "I've won our last four contests."

"Don't remind me," said Quintillius. "Let's just hope I win the one that counts."

"Oh?" asked Mafuta. "What did you write in your message?"

Quintillius told her.

Mafuta held her sides and laughed loud enough for a guard to stick her head inside the tent and be dismissed.

"Quin, Quin, Quin," said Mafuta between bouts of laughter. "You are in *so* much trouble. If you don't win, Laetícia will kill you."

Chapter 42

Damon and Dârio

Damon and Dârio were flying north toward the Dâron army's camp. The young king had his arms around the old wizard's waist and was reveling in the view of the countryside below from Damon's flying disk.

The counties south of Brendinas along the river were largely agricultural, filled with large estates and dotted with small towns and freeholders' farms. In the waning light, Dârio could see plowed fields with their dark soil beginning to turn green as early shoots emerged from the ground. Castles occupied several natural and human-or-wizard-made high points in the area's topography.

The royal army was encamped west of the main road leading from Brendinas to the southern reaches of the kingdom. Troops organized by feudal units had set up tents on a field belonging to the Earl of Claddarch. A well lined with blue-veined granite in the center of the encampment provided fresh water. *The stones were probably dug from the quarry near the Dormant Dragon,* Dârio supposed.

Damon descended toward a collection of marquees and pavilions decorated with pennants and heraldic banners. Even at sunset, Dârio could read them as easily as he could a book. He knew at a glance which of his nobles were at the army's headquarters. Duke Háiddon's banner, a dark-blue rose on a white field, was particularly prominent. A horizontal blue sword was painted above the rose. It marked the duke as the kingdom's earl marshal and commander of the royal army.

Dârio heard shouts from men and women-at-arms as they landed. "The king! The king! Dârio is here!"

He could sense a buzz of reports radiate out across the camp.

Rumors travel faster than wizards, thought Dârio.

He smiled when he realized he was riding behind the infamous author of that epigram.

Duke Háiddon stepped out of a large, rectangular marquee flying dark and light-blue pennants to greet the young king and master mage. The duke was in his early forties, the same age Dârio's late father would have been. He was of average height but had long auburn hair that made him look like an older, but still powerful lion. His physique reflected four decades of intense martial training and he wore a coat of blued mail over a white padded gambeson.

"Your Majesty," said the duke, extending his hand.

Dârio shook it, and introduced Damon. The duke bowed to Damon and shook his hand as well.

"We've met, Master Mage," said Duke Háiddon. "I was with Crown Prince Dâroth when you froze the Abbenoth. I'm glad you've returned to help Dâron in our present generation's hour of need."

"Yes, yes," said Damon. "Glad to assist and all that. Let's go inside." The old wizard paused and stared at the duke for a moment. "Has anyone ever told you that you resemble your father?"

Duke Háiddon laughed and so did Dârio.

"What?" asked Damon.

"There's a famous fresco of the duke's father on the wall of the great hall in his castle," said the young king. "He's been hearing that comparison for decades."

"Is there?" asked Damon. "I wasn't going by a fresco, I knew his father personally, and remember him when he was a young man not much older than you are now, Dârio. I hope Háiddon has inherited more than his looks from his father."

"My esteemed sire taught me many things," said the duke. "I hope I'll live up to his memory."

"You'd better," said Damon. "Or things won't go well in the morning."

The three men, each representing a different generation, walked toward the entrance to the headquarters tent.

"Do you think I could get a mug of cider?" asked Damon. "I've got a lot of news to share and talking is thirsty work."

"There's a standing order for a cask of Applegarth cider in the headquarters tent," said Dârio.

"In that case, make it two mugs," said Damon.

They stepped inside as guards were lighting torches on either side of the tent's entrance.

* * * * *

Damon was on his second mug of cider while the king and duke were still sipping their first. The master mage had established a sphere of solidified sound to prevent them from being overhead and had just finished updating the earl marshal, with assistance from Dârio. They were standing next to a sand table where their current location and the land on both sides of the river for five miles had been sketched. Small blue-painted rectangular wooden blocks marked as infantry, calvalry and archers, representing the forces of Dâron's royal army, were already in place on the expected site of the upcoming battle.

"See if I understand our tactical position correctly," said Duke Háiddon. "We're here." He pointed to the royal army's location. Damon and Dârio nodded.

"There are five hundred ships filled with bloodthirsty Bifurland warriors who may or may not decide to attack us *here*." The duke indicated several yellow blocks positioned in the "river."

Damon shrugged and opened his palms to confirm. Dârio shook his head slowly from side to side.

"The main strength of Tamloch's army is just north of us," the duke continued, placing green rectangles exceeding the number for Dâron's army immediately across a broad open stretch of sand. Dârio rolled his hands in a *yes, yes, get on with it* gesture.

Duke Háiddon reached out a finger to touch a collection of purple rectangles to the east.

"And our only allies are on the far side of the river, with the nearest bridge more than twenty miles upstream at the capital."

"That sums it up nicely," said Dârio.

"Except for the part about Verro having an extra surprise to spring on us," noted Damon. "We're not sure what *that* is."

"Oh joy," said Háiddon. His face looked anything but joyful as he finished his mug of cider. He frowned when he realized he couldn't get a refill until Damon dispelled the privacy sphere. The old wizard tipped an inch of Applegarth cider from his second mug into the duke's.

"What's your assessment of the situation?" asked Dârio.

"It doesn't look good," said the duke. "The royal armies of the two kingdoms are evenly matched. We've been trained to fight each other, and our wizards know the attacks and counters of their opposite numbers in Tamloch. The odds are good we'd end up with a stalemate, but we have to defeat them decisively, because they're between us and Brendinas."

"And city walls don't count for much against wizards," said Dârio. "Not that anything in Brendinas besides Dâron Castle is equipped to stand a siege."

"Correct," said Háiddon. "And the Bifurland fleet is still a wild card, plus that surprise you mentioned, which I expect won't be good for *us.*"

"A wise assumption," said Damon.

"So why aren't the two of you looking more worried?"

"Remember what Damon did a generation ago to help Dâron's army?" asked Dârio.

"He froze the Abbenoth..." said the duke. "Oh. And the Brenavon isn't as wide as Abbenoth. The legions will be able to support us and flank Tamloch's army. This could be entertaining."

"That's not *my* preferred choice of words," said Damon.

"Sorry," said Háiddon. "I meant it ironically."

"I know," said Damon. "I'm anxious about Verro and his surprise, but I have a surprise of my own to spring on *him.*"

"Eynon?" asked Dârio.

"Precisely," said Damon. "That young man has more raw power than any other wizard I've trained."

"He's got a *red* magestone," said Dârio. "He exploded a fireball above the Bifurland fleet that convinced them they didn't want to sack Brendinas."

"That was a wizard's fireball?" asked Háiddon. "We saw it from here. I thought it was a comet!"

"No, it *was* a fireball," said Damon. "My apprentice made it."

"I'm impressed," said Háiddon, "And I'm glad this Eynon lad is on our side. We'll take all the help we can get, and we'll probably need it. A *red* magestone, you say?"

"Like a ruby the size of a hen's egg," said Damon.

"Have you told Eynon that he's going to be a surprise for Tamloch?" asked Dârio.

"No," said Damon. "He's innocent and enthusiastic. I don't want him to worry—or get a swelled head."

"That makes sense," said Dârio. "You can tell him when he and Merry get here in the morning."

"Merry?" asked the duke.

"She's the daughter of..." began Damon.

"Salderwen, one of comrades in arms at the gates of Nova Eboracum," said Háiddon. "Now I remember. He's baron of the Upper Rhuthro now."

"He goes by Derry these days," said Damon. "His daughter is only fifteen, but shouldn't be underestimated."

"She sounds like her father," said Háiddon.

The duke stretched and covered his mouth to hide a yawn.

"It's probably best if we call it a night," said Háiddon. "I'll update the commanders, so they'll know what to do in the morning."

"Don't tell them what Damon is planning," said Dârio.

"I won't," said Háiddon, "but I will make sure they know Master Mage Ealdamon is here to help us to victory."

"That will do a lot to boost morale," said Dârio.

"They'll also be glad to hear *you're* with the army," said the duke. "Your armor and weapons and several changes of clothes are in your tent, Your Majesty. The Master of Stables has your warhorse groomed and ready."

Dârio looked carefully at the duke. His tone had been teasing and his eyes were dancing. Háiddon had a surprise planned for his king and Dârio hoped he'd enjoy it.

"Where's Inthíra?" asked Damon. "I need to give her an update, so she can inform the rest of the Conclave in the morning."

"Cancel the privacy sphere and I'll have servants escort you and His Majesty where you want to go," said Háiddon.

Damon gestured to dispel the sphere, then he yawned. Háiddon called for two attendants.

"Don't stay up late," said Háiddon. "You've got a lot to do tomorrow."

"I do indeed," said Damon. He sighed and followed a servant out of the brightly lit tent.

The second servant led Dârio in a different direction, to a large oval tent with dark and light-blue dagged trim. A dozen torches in front of it illuminated the royal standard, a light-blue banner bearing a dark-blue dragon with its right front foot raised, below a gold crown. Dârio sighed. He was tired, and the battle in the morning might decide the fate of the kingdom. He pushed open the tent flap and entered. The lighting was soft and low, just a few oil lamps, but it was enough for him to make out the location of the bed. Dârio stumbled toward it. Then he realized it was already occupied.

"I'm glad you finally made it, *Your Majesty,*" said Jenet with a smile. "I've been waiting for you."

Her uncovered shoulders peeked out above a heavy quilt.

"How did *you* get here?" asked Dârio.

"On the back of a flying disk with a wizard who'd showed up late for the meeting of the Conclave," she said. "I thought it would be a good idea if I wasn't where Princess Gwýnnett could question me further."

"That makes sense," said Dârio. "You're as wise as you are beautiful."

"Thank you," said Jenet. "It's checkmate in three moves."

"I know," said Dârio. "I concede. You win." He tipped an imaginary chess piece.

"You might be able to win at *something* tonight." said Jenet.

"Oh? Do tell."

"Of course, *my king.* My father suggested I might divert your attention with another sort of game to help you relax and sleep well before battle."

"Of course he did," said Dârio. "That sounds *exactly* like something your father, the kingdom earl marshal, would tell you."

Dârio leaned down and kissed her gently.

"I may be putting words in his mouth," said Jenet.

She sat up, smiled at Dârio, and let the quilt slide down a few more inches.

"It was mostly *my* idea."

Chapter 43

Túathal and Gwýnnett

A single dim lamp burned inside the royal tent. Uirsé, a wizard Verro had assigned to the king, created a privacy sphere and took her leave. The dark-haired young woman had no interest in being anywhere near the king when her services weren't required.

"You seem to have lost something," said King Túathal to the image of Princess Gwýnnett inside the hoop of an expanded communications ring. "I thought you told me you had Dârio under control."

"I do," said Gwýnnett. "I've just misplaced him temporarily."

"Misplaced your son and the ruler of Dâron?" asked Túathal. "That's sloppy—and careless."

"I thought he was occupied playing *shah-mat* and bedding would-be queen candidates," said Gwýnnett, "but he's gone and I can't find him, *or* his favorite bedmate."

"I can reassure you he's safe," said King Túathal. "I've just received reports he's with Dâron's royal army encamped on the west bank of the Brenavon. I can't say about the bedmate."

"I don't care about his bedmate," said Gwýnnett. Her eyes flashed, and her voice grew hard. "I care about Dârio's defiance."

Túathal shook his head. "I thought you had your son under your thumb."

"*Our* son," spat out Gwýnnett. "When I get to him he'll be much more compliant—at least after his next meal."

"Nothing to harm his mind permanently," said Túathal. "He is, as you say, *my* son. Someday it will be his turn to rule Tamloch and Dâron. We can't live forever."

"I promise I won't damage him," said Gwýnnett. "I'll just make him more amenable to my suggestions."

"Be careful," said Túathal. "I think I know the drugs you plan to use. They have side-effects."

"Like making eighteen-year-old men even more interested in horizontal entertainments than they are under normal circumstances?"

One corner of Túathal's mouth turned up. Gwýnnett frowned.

"I thought Dârio was eating the special meals I'd prepared for him," she said. "Reports from his servants indicated the side-effects were clearly present."

"Or perhaps he was behaving like a normal eighteen-year-old man and you took his willingness to do what you asked as a sign of his suggestibility?"

Túathal began to laugh, then closed his mouth. "Dârio is devious, then," he said. "What else should we expect from *my* son—and yours, for that matter?"

"True," said Gwýnnett. She squared her shoulders. "I'll take a courier boat downriver immediately. I should be there to see to Dârio's breakfast before dawn. Tell your observers along the river to let me pass."

"I don't think that's a good idea," said Túathal.

"Going downriver?"

"No," said Túathal. "Joining Dârio. The royal army of Dâron's encampment may be overrun during the battle and I wouldn't want you to get hurt."

"Oh," said Princess Gwýnnett. Her eyebrows rose. "I didn't know you cared."

"I don't," said Túathal, "at least not in *that* way, as you well know. Don't flatter yourself."

Gwýnnett frowned again. For a moment, she allowed her mask to slip and her eyes to show her internal fury. Then her mask returned.

"What do *you* think I should do, then?" she asked.

"Follow your original plan and head south on the river," said King Túathal, "but allow my soldiers to intercept your courier boat and take you hostage. We can use that status as a bargaining chip with Dârio to make it easier to explain Dâron's surrender and my proposed solution, joining our kingdoms."

Gwýnnett nodded. "That might work." She shrugged. "Unless the boy decides he's glad to be rid of me and thanks you for removing me from his life."

"I don't see that happening," said Túathal. "For all that he's our son, Dârio is soft-hearted and an idealist. He won't want you to be executed."

"Executed?" asked Gwýnnett.

"A threat must be credible to be a threat," said Túathal

"Not exiled to a tower on the Isle of Vines?" asked Gwýnnett.

"I might start with that as a threat, then escalate as necessary," said Túathal. "We'll see how soft-hearted the lad truly is."

"I blame his great-grandmother," said Gwýnnett. "She filled his head with stories..."

"And encouraged him to read," said Túathal. "I know. My resources in the palace in Brendinas send me regular reports."

Gwýnnett nodded in acknowledgment. Of *course* Túathal had spies. *Everyone* had spies.

"Too much reading isn't good for a king," said Túathal. "It can give them ideas."

Gwýnnett laughed and her face contorted into what might have been a grin on someone less self-centered.

"Present company excepted, of course," she said.

"Of course," said Túathal. "Queen Carys is another crowned head who's done too much reading."

"That was never a problem for Prince Dâri," said Gwýnnett.

"Hah!" said Túathal. "Your late husband had *no* interest in reading. He only cared about three things—fighting, hunting, and drinking."

"There was a fourth thing," said Gwýnnett.

"Oh, really?" asked Túathal.

"At least until I started drugging his drinks when he couldn't give me an heir after two years of trying."

"I see," said Túathal, nodding. "We really *are* a well-matched couple."

Túathal smiled to himself. He'd never tell Gwýnnett that the ring of friendship he'd given Dâri at the feast in honor of their mutual victory before the gates of Nova Eboracum was actually a fertility prevention charm.

"Except for the fact that you prefer men."

"Except for that," said Túathal.

"So kind of you to make an exception for me," said Gwýnnett.

Túathal gave Gwýnnett a slight bow. Gwýnnett grimaced.

"What?" said Túathal. "Was my *exceptional* performance a problem?"

"Don't flatter yourself, either," said Gwýnnett. "Your performance was adequate—and Dârio was the result, so I'm more than satisfied."

"As am I," said Túathal.

"I've just been thinking about how long Queen Carys has been a thorn in my side. When will the old woman get on with it and *die*? I'll never be *queen* so long as she lives."

"You'll be *my* queen," said Túathal. "That's our mutual arrangement. Soon *you* will be the Old Queen of our united kingdoms."

"I could do without the adjective," said Gwýnnett.

"Too late for that, my dear," said Túathal. "You should have poisoned the Old King, instead of your husband."

"But I didn't poison Dâri," protested Gwýnnett. "A blood clot moved from his knee to his lungs."

"Of course it did," said Túathal. The true manner of Dâri's death was something else he'd never tell Gwýnnett. He hadn't even told Verro.

Gwýnnett's face clouded. She knew she was being mocked. Túathal distracted her with a new question.

"What do you know about the Old Queen's personal wizard? My sources haven't been able to learn much about her."

"Astrí?" asked Gwýnnett. "She's another pain in my..."

"Astrí," said Túathal, considering the name. "Is she skilled?"

"She knows how to detect adulterated food and drink, at any rate," said Gwýnnett.

"You haven't been able to poison or control Queen Carys because of her and resent it."

"That's one way of putting it," said Gwýnnett. "My spies haven't learned anything more about her than yours have, I expect. She just appeared more than two decades ago like she'd stepped out of the mist."

"I don't like surprises," said Túathal. "And I don't like *not* knowing who she is or why Queen Carys trusts her."

"A sentiment we share," said Gwýnnett.

"I'll just have to be content with the surprises Verro has planned for the royal army of Dâron in the morning," said Túathal.

Gwýnnett nodded. "And I'd best get started downriver," she said. "Tell your observers I'll have blue lamps set fore and aft on my courier boat."

"I'll pass the word," said Túathal. "It shouldn't take you more than four hours to get here. That will be well before dawn."

"Perhaps I can make *you* breakfast in the morning?" said Gwýnnett.

"I think not," said Túathal, ending the connection.

Chapter 44

Quintillius

"King Bjarni agrees, Governor-General," said Felix. "But he has stipulations of his own."

"Such as?" asked Quintillius. He was pacing back and forth along the map table in his command tent. Mafuta stood beside Felix as the younger wizard shared his report. Her glowing light spell made the tent much brighter than the lamps on the table.

"The contest must be held on his flagship."

"I can live with that," said Quintillius.

"And you can bring no more than five guards and three wizards."

"Tell him I'll only need *two* wizards." Quin nodded at Felix and Mafuta.

Mafuta inclined her head, confirming she'd come along to visit the Bifurlanders. She knew she'd have her own part to play if, no *when,* Quintillius won.

The Governor-General consulted his guard captain.

"I need five guards to travel with me to the Bifurlander fleet," said Quintillius. "Get me two of your tallest, plus two warriors from the Little People and Deena, in full kit."

"Tonight?" asked the guard captain.

"Immediately," said the governor-general. "The fate of the province may depend on it. Get moving!"

"Yes, Governor-General!"

The guard captain sprinted out of the command tent to find Deena and the others Quintillius had requested. Quintillius turned is attention back to Felix.

Mafuta laughed. "You're bringing the small warriors to signal your disdain?" she asked.

"Not at all," said Quintillius. "I want to shatter their expectations that everyone in Occidens Province is tall and carries *gladius, pilum* and *scutum.*"

"That explains the small warriors," said Mafuta. "What about Deena?"

"She's in love with the legends of the women warriors in the old Athican stories," said Quintillius. "Her kit is impressive, and so is her physique. Bifurlander women like a good fight every bit as much as their men. I want them to see Deena, so they'll know we Roma feel the same way."

"And it's hard to tell women from men in the legions because everyone is in armor," contributed Felix. "Deena stands out."

"She certainly does," said Mafuta, remembering Deena's exaggerated, anatomically-correct bronze breastplate.

"What form of competition did King Bjarni select?" he asked. "*Shah-mat?* Archery? Single combat with sword and shield?"

"No, Governor-General," said Felix. "None of those."

"What then?"

"Tell him," said Mafuta. "It's not wise to annoy a provincial governor."

"Very well," said Felix.

He took a deep breath and struggled to replace his grin with a stoic expression worthy of Marcus Aurelius. When he succeeded, he spoke.

"King Bjarni wants to arm-wrestle, Governor-General."

Quintillius began to laugh. So did Mafuta. Soon Felix joined in. The three of them laughed for more than a minute before the chortles faded to guffaws and then to near-silent chuckles.

"He wants to *arm-wrestle* me to determine whether or not he and his fleet will help me defend Occidens Province?"

"I believe so," said Felix. "He's reputed to be quite good at it."

"Arm-wrestling is more a game for soldiers working off their aggression than for rulers settling the merits of their proposals," said Quintillius. He stretched his shoulders and flexed his biceps without realizing he was doing so.

Mafuta smiled. "King Bjarni thinks to put you at a disadvantage, Quin." She raised an eyebrow, appraising him. "The Bifurlanders' monarch may be underestimating you."

"What makes you think that, 'Futa?" asked Quintillius.

Mafuta didn't answer him and questioned Felix instead.

"Were you able to see King Bjarni when you delivered your message?" she asked.

"Yes," said Felix. "I constructed far-seeing lenses, even though I kept my distance when my solidified-sound golden dragon landed before the king and queen's thrones."

"Excellent," said Mafuta. "What did he look like?"

"The king?" asked Felix. "He was solid, an old warrior. With massive arms—probably from axe-work. He wore lots of gold rings from elbow to shoulder on both sides."

"Old?" asked Quintillius.

"Close to forty, I think," said Felix.

Mafuta and Quintillius flashed each other quick smiles. Mafuta's student was not yet twenty and everyone over thirty must seem old to him.

"He must be positively ancient," said Mafuta. "Perhaps he won't be strong enough to defeat Quin."

"King Bjarni seemed strong to me," said Felix. "His arms were larger than my thighs."

"That's not saying much," Mafuta teased. Felix was quite skinny and self-conscious about it. He shrugged.

"True enough," said Felix. "But I had the sense he could snap me in half like a twig if he'd wanted to."

"So King Bjarni is strong—*for an old man*," said Mafuta, "but that's not the most important question."

"Which is?" asked Quintillius.

"Is he tall?" responded the older wizard.

"Oh," said Felix. "Maybe."

The others regarded him, waiting for more.

"He's not as tall as I am. Probably close to six feet, if I remember correctly."

"And you're what, six and a half?" asked Quintillius, narrowing his eyes and taking the young wizard's measure.

"Six-foot-six and a quarter," said Felix with a grin.

"But who's counting," said Mafuta. "You may even have a bit more growing to do."

"I'd like that," said Felix.

"Why does it matter how *tall* King Bjarni is?" asked Quintillius. "Especially if his upper arms are massive."

"Because of *you,* Quin," said Mafuta. "You're *very* tall."

"You must be over seven feet," said Felix.

"Seven-foot-one," said Quintillius. "How is that relevant?"

"Arm-length correlates to height," said Mafuta. "Your forearms will be quite a bit longer than King Bjarni's."

"So?" asked Quin.

"That may give you the advantage," said Mafuta. "And you're strong, *at least for an old man*."

Quin wagged a finger at Mafuta and she grinned at him. They'd been through enough campaigns together for this sort of banter to be commonplace.

"All right," said Quintillius. "I'm strong, but King Bjarni's probably stronger. How does having longer forearms give me an advantage?"

"Simple, Imperial Governor-General, sir," said Mafuta. "Leverage."

Chapter 45

Eynon's Idea

Eynon tapped tentatively on the door to the room just beyond his. He'd heard Doethan's footsteps outside his own earlier, and then the squeak of the neighboring door.

"Doethan?" he asked softly. "Are you awake?"

"That's not how it's done," said Merry, easing him to one side. She pounded on the door with the bottom of her fist. "Doethan! Wake up! There's a hungry dragon at the gate!"

"What?" came Doethan's groggy voice through the thick wood. "A dragon? Where?"

"Get *up*!" said Merry. "Eynon has an idea."

Doethan cracked the door and peered out. "From what I hear, Eynon *always* has ideas," he complained.

"Right," said Merry. "But this is a particularly good one, and we need your help. Get dressed and meet us in the common room."

"Fine," said Doethan, sounding both more perturbed and less asleep. "I'll be down in ten minutes."

"Make it five," said Merry.

"Hrrumph," said Doethan. He closed the door.

"Let's see if Nûd and Fercha are still downstairs," said Merry.

"That wasn't very nice," said Eynon.

"We don't have time to waste being *nice*," said Merry.

"My mother says there's always time to be nice," replied Eynon.

"Your mother never had to fight a battle to save the kingdom," said Merry. She took Eynon's hand and dragged him toward the stairs. "Come on!"

Eynon stood fast and Merry jerked back when she realized he wasn't moving.

"What?" she asked.

"You don't have to be obnoxious to get things done. Is that how your father leads his barony?"

"Uh, no," said Merry. "He convinces people to do what's necessary. He doesn't yell at them."

"I thought so," said Eynon. "Leaders in the Coombe know how to be effective and *nice,* too, or we don't let them lead."

"Maybe I should spend some time in the Coombe when all this is over?" mused Merry.

"It wouldn't be a bad idea," said Eynon.

It was dark in the hallway. Eynon invoked a light spell. "Llachar!" He used his free hand to wave the glowing sphere to follow them.

"I think I hear their voices," said Merry.

"Walk softly," said Eynon.

"I *am* walking softly," said Merry in her normal speaking volume. "Oops," she said. They turned the corner into the common room, with Eynon bumping into Merry's back.

"I thought the two of you were otherwise occupied," said Fercha.

Nûd, pacing near Fercha, stopped moving and grinned at Eynon. "This must be *really* important for you to stop what you were doing."

"We were. It is," said Merry. "Doethan's coming down soon. When he's here, Eynon will explain his idea. We'll need your help to pull it off."

"I'd be glad for the distraction," said Nûd.

"What have the two of you been talking about?" asked Eynon.

"This and that," said Fercha.

"Family stuff," said Nûd.

"Fine, don't tell us," said Merry. "Fercha, what do you need to construct a wide gate, like the one you used to get the Roma legions here faster?"

"Two rectangles coated in powdered magestones, one on either side of the gate," said Fercha. "Plus wizards at either end to invoke the congruency and keep it stable."

"Can you get sacks of powdered magestones in Melyncárreg?" asked Merry.

"Damon would know if any are kept on hand," said Nûd.

"Don't worry about it," said Eynon. "I know where to find plenty of tiny magestones we can crush."

"Near the mudpots and the spring of many colors?" asked Nûd.

"Uh huh," said Eynon. "I didn't know what I was seeing when I went there to find *my* magestone, but now that I know how to recognize magestones, I remember seeing blue and green and yellow sparkling grains around several of the hot springs."

"You can gather them up," said Merry. "I expect Doethan and Fercha will know where to find more at the headquarters for the Conclave for this side of the gate."

"Why do you want to construct a new wide gate?" asked Doethan from the foot of the stairs. He'd put on his wizard's robes, but his hair was still tousled, at least what was left of it.

"Eynon will explain everything," said Merry. She waved to Nûd and Doethan. "Sit down. I'll get you some cider."

She moved behind the bar and started filling five mugs.

"Please be ready to enclose us in a privacy sphere when I'm back," said Merry.

"If I must," said Fercha.

Merry saw Eynon give her a stern look from the kitchen.

"I'd really appreciate it, Fercha. Thank you so much," she said.

Eynon smiled. "It would be a good idea to keep this private," he said. "We don't want word getting back to Tamloch. It would ruin the surprise."

"Could you see if the cook has any more of that chicken-and-egg pie left?" asked Doethan. "If I'm going to be awake, I could use a snack."

"I'll see," said Merry.

"I can help," said Eynon. He stepped into the kitchen and searched for a pie safe. He found it and removed half of one of the savory pies and three-quarters of a loaf of dark bread that seemed fresh enough to have been baked that morning.

Chee swung down from the rafters and jumped from the bar to the pass-through to the kitchen. Eynon snagged one of last year's apples from a bowl on the counter and tossed it to the raconette. He promised himself he'd find a way to thank the cook and innkeeper for their hospitality and remembered the small ball of solid gold in his pouch.

It's too much for a few meals and night's lodging, thought Eynon. *Maybe I can collect some gold dust for them if I have time when I'm in Melyncárreg—or bring them some flathorn antlers? They'd look impressive over the fireplace and bring in business. I'll have to ask Nûd if they shed.*

"Eynon, dear, are you coming?" asked Merry. Her tone didn't match her endearment.

"Is there pie?" added Doethan.

"Just a moment," said Eynon. He caught Merry's eye.

"Thanks for your help getting food for us," Merry added, shrugging her shoulders and smiling.

Eynon smiled back. He picked up plates, a sharp knife, and a crock of butter—not from Flying Frog Farms, he realized—and brought everything to the table. Merry had already served the mugs of cider.

"Fercha?" asked Merry.

Seconds later, a privacy sphere surrounded them and things beyond it were difficult to see. Chee had joined the gathering just before the sphere snapped into place. He was eying the chicken-and-egg pie and Eynon wagged the knife in Chee's direction.

"This is *people* food, Chee," said Eynon. "Enjoy your apple."

Chee made a face at Eynon and sprawled in the middle of the table, staring at the pie.

"Who wants pie and who wants bread?" asked Eynon.

"Here," said Merry.

She took the knife and deftly cut the half-pie into five wedges and sliced off the same number of slices of the dark bread.

"Doesn't anyone else have a sense of urgency?" she asked. "Take whatever you'd like, friends. Eynon, tell Nûd and Fercha and Doethan your plan."

Eynon understood Merry's concern and gave her the benefit of the doubt. Sometimes you had to push to get things done, and Merry was doing the pushing. Eynon gave Merry a brief hug, sat up straight, and explained.

"Nûd gave me the idea," said Eynon. "He said we should have some sort of surprise of our own to counter Verro's."

The others nodded.

"I'd love to turn the tables on Verro," said Fercha.

"I'd like to know how I can help," said Doethan.

"I'd like to save soldiers' and wizards' lives," said Nûd. "If we can end this war before anyone gets hurt, I'm all for it."

"Tell them the details, please," said Merry.

Eynon did.

The other wizards' expressions were encouraging. Doethan was stroking his chin.

"I'll handle the gate at this end," he said.

"That would be great," said Eynon. "You should be able to find wizards to help you…"

"…at the royal army's encampment to the north, I know," said Doethan. "After I return to the Conclave's headquarters for powdered magestones."

"Fercha will build the gate in Melyncárreg," said Merry. "I'll help her." She put her arm around Eynon and gave him a hug. "You and Nûd can collect magestones to powder near the hot springs and mud pots, then round up the remaining component of our surprise with Rocky."

"That should work," said Fercha. She faced Nûd a few seats down across from her. "Does the old man keep rope in the castle?"

"There should be plenty," said Nûd. "It's something that's always useful. I remember ordering more in our last shipment of supplies from Brendinas."

"Great," said Merry.

"How do we get Rocky back to Melyncárreg quickly," asked Eynon. "It would take too long to fly to the Blue Spiral tower."

"Don't be ridiculous," said Fercha. Then she stopped herself from insulting Eynon further. "That's right. You don't know. There's a large gate in the rear of the Dormant Dragon. I made it years ago. It connects to the storeroom next to the kitchen. We can use that to get to another inn back in the capital, then take the gate used to transport supplies to Melyncárreg from there. It's just two jumps."

"Let's go," said Merry. "We've only got a few hours and it's harder to work in the dark. Wake up Rocky and bring him to the doors to the supply room," she ordered Eynon. "You help him," she told Nûd.

"I hear and obey," Nûd replied with a smile.

"Right away," said Eynon. "I hope Rocky cooperates."

"I'm sure he will," said Nûd. "He's a good boy."

"I'll go upstairs and collect my things," said Doethan. "Fercha can contact me."

"Eynon may need to contact you, too," said Merry. "Take your ring back, for now, so he can reach you."

"Fine," said Doethan. He took the ring from Merry, then stood up and tilted his head toward Fercha. She canceled the privacy sphere and the older wizard headed toward the stairs.

A few minutes later, Nûd, Fercha, Merry, Eynon, Chee and Rocky—under protest—went through the large gate in the inn's storeroom. Rocky's complaints when he had to tuck in his wings and cross the gate's interface made Doethan smile a floor above.

When Doethan came downstairs, the innkeeper, her wife the cook, and their two children were in the common room.

"Your wyvern's loud," said one of the children.

"Will he be coming back?" asked the other. "I want to ride him."

"He will," said Doethan. "And I'm sure you can get a ride on Rocky's back. It's the least we can do for your hospitality."

"Speaking of that," said the innkeeper. She smiled at Doethan and quoted a sum for the rooms and meals.

"I'll be back with payment for you soon," said Doethan. "First, I have to go to Brendinas to find powdered magestone, then I have to help save the kingdom."

"Powdered magestone?" asked the cook. Her hair looked almost as tousled as Doethan's. "Why would you need to go to Brendinas for powdered magestones when we have a whole quarry full of the stuff just west of here?"

Doethan smacked the heel of his palm against the center of his forehead.

"Blast me for a fool," he said. "If I light our path, can you show me the way?"

"We'd be glad to," said the cook and the innkeeper simultaneously.

"Can I have a piggyback ride?" said one of the children to Doethan.

"No, me," said the other.

"How would you like to ride on a flying disk instead?" asked Doethan.

"Can we, can we, huh, mothers?" asked the children in pleading, high-pitched tones.

"So long as you do everything the wizard says," said the innkeeper.

"And don't go too high," said the cook.

"I'll take good care of them and stay just two feet off the ground," said Doethan. "Let's go!"

Chapter 46

Quintillius and Bjarni

The borrowed boat holding Quintillius, Mafuta, Felix, and the five guards was nearly silent as it moved downriver toward the Bifurlanders' fleet. Felix, who had grown up with boats on the north shore of Insula Longa, the huge fish-shaped island that stretched over a hundred miles from Nova Eboracum to the coast of Tamloch, guided the pull-stone. Behind him were the guard captain, who was nearly as tall as Quintillius, and a second guard of equal height.

Quintillius knew the guard captain would select himself. That was to be expected, as was the other guard the captain had selected. They were both excellent in individual combat as well as the tight formations that had made Roma's legions feared in the lands of the west and across the Ocean.

The two tall guards were inspecting the edges of their swords in the light from the glowing sphere floating above Mafuta, who was seated with the governor-general in the middle of the boat.

"You missed a spot, lad," said the guard captain, pointing out a small scratch in the other guard's blade.

"Yes, sir," said the second guard. He applied his whetstone to the offending scratch until it was gone.

Quintillius smiled at Mafuta and the middle-aged wizard frowned at him. Quintillius was a provincial governor now, not a legionnaire. There was a certain *dignitas* to be maintained, which would always be a struggle for Quin. She knew he wanted to jump into the guards' conversation, but decided against it after her silent admonishment.

Mafuta could hear the two little people, the *Parvi,* talking quietly in their own language behind her. They were a married couple and Mafuta recognized enough words to know they were trying to determine their odds of escaping the Bifurlanders' flagship alive.

She wished she was confident enough of the outcome of tonight's adventure to reassure them—and herself.

Deena stood on the thwart across the rear of the boat, practicing with her longsword and round shield. Her anatomically correct, or perhaps exaggerated breastplate was only painted to look like bronze. It was good steel underneath. Mafuta admired the younger woman and understood her armor as an excellent tactic to distract her opponents. There was no arguing with the martial skills she demonstrated with each practice attack and block.

Mafuta looked south along the length of the Brenavon. The older wizard didn't need to create distance, night-seeing lenses to make out the Bifurland flagship. It was lit with three dozen torches and easy to spot, anchored in the center of the river with hundreds of other torch-lit dragonships stretched out behind it. She made the glowing ball above her head brighter. They weren't trying to sneak up on the Bifurlanders—this was a prearranged meeting.

"Bring us around to their starboard side," Quintillius instructed Felix. "They've dropped a net we can climb to get on board." Quin turned to Mafuta, who carried more than a few extra pounds under her purple robes. "Climbing a net won't be a problem for you, 'Futa, will it?"

She tapped the flying disk strapped between her shoulders.

"No problem at all, Quin."

The governor-general laughed. "Of course," he said. "I'm a fool. I hope I retain more of my wits when I negotiate with King Bjarni."

"So do I," said Mafuta. Both of them laughed to break the tension.

Bifurland warriors—not in armor—were waiting at the bottom of the netting to assist the visitors in ascending. None of the Roma needed their assistance, however. The *Parvi* climbed the net as fast and sure as squirrels up a tree with their long-tubed weapons strapped across their backs. The two tall warriors didn't have as far to go to reach the deck and made it up the nets with ease, carrying their full kits, including their six-foot-high scutums.

Deena decided to show off and swung herself up the knitted ropes using only her hands, not her feet. She winked at the two

Bifurland warriors there to assist and did a handstand on the ship's railing before landing on her feet on the deck.

Quintillius, with some coaching from Mafuta, ascended with one foot on each wizard's flying disk. He stood tall as the disks rose several feet above the railing before descending to land near the mainmast. King Bjarni and Queen Signý stepped forward to meet Quintillius. No handshakes were exchanged, but three small nods were given, followed by three slight smiles.

"I'm pleased you decided to keep our bargain," said King Bjarni, "though I've always wanted to test my soldiers' skills against your legions."

"You'll have to settle for testing *your* skill against mine," said Quintillius. Felix had been correct. He *was* a foot taller than Bjarni and his forearms were much longer as well.

"May the better man win," said Mafuta.

"And the better realm," responded Queen Signý. She turned to Quintillius. "Does your lady wife know of your wager?"

"I've kept her apprised of the situation," said Quintillius.

Signý touched her husband's arm. "That means Laetícia doesn't know."

"What of that is your concern?" asked Quintillius, frowning.

"I just want to ensure you live long enough to hold up your end of the bargain," said Queen Signý.

Mafuta chuckled and answered. "Laetícia may *threaten* to kill him if he loses, Your Majesty, but I doubt she'll carry out her threat."

"Are we talking about the same Laetícia?" asked Queen Signý. "That's not her reputation."

"I assure you, she has a deep affection for her husband," said Mafuta. "She wouldn't kill him."

"Wouldn't kill him *lightly*," said Signý. "I've read books on Imperial history."

"And I've read accounts of your sagas, good queen," said Mafuta. "Both our peoples aren't strangers to familial violence."

"True," said King Bjarni. "Quintillius has a reputation as a man of his word, or else I wouldn't have accepted his offer. It's a simple-enough deal. A certain piece of land wagered against support from our fleet, though sometimes I wonder if it might not be wiser to let Tamloch defeat you and strike a bargain with them instead."

"They'd never offer you what I've proposed," said Quintillius. "It's excellent farmland, close to the sea."

"Yes, yes," said the king. "I've already determined which of my thains will receive it."

"Don't count your chickens before..." began Queen Signý.

"You mean *ducks,* in this case," said King Bjarni. "I hear the land is question is teeming with them."

"It is," said Quintillius.

"My understanding is that Tamloch's fleet is nearly to Nova Eboracum," said Queen Signý. "How would you expect us to get *our* fleet there fast enough to defeat them?"

"My wizards assure me they have a solution to that logistical challenge," said Quintillius. He moved to put a hand on Mafuta's shoulder, but she leaned away to avoid it. She had her own *dignitas* to preserve.

The three Bifurlander wizards in gold robes moved forward and whispered to Bjarni and Signý. Mafuta assumed they were telling their monarchs they'd be able to copy the magics once they'd seen them performed, just as Mafuta had learned them from Fercha and Doethan.

The three gold wizards withdrew a few paces. They were all women, Mafuta observed. At least she *thought* she saw women's faces under their hoods.

"Shall we get on with the contest?" asked Quintillius.

King Bjarni didn't reply at first. He looked over the five guards in the governor-general's retinue, especially Deena and the Parvi. Then he turned around to review two dozen of his own warriors crowded behind him on the deck.

"If I'm not going to have the pleasure of testing my army against yours," said the king, "I'd like to be entertained by seeing how your guards fare in combat against an equal number of *my* warriors."

"With what stakes?" asked Quintillius. "It can't affect the outcome of *our* competition."

"No, no, merely as a preliminary," said the king. "Fights before the main fight, so to speak."

Quintillius glanced down at Mafuta. She nodded her head almost imperceptibly.

"Very well," he said. Quintillius addressed his guards. "Are you willing to show our hosts why Roma's legions deserve respect?"

All five pounded their hearts with their right fists. Deena made an echoing clang when her bronze-plated steel vambrace hit her breastplate.

"*Ave* Quintillius! *Ave* Imperator!" they shouted.

Quintillius smiled warmly. Someday, he hoped *he* would be the emperor.

"There's not enough room on deck for five against five," said King Bjarni. "Shall we do two pairs, and then the woman armed like an Athican against one of my warriors in single combat?"

The guard captain signified his assent and Quintillius approved. King Bjarni signaled a pair of his warriors to step forward. His trio of wizards created glowing spheres that made the deck of the flagship as bright as daylight. The first two Bifurlander warriors were almost as tall as the men from Occidens Province. One carried a double-bladed axe, the other a sword. Both held round shields in their off-hands.

Instead of the two tall legionnaires the Bifurlanders were expecting, only the guard captain stepped forward, protected by his raised rectangular scutum. Quintillius could practically read the warriors' minds—*two against one would make this easier*. They approached to engage the guard captain, but when they were a dozen paces away, he lowered his shield a few inches, revealing one of the Parvi with a blow gun. Two quick darts hit exposed skin on upper arms. Soon, both axeman and swordsman were asleep on the deck.

King Bjarni clapped his delight as their bodies were removed.

"I love it," he said. "They shouldn't have underestimated you."

The guard captain and his Parvi comrade, now sitting on his shoulder, bowed and stepped back, leaving the younger tall legionnaire and the other Parvi, the first one's wife, to fight King Bjarni's next pair of champions. They both knew it wouldn't be as easy this time, without the element of surprise.

The king spoke to one of his thains, then selected an odd-looking pair of warriors. One was of medium height with long arms carrying two spears, with half a dozen more strapped to his back. The other was a short, wide man with a short sword and a whip on his belt. He held two captured Roma scutums, each taller than he was. The shields had spikes in their centers.

Quintillius caught Mafuta's eye and an unspoken concern flashed between them. The Bifurlanders had a trick of their own planned, he was sure.

The short Bifurlander anchored the bottoms of both shields against the deck and inched forward toward the legionnaire and the Parvi. His companion crouched behind him until they were within ten paces of the Roma guards. Then the crouching Bifurlander rose and hurled a spear at the top of the tall legionnaire's scutum. It's point pierced the reinforced wood of the shield and the Parvi hiding behind it cried out and denigrated the ancestry of the spear-thrower.

The tall Roma guardsman rushed toward the pair of Bifurlanders, hoping to knock over the braced shields and flip the short warrior on his back. Instead, the short warrior allowed his comrade to hold the shields while he stuck his head out near the bottom of the right-hand shield and twisted the end of his whip around the tall legionnaire's exposed ankles. The guardsman fell forward, propelled by his own momentum, and fell on the injured Parvi, pinning her between his body and his scutum.

The two Bifurland warriors stepped forward and held both Roma down with their boots and the bottoms of their shields.

"Nicely done," said Quintillius, complimenting the Bifurlanders, just as Bjarni had admired his men's victory earlier.

He turned to his guard captain. "Remember that trick with the whip," he told him.

The guard captain just grinned. Other legionnaires would buy him drinks for a month to hear him tell the story. Quintillius assumed he was already figuring out how to work it into future training sessions.

The two Bifurlanders helped the legionnaire and the Parvi back to their feet. All four shook hands—there were no hard feelings. The Parvi was bleeding from a scratch on her side and Mafuta signaled to Felix that he should help heal her.

Now it was Deena's turn to show her skill at arms. Her success or failure would determine which side had the psychological advantage when Bjarni and Quintillius began *their* contest.

The young woman in Athican armor stood eagerly waiting for her Bifurlander opponent to appear. Queen Signý, not King Bjarni, was making the selection. Deena's eyes went wide inside her helm when a young woman wearing only a loincloth walked out to stand at the other side of the deck. Her body was lithe and strong, and her small breasts were a contrast to the ones on Deena's breastplate. She carried two metal rods in her hands. Each had a leather strap riveted to one end. A coiled rope hung from the wide belt that supported her loincloth.

"Wonderful!" shouted Deena. "I love your kit. I've always wanted to fight a bull-dancer. I had no idea there was anyone interested in that style in Bifurland."

Her opponent bowed slightly then stretched up on the balls of her bare feet and spun toward Deena. The near-naked woman was faster than the Roma, whose breastplate, helm, and armored limbs slowed her down. Deena ducked, but the other woman still managed to land blows on the side of Deena's helmet and her right shoulder.

"Get her, Ríga," shouted one of the women standing behind the queen.

Deena turned to keep Ríga in front of her. She had her sword and shield up, ready to block as Ríga raced across the deck, jumped above the point of the sword, and whacked Deena on the back of the helmet as she descended.

Bull dancing, thought Deena as she shook her head to clear. *How wonderful! And my sword substitutes for horns...*

Aesthetic admiration for Ríga's form aside, Deena knew she'd have to work hard *and* smart to earn victory. The next time Ríga danced in to attack, Deena threw her shield, not at where her opponent was, but where she expected her to be. The heavy disk caught Ríga in the ribs and knocked her to her knees. Deena closed quickly to end the fight with a stroke using the flat of her blade, but Ríga caught her behind the knee with a blow from one of her metal rods.

Now both women were on their knees, but Deena thought she still had the advantage. She leaned her torso against Ríga's, the weight of her breastplate pushing Ríga backwards. Deena used the vambraces on her forearms to block blows from Ríga's rods and keep pushing her over. Ríga's back was at a forty-five degree angle to the deck and Deena was confident the bout would soon be over.

Ríga had a different idea, however. She pulled the coil of rope from her hip and looped it over Deena's neck. The loop tightened as Deena pushed Ríga farther down. Deena was gasping while Ríga's shoulders were getting nearer and nearer to touching the deck.

Without air, Deena was weakening. Acting on reflex and training, she pulled a tab at her right wrist and a blade snapped out along one edge of her vambrace. Deena cut the ends of the rope Ríga was pulling and was suddenly able to draw in a deep breath. Reenergized, Deena pushed Ríga's shoulders all the way to the deck planks and put the sharp edge of her vambrace against Ríga's throat.

"Do you yield?" Deena asked.

"I yield," said Ríga. "Well fought."

"Thank you," said Deena as she stood up and retracted the blade on her vambrace. She helped Ríga rise.

"I would have done better not to get so close to you," said Ríga.

"You would have done better to remember that shields are distance weapons, not just tools for close defense," said Deena.

"Let me get you a mug of mead," said Ríga as Deena retrieved her shield and the two women pushed through the crowd behind Bjarni and Signý.

"I think I'd prefer wine, if you have it," said Deena, excitement making her voice loud. "It's more Athican."

"Wine it is," said Ríga. "You can tell me more about how you made your armor."

Quintillius, Mafuta, Bjarni and Signý's eyes tracked the two women as they left. Signý covered her mouth to hide her grin, but the other three didn't bother. Mafuta considered it a major plus that the two former opponents were now on their way to being friends.

"Ready?" asked King Bjarni. He waved to a pair of soldiers and a sturdy table and two stools were positioned near the mainmast. The table had a pair of thick pegs coming up from opposite corners.

"I am," said Quintillius.

The night was cool, but he still took off his toga and linen tunic, leaving him wearing not much more than Ríga. He was pleased to overhear admiring comments from Bifurlanders, men and women alike, over his chiseled muscles and smooth chest. He was in excellent shape for a man close to forty and kept up a diligent daily program of martial conditioning. He removed three rings and gave them to Mafuta for safekeeping, then sat on one of the stools and waited.

King Bjarni decided he'd take off his robes and shirt as well. The Bifurland monarch wasn't chiseled, precisely. His body looked more like it was formed from clay, with a bit extra daubed on here and there. His back and chest were covered in thick hair. It was hard to tell where his beard ended and his chest hair began. As Felix had reported, the king's forearms *were* larger than his thighs. They were larger than Quin's thighs, for that matter. Bjarni's biceps bulged when he flexed them as he took the stool across from Quintillius.

"How does this work?" asked Quin.

"I'll show you," said Queen Signý. She looked at his forearms, then her husband's and took four one-inch thick disks of braided horsehair from a servant and put them under Bjarni's right elbow. "There. That should make it easier for you to clasp hands without twisting your wrist down. Grab hold."

Blast! thought Mafuta. *So much for leverage.*

Quintillius did. He and the king both shifted to find a firm, comfortable grip.

"What are the rules?" asked Quintillius.

"Grip the peg with your left hand," said the queen. Quintillius did. "If you release the peg, you lose. If you lift your elbow, you lose. If you break your grip, you lose."

"How do I win?" asked Quin.

"By pinning the back of my wrist to the table," said Bjarni.

"How do *you* win?" asked Quintillius with a smile.

"By having new land to give to my thains," said Bjarni. "I may even keep a farm there for myself." He tightened his grip. Quintillius did the same.

"What if neither one of us can pin the other?" asked Quintillius. "What happens then?"

"It never happens," said Queen Signý. "Someone tires eventually."

I hope it's not Quin, thought Mafuta. She was pleased to see that even Deena and Ríga had come back to watch the contest play out. She wished she had a goblet of wine, or even a mug of mead for herself.

Queen Signý held up a gold coin. "I'm going to drop this on the table. When you hear it strike the surface, begin."

Mafuta had done her research. Traditionally the coin went to the victor. Now the stakes were a great deal higher.

Signý held the coin lightly between her pinched fingers and let it drop. Mafuta was sure she heard a hundred spectators inhale as the coin descended. She was one of them. Then the coin struck the table with a muted clunk and the competition began.

Mafuta was most worried about the first fifteen seconds. She'd learned that many arm-wrestling bouts were decided by an initial surge by one participant that overwhelmed his opponent. She was pleased to see that Quin was holding his own past that point, and then past half a minute. Quin's greater leverage, of sorts, was compensating for Bjarni's raw strength.

She had advised Quintillius to seek out the best arm wrestlers in the legions and learn their tricks. Quin had been wise enough to do so, taking half an hour while a boat was located.

Traveling by water had made more sense than flying, given the size of their party. Quin's scouts had found a fisherman willing to rent them his boat for the evening. The legionnaire designated to handle the negotiations said the fisherman had been quite accommodating and pleased with the proposed rent, though the rest of the squad of soldiers with the negotiator may have provided encouragement.

Mafuta had watched grizzled veterans from the legions show Quintillius how to twist his wrist, vary his force, and appear to lose, only to redouble his efforts and pin his opponent. She hoped the veterans' quick lessons would be effective.

Back at the table, both Bjarni and Quintillius were starting to sweat. It was cool enough that you couldn't see any droplets on their torsos, but their furrowed foreheads were slick with perspiration. Mafuta was pleased she'd given Quin a mixture of fruit and vegetable juices to drink before the competition. It might help him last longer.

She looked away for a moment to observe the queen and the crowd. Every eye was focused on the two straining men. She heard Signý gasp and quickly turned back to the table. Quintillius was forcing Bjarni's wrist down toward the table. Already, it was halfway there. Bjarni was struggling to keep the back of his hand from touching. He looked at Quintillius imploringly. Quin nodded in a way that made it seem like it was just part of his effort to defeat the Bifurland monarch.

Mafuta saw Signý's face brighten as Bjarni struggled back. He forced Quin's arm up and back to vertical, then past vertical. With a tremendous effort and shout, Bjarni pressed the back of Quin's hand into the wood of the tabletop. The gold coin bounced and rattled from the impact. Cheers erupted from from the Bifurlanders. Queen Signý clapped and so did a young girl with blonde braids like Signý's who'd recently taken a spot on the queen's lap. *A daughter,* assumed Mafuta. Then the wider implications struck her. *Laetícia's not going to be happy.*

Bjarni jumped up and embraced Quintillius.

"Well fought," said the king. "Well fought indeed." He pounded Quin's back.

"And you, my *friend*," said Quintillius.

"Yes," shouted Bjarni. "The Roma are now our friends. We will get our new lands—half of one of Occidens Province's greatest treasures."

There was more cheering across the ship. Bifurlanders were shaking hands with the guards. Some even went to their knees to hug the Parvi, including the one with the deep scratch Felix had just healed. Others brought drinks to Ríga and Deena. A thoughtful woman approached Mafuta with a goblet of wine. The older Roma wizard quickly checked it for poison, found none, and drank three swallows. She was still worried about Laetícia's reaction.

With help from a few warriors, Bjarni climbed up on the table and stomped his foot for attention. Only three-quarters of the people on the flagship noticed, but that was enough to lower the noise level so his next words could be heard.

"Yes," he said. "The Roma are now our friends—and that is why our fleet will soon go to Nova Eboracum to engage Tamloch's fleet and ensure the treasure is still Quintillian's to give."

The king's announcement earned still more cheers. *Bifurlanders love a fight,* thought Mafuta. *This should make Laetícia a lot happier.*

* * * * *

Dawn wasn't far off when the Roma travelers were back in their borrowed boat heading north up the river. Mafuta and Quintillius spoke softly from their seats side by side on the middle thwart.

"Why did you lose on purpose?" asked Mafuta.

"King Bjarni didn't want to lose face in front of his people," said Quin. "He made that plain to me with his expression. I knew he'd make good on supporting us with his fleet if I did."

"That was a lot to wager on reading someone's face," said Mafuta. "What if you were wrong?"

"I wasn't wrong," said Quintillius.

"What is this chunk of land that's a treasure of Occidens Province you're giving away? I want to know how far away I should get when you tell Laetícia."

"She knows my plan," said Quintillius. "She even helped me refine it."

"That's reassuring," said Mafuta.

Quin told her.

"You gave Insula Longa to the Bifurlanders!"

"Only the eastern half," said Quintillius. "That part of the Long Island is across the sound from Tamloch and there are plenty of Tamloch settlers already there. Bjarni's thains will help me clear them out and provide a buffer for us against future Tamloch attacks."

"Until they're dug in and their harbors become staging areas for future attacks from Bifurland," said Mafuta.

"That's what I like about you," said Quin. "You always see the bright side."

"It's not funny, Quin."

"I know," said Quintillius, "but take an even longer view and consider how valuable a fleet of five hundred or a thousand dragonships would be when its time for me to cross the Ocean and claim the imperial throne."

"Oh," said Mafuta. "That's different."

Chapter 47

Doethan

"Higher," chirped one small child.

"Up, up!" exclaimed the other.

"Later," said Doethan. "It's dark and I want you both to be safe."

"You make light," said the first child, pointing at the glowing sphere above Doethan's head.

"More light than when we're up to feed the chickens," said the other.

"Shush, children," said the innkeeper.

"Plenna, Mercha, pipe down and don't annoy the wizard," said the cook.

Doethan smiled. At least he knew the children's names now, though he didn't know which name went with which child. Come to think of it, he didn't know their mothers' names, either. Both problems could be addressed easily.

"Good ladies," said Doethan, "I've enjoyed your cooking and your hospitality—and your children, for that matter—but we haven't been formally introduced. If we're going to be exploring an old quarry together close to midnight, the least I could do would be tell you my name. I'm Doethan."

"Wizards are funny," said one small child.

"He could have said, 'My name is Doethan. What's yours?'" said the second child.

"I'm Plenna—she's Mercha," said the first child who seemed indistinguishable from her sister. "I want to be a soldier," she continued.

"I want to be a *cook*," said Mercha.

"Both are respected professions," said Doethan, smiling to himself so the girls didn't think they were being patronized.

"I'm Coegi, and my wife is Gwest," said the thin, long-haired cook. The two women had empty rough-woven bags in each hand, the kind grain was stored in for transport.

"The girls can be a handful," said Gwest. Dimples formed in her cheeks when she smiled.

"We're a handful and a half," announced Mercha proudly.

This time, Doethan couldn't keep from smiling.

"I hope you young ladies are good at collecting blue pebbles," he said. "I'm going to need a lot of them."

"We are, we are," said Plenna. "We feed them to the chickens for their gizzards. It makes their eggs extra special."

"I'm sure it does," said Doethan. He wondered if that contributed to the taste of Coegi's excellent chicken-and-egg pie.

"You've been to the quarry before?" he asked the girls.

"Lots of times," said Plenna.

"But not after dark," said Mercha. "We're afraid of the monster."

"It snores," said Plenna.

"I'm afraid of you falling in the lake," said Gwest.

"I wouldn't like that either," said Plenna. Doethen looked down and saw the girl shake her head. "You won't let us fall in the lake, will you, good wizard?"

"I won't let you fall in the lake *or* be eaten by a monster," he said.

Plenna and Mercha smiled at Doethan and squeezed his hands. The two didn't take up much room on his flying disk.

The girls and their mothers were quiet for a few minutes as they walked along and skimmed above the gravel road heading west from the Dormant Dragon. Doethan saw steep cliffs rising ahead of him. He made his sphere of illumination glow brighter and realized they were more than two hundred feet tall, with a wide opening ahead, like someone had cut a wedge out of a pie.

I shouldn't snack after bedtime, thought Doethan. *Everything reminds me of food.*

"The quarry is just through that gap," said Mercha.

"Both our moms won't let us go there by ourselves," said Plenna.

"Your mothers are wise women," said Doethan. "You should aspire to be like them."

"What does *aspire* mean?" asked Plenna.

"I know," said Mercha. "It's like a tower at a castle."

"That's *a* spire," said Coegi.

"I mean you should hope you grow up to be as wise as they are," said Doethan. He was enjoying himself. He hadn't spent time with small children since Salder and Merry were little.

A few minutes later, they were in the gap in the cliff wall. Doethan's glow light seemed brighter, reflecting off the stone walls that ranged in color from white to dark-blue. Doethan was impressed by the way the layers of rock seemed to be folded on top of themselves, like the blankets on a haphazardly-made bed. He resolved to return to the quarry in the future for a more detailed inspection.

If I live through the upcoming battle, he considered.

Soon the gap opened into a broad bowl-shaped quarry with high walls and a lake taking up two-thirds of the bottom. Tens of thousands of stones, from dust to boulders, covered the quarry's floor. *It shouldn't take long to gather enough magestones for his needs,* thought Doethan. He lowered his flying disk and the girls ran off to hug their mothers.

"What do you say to forming mother-daughter teams to look for stones," said Doethan. "I'll give each team its own ball of light."

Gwest and Coeli nodded. Doethan could see they didn't want the girls to wander off as their own team. He said *Llachar!* twice and made two new glowing spheres above the women's heads, keeping the original sphere for himself.

"Only gather the stones and pebbles that are blue," said Doethan. "The deeper the color the better. The gray and white ones don't have magic in them."

"We can do that," said Plenna. She tugged Gwest off to the left.

"Here's a sack for your collection," said Coegi, tossing one to Doethan as she was pulled to the right by Mercha.

"Thanks for your help," he said softly. The mother-daughter teams were already too far away to hear him.

Doethan modified his glow sphere to shine a bright beam of light on the ground in front of his eyes. He paced forward slowly, bending down to pick up promising blue rocks and pebbles when he saw them. He wondered why the quarry was no longer used for magestones. He was only familiar with Melyncárreg and three quarries northwest of Brendinas used by most wizards in Dâron's Conclave. He'd found his own magestone in the middle one of the three more than a quarter of a century ago.

The stones he was collecting were small, but seemed of high quality. He'd have to ask Damon why it had been abandoned. Damon might know, unless it had happened before *his* time. Doethan's light touched the edge of the lake and he smiled. Perhaps part of the quarry filling with water had something to do with it.

He walked back and forth in a zigzag pattern between the lake and the gap until his sack was half full and growing heavy. He made a megaphone of solidified sound and called to his companions. "Time to go!" he shouted. His words echoed off the quarry's vertical walls. They seemed louder than they should because everything else around him was quiet, including his new friends.

Then he heard Mercha's voice off to the right.

"What *is* it, Mother?" she asked.

Doethan left his sack near the gap and ran toward the glowing ball above Coegi and Mercha. He could hear footsteps that must belong to Plenna and Gwest behind him.

"I don't know," he heard Coegi answer as he got closer. "It doesn't feel like stone."

Doethan saw what they were looking at—an odd blue triangle poking out from the floor of the quarry. It was big, nearly four inches thick, as tall as his outstretched arm, and as wide at the base as the distance from his fingertips to his elbow.

"I wouldn't touch that," he said.

Coegi removed her fingers from the triangle and held Mercha back when she reached for it.

"Wow!" said Plenna, who had just arrived. She stepped toward the triangle with her hand stretched toward it. Gwest put her arms around her daughter's waist and lifted her up. Plenna's legs still churned below her.

"What *is* it?" Mercha repeated.

"I don't know, and we don't have time to investigate tonight," said Doethan. "Please stand back. I'm going to ensure it's not disturbed until I return."

Coeli and Mercha moved five steps away. Both mother-daughter teams stared at Doethan as he created a solid-blue sphere of solidified sound around the triangle to protect it from small children *and* their parents.

"Did you find lots of stones?" he asked.

"Lots and lots," said Mercha.

"I can hardly lift my bag," said Plenna, pointing to it proudly.

"Excellent," said Doethan. "So did I. Now I have to join the king and the royal army. I have plenty left to do tonight, and these stones will help me do it. You've all been a big help, thank you!"

"Yay!" shouted the girls.

"I'm going to put the bags on my flying disk and head back at high speed," said Doethan. "Your glow spheres should stay in place for a few more hours to light your way back. I promise I'll return to give you girls a ride high in the air in daylight."

"That will be *fun!*" exclaimed Mercha.

"And a wyvern ride!" added Plenna.

"I'll talk to Eynon and see what can be arranged," said Doethan.

He hugged the girls and nodded his thanks to their mothers, then hefted the sacks of stones onto his flying disk, rose up and flew northeast. Cooking fires should make it easy to spot the army's encampment from the air. Someone on Duke Háiddon's staff would be sure to know a good place to establish the gate at *this* end.

Chapter 48

Túathal and Gwýnnett

"Hello, my dear," said King Túathal when Princess Gwýnnett was escorted into his tent. Her gown and coat were soaked and water from her wet hair dripped down her back. She did *not* look happy, but she waited until the servant withdrew before sharing her thoughts with the king.

"You despicable cross between a skunk and a scorpion," she began. "How dare you…"

The intensity of Túathal's harsh gaze closed Gwýnnett's mouth momentarily. The king clapped his hands twice, sharply, and Uirsé, the dark-haired young wizard Verro had assigned him, entered the tent and looked at Túathal for instructions.

"Privacy sphere, now, for half an hour," said the king. "Then get out."

The dark-haired wizard nodded, created a sphere large enough to include most of the tent, and left.

"*Now* feel free to tell me what you think of my nature and ancestry," said Túathal. "It wouldn't do to air such phrases in front of the encampment. Tents have thin walls, you know."

Gwýnnett glared at Túathal and spun around three times on the balls of her feet. She could feel her toes squish inside her damp shoes but took satisfaction from the way drops from her long, wet hair sprayed across the king's fine robes and face. Túathal wiped his cheeks and forehead with a green, bell-shaped, ermine-trimmed sleeve.

"Everything out of your system now?" he asked in a matter-of-fact tone.

"Not at all," said Gwýnnett. "Why did your soldiers have to drop me in the river getting me out of my boat? It's undignified. And I'm *wet*."

"My apologies," said the king. "That wasn't my intent, or my instructions, but you have to admit, it makes the notion that you were taken hostage easier to believe."

Gwýnnett sniffed, then sneezed. Túathal took advantage of her pause in their exchange and continued talking.

"I understand that your guards tried to fend off my soldiers with swords and spears," he said. "You're lucky the boat tipped over near the shore."

"*You're* lucky my traveling chests are mostly waterproof," said Gwýnnett. "I need a bath and time to change into something more suitable…"

"And less soaked," added Túathal. "The wizard who made the privacy sphere can heat you some water, but don't keep her too long. I may need her."

"Yes, Your *Majesty*," said Gwýnnett. She added an ironic curtsy and took off her coat, dripping more water across the tent's canvas floor. "Far be it for your future queen to inconvenience you."

"Far be it," said Túathal. He raised an eyebrow and Gwýnnett grimaced. She saw the sand table behind Túathal and walked closer to inspect it.

"Don't drip on my armies," he said.

"I wouldn't dream of it," Gwýnnett replied. She pushed her sleeve back so water wouldn't drip on the sand and saw the small blocks representing the Tamloch army and the army of Dâron on the west bank of the Brenavon. The armies were almost equal in size and composition. *Too many years of primarily fighting each other,* she thought.

Why would Túathal and Verro force battle with Dâron without overwhelming odds in their favor? she wondered. Then Gwýnnett saw the Bifurlanders' dragonships to the south on the river and began to smile. The smile vanished when she took in the Occidens Province legions on the east bank. She frowned at Túathal. He moved to stand beside her at the sand table.

"It's not like you to fail to account for every contingency," said Gwýnnett. "How do you plan to win if the Roma manage to cross the river?"

"Remember, my dear," said Túathal, "you and I can win, even if we lose—not that I intend to."

He reached below the sand table and came back holding a small cloth drawstring bag. He pulled square after square of dark-brown irregular infantry tiles representing warriors from the southern Clan Lands from the bag and positioned them on the west bank just down river from Dâron's army.

"Behold Verro's surprise, my future queen," said Túathal. "The army of Dâron will be trapped between Tamloch's army, a horde of barbarian Clan Landers, and the Bifurlanders on the river." One eyebrow arched up and he grinned. Gwýnnett felt a cold shiver go down her back. "I expect Dârio's surrender by noon."

"And for your foes to accept your gracious offer to make our son high king of both realms by mid-afternoon?" asked Gwýnnett.

"Precisely," said Túathal.

"What about the Roma?"

"I've arranged a distraction for them," said the king. "They'll be turning around and marching back to Nova Eboracum as soon as they get word of *my* fleet's movements."

"They're blockading the Roma capital?" asked Gwýnnett.

"Supported by the northern Clan Lands' warriors sweeping their way south," said Túathal.

"You *are* a devious man. I thought you were waiting to consolidate Tamloch and Dâron before taking on Occidens Province."

"Once one stone falls there's no reason not to encourage an avalanche," said Túathal.

Gwýnnett smiled. "I admire a man with ambition," she said. "I also like the sound of *Gwýnnett, Queen of All Orluin*."

"Not planning to allow Dârio to marry?" asked Túathal.

"Don't spoil my daydreams," said Gwýnnett. "I know Dârio must marry, and *his* wife will be queen, but grant me a moment to enjoy the title without adding an adjective describing my age."

"Yes, *Gwýnnett, Queen of All Orluin*," said Túathal. He gave Gwýnnett a mocking bow. She stroked the heavy ring on her left hand that bore the Dâron dragon carved into a sapphire and gave him a regal nod.

"When it's over, I'll have Queen Carys eliminated," said Gwýnnett. "And her personal wizard, too, if Verro can manage it."

"I assumed you would," said Túathal. "You won't want either of them stirring up trouble for you back in Brendinas."

"Don't let them put up a statue to her," said Gwýnnett. "I'd hate to see it when I left the palace."

"Don't worry," said Túathal. "If one must be erected, I'll have it placed above her tomb. You're not likely to spend any time there."

"Thank you," said Gwýnnett. "Do you have anyone picked out?"

"Picked out for *what*, my queen-to-be?"

"Dârio's bride, of course. I assumed you'd want to marry him to a Tamloch noble's daughter to cement the alliance between the kingdoms."

"Perhaps I'll have him wed the daughter of Quintillius and Laetícia to strengthen the hold I expect to have on the Roma."

"She's only five," said Gwýnnett.

"I didn't think you were in a hurry to be the new Old Queen?"

"I'm not in a hurry, but keeping Dârio from marrying for ten years might be stretching my influence over our son."

"I'm sure suitable candidates can be found when the time is right," said Túathal.

"And I'm sure the time is right for me to get out of these wet clothes," said Gwýnnett. "Do you have your knife?"

She turned her back on Túathal and waited. He stepped behind her with his personal blade to her neck and his arm around her waist.

"Don't tempt me," he whispered. Gwýnnett felt his breath on her neck.

"Slash my laces, not my throat," said the princess. "We still need each other."

"Yes, *my queen*," said Túathal.

Gwýnnett felt her gown's laces part as Túathal ran his dagger up her back. She'd have a servant re-lace it after it was cleaned and dried. She shrugged her shoulders and the gown slid down to the tent's canvas floor. The princess was dressed in a wet linen shift that revealed her figure.

"Are you sure I can't talk you into another *exceptional* performance to give Dârio a younger brother or sister?" Gwýnnett asked.

"I think not," said Túathal. "Once was enough."

Gwýnnett turned to face Túathal and stretched her body like a cat. She put her hands on his chest, then ran them sensuously down toward his waist and beyond. The king was unaffected. Gwýnnett started to kneel in front of him and licked her lips, but Túathal sheathed his dagger and pushed her away.

"You're embarrassing yourself," he said. "I said it would only happen once."

"Oh, all right," said Gwýnnett. "If that's the way it has to be."

"Good," said Túathal.

"Fine," said Gwýnnett.

"I need some tokens to convince Dârio you're our hostage, my dear lady," said Túathal. "A lock of your hair. A ring, like that blue dragon signet you're wearing."

"Not that ring, *this* one," said Gwýnnett, pointing to a smaller band with interlaced knotwork. "Dârio knows Crown Prince Dâri, the man he thinks is his father, gave it to me. It will have more sentimental value."

"As you wish," said Túathal. He took the ring Gwýnnett offered and cut off a larger section of her hair then she appreciated. Gwýnnett knew Túathal had only done it to annoy her, and she wouldn't give him the satisfaction of knowing he'd succeeded. The privacy sphere ended, and they could hear sounds from the encampment again.

Uirsé, the dark-haired wizard, came back to see if the king wanted the privacy sphere renewed. Túathal glared at her and left to enter his personal sleeping chamber. She saw the princess shivering in her wet shift.

"Follow me," she said to Gwýnnett. As Uirsé left, she took great care not to let on that she'd seen the dress with split laces puddled on the tent's floor.

Chapter 49

Back to Melyncárreg

Eynon tried to focus when they led Rocky through the nearly deserted streets of Brendinas close to midnight. He followed Fercha as she wended her way from the Passant Tyger, the inn at the other end of the gate they'd just taken, to find the warehouse for the wholesaler who kept Damon's castle and the Academy back in Melyncárreg supplied with flour, butter, and beer. Nûd walked beside him, talking softly to Rocky from time to time.

Eynon asked Nûd a question, keeping his voice low so as not to attract any more attention than Rocky did by his mere presence.

"What's *passant?*"

"What?" asked Nûd.

"I think I know what *dormant* is," Eynon continued. "That's when an animal on a shield is sleeping, like the blue dragon on the tapestry."

"Oh," said Nûd. "I'm surprised you never picked that up in your reading. *Passant* is when an animal has three legs on the ground and one up, like the dragon on Dâron's royal arms. It's usually the right front foot that's raised."

Eynon nodded and rubbed his chin as he walked. He looked at Rocky, then at Nûd.

"I guess that means wyverns can't be *passant* then," said Eynon.

"Why not?" asked Nûd. "They're animals."

"Yes, but they only have two feet," Eynon answered.

"There are books on heraldry in the library in Melyncárreg," said Nûd. "We could look up the heraldic postures that work for wyverns."

"Later," said Eynon.

"Right," said Nûd.

"I'm glad you said it so I didn't have to," said Merry as she caught up to the rest after checking out the titles in bookshop windows along their way. She had a dim glow sphere above her head, but they were relying on light from Fercha's sphere for navigation.

Chee was above and behind the three young people, perched on top of Rocky's head. The raconette was excitedly taking in all the sights and smells of Brendinas. He turned his own head from side to side, trying to absorb everything at once.

"There it is," said Fercha, pointing to a long, low wood-frame building on the river. *Serendipity Suppliers* read a sign above the front entrance.

"Curious name," said Eynon.

Nûd smiled. "It's a family joke."

Fercha frowned at her son but opened the door with a key from her pouch.

Why would Fercha have a key to this particular warehouse? Eynon wondered.

Fercha went through the door and a few moments later one of two wide doors farther down the block opened. Nûd rushed ahead to help his mother open the other one and Eynon, Merry, Rocky and Chee used the larger entrance to step into the warehouse. It was filled with crates, barrels, sacks, bottles, jugs and boxes of all shapes and sizes. They cast intriguing shadows in the light from Fercha's glow ball.

"The gate's over here," said Fercha, pointing to the left.

"No, Mother, you've got it backwards. It's on the right," said Nûd. He moved in that direction and the rest of the party followed.

"Sorry," said Fercha. "I haven't been here in decades."

"So long as it's a mistaken memory, not impending senility," teased Nûd.

Fercha seemed ready to reply, but thought better of it. The gate was formed by two massive old-growth timber uprights, a cross-beam twelve feet above, and a sill-beam running along the floor from upright to upright.

"Do you remember the trigger phrase, Mother?" asked Nûd. "Damon never gave it to me. I think he was afraid I'd leave his protective custody."

"I do," said Fercha. "You know we only kept you in Melyncárreg for your own safety."

Nûd grimaced at her and put his hands over his ears.

Fercha nodded at Nûd, then turned to face the gate and recited ten clear syllables. Eynon could see Merry working to memorize them, just as he was. Knowing how to operate a gate from Brendinas to Melyncárreg could be useful.

"Is it active?" asked Nûd.

Fercha turned and spoke.

"It is," she said.

Nûd lowered his hands and stroked the side of Rocky's neck.

"Come on, boy," he said. "It's just another gate. You've been through lots of them lately."

The wyvern bent his head and rubbed the side of his scaly jaw against Nûd's palm. Chee took advantage of his position to muss Nûd's hair. Nûd grabbed Chee with his free hand and tossed the raconette to Eynon. Chee squeaked and settled into his usual spot on Eynon's shoulder.

Now that Eynon was more experienced with wizardry, he could detect the subtle channeling of power that marked an active gate. *Someday I'll have to learn how to create them,* he considered.

Chee seemed as fascinated by the gate as he had been by the sights and smells of the city. He leaned forward eagerly, ready to transition.

"No time like the present," said Fercha.

They stepped through the gate, with Fercha continuing to lead the way.

They came out through another blank wall at the end of a wide corridor in Melyncárreg's labyrinthine pantries. Nûd stepped past his mother with Rocky and Chee behind him until they were in the castle's commodious kitchen. Everyone else followed, taking care to avoid being inadvertently smacked by Rocky's swinging tail.

"Do we need to get Rocky outside?" asked Nûd.

"I'm afraid so," said Eynon. "He's vital to our plan."

"*Your* plan," said Merry, squeezing Eynon's hand.

Eynon looked embarrassed. Merry continued.

"Eynon, you and Nûd and Rocky and Chee should gather small magestones to powder. You said you knew where to find some." Merry took a breath. "Fercha and I will find a good spot to start building the wide gate."

"*I* will find a good spot for the gate—I grew up here just like Nûd, you know—and Merry will assist *me* in gate preparations," said Fercha. She gave Merry a look that reminded the younger wizard of her mother's expression when she needed to tone down her exuberance.

"Yes, Fercha," said Merry. She smiled at Fercha and Fercha grinned back. Merry reminded Fercha of herself as a girl, though with a more loving relationship with her father.

"Would the second plateau above the castle work well?" Fercha asked Nûd.

"That would be perfect," he replied.

"Excellent," said Fercha. "It's best you get flying. The sooner you're back with magestone dust, the sooner we can pull our surprise and get back to Dâron.

"Will you need to coordinate with Doethan at the other end?" asked Eynon. "I can loan you my ring if you need to connect with him."

Fercha held up her left hand, revealing several small gold rings. "Doethan and I have a connection in place already," she said. "Get moving, and watch out for basilisks."

"Yes, Mother," said Nûd in a voice more like his childhood self than his current adult status.

Eynon laughed and guided Rocky toward the kitchen wall that led to the banquet hall and the outside world. He climbed on one side of Rocky's back and fastened his new leather harness. Nûd did the same on the other side. Chee moved from Eynon's shoulder to Rocky's neck and held on.

With a gesture, Eynon crafted a tasty magical sphere against the wall and Rocky launched himself forward to reach it. They transitioned into the banquet hall. Solidified sound constructs opened the outer doors of the hall and soon the four of them were flying northwest toward the field of geysers, hot springs, mud pots and magestones.

Chapter 50

Fercha and Merry

"You've never been to Melyncárreg, have you?" asked Fercha. "It wasn't a great place for me when I was a student."

"I have, actually," said Merry. "Damon brought me here when we came back from Riyas, before we gated to his private quarters in the royal palace in Brendinas. I didn't get to see much. We were only here for a few minutes."

"That's still too long as far as I'm concerned," said Fercha. "I'm only here now for the good of the kingdom and to stick it to Verro."

"Is there a particular reason you don't like him?" asked Merry. "Besides him stealing magestones and attacking us?"

"Yes," said Fercha, "It's a long story and not worth getting into. We have more important things to deal with."

"Agreed," said Merry. "How can I help?"

Fercha paused to lean on one of the kitchen worktables. Merry could see she was thinking so she kept quiet.

"Blast!" said Fercha. "We need rope. I know Nûd said he'd just received some in a shipment of supplies, but I forgot to ask him where he stored it."

"Do you want me to use my ring to contact Eynon?" asked Merry. Then she remembered. She'd loaned her ring to Doethan.

Fercha smiled at her. "I see you remember that's not an option."

"Ah, well," said Merry. "Let me help you search. I wonder where Nûd would store non-food items?"

"Things that aren't food?" asked Fercha. "They don't make rope soup in Applegarth?"

"What?" said Merry. "Rope soup? You're kidding!"

"Uh huh," said Fercha, grinning at Merry. "Got you!"

Merry looked at Fercha and started laughing. It took her several seconds to stop.

"What?" asked Fercha.

"You made a joke," said Merry. "I've never heard you joke before. You're always so serious, about my magestone and setting, about my training, about Damon and Nûd and now Verro. It's nice to know you *have* a sense of humor."

"Am I really that bad?" asked Fercha.

Merry stared at her.

"Alright, maybe I have been," Fercha continued. "Sorry."

"It was a good joke," said Merry. "Even better because it was unexpected. It won't be such a shock the next time."

"If there *is* a next time," said Fercha. "I have a quota and am only allowed to tell one every twenty years."

"There you go," said Merry. "You've told another one—a joke by exaggeration."

"I guess I did," said Fercha, smiling. Then her serious mask returned. "Enough of that," she said. "We need Nûd's rope."

"Do you start with a chicken or a beef stock?" asked Merry.

"Either one will do," said Fercha. "You just need to let it simmer in a cook pot for seven or eight days until it's tender. If you don't, it gets stringy."

"Ouch!" said Merry. "That's even worse, which means better!" She stopped to laugh again, then decided to add to the recipe.

"I'd toss in spring onions, for extra flavor."

"And chopped garlic cloves," said Fercha.

The two women were smiling and making faces at each other.

"And a braised rabbit," said Merry, feeding Fercha a straight line.

"No, not a *rabbit*," said Fercha.

Merry grinned. "Why not?"

Fercha started but they both completed, "Because no one likes finding a hare in their soup."

Merry hugged Fercha as they both moved from guffaws to plain laughing to giggles. After a minute, Fercha put Merry at arm's length and leaned back against the kitchen worktable.

"Thank you, I needed that," said Fercha.

"We *both* did," said Merry. "I haven't heard that joke since my father told it to Salder and me when we were small."

"I heard it from my mother," said Fercha. "My father went in for lectures, not funny stories."

Fercha's face brightened.

"Our humorous diversion was just what I needed to remember where Nûd was likely to store the rope," she said.

"Where?" asked Merry.

"In the castle's laundry," Fercha replied. "You always need lots of rope for clothes to dry on out here."

"Why not dry it with wizardry," asked Merry.

"That stopped back when the Academy was more active," said Fercha. "An apprentice was put in charge of drying clothes with wizardry and instead the undergarments for every man and woman in Melyncárreg were turned to a fine gray ash by an overzealous application of heat."

Merry laughed again. It felt good to be laughing as much as she had when she'd been traveling down the river with Eynon.

"Let me guess," said Merry. "It was Hibblig. He seems to carry a perpetual chip on his shoulder."

"No," said Fercha. "Wizards from Gwýnnett's faction don't train here. They have their own school built on swampland along the first big river south of the Moravon. You could inhale a quart of mosquitoes in a single breath there if you didn't keep your shields up."

"Why don't they drain the swamp and make it a better place to live?" asked Merry. "My da drains more swampland across the Rhuthro every season, with help from Doethan."

"Your father is a wise and practical man," said Fercha. "The wizards in Gwýnnett's faction aren't. They take after their patron."

"I see," said Merry. "All the more reason for us to win, then."

"Correct," said Fercha. "Time to visit the laundry."

* * * * *

"Can you tie a tautline hitch?" asked Fercha. She was on her flying disk, floating near the rough bark of a sizable spear-pine, a tree that grew perfectly straight and only retained branches on the upper third of its trunk. This specimen was sixty feet tall and Merry was floating halfway up its length, guiding her flying disk above the floor of a broad valley. She was wrapping one end of the long rope they'd found around the tree's two-yard circumference.

"I can, and I have," said Merry. "We can tighten it when I fasten the other end."

Far in the distance they could hear sounds of a herd of large herbivores grazing at the other end of the valley. It was still dark as a mineshaft in the middle hours of the night, but Fercha and Merry each had glowing spheres floating above their heads that provided sufficient illumination for the two wizards to accomplish what was necessary. Merry let the dangling rope coiled on her flying disk pay out behind her as she and Fercha headed for a second stand of spear-pines on the far side of the valley.

The rope was covered in powdered magestones. It glittered in the light from their glow spheres. Fercha had found a small bag of magestone shards in the Academy's artifact studio. It was enough to coat the rope, but not enough for the rest of the gate.

"We were lucky to find two crocks full of waterproof glue in the laundry near the rope," said Fercha.

"They were *huge* crocks," said Merry. "It looked like Nûd made the glue himself, too."

"When you hunt wisents, you get a *lot* of horns and bones. It's easier to made big batches," said Fercha.

"Why would he need so much glue?" asked Merry.

"I'm not sure," said Fercha, "given Damon's odd whims and strange projects, but my memory is that it helps keep canvas waterproof. I remember getting lots of bad weather in Melyncárreg, so it would be useful."

"I remember making glue outside in a cauldron with my mother back at Applegarth," said Merry. "We'd boil out the gelatin, add spoiled milk, and include oil of wintergreen so it wouldn't smell so bad."

"Wintergreen glue sounds intriguing," said Fercha. "You've got a wise mother."

"She has her good points," admitted Merry.

"Once you tie off the other end of the rope, there's not much we can do until Nûd and Eynon come back."

"You could teach me how to make wide gates," suggested Merry.

They'd reached the spear-pine they'd selected on the opposite side of the valley more than a hundred yards away. Nûd had ordered a full spool of rope, so it was just enough to reach. Merry tied another tautline hitch and tightened it as Fercha watched her.

"I could do that," said the older wizard. "It's the same general principle as making smaller gates."

"But you haven't taught me *anything* about making gates yet," said Merry.

"Oh! You're right. What kind of mentor *am* I," said Fercha. "We'll remedy that lack right now. Let's descend and I'll show you."

"Great!" said Merry. She circled down in exuberant spirals to land next to Fercha. The two wizards moved their flying disks to their backs and found a pair of convenient rocks to sit on a few feet beyond the spear-pine.

"There are three kinds of gates," Fercha began. "Standard gates, wide gates, and emergency gates. They all open congruencies connecting one place with another."

Merry nodded and leaned forward.

"Standard gates," Fercha continued, "are powered by magical energy from their creators. They remain in effect as long as the wizard who made them lives. They're usually circles, squares, or rectangles with magical anchors at the corners or at cardinal points, for circles— and sometimes ellipses. You can use those, too."

"You'll show me how to set those anchors?" asked Merry.

"After I finish explaining things," said Fercha. "And if we have time. The wizard who creates the gate can set it to be always open, locked, or only locked in one direction."

"I can see why the ability to lock gates is essential," said Merry. "Go on. Do you need to have wizards at both ends of a standard gate?"

"No," Fercha answered. "That's only required for wide gates, but it is possible. If two wizards create a standard gate, it breaks when one of them dies. I've done my share of reestablishing gates when their creators are gone. It's young wizards' work."

"Don't young wizards tend to die in battle?" asked Merry.

"They haven't for a generation," Fercha answered. "Though that may change in the morning."

"Yes. It might," said Merry. She shook her head slowly.

"Wizards need to touch the four anchor points at both ends and power the gates with their magestones," said Fercha. "The directional and locking settings are added afterward."

"I can't wait to learn," said Merry.

"Wide gates need a continuous circuit of magical energy from powdered magestones to keep them operating," said Fercha. "It takes at least two wizards on both sides of the gate to power one up, though four would be even better. When we get more powdered magestone, we'll paint the tree trunks with glue, then coat them with the powder. Then we'll need to dig a trench between the trees and sprinkle more powder along its length, so the magical energy can flow all around the gate."

"Oh," said Merry. "We have to dig a trench? We need to get started—and we forgot to bring shovels."

"Stop," teased Fercha. "Think."

"Oh," said Merry. "That's right. I need to think like a wizard now. I guess it takes practice."

"Unless you were *raised* by wizards," said Fercha with a wan smile. She nodded toward the space in the wide valley between the trees. "Go ahead, young wizard. Show me."

"Let's see," said Merry. She held her arms out wide then brought them out in front of her with her fingers outstretched. Bright blue beams of tight light shot out from each hand and cut into the ground six inches apart. Fercha sent her glow sphere across to the far side of the valley so Merry could keep the path of her beams straight.

"Very good," said Fercha. "Now flip it up so we can see the channel where we'll spread the powdered magestones."

Merry concentrated. Using only blue tight-light force beams from her left hand, she lifted her hand and turned it in a smooth, even motion. A triangular line of grass and soil extending across the valley flipped up, revealing a v-shaped hole that would be perfect for receiving powdered magestone.

"Excellent," said Fercha. "Now you're thinking like a wizard."

Merry smiled and nodded her appreciation of Fercha's praise. "Do wide gates have to be the same dimensions at either end?" she asked.

"Not exactly," said Fercha. "It can be a problem if they're off by yards, but a foot or two won't matter."

"That's why we need to reach Doethan? To tell him the dimensions of our gate?"

"Correct," said Fercha. "They have more flexibility at their end, since they'll be using logs, not trees for uprights."

"Got it," said Merry. "What about emergency gates?"

"Those are different, sort of," said Fercha. "They require only *one* set of anchor points, but the connection to the destination location has to be *very* strong."

"Like my connection to Applegarth?" asked Merry.

"No, not an emotional connection. A place where the wizard has spent a lot of time investing energy at one end of a gate without having a permanent matching gate at the other end. In a way, the wizard herself is the other side of the gate. Additional corners or cardinal points aren't necessary. Most wizards can only manage to establish one or two such gates."

"Most wizards?" asked Merry. "There are exceptions?"

"Damon is quite skilled at it," said Fercha. "So is Verro. It makes them both particularly dangerous men."

"I see, I think," said Merry. "What should I look for in an emergency gate destination?"

"Somewhere hidden," said Fercha. "Somewhere safe that only you know about. That's the best way."

"Yours must go to your tower," said Merry.

"I won't say, and neither should you when you build yours. Emergency gates are for just that—emergencies," said Fercha.

"Too bad I won't be able to create one before morning," said Merry.

"True," said Fercha. "You'll just have to be careful."

"Where's the fun in that?" asked Merry with a grin.

She saw a flash of red light in the sky above Fercha's head and sent up an answering flash of blue.

Nûd and Eynon and Rocky and Chee were back. They still had enough time. Eynon's idea was going to work!

Chapter 51

Nûd and Eynon

Nûd and Eynon were flying northwest on Rocky's back over a snow-covered landscape, heading for the hot springs and mud pots. Chee, sensibly, was strapped in, sleeping on the wyvern's wide neck. His front and back paws were locked to ridges of bone along Rocky's spine. Eynon directed an extra-bright sphere of illumination close to the ground ahead of them to light their way.

"It's easier flying than walking," said Eynon, "especially since I didn't really know where I was going when I left to find my magestone."

He adjusted the straps on his backpack where they bit into his shoulders. Eynon wasn't quite sure why he had put it back on instead of stowing it somewhere on Rocky's harnesses, but it felt reassuring to have it where it had been the day he set out on his wander year.

"Damon sent you by the route that went *over* a couple of mountains instead of around them," said Nûd. "The snow was deeper that way, too."

"Why would he do that?" asked Eynon.

"The old man likes to push apprentices, physically and mentally," said Nûd. "He says it reveals and refines character."

"What did it reveal about *me?*" asked Eynon. He tilted his head, waiting for Nûd's answer.

"It revealed more about Damon than you and proved the old buzzard could still be surprised."

"What do you mean?" asked Eynon. "*I* don't feel like I'm that surprising."

Nûd laughed. "And that's part of what makes you so refreshing! I've grown up surrounded by wizards. They're grumpy and devious and egotistical and domineering."

It was Eynon's turn to laugh as he tried to match up Nûd's adjectives with Damon and Fercha. He thought he had a good guess which ones went with which wizard.

Nûd continued. "Please don't get a swelled head, but you're a *very* powerful wizard, Eynon. You're good at thinking on your feet and coming up with creative ways to use magic that no one has ever tried before."

"I guess I don't know what other wizards have done before, so I just try what makes sense to me," said Eynon

"Precisely," said Nûd. "You don't know how it's always been done, so you just do it—your way." Nûd stretched against his flying harness. "The last wizard with close to your raw potential was Damon himself, and he ended up as master mage of Dâron."

"Stop teasing," said Eynon. "I'm just a novice."

"A novice who scared the Bifurlanders into calling off their attack."

"But we *paid* them to do that," said Eynon.

"That fifty pounds of gold wasn't going to be enough for them to give up on sacking Brendinas until you threw your fireball," said Nûd.

"Damon has ten times the knowledge of wizardry I do," protested Eynon from the other side of Rocky's back. "Maybe a hundred times more."

"Maybe so," said Nûd, "but Damon's getting old. He's got the knowledge, but you have the raw power—and with Fercha's magestone in addition to your own, you have plenty of knowledge, too. That's an impressive combination."

"I don't *feel* impressive," said Eynon.

"If we weren't strapped in, I'd hug you," said Nûd. "You're *not* full of yourself. You're not arrogant. Do you know how rare that is among wizards?"

"No," said Eynon.

"Don't ever change, my friend," said Nûd. "Stay true to yourself." Nûd paused and stared down, then shouted, "Look, there are the hot springs!"

"Down, Rocky!" exclaimed Eynon. He'd seen the glint of water and flashes of color, too. He sent the tasty ball of magic downward and the wyvern followed.

"Good boy," said Nûd, encouraging the great beast.

"Where should we land?" asked Eynon. "I don't want Rocky to fall into a hot spring or mud pot by accident."

"Bring him down at the top of the hill," said Nûd. "We can send him off to hunt and take your flying disk the rest of the way."

"Good idea," said Eynon. Moments later, Rocky touched down at the specified landing site. Nûd and Eynon dismounted. Chee woke up and jumped to Eynon's shoulder.

"Blast," said Eynon as he unstrapped his flying disk and stepped on to it. "I forgot to pick up bags for collecting the magestone fragments."

"Hang on," said Nûd. He returned to Rocky and rummaged in the gear they'd reorganized after the Bifurland dragonriders had given Rocky his beautiful new gold-painted leather harnesses. "Here they are," said Nûd triumphantly. "The last two pillowcases."

"You mean we didn't use all of them for carrying gold?" asked Eynon.

"No," said Nûd. "I was saving these and didn't really want to use them. They're mine, and were embroidered by my great-grandmother."

Eynon looked at the design stitched along the hem at the open end of the pillowcases. It was dark-blue Dâron dragons alternating with gold crowns. "They're pretty," Eynon offered. "I can see why you don't want to get them dirty with chunks of magestones."

"Don't worry," said Nûd. "I'm sure my great-grandmother would tell me to use them. It's in a good cause."

"Your great-grandmother sounds like a wise woman," said Eynon.

"She's that," said Nûd. "And a lot more."

Nûd patted Rocky's neck. "Go get something to eat, boy," he said. "But don't spook the wisent herds."

Eynon looked at Nûd and winked. From everything they'd seen, the wyvern was a judicious hunter. He'd find a pronghorn or flathorn or some other large mammal for a late dinner. He hadn't had anything to eat since the pair of goats he'd consumed on the Bifurland flagship this afternoon—*and a sturgeon,* Eynon remembered.

Rocky launched himself skyward and circled up to hunt, his eyes already adapted to nocturnal searches for prey, while Nûd climbed on Eynon's flying disk and the two of them, with Nûd carrying a pair of pillow cases, skimmed down the snow-dusted slope into the basin.

"Watch out for basilisks," said Nûd.

"Speaking of basilisks," said Eynon. "Why didn't you warn me about them before I set off to find my magestone initially?"

"Damon wouldn't let me," said Nûd.

"More of his character building?"

"I think it was more like destructive testing," said Nûd. "Any would-be apprentice who couldn't make it back alive wasn't true wizard material."

"That's a callous approach to teaching," said Eynon. "How many apprentices never came back?"

"About one in five," said Nûd. "I thought it was cruel, but I was overruled. Damon said any would-be wizard stupid enough to be petrified by a basilisk didn't deserve to be a wizard."

"He let the basilisks kill them?" asked Eynon.

"I didn't say *kill,* I said *petrify,*" noted Nûd. "Damon would turn failed candidates from stone back to flesh, then send them through the nearest gate to Brendinas or Tyford."

"We'll have to be extra-careful around the basilisks then," said Eynon.

"Because Damon is busy with the royal army?" asked Nûd. "Fercha might unpetrify you as a favor to me, but I wouldn't count on it."

"I'll keep that in mind," said Eynon. "I'm going to put us down on the far edge of the circle around the big geyser. It's close to a field of mud pots, but there are mud pots all over the basin. I remember sensing something that must have been magestone fragments near there, but I was too inexperienced and too worried about basilisks to know what I was detecting."

Nûd stepped off Eynon's flying disk first.

"How will I know which stones are magestone fragments when I see them?" asked Nûd.

"That's right. I'm sorry. You can't sense them like I can," said Eynon. "Let me think."

Eynon tried the solidified sound lenses that helped him see at night and far away, but neither of those helped. Then he tried varying the quality of the light from the glowing sphere above his head. He made a similar sphere for Nûd.

At one point as he shifted across the spectrum he saw a flash on the ground beyond the glazed circle around the geyser. He tuned back to focus on that style of light and increased the sphere's altitude and brightness. Thousands of tiny fragments glittered blue, green, purple and gold near the closest hot spring.

"That will help," said Nûd as his glowing sphere matched Eynon's.

"Glad to be of service," said Eynon.

Then they both heard a slapping sound, like a sandal flapping against mud. Chee started a frantic chorus of *chee-chee-chee-chee* next to Eynon's ear.

"Uh oh," said Nûd. "We've got company. Don't look directly at them."

Basilisks! thought Eynon. *One basilisk, anyway. Where there was one, there would be more.* He threw up a hemisphere of translucent solidified sound between them and the slapping sounds.

"Any great ideas?" asked Nûd. "It won't be easy to gather magestone fragments while we're dodging basilisks."

"Hmmm..." said Eynon. "Basilisks eat us—I wonder what eats basilisks?"

"Nothing we'd like to meet in the dark, that's for sure," said Nûd. "I don't think Rocky would eat them. They can't taste very good living in all that sulphurous muck. It's too bad we can't just lock them in their mud pots somehow."

"Thanks for the great idea," said Eynon. "My red magestone is great at *generating* heat. I wonder how good it is at absorbing it."

"Oh!" said Nûd. "That could work. I'll keep an eye on the one that's out. Why did I leave my crossbow on Rocky's back?"

"Because you knew you'd need both hands to gather magestone fragments," said Eynon. "Let's get back on my flying disk so we don't have to worry about the basilisk that's stalking us."

"I'm in favor of that," said Nûd.

He stepped onto the disk and waited for Eynon to join him. Soon they were twenty feet above the circle of hard white ground around the geyser. Eynon shifted the translucent hemisphere of solidified sound to track below them so they didn't catch the gaze of the lone basilisk inadvertently.

"Nudge me if you think I'm taking *too much* heat away," said Eynon. "I want to slow down the basilisks who want to eat us, not kill them all. They must have some role in the natural order in this basin and I don't want to upset it."

"Most wizards wouldn't care," said Nûd.

"I guess I'm not most wizards," Eynon replied with a smile.

Nûd grinned, but Eynon couldn't see him. Their flying disk had drifted to the center of the hard-crusted white surface around the geyser, above a small tower of rock. Eynon looked past the translucent sphere to the field of mud pots and consulted his blue magestone, then drew on the power of his red stone to suck heat out of the top layers of the mud. In seconds, the mud pots stopped bubbling. Then they crusted over and a rime of white, like frozen dew, formed on the surface.

"You can stop now," said Nûd, tapping Eynon's shoulder. "That should do it."

"Right," said Eynon. He shook his head, clearing his mind of the magic he'd just worked.

The events of the next five seconds did even more to clear his mind, replacing coherent thought with panic. Removing heat from the field of mud pots had triggered the geyser. A huge jet of boiling, mineral-laden water shot up from the tower of rock and caught the bottom of Eynon's flying disk, sending it a hundred feet higher. Nûd was caught off-balance and fell to his knees, though he managed to grab Eynon's shins before he fell off. Then Eynon slipped through Nûd's arms and was gone.

"Eynon!" shouted Nûd. But Eynon wasn't there. A gryffon twice the size of a wisent had Eynon's backpack in his talons and was carrying him north beyond the basin. Nûd didn't have time for more than a glance skyward, however. It took all his skill to keep the flying disk balanced atop the geyser's jet and not fall to his death. It was a long way down.

Chapter 52

Doethan

"Come no further!" shouted a wizard from the darkness as Doethan flew close to the royal army's encampment. "Friend or foe?"

"If I were a foe, would I tell you?" asked Doethan. "What kind of challenge is that? If I were trying to sneak into camp, would I have a light over my head announcing my presence?"

"Doethan, good to see you!" said Inthíra from her flying disk. She triggered a glowing sphere above her head now that remaining hidden was no longer necessary. "It sounded like a good challenge, but now that you mention it, any foe would just lie. I'd thought it was you when I saw you, but was sure when I heard your voice."

"That's how I knew it was you, too," said Doethan as he brought his flying disk alongside Inthíra's. "You need to implement a system of passwords. We can worry about that later, if the kingdom survives the day."

"Always the optimist," said Inthíra.

"I didn't say I thought Dâron *wouldn't* survive," said Doethan, "but if it doesn't, passwords will be the least of our worries."

"Always wise, too," Inthíra responded. "I assume you're here to see King Dârio and Master Mage Ealdamon? I can take you to them."

"Duke Háiddon, too," said Doethan "I'll need help from his people who know the land west of the Tamloch army's encampment. I'll also need your help, plus assistance from other trusted members of the Conclave."

"Follow me down," said Inthíra. "I'll get you to the headquarters tent. Everyone you want to talk to is there."

"Be sure to send up another wizard to look for spies," said Doethan.

"Always responsible too, my friend," said Inthíra. "I will." She turned her head so Doethan wouldn't see her smile.

* * * * *

"That's quite clever," said Duke Háiddon after Doethan explained why he needed assistance. "Quite devious, too. It sounds like something *you'd* come up with, Ealdamon. Are you sure this wasn't your idea?"

"Quite sure," said Damon. "My new apprentice came up with it all on his own."

"He claims Nûd gave him the idea, Your Grace," said Doethan. "The particular solution he selected is all on Eynon."

"I'm looking forward to meeting this young man with a red magestone," said Duke Háiddon. "And that other fellow who inspired him. Nûd, you said his name was, Master Mage? Who is *he?*"

"My servant," said Damon.

Doethan raised an eyebrow.

"My associate, really," Damon revised. "He keeps me organized."

"Another wizard in training?" asked Duke Háiddon.

"More like a close friend of the family," said Damon.

"He's not a wizard, but Damon would be lost without him," said Doethan.

"And so might the kingdom, if not for Nûd and Eynon," asserted the Duke. "Their plan is ingenious. *Confusion to the enemy!*"

"*Confusion to the enemy,*" everyone repeated.

"Where do you intend to spring the trap?" asked Dârio. "Where the Tamloch army is encamped now, or where they will form up for their attack?"

"Eynon wasn't sure, Your Majesty," said Doethan. "He said that answer was best left to people more experienced with military strategy." Doethan yawned and covered his mouth then continued. "I'd expect it best to attack them after they were formed up, but before they engaged, though I could see it either way. We're just not sure we can have everything in place before first light so we would even have the option of attacking the camp, not the ordered troops."

"What do you advise, Your Grace?" asked Dârio.

Damon smiled at the young king. He was learning.

"I second Doethan, Your Majesty," said the duke. "It will have a greater impact on their morale to hit them after they're assembled.

If we attack their camp, they'll scatter and we'll be rousting Tamloch soldiers out of farmers' barns from here to the Coombe before they're all accounted for."

"Very good," said Dârio. "Take the people and resources you require and make the necessary preparations quickly. We want this surprise to truly be a *surprise*."

"I think we can count on that," said Damon. "I wonder what Eynon will come up with *next?*"

"I'd be more worried about that if I were Túathal and Verro," said Inthíra. "How many wizards will you need?"

"Six more, in addition to the two of us," said Doethan. We could get by with two, or four, but eight is even better."

"Plus some soldiers to defend us," suggested Inthíra.

"But not too many," said Duke Háiddon. "This little project needs to rely on stealth, not force of arms."

"Of course, Your Grace," said Doethan. "A squad of archers and one with swords and shields should do nicely. Preferably ones who know the area."

"I'll inform their commanders," said Háiddon. "Let's get about it."

"How can I help with Eynon's surprise?" asked Damon.

"Oh no you don't," said Dârio. "You're not heading off over the countryside. You're sticking close to me so you can focus on *your* surprise, the one that will let the Roma legions from across the river join forces with us."

"Forgive me, Your Majesty," said Damon with a smile. "I *do* have a surprise of my own to manage, don't I?"

"Yes," said Dârio with a tone of finality. "You do."

Damon bowed to the king and smiled. Dârio raised both eyebrows while Damon turned up his palms in a gesture of acceptance. He'd be ready to freeze the Brenavon in the morning.

"Inthíra," said Duke Háiddon as that worthy wizard was about to leave with Doethan. "Redouble the patrolling wizards in the skies. We don't want to be caught out by any Tamloch trickery."

"Of course, Your Grace," said Inthíra. "We don't want to be caught unawares while we're doing the same to Tamloch."

"Remember, good duke," said Doethan. "Our sources tell us that Verro has a surprise of his own planned for us."

"More than one, probably," grumbled Damon. "We all need to stay alert and ready to cope with whatever happens."

"And there's no chance of a good night's sleep for any of us," added Duke Háiddon.

"I'll be ready when necessary" said Dârio. "It won't take me long to put on my armor when the time comes."

"Of course, Your Majesty," said the duke. "I'm counting on you to stand by me to inspire the troops."

"I intend to do more than inspire," said Dârio. "I plan to fight."

"So long as you remember you're a king, not a common soldier," said Duke Háiddon. "And keep your shield up the way I taught you."

"Yes, Your Grace. I'll remember," said Dârio. He saw that Doethan and Inthíra were still standing by the door to the headquarters tent. "Hurry, my friends," said the king. "We're counting on you!"

"As His Majesty commands," said Inthíra. She gave a quick bow and dragged Doethan out of the tent behind her.

Chapter 53

Verro

"We're clear then?" asked Verro. He was standing by a campfire, fifty feet away from the others, at a large encampment of southern Clan Landers.

"Yes," said Fox from the Mastlands. "We come in behind the Dâron royal army while you attack them from the front."

"Don't stop to pillage their encampment," Verro reminded. "There will be plenty of Dâron loot to go around when the battle's won."

"Of course," said Fox. "The Clan Landers—*we Clan Landers*—know our business, even if we don't march on command like the kings' armies. The clan chiefs want land more than loot, and that's what you've promised."

"I'll see that you get it, too," said Verro. "All the way to the Rhuthro valley."

"The barony of Upper Rhuthro and Applegarth are to be mine," Fox asserted, "and all the lands on the west bank up to Flying Frog Farms, including Mastlands."

"You shall be a Duke of the Rhuthro, if Clan Landers have such a title," said Verro. "So long as you and your forces help us crush Dâron's army."

"Just keep their wizards off our backs and we will," said Fox.

"Dâron's wizards will be busy elsewhere fighting off Bifurland raiders and Tamloch's wizards," said Verro. "They won't have time to bother you."

"Good," said Fox, tugging his pointed beard. "A pair of wizards cost two of my brothers their toes and I have a score to settle."

"You'll have to tell me that story over a beer someday," said Verro.

"If you're buying," said Fox.

"Gladly," said Verro. The Tamloch wizard stretched his long frame and regarded the smaller man.

"I have a personal question for you, if you don't mind me asking," said Verro.

"That depends on the question," said Fox.

"You just arrived in the south," said Verro. "You haven't been in the southern Clan Lands for a fortnight. Why did the chiefs appoint *you* as their go-between and spokesman?"

"There's a simple answer to that," said Fox, "and I don't mind the question." Fox looked around to ensure other Clan Landers weren't close by. Reassured, he continued. "None of the clan chiefs particularly trust each other," he said. "I'm a newcomer, with a grudge against Dâron. Choosing me meant *not* choosing one of them, which would have given the chosen chief an advantage. With me, the balance of power among the clans stays as it was."

"That makes sense," said Verro.

"There's also the small matter of the south Clan Landers' accent," said Fox. "It took me more than a week to understand what they were saying, and they figured I'd do a better job of serving as their liaison to Tamloch since you could tell I wasn't insulting your mother when I spoke."

"Lucky you," said Verro. He found the dialect of the southern Clan Lands intelligible, if he paid attention, though it could be hard to decipher when they'd been drinking.

"Not at all," said Fox with a sly grin. "It was a matter of seizing an opportunity."

"Like the chance to gain half the Rhuthro valley?" asked Verro.

"The clan chiefs don't care about the Rhuthro," said Fox. "They want the good farm lands in the Coombe."

"So long as they know the quarry to the northwest of that territory is off-limits," said Verro.

"I've told them, and they've agreed," said Fox. "The clans don't have much use for rocks—and you do. Why do *you* want rocks?"

"It's a wizards' matter," said Verro, "and not your concern if you want to be Duke of the Rhuthro."

"Alright, alright, I was just asking," said Fox. "I hope I'll find the two wizards who chopped off my brothers' toes tomorrow. I'll chop off more than their toes, you can be sure of that."

"What do these wizards look like?" asked Verro. "I'll keep an eye out for them and give you a chance at payback if I can manage it."

"That would put me in your debt if you could," said Fox. "They're both young—fifteen or sixteen. A man and a woman. He's tall and thin, with a Coombe accent. I know the woman. She's Meredith, the daughter of the baron of the Upper Rhuthro, and goes by Merry. She has auburn hair and a smart mouth—she thinks she's better than the rest of us. Rumor says she spends time with a hedge wizard named Doethan who has a tower on the Rhuthro. She might be his concubine."

"I saw them this morning," said Verro. "And I doubt she's his concubine, though she may be his apprentice."

"I don't care if she sleeps with wizards or goats, so long as I can have a few hours alone with her to teach her proper manners," Fox replied. He spat and wiped his mouth.

Verro looked away to hide his distaste. *Battles made strange bedfellows, or something like that,* he thought. *Not something for Ealdamon to add to his next book of epigrams.*

"Where did you see them?" asked Fox.

"At the quarry near the Coombe at first light," said Verro.

Fox's eyes lit up with anticipation. He rubbed his palms together in excitement.

"They're not there now," said Verro. "Given their traveling companions, I expect you'll find them with the Dâron royal army in the morning."

"I hope you're right," said Fox. "You'll make sure I get them if they're taken captive?"

"I will," said Verro, though he resolved he'd tell Fox he found their bodies dead on the field before giving them to this repulsive little man.

"That would be worth a tun of Applegarth cider once I'm the Duke of the Rhuthro," said Fox. "That's the best cider in Dâron."

"I've heard," said Verro. "Just have your new *associates* armed, massed and ready to run through the gate as soon as I trigger it. Make sure they run *through* Dâron's encampment and attack their army."

"So you've said," said Fox. He looked around for listeners again before he spoke. "I can understand why you keep telling me. I have to keep telling the clan chiefs as well. They follow their own minds in almost everything. It's like herding wildcats."

"Do *you* think they'll follow my instructions?" asked Verro.

"Yes, yes, I'm sure they will," said Fox. "You've kept them simple enough. Through the gate, don't stop to loot the encampment, hit the Dâron army. I think they can manage it."

"I'll hold you to it," said Verro.

"And I'll hold you to my prisoners and dukedom," said Fox.

"See you at dawn, then," said Verro.

He stepped out of range of the firelight, mounted his flying disk, and flew up to vanish into a near-invisible gate, black against the black sky.

Chapter 54

Nûd

Thank goodness I've had so much practice riding flying disks with Damon, thought Nûd. He felt like a child tipping on a board placed across a log, trying not to lose his balance. Nûd didn't dare look down—it would distract him from staying atop the flying disk and remind him how far it was to the basin's floor—and the waiting basilisk.

"Eynon!" Nûd shouted again. There wasn't an answer, but he nearly fell off when he was surprised by a pair of small arms grabbing his leg. Chee must have jumped down from Eynon's shoulder when the gryffon captured his friend. Nûd heard soft, nervous chirps of *chee-chee-chee* below him and spared a few seconds of attention to say, "Hang on, little buddy, and don't move." He didn't receive a response, but the raconette's arms squeezed his leg tighter.

Nûd made his stance wider and that gave him more control as the geyser's jet began to weaken. Now they were only eighty feet above ground, then fifty. *Thank goodness Eynon's glow sphere is still above my head,* thought Nûd. *I'd hate to deal with a hungry basilisk in the dark. Damon would tell me it builds character,* Nûd considered. *Maybe Damon should be balancing on a flying disk above a geyser!*

The flying disk continued to descend as the flow from the geyser diminished. Nûd had figured out how to control the disk and could spare a few seconds to think on what would happen when he touched down. *The basilisk will charge,* Nûd decided. He'd seen them take down a flathorn who'd had the misfortune to enter the basin when he'd been repairing the railing by the steps leading down the hillside. It hadn't been pretty. *At least there's only one of them to deal with,* he considered.

What are my resources? Nûd asked himself. *A flying disk that I can't make fly. A frightened raconette. The clothes on my back. My belt knife. And two embroidered pillowcases from my great-grandmother to guilt me into remembering I'm the rightful king of Dâron. Blast! Maybe it would be better just to let the basilisk eat me.*

No, Nûd determined. *I'm not ready to die even if I'm not planning to take the throne. Dârio is welcome to it. I have too many things to learn ahead of me.*

The geyser's flow sputtered out, flinging water left and right like a wet dog shaking. For a few heartbeats, the flying disk balanced on the lip of the geyser's tower, then it tipped over away from the mud pots and the basilisk. Nûd rode it down like a sled on a steep slope, keeping the tower between himself and the mud-covered monster.

Don't look at it. Don't look at it. Don't look at it. Nûd repeated the words softly. He tucked the pillowcases into his belt and rubbed Chee's head, giving the small creature a reassurance he didn't feel himself. Chee climbed on his shoulder then found his way inside Nûd's jacket to hide. *Just as well,* Nûd realized. *Now the raconette wouldn't be petrified by the basilisk's gaze.*

Nûd held the flying disk in front of him by the straps Eynon used to put it on his shoulders over his backpack and pulled out his eating dagger. *I wish I'd done more practicing with sword and shield and less reading about styles of combat,* thought Nûd. *It was hard enough to get Damon to give me time to practice with my crossbow.*

The surface below his feet was smooth, white and slick, like the porcelain pitcher from across the Ocean that Damon kept in a glass-fronted cabinet with a set of gold-plated serving dishes. The cabinet hadn't been opened in Nûd's memory. The area around the geyser's tower was slippery with mineralized water. Nûd strained to hear the basilisk's approach over the final fitful hisses and pops of the geyser.

A wet, slithering sound was his only warning before something heavy slammed into the flying disk and knocked Nûd on his buttocks. He skidded across the smooth surface of the white circle around the geyser until his back slammed into a rock around its periphery. He could feel the basilisk scrabbling forward, its front legs brushing his own as it drove against the reflective bottom on Eynon's flying disk.

Nûd forced his arms to keep the disk between himself and the attacking monster. It was the only thing preventing his evisceration and he could think of better ways to go. His knife was pressed flat against his stomach and he could feel Chee climb out of his jacket to escape the pressure. To Nûd's surprise, he felt the raconette's front paws pry at his fingers to get at the knife. He released his grip. Chee took the knife and escaped along Nûd's left side.

"Be careful, little buddy," he said.

I don't have a magestone, but I've got a strength of my own, thought Nûd. *I've chopped enough wood and hauled enough pronghorn carcasses to fight off a basilisk.* He flexed his forearms and turned the top edge of his makeshift shield out, forcing the basilisk's head down into the hard ground.

Nûd anchored one end of the flying disk in the mineralized surface to give him more leverage and pushed, trapping the monster's head beneath the disk. The basilisk worked its legs furiously, trying to drive past his prey's defenses, but its claws couldn't get traction on the slick coating covering the area around the geyser.

The rock behind Nûd wasn't going anywhere, no matter how hard the basilisk struggled. From the other side of the flying disk, Nûd heard a triumphant cry of *chee-chee-chee-CHEE,* then the basilisk stopped pushing and gave only a few more scratches with its front claws before ceasing to move. He sat up straight and peered over the top edge of the flying disk. Chee had stuck Nûd's eating dagger in behind the basilisk's skull, severing its spinal chord.

The raconette was dancing on the basilisk's back, looking quite proud of himself. *Chee?* he asked.

"*Chee-chee-CHEE!*" Nûd replied, hoping his tone would convey his appreciation. He picked up Eynon's familiar and stroked his fur until the raconette was humming with pleasure. "Thank you, little fella," he said. "I'll get you a bag full of dried cherries as soon as I can."

"Chee," said the raconette softly.

With a struggle, Nûd twisted his body out from under the shield and basilisk and stood. Chee climbed on his shoulder and stroked his hair, imitating what Nûd had done to the raconette.

Nûd removed his eating dagger from the basilisk and observed the beast's dark blood with distaste. He wiped the knife on some moss that must have been shaded by the rock behind him and reluctantly put it back in his belt. He promised himself he wouldn't use it to eat with in the future.

Chee jumped down to the top of the rock to explore on his own while Nûd considered what to do next. His heart wanted to follow the gryffon and rescue Eynon, but he didn't have any way to fly now, at least not until Rocky returned. There was no telling when the wyvern would come back. His head said Eynon would escape the gryffon on his own and make his way back, flying disk or not, and the most important thing was to collect magestone fragments now, so they wouldn't lose any time. Eynon's surprise for Tamloch depended on it.

Reluctantly, Nûd pulled a pillowcase from his belt and left the smooth ground around the geyser. When he reached the space near a hot spring, he bent to pick up glowing stones. Chee scampered over, begged for the other pillowcase, and joined him.

Chapter 55

Eynon

Eynon woke when he fell on a thick mat of grass and leaves lining the gryffon's nest, though he didn't realize where he was at first. Then he saw three hungry chicks with eagle's heads and lion's bodies pecking at his boots, trying to determine how edible he'd be and jockeying to see who would take the first bite. He pulled in his feet and tried to stand up but couldn't. A large claw belonging to momma or papa gryphon pressed down on his head. Chee was nowhere to be seen. Eynon hoped he hadn't been an appetizer.

"No thank you, I don't care to stay for dinner," said Eynon. "I'm even less interested in *being* dinner."

One of the gryffonlets growled like a big cat while another screamed like a hunting raptor. Neither sound was particularly reassuring, though Eynon had always assumed gryffons only made calls like eagles, because their heads were avian.

Stop thinking about gryffons' vocalizations and start thinking how not to be eaten, Eynon told himself.

He crafted a shield of solidified sound around his body and gently expanded it to push the chicks over to the other side of the nest and force the big gryffon's claw away from his head. When he looked more closely, he realized the chicks weren't really chicks any longer. The were fully fledged and of a size that seemed ready to fly off on their own, at least if they were anything like the seed-eaters and songbirds Eynon was familiar with from back in the Coombe. *Perhaps I'm the last meal they'll be offered by their parent,* Eynon considered.

The big gryffon was a momma bird, Eynon decided. Male gryffons had tawny feathers near their shoulders like male lions' manes, at least according to the pictures he'd seen in Robin Goodfellow's *Peregrinations.* The feathers on this gryffon's head were white all the way down.

The chicks still looked at him like he was lunch, or breakfast, given the darkness and the early hour, while the momma gryffon eyed him warily, ready to strike if he made a move to harm her off-spring. Eynon laughed with a sudden realization, and the big bird took a step backward. "Now I know what eats basilisks," he said. "You do."

The gryffons, young and old, stared at him. Then the biggest chick pounced and knocked Eynon over, back into the vegetation that padded the nest's interior. The chick pecked at Eynon's head with his beak and was joined by the other two, holding down his arms with their forepaws and turning their heads to strike at his neck. If Eynon hadn't had his shields in place, he'd be dead.

Pushing his shields away from his body, Eynon was able to make enough space for him to stand again. He tried a trick that had kept Rocky entertained and hoped it would distract the gryffons. He generated seven balls of solidified sound, each in a different color, and sent them spinning in intricate, hypnotic patterns. The momma gryffon was entranced, but the chicks pounced on him again and rebounded against his shields. Eynon realized he needed to escape the nest before he could decide what to do next.

He looked over the side of the nest to see where he was, but the only thing that confirmed was that it was dark all around him. He made the glowing sphere above his head larger and brighter and saw the nest was built on a shelf of rock sticking out three-quarters of the way up the side of a cliff in the mountains north of the basin. He saw dim light from fumaroles in the distance and hoped one of them belonged to the glow ball above Nûd's head.

The momma gryffon and her chicks had backed away from the brighter light, so Eynon transformed his shield into a hemisphere that took up half the surface of the nest and gave him room to move around. A few bones from what Eynon supposed were basilisks crunched beneath his feet. It would be a challenge to get down from here without his flying disk. He didn't have time to try making his way along the cliff face. He didn't have the skill to attempt it, either.

Eynon stretched his shoulders and rubbed his head where the momma gryffon had stunned him with her balled claw on her initial dive. He'd have to see if he could get some willow bark back at the castle if they had time, or maybe Merry had learned something about reducing pain from Doethan that would help. He took off his pack to see if anything he'd stored inside could help him.

Once the pack was on the bottom of the nest, Eynon saw the solution to his problem—the large shard of unknown material he'd found by the fireball-blasted oak the first day of his wander year was strapped across it. *It's part of a shattered flying disk,* he realized. *Maybe it's enough to fly me down.*

The shard was wide at one end and narrow at the other, like swords he'd seen pirates use on an illustration in *Peregrinations.* Handling it carefully, because of its sharp edges, Eynon put one foot on an angle across the wide part at the front and the other in line at the back. Part of the sole of his boot was over the sides of the shard, but he hoped it would be enough to support him. Using the same channeling of his mind and his magestones he used on his unbroken flying disk, he willed the shard into the air. To Eynon's pleasure and surprise, it rose.

Eynon eased himself up and over the side of the nest and tipped the shard down at an angle toward the distant lights, like one of his uncles strapping long boards to his feet to slide on snow-covered mountains. It was something his relative had heard the Bifurlanders did. *Thank goodness the baron's hedge wizard had been in the vicinity to set his uncle's leg.*

After leveling out a hundred feet above the treetops, Eynon heard screeches and growls behind him. He carefully turned his head and saw all four gryffons chasing him. Momma could have caught him, but she was apparently teaching her chicks how to hunt. Eynon centered his body and modified his shield of solidified sound until it formed a vertical wedge-shape around him. Air flowing around the wedge pushed on him evenly from both sides and kept his flight stable, despite the inherent wobbliness of the shard's geometry.

Stability was impermanent, however, once chicks began to batter at his shields from all directions. Their screeches and growls grew louder, overpowering the wind noise of his passage. *If I was as good at manipulating tight light force beams as Merry, I could push the gryffons away without hurting them,* thought Eynon.

A particularly bright light sparkled below and to the right. Eynon shifted his balance and twisted his feet while trying to dodge more gryffon chick attacks and headed toward it. *Wait,* he thought. *I don't want to bring hungry gryffons close to Nûd.* Unfortunately, the shard's downward course didn't give him many options. It was barely steerable even with the wedge of solidified sound in place around Eynon.

Luckily, Eynon didn't have to worry about protecting Nûd from the gryffons, too. Rocky, drawn by the gryffons' hunting cries, came hurtling down out of the dark sky, scattering them like hens running from a fox in a barnyard. The momma gryffon screamed at Rocky, but chose to follow her chicks instead of give battle.

Eynon made an ungraceful landing on the circle of slick white ground around the geyser, almost colliding with the near-invisible dead basilisk as he did. Rocky landed gracefully beside him. The wyvern sniffed at the dead basilisk, but turned up his nose in disgust.

"It's about time you got back," said Nûd from the field of sparkling magestone fragments.

"Chee!" shouted Chee from a few feet away.

"You're alive," said Eynon. "Thank goodness!"

"I didn't know you cared," said Nûd with a grin.

"Not you," said Eynon. "I was talking to Chee."

"Chee," the raconette repeated.

"In that case," said Nûd, "I won't tell you we've filled two pillowcases with magestone fragments."

"Be that way," teased Eynon.

"Good," said Nûd.

"Fine," said Eynon.

"Chee," said Chee.

"Let's get these to Fercha right away," said Nûd, holding up the bulging pillowcases.

"Great idea," said Eynon, waving at Rocky and retrieving his flying disk. "Mount up!"

The wyvern roared at the retreating gryffons and waited eagerly for Nûd and Chee and Eynon to climb on.

"Who's a good boy?" asked Nûd. The wyvern made a happy rumble deep in his chest.

"Go find Fercha and Merry," Nûd added. "Find them, boy. Find them fast."

Rocky launched himself into the sky and set his own course southeast, his wings beating fiercely.

Eynon would send up a glowing red sphere when they got closer. He knew Merry would answer.

Chapter 56

Doethan

"Fercha says to tell you that your end of the gate needs to be a hundred yards wide," said Merry from inside the golden hoop of a communications ring she'd borrowed from Fercha. Fercha recited more measurements. "And thirty feet high," relayed Merry.

"Got it," said Doethan quietly. "We'll be ready."

"Thanks," said Merry. "We're almost done here."

"Inthíra thinks we'll need another half an hour at this end, once the pole is sunk, and that should only take a few minutes," whispered Doethan. "We had to wait until you gave us the dimensions."

"You're just west of where Tamloch's army will assemble in formation?" asked Merry.

"Yes, that was the plan. Duke Háiddon has soldiers who know the territory. They selected a great spot," said Doethan.

"You'll keep us *posted* as soon as the pole is sunk and your side is ready?" asked Merry.

Doethan ignored Merry's pun. "We'll be ready before sunrise," he said. "Remember, you'll need to trigger the surprise at your end well *before* dawn. Melyncárreg is far to the west of this end of the gate. It will take several more hours for the sun to get there."

"I remember my geography lessons," teased Merry. "Imagine a fly walking around the middle of an apple..."

"Good," said Doethan. "You always did pay attention to your tutors—even me."

"Especially you," said Merry. "You were teaching me wizardry."

"Until you left me for Fercha," said Doethan.

Merry stuck her tongue out at Doethan from the other side of the interface.

"You could have her back if you want," came Fercha's muffled voice.

"Hey," said Merry. "I'm pleased to have you both as mentors. Now I have to get back to touching up spots I missed on a couple of spear-pines."

"Good luck," said Doethan.

"You, too," said Merry. "See you in the morning."

The interface went dark and Doethan closed the hoop back into a small gold ring. He reminded himself to teach Merry how to make communications rings of her own once they'd dealt with the current unpleasantness. *Who am I kidding?* he asked himself. *The more relevant question is if both of us survive.*

Two of Inthíra's friends had crushed the blue magestone fragments Doethan had found at the quarry near the Dormant Dragon. Doethan promised himself to consult the royal library to see if he could learn when and why the quarry had been abandoned. It could be as simple as them excavating down to the water table, but that didn't match up with Doethan's observations—*in the dark*, he told himself. He'd investigate later.

Doethan hadn't given Inthíra's friends every stone or fragment he'd brought north. One of the little girls or their mothers had discovered a blue rock so big he could barely hold it comfortably in one hand. He'd found it at the bottom of one of their sacks and could feel that it contained a magestone—a sizable one. Doethan wedged the rock into his pouch and promised himself he'd analyze it later, when it wasn't so dark and he'd had more sleep.

Inthíra and four other wizards she'd recruited had generated lenses to help everyone on their team see despite the lack of light. He'd come along because he could connect with the wizards on the other side of the gate. He'd told Inthíra the details of Eynon's plan, but the rest of the wizards and soldiers didn't know what was in store for Tamloch's army. It was better that way, in case any of them were captured.

Eynon's surprise wasn't unprecedented, Doethan considered. He'd read about the tactic being used on a smaller scale in battles across the Ocean, but doubted Eynon had ever read the obscure texts Doethan had discovered that recounted its use. The Athicans hadn't used it during their legendary conflict with the ancestors of the Roma, though they had pulled off a major deception involving a large wooden horse.

Deception wasn't Eynon's style, though. His surprise was more straightforward. If the timing worked, it would be a thing of beauty to watch unfold.

Damon still had a part to play in all this, too. Doethan had been with the royal guards when Damon froze the Abbenoth. The Master Mage had been at the peak of his power then and the river was wide. Doethan still marveled at how Damon had frozen a bridge two hundred feet wide, eight feet thick, and four hundred and fifty feet long. Doethan and his comrades had marched across it quickly, before the legionnaires could muster to meet them. There were stories about Ealdamon collapsing after the effort. Years later, Doethan had never asked Damon what it took out of him to work that wizardry.

Someone touched Doethan's shoulder. It was Inthíra. He turned to face her as she pointed and whispered.

"What do you think about the placement of the second pole," she said. "Is the angle right?"

Doethan saw a small circle of light as round as a pie plate nearby, projected by one of the other wizards.

"That should be fine," he said. "It's not like we're aiming a crossbow. A few degrees this way or that won't matter."

"True," said Inthíra. "I thought I'd ask just in case."

"The most important thing is that the pole is sturdy and well-secured," Doethan noted. "We'll want to protect the inner surface of the poles with shields, too, if your friends can stay nearby?"

"They'll stay," said Inthíra. "When this is triggered, it should keep our kingdom's casualties to a minimum."

"We can hope," said Doethan. He spared a moment to worry about the rumors of *Verro's* surprise. *What would he do if he were Tamloch's Master Mage to cause the most damage to Dâron?*

He looked southeast, beyond the fires of the Dâron army's encampment.

Fercha knows Verro's mind better than I do, Doethan decided. *I'll ask her advice when Merry contacts me again. Better yet, Fercha could join me on this side.*

"Do you have enough wizards to spare that you could fly a few through to the other side of the gate when it opens?" he asked Inthíra.

"I should," said Inthíra. "I brought eight, plus the two of us. What are you thinking?"

"I'm thinking having Fercha on our side would be a nice insurance policy," Doethan replied.

"Having Fercha on your side is *always* a plus," said Inthíra. "I'll make the arrangements."

Chapter 57

Túathal and Verro

Túathal sensed the change in air pressure when Verro gated into his sleeping chamber. He'd been asleep for three hours and felt recharged and ready for what was to come.

"Everything is in place, brother?" asked the king.

"It is," said Verro.

"No surprises?"

"Only for Dâron," Verro replied.

"Good," said Túathal. "Any word about their Master Mage?"

"Ealdamon hasn't been seen in more than twenty years, brother. None of the rest of Dâron's Conclave can work wizardry on his scale."

"Excellent," said the king.

Túathal had been sleeping in his clothes and sat up, stretching his muscles and rotating his shoulders.

"The legions are still on the east bank?"

"They are," said Verro. "And the Bifurland fleet control the river. The Roma won't be crossing."

"Excellent," said Túathal. "When did you last speak with King Bjarni?"

"At noon yesterday," said Verro. "I could see how eager he was to sack Brendinas."

"Not that we'd let him pillage our new southern capital..." said Túathal, his voice trailing off.

Verro smiled.

"You don't think the legions' arrival will change his mind?" asked the king.

"If anything, that will make him *more* eager to fight," said Verro. "King Bjarni has never tested his troops against the legions."

"Perhaps we can encourage him to land his warriors on the eastern shore..." said Túathal.

"...and kill two foes with one bolt," Verro completed.

"Please," said Túathal. "The King of Bifurland is our ally."

"Of course," said Verro, giving his brother a mocking nod.

"Still," said Túathal, "send a wizard to the fleet to confirm the Bifurlanders are ready to do their part. They're like children who decide to chase butterflies instead of doing what they're told."

"I'd have said battle-axes rather than butterflies, but I know your meaning," said Verro. He gave his brother a hand to help Túathal to his feet. "I'll send one now."

Verro turned to leave, but Túathal caught his arm.

"Don't send that dark-haired mage you've got managing my food and wards and privacy spheres," said Túathal. "She doesn't say much, but I love to bait her. She frowns at me when she thinks I can't see her."

"Uirsé is one of my best," said Verro. "And you must know your moral compass hasn't pointed true north since you were born. Of course she frowns at you. Half the time *I* frown at you and your methods."

"Small disagreements within the family only, of course," said Túathal.

"Sometimes not so small," said Verro, staring hard at his brother.

"Trivialities," said Túathal.

Verro shook his head.

"Maybe if you'd treat my wizards with respect instead of abusing them, you'd get better service from them," he said. "No one likes being ordered about like a Bifurland thrall."

"So long as she does her job," said Túathal. "It's all for the greater glory of Tamloch."

"And Túathal," said Verro.

"As you say," said the king, extending his hands as if Verro's statement was self-evident.

"Anything more I should know, dear brother?" asked Verro.

"Princess Gwýnnett is my captive. She's in the next tent."

"My, you *have* been busy," said Verro. "How did you manage to arrange that?"

"It was Gwýnnett's idea, of a sort."

"Oh?" asked Verro.

"She suggested she should join Dârio with the army," said Túathal. "I encouraged her to stop here instead."

"Making Gwýnnett a new pawn in your long game of *shah-mat?*" asked Verro.

"She's been one for years now," said Túathal.

"Eighteen years, brother?"

"Nearly nineteen, if you go back to that part of my plan's inception," said Túathal.

"And Dârio's," said Verro.

"Yes," said Túathal, "I'll soon be able to instruct my son personally, and develop him into a worthy heir."

"Unfortunately, you have to take Princess Gwýnnett as part of the bargain," said Verro.

"For now," said Túathal.

"Watch your back," said Verro.

"And anything I eat or drink," said Túathal. "I know enough to be wary of a rattle-viper. She'll help me convince Dârio to take my compromise once we win."

"Only you would doubt that the loser would accept a compromise that makes him ruler of *two* kingdoms."

"Dârio is *my* son, he'll look for the worm in the apple."

"You'll just have to make sure he eats it anyway," said Verro. "You do *your* part. You can count on me to do mine."

"I will," said Túathal. "And let me know what the wizard you send to the fleet reports."

"I hear and obey, mighty king."

Verro departed through a personal gate.

In the darkness outside the Tamloch command tent, Salder and Uirsé embraced.

Dawn would soon arrive and much remained to be done.

Chapter 58

Melyncárreg

Chee was enthusiastically crushing multicolored magestone fragments with a rock as big as his head. Each time he brought his makeshift hammer down he said, "Chee!" The blows and sounds came faster and faster until they blurred into a *bang-bang-bang chee-chee-chee* chorus.

"Someone's having fun," said Merry.

Rocky leaned over and nudged the little raconette, who stopped crushing fragments.

"Let him enjoy himself," said Nûd, stroking the wyvern's neck. "We need the powdered magestones for the gate."

Merry moved handfuls of sparkling fragments into a pillowcase and noticed the embroidered crowns and blue dragons. She gave Nûd an odd look, then prepared to hop on her flying disk and fly to the nearest spear-pine to add more magestone powder to what she'd already glued in place.

Eynon and Fercha were twenty yards away talking to Doethan through Eynon's ring. They'd moved away from the *bang-chee* sounds so they could hear Doethan speaking.

"That would work," said Fercha. "Once the gate is up, we can trade off with the wizards Inthíra sends through. They'll just have to maintain the gates and make sure they're not damaged."

Merry couldn't hear what Doethan was saying. She supposed he must be whispering. Eynon's voice was easy to pick out, though.

"You want me, too?" said her lover. "To help Damon? Why would he need *my* help?" She saw Eynon nod. "I can do that. Just in case," he said.

Nûd spoke to Merry from his spot next to Rocky.

"The wizards are saving the world, it seems."

"I'm a wizard, too," said Merry. "And I'm certainly interested in saving the kingdom, if not the whole world."

"Of course," said Nûd. "You're one of them—and a baron's daughter. You can make a difference."

"What did I do to get on your bad side?" she asked. "You're Eynon's friend. I'd hoped you could be my friend, too. And anyone who sets their mind to it can make a difference."

"I'm sorry," said Nûd. "Forgive me. I must sound as grumpy as Damon."

"You're not even in his league yet," teased Merry.

"Thank you for that," said Nûd. "I just have a lot on my mind, trying to come to terms with something my mother told me earlier at the inn."

"Would it help to talk about it?" asked Merry.

"Probably not, but I appreciate the offer," said Nûd. "Things would be different if I'd grown up around nice, normal people, like Eynon."

"You think Eynon is *normal?*" asked Merry. She could see that Eynon and Fercha were still talking to Doethan.

Nûd laughed. "Not that way. It's clear he's an exceptionally powerful wizard. It's just that he's so *nice.* None of the people I grew up with were nice." He stopped and looked at Merry. "Are *you* nice?"

Merry grinned back. "Probably not," she said. "My parents were looking forward to having me out of their hair when I started my wander year. That should start any day now, I think. I've lost track."

"It seems like you started yours a few weeks early," said Nûd.

"Meeting Eynon started a lot of things," Merry replied.

Nûd raised an eyebrow and Merry blushed.

"I mean about having adventures and learning wizardry and such."

"I think you're nice," said Nûd. "Nice to talk with, anyway. Eynon says you like to read, too?"

"Every book I can get my hands on," said Merry.

"Me, too," said Nûd. "Did you get a chance to see the library in the castle when you were in Melyncárreg with Damon?"

"I didn't get to see much of anything except the inside of a room and a courtyard," Merry answered.

"It may be the biggest library west of the Ocean," said Nûd.

"How many of Orluin's libraries have you seen?" asked Merry.

"One," said Nûd. He smiled at Merry and she smiled back.

"Maybe I can show you around the street of the booksellers in Tyford," she said. "You and Eynon, both."

"I'd like that," said Nûd. "I wonder if there's a street full of booksellers in Brendinas, too."

"I expect there is," said Merry. "If not more than one. Is Damon really writing a second book of epigrams?"

Nûd tilted his head and rubbed under Rocky's long jaw. The wyvern yawned. So did Nûd and Merry.

"He says so," Nûd reported. "But he says a lot of things that aren't so."

"Why is Damon so grumpy and sad all the time?" asked Merry.

"Ask Fercha," said Nûd. "It's her fault."

"What do you mean?"

"She wanted to go back to court after I was born and Damon wouldn't permit it."

"I'll bet that went over well," said Merry.

"Like a hedgehog on a royal throne," said Nûd. "She went to court anyway, and Damon's been permanently out of sorts ever since."

"Damon must have been rough on Fercha during her training," said Merry. "Especially if he thought he could boss her around like that."

"It's more complicated than that, but you're right," said Nûd.

"He's the famed Master Mage who froze the Abbenoth," said Merry. "I don't expect he'd be easy to live with. Not like Eynon."

"Nobody is like Eynon," said Nûd.

"True," said Merry. *"Very* true."

Chee let out a particularly long string of bangs and commentary. Rocky leaned down to nudge him with his snout again. Nûd didn't try to stop him.

"That's pretty embroidery on that pillowcase," said Merry. "Is it yours?"

"Uh huh," said Nûd, reluctantly. "Damon told me my great-grandmother made it for me."

Merry remembered Queen Carys doing embroidery during her meeting back in the palace. It seemed like that had been ages ago, but it was only this morning. She looked at Nûd with appraising eyes. Nûd noticed.

"What?" he said.

"Nothing," said Merry. "You'll tell me if you want to tell me."

Nûd shook his head, slowly. "I'm not even sure I want to tell myself."

"You're one of Crown Prince Dâri's bastards?"

A wide grin spread across Nûd's face. "If only," he said. "I don't think he had any."

Nûd waved toward Eynon and Fercha. "Looks like they're almost done. You'd better finish your touch-up work with glue and magestone fragments before Fercha gets back."

"Right," said Merry. "Later."

Nûd watched her ascend and went back to rubbing Rocky's jaw. The big wyvern rumbled his contentment. Nûd wished he could share the feeling.

Chapter 59

Háiddon

Duke Háiddon had managed to sleep for a few hours before an aide woke him up near dawn. He dressed in his gambeson—the padded garment that went under his armor would be sufficient until it was time to don his full kit. It was a cool and foggy morning with frost just beginning to melt off the grass between the pavilions. He saw a lamp was burning inside the young king's tent and expected that Dârio was feeling the full weight of his crown as the royal army prepared to take the field in a few hours.

Several soldiers were up and about. The duke stopped at a nearby campfire to encourage them and wish them well. Morale was critically important for any army, and this one hadn't been tested, except for skirmishes with Clan Landers on the western borders and occasional disputes with Tamloch's garrisons at the forts near the great falls to the northwest. Háiddon was pleased that the soldiers seemed confident and ready to fight for crown and kingdom. Dârio's false reputation as a petulant and juvenile womanizer didn't seem to affect his standing with the troops.

The duke wished he felt as confident about his own performance as the soldiers seemed about the fight ahead. He reviewed the disposition of his troops for the upcoming battle. His heavy cavalry—knights in service to nobles and the crown—would be in the center, surrounded by his most-experienced infantry. Lighter troops with longbows and crossbows would be positioned behind the massed infantry, while less experienced local levies, supported by light cavalry, would make up the army's left and right flanks. He planned to have a contingent of wizards stay near the king and the army's commanders near the van, while other wizards would fly above the army, ready to attack or defend as necessary.

"Are we going to smash 'em, Your Grace?" asked a well-muscled woman sharpening a sword.

"That's the general idea," said the duke.

"Is it true there are Roma legions on the east bank? Are they with us or with Tamloch?" asked a man with a scarred nose. He was eating cooked oats from a small bowl. Behind him, a third soldier was stirring something—probably oats—in an iron pot with a long wooden spoon.

Duke Háiddon laughed. "You'll just have to count on me knowing how to give us every possible advantage," he said. He rubbed his padded arm and smiled, then raised an eyebrow. "I've got a few tricks up my sleeve to make Tamloch's troops miserable."

"I'll bet you do," said the well-muscled woman, putting extra effort into the strokes of her oiled whetstone.

"I've heard the young king will be fighting with us," said the man with the scarred nose.

"I'm trying to keep him from being the first to hit Tamloch's shieldwall," said Duke Háiddon.

"You're a wise man," said the well-muscled woman. "It wouldn't do for the kingdom to lose its king in the first five minutes of battle."

"Especially without a designated heir," added scarred-nose.

"I'll call for you if King Dârio proves to be too stubborn for his own good," said the duke.

"Did I hear my name?" came a familiar voice. Duke Háiddon saw King Dârio and the duke's dark-haired oldest daughter, Jenet, standing behind the soldiers at the campfire.

"Your Majesty," said the scarred-nose man without rising. He held up his bowl. "Would you and the lady care for some oatmeal?"

The king and Jenet were wearing thick robes over long night-shirts. Both looked tousled, which earned them smiles from the soldiers. Dârio offered a small earthenware crock to the man with the scarred nose.

"Oatmeal sounds good," said the king.

"It will be even better with this honey," said the soldier, accepting the crock. "Some for you, too, m'lady?"

"I'd appreciate it," said Jenet, "So long as my father remembers to eat breakfast as well."

"Your father, m'lady?" asked scarred-nose.

"She means me," said Duke Háiddon. He reached into his pouch and removed a small bag of raisins which he offered to scarred-nose. "These should help you stretch your breakfast."

"Don't be a fool and lead the first charge, Your Majesty," said the well-muscled woman. "Wait for the second or third engagement."

"That's good advice," Dârio replied.

"And you may want to wait until you've put on your armor," added scarred-nose.

Jenet laughed and bowed to the soldiers, flashing a smile at each of them.

"With the two of you to advise our king, the kingdom is in good hands," she said, then turned to Dârio. "If the king is wise enough to listen."

"I'll listen better after I've dressed and have breakfast," said Dârio.

"Did someone mention breakfast?" said Damon as the old wizard came into the firelight. He was wearing a long nightshirt, like Dârio's. In fact, it was one of Dârio's, borrowed from the king's supply of extra garments. He didn't wear a robe and his body seemed to glow from the heat field he'd placed around him.

The soldier stirring the pot filled four bowls with cooked oats and handed them to Dârio, Jenet, Damon and the duke. Scarred-nose came by to add raisins and honey to each bowl. The well-muscled woman put her sword down on a rock and distributed spoons to the newcomers. After that was done, she found four two-foot lengths of tree-trunk and placed them near the fire for their visitors to sit on.

Dârio turned to Damon. "I'm glad you're up. You need to be in position by the river before dawn. Wear that fancy robe, if you can. It's impressive."

"Good morning to you, too, Your Majesty," said Damon. "I know my job. Don't teach your grandmother how to bake pies."

Dârio was about to offer a sharp reply, but Jenet touched his arm and he spooned up sweetened oatmeal instead.

"I don't think my grandmother ever baked a pie," mused the young king. "Neither did my great-grandmother."

"I can bake pies," offered Jenet. "Both fruit pies *and* meat pies."

"Wait until you try the chicken and egg pies from the Dormant Dragon Inn," said Dârio. "You'll have to get the recipe."

"I'll put that on my to-do list," said Jenet. "Maybe I'll wait until *after* today's battle."

"Probably wise," said Dârio.

Duke Háiddon covered his mouth with his hand and coughed softly to hide a smile. Dârio was clearly nervous about what was to come and seizing on trivial matters to distract himself. Somehow, he'd thought his daughter would provide quite a bit of distraction on her own. Thinking of his daughter reminded him to ensure three or four wizards were tasked with protecting his daughter and others who'd be left behind in the encampment when the army mustered on the open field to the north. He ate some cooked oats and realized they were quite tasty—and that he was hungry.

"You'll work with Damon?" the duke asked Dârio. "I have to talk to my unit commanders."

"We'll head for the river as soon as I finish my oats and get dressed," said the king.

"And as soon as *I'm* ready," said Damon. "It will take me a few minutes to get into my Master Mage's robes."

"May I assist you?" asked Jenet.

"If you'd like," said Damon. He put his spoon in his empty bowl and placed both on top of his length of tree trunk after he stood. He began to walk away, and Jenet quickly rose to follow.

"Now who will help *me* get dressed?" protested Dârio with a smile.

The well-muscled soldier got up, put her sword in its sheath, and loomed over the young king.

"I'll help," she said. "Maybe I can give you more good advice while I do."

Chapter 60

Eynon

"Is it working?" asked Merry.

"I can't tell," said Eynon. "All I can see on the other side is a white mist."

"Did you consider that it might be foggy along the Brenavon?" asked Fercha. "I know that gate is working properly. Once you've made enough gates you can feel it when everything is congruent."

"Maybe I'll be able to tell when I'm as old as you are," said Merry.

"Whatever happened to respectful apprentices?" Fercha mused.

Merry stuck her tongue out at Fercha and grinned. Her mentor copied Merry's gesture. Both laughed.

Taking another look at the wide gate, Merry could tell that Eynon was right about the scene on the other side of the gate looking like so much mist or fog. It roiled about beyond the interface like low-flying clouds.

Chee was sleeping on the padded saddle in the middle of Rocky's back, while the big black wyvern was stamping back and forth, sniffing the air, as if sensing prey nearby. Nûd was keeping pace with Rocky's movements, speaking soothing syllables to help the wyvern remain calm. "Who's a good boy?" asked Nûd. *"You're* a good boy," he answered.

Fercha glanced at Eynon, shook her head, then walked through the gate and disappeared into the white mist.

"Did I do something wrong?" asked Eynon.

"I think you did the absolute minimum necessary," said Merry. "You should have called out. Doethan is supposed to be on the other side."

"I didn't want to shout because I was afraid my voice would carry and Tamloch wizards or soldiers might hear me," said Eynon.

"That was wise," said Merry.

"When do you think Fercha will be back?" asked Nûd. "She's the only one who knows how to rebuild the gate if anything happens at this end."

"I might be able to do it," said Merry. "I was watching her closely when she triggered the connection."

"So long as you don't end up sending us into the middle of the harbor at Riyas," teased Nûd.

"I'd be more likely to drop us in the Rhuthro," Merry noted. "But since the gate is already established, the odds are good I'd get us back where Fercha made the original connection."

"Good to know," said Eynon. "I hope Fercha will teach me how to set up gates, too."

"What did Doethan ask you?" said Merry. "You were talking to him for a long time."

"He's concerned about Damon," Eynon replied. "He thinks it would be a good idea for me to be there when he freezes the Brenavon."

"Have you ever frozen anything?" asked Merry.

"He froze a field of mud pots tonight to prevent a hundred basilisks from attacking us simultaneously," said Nûd.

"So you know the general concept?" asked Merry.

"Or my blue magestone does," said Eynon.

"Your red magestone is pulsing," said Merry. She pulled Eynon's red and gold artifact out from under his jacket and linen shirt. Eynon could see crimson light flash across her face in time to his heartbeat.

"What does it mean?" Eynon asked.

"My guess is it's telling you it's full of heat energy," said Nûd. "Damon's would do that when he taught apprentices how to freeze water. You'll want to figure out a way to release it soon."

"Maybe shoot a fireball at the far end of the valley?" suggested Merry. "It would help with your surprise."

"I'll have to wait a bit, then," said Eynon. "It's still at least an hour before the sun's all the way up back east, even if there were hints of light when I stepped through into the fog."

"You need to leave now," said Fercha to Eynon as she stepped across the interface. Four wizards Merry remembered from the Conclave's headquarters were behind Fercha. The two men and two women all had solid sky-blue robes.

"But I need to..." began Eynon.

"You need to help Damon," said Fercha. She moved behind Eynon and began to push him toward the wide gate. He resisted and turned to face her.

"Where do I go when I get there?" asked Eynon.

"Doethan will give you directions," said Fercha, "but it's simple. Just head east until you get to the river then look for Damon's sparkling robes."

"That should be easy," Eynon replied. "Those robes would be visible from halfway to the moon."

"Just get going," Fercha insisted. "Damon's planning to start as soon as a sliver of sun shows above the horizon. You don't have time to waste."

"Will you and Rocky be ready?" Eynon asked Nûd.

Chee raised his head from the saddle on Rocky's back, then lowered his head and went back to sleep.

"We'll be fine, won't we big guy," said Nûd to Rocky. The wyvern licked Nûd's face with his long, forked tongue. "Good boy," said Nûd. Rocky rubbed his head against Nûd's outstretched palms.

"Go," said Merry. "Fercha and I can help get things moving at this end."

"You'll have to do that on your own, with help from these fine wizards," said Fercha, indicating the men and women in wizard's robes who'd crossed over with her. "I'd use lightning, not fireballs, by the way."

"Where will *you* be?" asked Merry.

"Doethan asked for my help, too," said Fercha. "With luck, we'll surprise Verro before *he* can surprise *us*."

"Safe travels," said Nûd. "Watch out for Tamloch wizards on flying disks guarding their army, Eynon."

"I will," said Eynon. He blew Merry a kiss and stepped through the gate before Fercha could push him through. It was still foggy on the other side. He reduced the glow of the sphere above his head to the equivalent of a single candle. "Hello?" he whispered.

Fercha took Eynon's elbow and tugged him to the right, away from the front of the wide gate. "Doethan?" she asked. "Inthíra?"

"Over here," said Doethan to Fercha. "Eynon, you're here! Head east as fast as you can, look for..."

"Damon's sparkling robes, I know," said Eynon. "I'll find him."

"Good," said Doethan. "Be ready to help, but only if he needs it."

"I'll do what I can," said Eynon, "but I don't understand what Damon would need *my* help with."

"He's an old man, lad—a *lot* older than I am—and he hasn't worked this level of magic since before you were born," said Doethan. "Lend him strength Eynon, but only if he needs it."

"I'll try my best," said Eynon, "but who will tell Merry when Tamloch's army is in place on this side of the gate."

"I will," said Inthíra. "Five of us will stay here and let her know."

"Good," said Eynon. He didn't want anything to interfere with the successful execution of his plan. Doethan spoke up and interrupted Eynon's review of the things that could still go wrong.

"Climb to thirty or forty feet and head east until you hear the river," said Doethan. "Damon will be nearby."

"If you see legionnaires, you've gone too far," said Fercha with a smile.

"How much of the river will Damon try to freeze?" Eynon asked.

"From shore to shore and two hundred feet along the banks," Doethan replied.

"How deep?" asked Eynon.

"Two or three feet should be enough," said Fercha. "More would be better if you can manage it."

"Me?" asked Eynon. "The only thing I've ever frozen is mud."

"It's the same thing," said Fercha.

"Not exactly," said Doethan, rubbing his chin. "The solids in the mud vary its properties when you lower its temperature, so it's actually *harder* to freeze mud than water."

"Whatever," said Fercha. "Just go. Help Damon. We have to head south to thwart Verro."

"Verro's attacking from the south?" asked Eynon.

"Not your problem," said Fercha. "Help Damon."

"On my way," said Eynon, climbing on his flying disk. The others mounted theirs as well.

As he sped toward the river, Eynon looked over his shoulder and saw the glowing balls above Doethan and Fercha's heads fade into the mist to the south. With a smile, he realized he'd be able to see *his* surprise play out from *this* side of the gate once Damon worked his wizardry.

Chapter 61

Túathal

Túathal was dressed in an impressive green robe trimmed with gold. It was covered with hundreds of rounded quatrefoils, stylized clovers, picked out in gold thread. The robe had long, deep sleeves, with slits where he could slide his arms out. That made it much easier for him to eat and sign documents without dragging his robe's fancy sleeves through sauces or ink. The king's undertunic was dyed a rich gold and the buttons holding the tight sleeves of that garment closed were enameled green quatrefoils that matched his robe. It wasn't something to wear under armor. Túathal had knights and soldiers to do his fighting for him.

He stood in an otherwise open section of the headquarters tent, beside one end of a trestle table set with ten places. Tibbo and Tannis were transferring platters with dried fruit, rolls and sausages to the table from a small wheeled cart. Salder had arranged for the staff of the Blue Whale inn to cater to Túathal's every culinary need, ensuring that the king was well-fed while in the field. If that meant more ears to overhear Túathal's plotting, so much the better.

A few minutes later, Salder himself arrived, escorting a now less-bedraggled Princess Gwýnnett. Túathal gestured that Salder should seat her on a folding chair with curved arms at the opposite end of the table. The king knew the chair wasn't particularly comfortable, especially without the pillow that was on the chair beside him. Gwýnnett sat, glaring at Túathal. She understood the game he was playing, or thought she did.

Salder moved to assist Tibbo and Tannis by finding a gold-plated pitcher and pouring cider into mugs at each of the ten places.

"Did you sleep well, *my dear?*" asked Túathal with a slight sneer.

"Like a babe," said Gwýnnett, offering an insincere smile. "I hope you can't say the same."

"Sheathe your claws, little kitten," said Túathal. "There are other ears to hear."

"A prisoner should strike whatever blows she can to gain her freedom, wouldn't you say?" offered Gwýnnett.

"But an honored noble guest should mind her manners," countered the king.

Their exchange was interrupted by Uirsé, the dark-haired young wizard, entering the tent. She bowed to Túathal.

"Your commanders await your pleasure outside, Sire," she said.

"Send them in," said the king, "then check my breakfast for poisons. Pay particularly attention to anything at *her* end of the table," he said, nodding toward Gwýnnett.

The princess gave the young wizard a saccharine smile and lifted her hands above the table, palms up. Uirsé didn't meet Gwýnnett's eyes, but noticed the heavy rings she wore on both hands.

Uirsé stepped out of the headquarters tent momentarily, then returned with eight hard-looking men and women wearing gambesons or archers' leathers, with Duke Néillen, the senior-most commander in the lead. The duke passed much closer to her than necessary. Uirsé felt his hot breath on her bare neck. She held in a shudder and stepped farther away until she stood behind the king while the rest of the commanders found their places. When everyone was seated, Uirsé used her wizardry to carefully scan the table for poisons, paying particular attention to Gwýnnett's rings. There was no telltale glow to Uirsé's magic-augmented sight.

"Enjoy your meal, good gentles," said Uirsé, giving her assent to proceed.

"Took you long enough to complete your scan," muttered Túathal to Uirsé when she'd finished. "Don't bother with a privacy sphere," said the king. "There's not much Dâron can do to stop me now, anyway."

Uirsé said nothing. She just withdrew to stand near Salder, Tibbo, and Tannis, where she could inspect any new food or drink before it reached the table. She was privately amused by Túathal saying, "stop *me* now," rather than, "stop *us* now," even with the leaders of his army arrayed before him. Her loyalty was to Verro, not his older brother. Túathal was not a man to inspire such feelings.

Without waiting for Túathal to start, Princess Gwýnnett plucked a dried peach from a platter and nibbled it suggestively, trying to keep and hold eye contact with the king as she did. Túathal ignored her. Instead, he speared a sausage with his eating dagger and took a roll from a platter. He spread butter on the roll and watched the others at the table break their fasts. Dawn wasn't far off and this would be his last chance to confirm the military side of his long campaign was ready. The commanders reassured Túathal that their forces were prepared for battle and knew the roles they must play. The king smiled as each reported. Túathal's expression held just enough malice to ensure the men and women around the table wouldn't dare to disappoint him.

"Return to your troops," said Túathal once the last commander finished. "You know where to muster. Do your part and we will crush Dâron on the field of battle. Today is the day we unite north and south by the sword. Tamloch and victory!"

"Tamloch and victory!" said the commanders, raising their goblets and saluting their king.

Túathal gave Duke Néillen and his other, less senior commanders a malice-free smile as they departed. Once they'd left the tent, he reflected that Verro's report given a few hours earlier was the most important one. The southern Clan Lander barbarians attacking Dâron's army from behind would truly turn the tide.

He hoped his brother would get him word from the blasted Bifurlanders soon. They were the only detail he hadn't fully confirmed. He'd have to trust them to hold firm to their allegiance from noon on one day to dawn on the next. Still, Túathal felt uneasy. Trust was not something he extended often. While he waited for word, he decided to amuse and distract himself with the princess.

"Would you like a good seat for the battle?" he asked. "You can sit by my side on the viewing platform I've erected."

Princess Gwýnnett raised an eyebrow at Túathal's choice of words and bit into a sausage, chewing sensuously before she licked her lips and swallowed.

"Do you intend to show off your captive?" she asked.

"I intend to remind Dârio that I'm holding you, while having my future queen next to me as all my plans are realized," Túathal answered.

"I suppose we both can gloat at Dâron's loss and our gain," said the princess. She licked grease off her lips and looked suddenly thoughtful.

"What?" asked Túathal.

"How do you expect to ensure our son isn't killed or injured?" asked Princess Gwýnnett, all mis-guided attempts at seduction put aside. "If he dies..."

"Don't worry," said Túathal. "Duke Háiddon would never let Dârio enter the battle."

"Hah," said Gwýnnett. "You don't know our son as well as I do. He *will* fight. How do you propose to protect him?"

"I can tell all our commanders not to engage any unit Dârio is part of," said Túathal, tentatively. "I'll give orders to take him alive if they somehow do engage with him."

"Will you give the same order to the southern Clan Land chiefs?" asked Princess Gwýnnett.

"You have a point," said Túathal. "Verro can gate him away from the battle as soon as the Clan Landers come through their gate. I'll let him know I'm adding one more thing to his list."

"You depend on Verro for so much," observed Gwýnnett. "I hope he doesn't break under the strain. He's too handsome a man to waste—and *he* likes women."

"Don't get any ideas," said Túathal. "He's in love with someone else. You're not in her league."

"We'll see," said Gwýnnett. She stood and motioned to Salder. "Escort me to my tent. I have to prepare to watch a battle."

Salder started to cross to join the princess. Uirsé glanced at Salder and raised an eyebrow as he passed her. He returned the same expression.

Dârio of Dâron was King Túathal's son? Her king was plotting with the king of Dâron's mother? She had to tell Verro.

Chapter 62

At the River's Edge

"I'm ready," said Dârio as Damon emerged from his tent. "Are *you?*"

"Of course, Sire," said Damon. He extended his arms to give the shimmering fabric of his robes a chance to shake out and drape properly. "Is it time?"

"It's nearly dawn," said the young king. "Time to earn your title."

"You can *have* my title," said Damon. "I'm planning to give it up soon anyway."

"Who do you have in mind for the job?" asked Dârio.

"There's only one suitable candidate," said Damon.

"You're probably right," said Dârio, "but it still seems odd for a sixteen-year-old to start at the top."

"Says the man who was king of Dâron at that age," noted Damon.

"You've got a point," said Dârio.

"The role has little to do with experience and everything to do with raw magical power," said Damon. "Your grandfather handed it to me before I was twenty."

"Then prove his confidence in you was well-founded," said Dârio.

A few minutes later Damon was on his flying disk heading northeast toward the river with Dârio holding on behind the Master Mage. They flew through thick white fog that flowed up from the riverbank like clouds climbing up the slopes of a high mountain. A glowing ball above Damon's head didn't help Dârio see farther than Damon's iridescent robes in front of his nose. The old wizard seemed to know where to land, even if everything looked the same to the king in the featureless mist.

Dârio scraped his boots across a wide flat rock that his companion had selected as a landing site. The king could hear and smell the river rushing by, just beyond Damon.

"Put my flying disk on my back, please," said Damon. "These robes make it harder for me to do it for myself."

"Certainly," said Dârio. He took in the wizard's bent shoulders. Damon looked tired. Dârio wondered if it was fair to expect a man his grandmother's age to do what he'd been asked to accomplish. He gently lowered Damon's flying disk over his shoulders by its straps.

"Are you sure you're up for this?" asked Dârio. He patted the flying disk, then realized the old wizard probably couldn't feel his touch through the layers of sparkling fabric in his voluminous multi-colored robe.

Damon had felt it, however. He turned to face Dârio.

"I know why *I'm* here," said the old mage, "but why are *you* here?" Damon looked Dârio over from his boot soles to the top of his quilted arming cap, designed to fit under his helm. "Shouldn't you be by Duke Háiddon's side, inspiring the army?"

"There's time for me to do that when we finish," said Dârio. "I want to make sure you don't overextend yourself..."

"I beg your pardon?" Damon objected. "You asked me to freeze the Brenavon—I'm going to freeze it. Don't worry about me."

"But I do worry about you," said Dârio.

"And so do I," said a soft alto voice from the fog. A woman in dark-blue robes and a deep hood stepped up onto the rock. Her movements were slow and deliberate.

"Astrí," said Dârio. "Is everything alright? Did Queen Carys send you?"

"No," said Astrí. "I mean yes, everything is fine, but your great-grandmother didn't send me. I came because of him."

"You mean Damon?" asked Dârio. "I didn't even know you knew him."

Damon stared at Astrí like a mother recognizing her long-lost child. His eyes were wide, and his mouth hung open.

"Damon and I are acquainted, Your Majesty," Astrí replied after a few seconds. She turned her body to face Damon. "Close your mouth before you swallow too many midges," she instructed the old wizard. Damon obeyed.

"I thought I'd never see you again," said Damon. "My heart broke when you left."

"You could have seen me any time you wanted," said Astrí. "I know you have a gate from the castle in Melyncárreg to your quarters in the royal palace in Brendinas. I wasn't hiding from you."

"But the risk was too great," said Damon. "If anyone had recognized you and connected us…"

"I was eighteen when I left court," said Astrí. "I walked through that gate you made and into another life with you in the far west. No one would recognize the girl I was in the old woman I am."

"You're not old," protested Damon.

"Yes I am," said Astrí as she threw back her hood. Only a few traces of red remained in her short white hair, along with wisps of gray. Damon stepped toward her.

"Can you see now," she said. "I wasn't protecting me—I was protecting you, and our daughter."

It was Dârio's turn to stare. He'd never seen Astrí without her hood on. It wasn't hard to see the resemblance between the gilded statue of the young princess that stood in front of the palace and Astrí's face and form.

"You're her," said Dârio. "You're Princess Seren."

Astrí sighed. "I once was. I fell in love with magic—and this dashing young mage." She gestured in Damon's direction. He took two steps toward her and gave a small bow.

"Being young and foolish is one thing," said Damon. "But keeping it up over the years takes real talent. There's no fool like an old fool." Damon shook his head slowly, but didn't take his eyes off Astrí. "It's been twenty years since I last saw you."

"You didn't need to worry," said Astrí. "I kept up my masquerade and ensured my identity stayed secret. I was also there to watch over our daughter at court. My mother was glad to have my counsel as well."

"Leaving me to raise our grandson on my own," said Damon. "That was no way to bring up a boy."

"Wait," said Dârio. "Who's your daughter? And your grandson?"

Damon and Astrí weren't paying attention. Astrí took a step toward Damon and reached for his hand. He took it and smiled, lines of pain and worry vanishing from his face.

"That was your decision, and Fercha's," said Astrí. "You didn't want our grandson anywhere near court."

"Would you want Princess Gwýnnett to guess his identity?" asked Damon.

"Fercha is my *aunt?*" asked Dârio.

"Not exactly," said Damon. "It's complicated."

Dârio looked like he'd been smacked across the back of his head by the flat of a sword.

"No, I most certainly do *not* want Princess Gwýnnett to guess his identity," said Astrí, getting back on track after Dârio's interruption. "That may be why I didn't fight you too hard when you were determined to keep him in exile and raise him in Melyncárreg."

"At least you kept this young fool from being the total ass he pretends to be," said Damon, indicating Dârio with two fingers.

"Hey," said Dârio. "Great-grandmother and Fercha and Duke Háiddon also helped with *my* masquerade."

"I'm grateful to them," said Damon, "and to you, lad, for heeding their wise counsel. You'll be a good king, I expect."

"Thank you," said Dârio. "I hope so." He noticed the fog was getting brighter, even though Damon hadn't adjusted the glowing ball above his head. Fingers of red appeared to the east in the direction of the Brenavon. Damon turned and reached the same conclusion as Dârio.

"Time to get busy earning my title, as you said, Your Majesty," Damon remarked.

"No," said Astrí. "Not by yourself. You weren't yet forty when you froze the Abbenoth and it almost killed you. It took almost a year for you to recover your strength. Let me help—I'll do what I can."

Damon leaned close and hugged Astrí.

"We both know your best magics have nothing to do with cold," said Damon. "You could barely chill wine before serving it."

"Then let me lend you what energies I can, and *you* direct them," said Astrí. "Let me be your battery."

"I'd rather you return to Melyncárreg with me, so we can spend our remaining years growing older together," said Damon. He shrugged his flying disk off his shoulders and handed it to Dârio, then shifted so Astrí could put her arms around him from behind and press against him.

"That's perfect," said Damon. "It's wonderful to feel you close again."

"You're supposed to be connecting to my magestone and its energy," said Astrí.

"That too," said Damon.

He looked over his shoulder at Dârio.

"You may want to step back, Your Majesty," he said. "I don't want to turn the king of Dâron into an icicle by accident."

"Good idea," said Dârio. He moved to the far edge of the flat rock, keeping as much distance between himself and the wizards as possible. He held up Damon's flying disk like a shield and saw Astrí's disk a few feet from him leaning against the edge of the rock.

"It's time," said Dârio, noting the increasing light to the east. The fog was clearing, and he could now see the river flowing by, its current strong.

"Lean in," said Damon. Astrí did. Damon extended his arms, faced the river, and opened a congruent connection to a place of cold. A chill wind blew out from him and swept across the river. A layer of ice formed across its surface. Damon bent over, coughing and shaking. Astrí helped him back upright.

"Did it work?" asked Damon.

Dârio looked out across the river. The ice coating the Brenavon was so thin it was almost translucent. A small dog would fall through its surface, let alone a Roma legion. Then they sensed a bright flash behind them. A second later, a loud boom shattered the morning silence and some of the nearest ice on the river.

All three turned and watched a huge red sphere of heat energy continue to expand, then contract in the sky not too far to the west.

"I hope that's who I think it is," said Dârio.

"So do I," said Damon.

"Merry's beau from the Coombe," said Astrí, matter-of-factly.

"A suitable candidate indeed," said the young king. "Do something to get his attention."

"As My Liege commands," said Damon.

"Just do it, old man," said Dârio. "Give him a squeeze to encourage him, *grandmother.*"

"You're not too old to be sent to your room without your supper," said Astrí with a smile.

"Yes, ma'am," said Dârio in a contrite five-year-old's voice.

Damon launched three blue streamers into the sky.

Chapter 63

Eynon

Eynon quickly realized that it was hard to keep his bearings flying through thick white fog. The glowing ball above his head didn't do much good—it just allowed him to tell the fog was cloud-white, not dark gray. He couldn't see farther ahead than the fingers of his outstretched hands and the sun was not yet up to provide a reference point. Hoping to see stars for orientation was so much wishful thinking. Eynon formed a wedge-shaped shield around his body, like he had when escaping the gryffons, but that only made his flight more stable. It didn't push fog out of the way, or if it did, there was more of the same fog ahead to replace it, so he dispelled the wedge.

Now what? thought Eynon. *I can't help Damon if I can't see where I'm going.*

He continued to fly in a direction he hoped was east, thinking about what to do next.

Wait! he realized. *This is just like trying to see the Bifurland golden dragons in the clouds.* He generated the same lenses he'd created the previous morning, but they didn't help much. There wasn't anything to see except white fog. Eynon still couldn't see far enough to find the river. Then he remembered how they navigated the way from Haywall village to the milking barn when heavy fogs like thick low clouds filled the Coombe's basin. One of the villagers would tap his or her way along with a stick and the others would trail behind, listening for the stick's scratching and the tapping of other villagers' feet in front of them.

That might work, Eynon considered. *I could use the listening spell Merry first taught me on the Rhuthro to hear the Brenavon.*

Eynon worked the simple magic needed to improve his hearing. He heard running water and knew for sure which way was east. He also realized he was being tracked by three Tamloch wizards.

They'd been keeping watch above their army's mustering field just out of range of his limited vision. *Blast!* thought Eynon. At least the scout-wizards' whispered warnings to each other noting his presence had given him a clue to their existence. The green-robed scouts had Eynon boxed in. *No,* thought Eynon. *They triangulated on him.* Eynon knew his Euclid.

Five tendrils of force—tight-light beams from the hand of the closest Tamloch wizard—cut in front of Eynon's path. The fog made the beams easier to see and avoid. Eynon dodged around them and accelerated. Going faster proved an unwise strategy, however. Eynon *had* been boxed in. There were four green wizards, not three. The one in front of him cast a hemisphere of solidified sound that Eynon slammed into at high speed. One of the trailing wizards cast a matching hemisphere, locking Eynon inside a spherical shield he didn't control. His opponents could direct the sphere's motion and send him to be inspected by the senior crown wizards at the Tamloch encampment.

Eynon didn't have time for that, not if Damon needed his help. He felt the heat-energy pulsing in his magestone after freezing the mud pot field, but wasn't sure where or how to release it. He didn't want to kill other wizards, even if they were from Dâron's traditional opponent. He just wanted to get out of the sphere. Eynon first tried to talk his way out. He waved until both wizards controlling halves of the sphere were watching, then he shouted.

"I don't want to hurt you, so please drop the sphere and get back. I don't know how long I can control it."

Eynon made sure the artifact with his red magestone was clearly visible on his chest and willed his stone to pulse even faster and brighter. The magestone's red light seemed to cut through the diminishing fog.

"That's a *red* magestone," said one Tamloch scout-mage.

"I don't like the look of it," said another.

"Maybe it controls the boy, not vice-versa," said a third.

"Stop scaring yourselves and squeeze that sphere," came a gruff commanding voice belonging to the fourth scout. "You can be sure

Túathal and Verro will want to inspect that red stone. There may be a bonus for us for capturing such an unusual prisoner."

The sphere around Eynon began to contract. Eynon knew he could open up a congruency to outside the sphere to get more air, but it would soon be harder to move inside. He crafted a sphere of his own just inside the Tamloch wizards' sphere and held it against further tightening. The third scout's observation had given him an idea.

"Please," he pleaded. "Let me go. The magestone *is* controlling me. It's angry and wants to release all its energy in one big blast. I'm trying to get to the river so I'm the only one it will kill when it does."

Eynon saw two of the scout-wizards look at each other uncertainly. He increased the speed and intensity of his magestone's pulses for emphasis and could feel that his fabrication wasn't completely fiction. His magestone *did* want to release its stored energy.

"I'm fine with this spy *leaving* the mustering field," said one of the uncertain scout-wizards.

"We're supposed to drive spies away, not capture or kill them," said the other.

"Capturing spies is part of our job, you maggots," said the gruff-voiced wizard. She continued her insults. "Any mage or mercenary with half a brain would know that."

"You don't have to call us names," said the third scout-wizard. "Verro doesn't call us names."

"When you act like sniveling, cowardly maggots, I'll call you whatever names I please," said the gruff-voiced woman wizard.

"Now you sound like Túathal, not Verro," said one of the others.

"I can't hold it back much longer," said Eynon. "It's going to explode. I don't want your deaths on my hands as well as my own."

"You're heading for the river," said one of the uncertain scout-wizards. "You promise?"

"As fast as I can get there," said Eynon. "Just drop your sphere and I'm gone." It was hard for them to see Eynon's face through the pulsing red energy filling the sphere.

"Go then," said the wizard who'd created the front half of the sphere. He dispelled his creation and sped west on his flying disk, away from Eynon. He was joined by the woman who'd made the other segment of the sphere. She dropped her spell once the leading hemisphere vanished and joined her departing associate.

The gruff-voiced wizard didn't say anything out loud, but Eynon's augmented ears could hear her mutter, "Cowards," at her departing squad members' backs. She threw a pair of lightning bolts at Eynon, one from each hand. Enough of the crackling energy penetrated Eynon's spherical shield—designed to protect against compression, not lightning—to set the hairs on his arms and the back of his neck standing. His red magestone pulsed still faster, and not by Eynon's direction.

"Get back!" shouted Eynon.

Something in his voice convinced the scout-wizard who'd remained with the gruff-voiced leader to send his flying disk west after his squad-mates who had disappeared into the fog. Even the squad-leader moved to put more distance between herself and Eynon.

Partly for dramatic effect, and partly because his red magestone wanted to release its stored energy, Eynon sent a ball of heat and light up and out from the stone and gold setting around his neck. He used the moderating power of his blue magestone to constrain the intensity of the release, making it more light than heat. He strengthened the sphere around him to protect himself from the coming blast.

The ball detonated high above him, making the pre-dawn night brighter than noon for an instant. Heat from the explosion evaporated the fog for several hundred yards. Eynon saw the gruff-voiced scout-wizard, protected by a green-tinted elliptical shield, spinning end over end to the west like a grain of wheat caught by a thresher. He turned and caught a glimpse of the river. At least he'd been headed in the right direction.

Then Eynon saw three blue streamers of light in the sky above the Brenavon and set off at speed to find Damon as the first hints of dawn appeared on the eastern horizon.

Chapter 64

Fercha and Doethan

Fercha and Doethan flew south side by side. It made it easier for them to talk.

"What's your theory?" asked Doethan.

"About Verro's surprise?" asked Fercha.

"No, about the fundamental nature of wizardry," said Doethan. "Of *course* about Verro's surprise."

"I think it connects to the southern Clan Lands, like Damon said," Fercha replied. "Verro has probably formed an alliance and arranged for them to attack Dâron."

"That's plausible," said Doethan. "If so, Verro must have a wide gate in place somewhere north of the Dormant Dragon."

"How *far* north is the question," said Fercha. "There's a lot of territory to cover in a heavy fog, even with special lenses."

"I know," said Doethan, "but I think we can narrow down its location. It will be as close as possible to the Dâron army's encampment while still being out of sight of our pickets and scout-wizards."

"That's as good a guess as any," said Fercha. "I'll change my lenses to look for magestones."

"If you spot a big rectangle, you've found it," said Doethan.

"Ha ha," Fercha replied in a monotone.

"While you're looking for the gate, I'll look for the wizards Verro likely has guarding it," noted Doethan.

"How far can *you* see through the fog," asked Fercha.

Doethan turned his head left and right.

"Maybe fifty feet," he said.

"You should look for magestones too, then," said Fercha. "You'll see the glow from wizards' stones in this fog sooner than you'll see their faces."

"True," said Doethan. He gestured to change his lenses then slowly rotated his flying disk once around. "No other wizards nearby," he said.

"Good," said Fercha once Doethan was facing in their direction of travel again.

They flew together in silence for more than a minute, scanning carefully.

"Verro is clever," said Fercha. "He may have more than one surprise planned."

"Is he clever, or crafty?" asked Doethan. "Do we need to look for something sneaky, or just unexpected."

"The latter," said Fercha. "Túathal got a full measure of fox. Verro is more straightforward. He's a mountain lion. You know he's hunting you—he doesn't need subterfuge."

She thought back to the first time she'd seen Verro, when the young Tamloch wizard and his brother, the crown prince, had visited the court in Brendinas. He was tall, dark-haired, and so handsome her breath caught when she noticed him enter the refectory that magical morning. Fercha had been thrilled when Verro had taken the seat beside her at breakfast. They'd discussed advanced aspects of wizardry over eggs and bacon and had agreed to meet somewhere more private later to continue their conversation. They'd done more than talk.

Barely more than a girl herself, just twelve months past her sixteenth birthday, Fercha remembered the fights she'd had with her father about leaving Melyncárreg. Damon hadn't wanted her to go to court. He'd said she looked too much like her mother and there would be questions, but she was ready to leave the confines of the Academy and prove herself in the wider world. She'd cut her hair short and charged it with a tiny bolt of lightning each morning, so the only thing people noted about her appearance was her resemblance to a dandelion in seed. It had worked. None of the nobles or servants had ever said, "You look just like Princess Seren," even though Fercha was the same age as the princess when she'd disappeared. *I have some of Damon in my face,* she thought. *That helped.*

Nûd, on the other hand, had Verro's height and coloring, but his face was a perfect match for the Young King's, save for his dark hair and Dârio's lack of it. His face also had a bit of Queen

Carys showing through.

That's why I didn't fight Damon over my son. If Nûd had come to court, the palace, and soon the whole kingdom would be buzzing, thought Fercha. She reminded herself how much Nûd and Dârio resembled each other. From what Doethan had told her about Princess Gwýnnett and Túathal, the two young men were first cousins. *It's a good thing Dârio keeps his head shaved or the resemblance would be even easier to spot.*

Fercha was glad Nûd was back in Melyncárreg, working on Eynon's surprise. Verro didn't know that Nûd existed, and Fercha wanted to keep it that way. It had been a relief to finally tell Nûd about Verro. She supposed that meant her son would seek out his father at some point and she'd have to answer for keeping their son secret from her husband, but with luck that wouldn't happen *today*.

"What are you thinking?" she asked Doethan to deflect attention from her own reverie. Somehow it was easier to talk with Doethan as they flew side-by-side through the fog instead of facing each other across an inn table.

"This and that," said Doethan, deflecting.

"You're thinking about *her,* aren't you? Princess Rúth."

"What if I am?" asked Doethan. "Don't remind me of our shared unrequited loves for Tamloch royals."

Fercha didn't think Doethan knew about the gate from her townhouse to Verro's apartment in the palace in Riyas. They were friends, but she didn't know if he'd approve of her continued connection to her husband, even if it was just to share a bed from time to time. *Then again, maybe he'd be more envious than angry?* she considered.

"When was the last time you spoke to her?" asked Fercha. She knew Doethan had given Princess Rúth one of his communications rings.

"More than a month ago," said Doethan. "Just before the preparations for war ramped up. I'm afraid Verro may have recognized the ring for what it was. I asked Rúth not to wear it, but she told me it reminded her of me and she wasn't taking it off."

"She *does* love you," said Fercha. "That's obvious. She never married, even with dozens of suitors put before her."

"I told her to pick one," said Doethan. "I begged her not to give up her chance at a family, but she wouldn't listen."

"You're saying she's as stubborn as you are?"

"I guess I am," said Doethan. "Túathal got guile, Verro got wizardry, and Rúth got..."

"You," said Fercha. She nudged Doethan's flying disk so he would glance over and see her smile.

"I was going to say *stubbornness*," said Doethan. "You're in much the same situation with Verro."

"There's plenty of that to go around," Fercha commiserated.

An unexpected flash of red light washed over them. Doethan and Fercha spun their disks around to face north in time for their ears to be assaulted by a giant *boom* that echoed across the mist-covered landscape. A glowing crimson ball was expanding high above the distant horizon.

"Eynon?" asked Doethan.

"Probably," said Fercha. "It resembles the one he cast above the Bifurland fleet. I hope the lad isn't hurt."

"I wouldn't worry," said Doethan. "With your old magestone and his red one, there's not much he can't handle."

"Maybe," said Fercha. "From what Merry's told me, he's far too trusting and inexperienced, like a puppy with big feet. I just hope he gets to Damon soon enough to be useful. The old man isn't as strong as he was, but he's too stubborn to admit it. He's at another level of stubborn from the rest of us."

"I can't disagree," said Doethan, "and I'm glad we've turned around."

"Why?" asked Fercha.

"We missed Verro's wide gate when we were distracted by the fireball," Doethan replied. "Look down there, between those trees. It's not far south of the Dâron army's encampment."

"As you predicted," said Fercha.

"Sometimes I hate being right," said Doethan. "How many wizards' magestones do you see?"

"Eight," said Fercha. "No, ten."

"Is one of them Verro?" asked Doethan.

"I'm not sure," said Fercha, "but I don't think so."

"Good," said Doethan. "Only five-to-one odds. Those aren't insurmountable. All we have to do is disrupt the gate's circuit. Ready?"

Fercha looked down. From their movements, it was clear that the wizards guarding the gate had spotted them.

"Ready," she said.

The upcoming confrontation didn't worry her. Fercha's larger concern did.

Where was Verro?

Chapter 65

Freezing the Brenavon

Eynon skidded his flying disk in for a landing on the broad flat rock next to the river. To his surprise, King Dârio caught his arm to keep him from tipping over.

"What are *you* doing here?" asked Eynon.

"Making sure our Roma allies can cross the Brenavon," said Dârio. "Why are *you* here? I thought the rest of you were coming to the royal army's encampment about this time."

"We were," said Eynon, "Then I got an idea for a way to surprise the Tamloch army and..."

"Wait, lad," said Damon. "Not out here in the open. Voices carry."

"Yes, sir," said Eynon. He just realized the Master Mage was standing nearby in a shimmering outfit, next to an older woman wizard in heavy dark-blue robes.

Damon gave Eynon an exasperated look and Eynon mouthed, "Yes, *Damon,*" to earn a smile.

"This is my..." began Dârio, extending an arm to indicate Astrí.

"...great-grandmother's personal wizard," said the woman in heavy robes. "I'm Astrí—and I've heard a lot about you."

"Really?" asked Eynon. "From whom?"

"I have my sources," said Astrí with a twinkle in her eye. "We can talk about it later. Now we need to freeze a river."

Damon stared down at the damp surface of the flat rock, not catching Eynon's eye. He seemed ashamed, but Eynon had never seen him express that emotion before.

Dârio used his arm to direct Eynon's attention again, this time to the Brenavon. Its surface was covered with a thin coating of ice, some of it cracked. Eynon could see through it. He looked at Damon, but the old wizard didn't raise his head.

Astrí spoke. "Damon's not feeling well today," she said. "He'd appreciate it if you'd freeze the river."

"Me?" asked Eynon.

"Yes, young man," said Astrí.

"But I only know how to freeze mud," said Eynon. "I've never tried to freeze a river. How is it done?"

Astrí touched Damon's arm. "Show the lad," she said. "You've always been a good teacher. You taught me."

Eynon looked at the two wizards together. They seemed to be much the same age. *Astrí must have been one of Damon's older students,* he considered. His eyes widened when Astrí took Damon's hand and tugged him to stand at the far end of the rock. She beckoned Eynon to join them. Dârio followed, observing from one side.

Astrí lifted Damon's head with her hand. It fell back. She did it again and this time, to Eynon's amazement, she *kissed* the Master Mage. It was a serious kiss and Eynon turned his head, but not before he saw Dârio grinning. Turning back for a quick glance, Eynon saw that Damon had put his arms around Astrí and was returning her kiss enthusiastically. Eynon focused on the river, trying to sense the structure of the ice and how it differed from liquid water.

A minute later, Damon coughed and Eynon turned back. The old wizard's posture was straighter, and his head was no longer focused on the flat rock. He had his arm around Astrí and a warm smile on his face.

"Let me show you how it's done," said Damon. He reluctantly released Astrí and faced the river. Eynon watched as Damon extended his arms. He sensed his mentor open a congruency to a place of intense cold and use patterns of solidified sound to channel a chill wind out over the water. Eynon felt a pulse from his blue magestone. It could help him do what Damon had done. The ice was getting thicker. You couldn't see through it in several spots.

Eynon realized the river was wider than he'd first understood. What appeared to be the far bank was actually a large island in the middle of the current. On either side of the island, Eynon could see the true far bank several hundred feet beyond. Damon's attempt at freezing had only managed to chill a fraction of the distance.

"See?" asked Damon. "Now you try."

"I'm confused," said Eynon. "That's not how I froze the mud pots."

"When were you back in Melyncárreg to freeze mud pots?"

"This morning," said Eynon. "It's part of my surprise for the…"

"That's not important," said Astrí. "How did you freeze them?"

Damon's face was returning to its usual dyspeptic expression. *Maybe Astrí should kiss him again,* thought Eynon.

"If I interpreted your magic correctly, you're adding cold to the water," said Eynon. "That only works slowly, from the top down, and the layer of ice at the top insulates the flowing water below."

"What do *you* propose?" asked Damon. He removed his arm from Astrí's shoulder, then crossed both of his over his chest.

Dârio was leaning forward, watching closely.

"Instead of adding cold, why not take away heat?" asked Eynon. "That's what I did with the mud pots, and they were hot to begin with."

"I'm not sure what you mean," said Damon. He rested his chin on one palm and put his other arm back around Astrí. Dârio saw that Astrí had been rubbing the small of Damon's back.

"I'll show you," said Eynon.

He adjusted his red magestone and centered its setting on his breastbone over his jacket. Then he extended his arms and threw out two huge transparent walls of solidified sound, five hundred feet up and down the river, from bank to bank, with the large island in the middle. The current stopped flowing. Eynon's blue magestone took over control of the walls, leaving Eynon and his red magestone free to absorb the water's heat.

Eynon took a deep breath. As he drew in air, he also drew in every calorie of warmth from the top two feet of water between the transparent walls. A layer of ice thicker than a barn's foundation stones snapped into place from shore to shore and more, drawing high up the river's banks to anchor it firmly in place.

The young wizard fell backward like a toppled tree. Only Dârio's quick-thinking assistance saved Eynon from hitting his head on the ground. The walls of solidified sound disappeared with a pair of *pops.* Beneath the sturdy sheet of ice the river began to flow again, with only a brief interruption.

Dârio carefully placed Eynon's limp body on the grassy bank. Astrí used her hood to pad Eynon's head. She listened to the young wizard's shallow breathing and felt his forehead. It was burning hot.

Astrí moved to sit behind the top of Eynon's head and put her hands on his temples. The others stood by, watching as she attempted to heal him. Her efforts appeared to be working. Slowly, his breathing returned to normal, but his temperature was still too high.

"Should we drag him out on the ice to cool him off?" asked Dârio.

"What?" asked Eynon, jerking his head up and away from Astrí's soothing palms. "No! Not ice!" he said before his head fell back.

"Rest," she told Eynon. "That was amazing. A tremendous feat of wizardry. Channel your body's heat to your magestone."

Eynon nodded weakly. He felt physically drained by his effort, but Astrí's healing touch was making a difference. Still, his red magestone was pulsing rapidly, sending out rhythmic flashes of crimson. He looked down and saw his stone seemed ten, or even a hundred times as full of energy as it had after he'd chilled a crust over the mud pots. The stretch of river he'd frozen had been a *lot* bigger.

Astrí addressed Dârio and Damon. "Did either of you think to bring something to eat on this expedition?"

Dârio and Damon both shook their heads.

"I can understand *you* not thinking ahead, Your Majesty," said Astrí. "But this old fool should know better. It takes lots of fuel to work wizardry on such a scale."

"There's some dried meat and hardtack in my pack," whispered Eynon weakly. "I put it there at the start of my wander year and never had a chance to eat it."

"Thank goodness for that," said Astrí. "No time like the present."

Astrí rummaged in his pack, taking care to avoid sharp shards of fractured flying disk, and found the meat and biscuits. She watched Eynon eat both as the eastern horizon revealed hints of a rising sun.

"I have to tell you about my surprise," said Eynon after a few bites.

Damon had been alternating between staring at the frozen river and staring at Eynon. Sometimes he shook his head. Once, he whistled.

"Just a moment, lad," he said. He threw up a privacy sphere around the four of them with a word and a gesture. "Now we can talk," he said.

Eynon told them about his plan. Astrí clapped her hands and grinned. Dârio pumped his fist and laughed, glad the noise wouldn't carry outside the privacy sphere.

"Brilliant," said Damon. "I'm impressed. You got Fercha and Doethan to help you?"

"I did," said Eynon. Astrí put her hands back on his head. He was starting to feel better, but kept eating. "Nûd gave me the idea."

"Did he now," said Damon. "Good for Nûd." He paced a few times and looked back across the ice-covered Brenavon. "I should tell our Roma allies about your *surprise*."

"I'll alert the Bifurlanders after I'm sure Eynon's well," said Astrí. "We don't want their dragonships running aground on the ice."

"I'm coming with you," said Dârio. "I want to see the looks on King Bjarni and Queen Signý's faces when you tell them. You can fly me back to the royal army when we're done."

"You're going directly back to camp, Your Majesty," said Astrí.

"Very well," sighed Dârio. "That's the wiser course, blast it."

Eynon finished his food and began to stand. Dârio helped him to his feet and shook Eynon's hand, then collected flying disks to distribute to Damon and Astrí.

Without external support, Eynon wobbled on his feet. Astrí reached out to help. She put one arm around Eynon to steady him, then one of her fingers touched Eynon's red magestone. Something crackled. Eynon felt her channel a tiny fraction of the magestone's power into his body, replenishing some of the energy he'd lost freezing the river.

Everything was different—brighter, stronger somehow. Eynon had yawned earlier, but now he didn't feel tired at all. He felt like he could wrestle a mountain lion and win two matches out of three.

Eynon straightened up, standing without need of assistance. He smiled a broad smile at Astrí, then gave her a hug.

"Will you be alright here, young man?" asked Astrí when they'd disengaged. "We should all be going."

"Don't worry about me," said Eynon. "I'm fine, thanks to you. I'll head back west to make sure my surprise comes off as planned in a few minutes. We've got time before both armies take the field."

"Perhaps an hour," said Dârio, noting the position of the sun. "Not more than that."

"Safe travels," said Eynon. He yawned, then smiled.

"And you," said Astrí from her flying disk.

Dârio, standing behind her, nodded.

"I have another job for you," said Damon as he mounted his own disk. "The details can wait, though. We can discuss it after the battle."

"Yes, sir," said Eynon. "I mean, 'Yes, Damon.'"

Eynon was still worried about his red magestone. Even with the small transfer, the energy inside it was like a captive thing that wanted to escape. He was afraid what might happen if he didn't release it soon, or if it broke free on its own in the wrong place. He didn't want it to be a threat to his friends or the kingdom.

His finger began to buzz. It was the ring he'd originally received from Doethan. He tugged on its band until it expanded. A battle was already in progress on the other side of the interface.

"Eynon," said Doethan as lightning blasts and fireballs filled the air behind him. "If you're here, come south. A mile or so below the royal encampment. We need your help. I've got to go."

The connection abruptly terminated, and the wide band shrank back down to ring-sized. Eynon returned the ring to his finger.

"On my way," he said to empty air.

As he rose, he spotted twelve small dragons high above him, their scales glinting red and orange as well as gold in the dawn light.

Eynon waved to Sigrun and Rannveigr and their friends and sped south.

Chapter 66

Túathal and Gwýnnett

King Túathal allowed Uirsé to lift him to the top of the royal observation platform on her flying disk. He didn't have the time or inclination to climb the four flights of stairs that would take him there. The upper level had a waist-high railing to prevent anyone from falling and provided a vantage point high enough for Túathal and Duke Néillen, his senior-most commander, to observe the course of the battle.

"Stay close in case I need you," said the king.

"Yes, Sire," said Uirsé softly. She put her flying disk on her shoulder and moved as far away from Túathal as she could manage on the twenty-by-twenty-foot floor of the platform.

"What about me?" shouted Princess Gwýnnett from the ground below. "You don't expect me to climb up there in a *skirt,* do you?" The soldiers standing guard on either side of her were laughing.

Túathal and Néillen, a compact man with huge scarred forearms covered in tattoos, exchanged smiles. Néillen was an experienced military commander. He'd been a young bravo from the streets of Riyas before he'd joined the royal guard. He'd fought beside Túathal and his father at the gates of Nova Eboracum. Túathal respected him, considering the man almost as crafty as strategist as he was. The king had made the rough-hewn soldier a duke after eliminating one of his nobles who'd been showing a stubborn tendency to follow his own counsel instead of doing what Túathal told him.

"Might as well lift her up," said Néillen, "if only to keep her quiet."

Túathal motioned to Uirsé, who reluctantly approached.

"Fetch the princess," he said, "but try not to give her a smooth ride."

"Yes, Your Majesty," Uirsé replied. She placed her flying disk on the platform and stepped onto it, lifting off, then descending to do as she'd been ordered.

Soon Gwýnnett's complaints stopped, only to be replaced by grumbles from her guards who now realized that *they* would have to climb four flights wearing mail. After a short debate, the guards decided the princess could be guarded just as easily from the base of the high platform as its top.

Gwýnnett dismissed Uirsé with a wave once she landed near Túathal and stepped off the wizard's flying disk.

"You're *so* kind to your captives," said the princess.

"Stay quiet and observe my victory," said the king.

"Our victory," said Gwýnnett.

Duke Néillen was wise enough not to say he agreed with the princess's way of putting things. He was privy to almost as much information about the king's plans as Verro and knew he was due to receive a much larger ducal estate in Dâron after Tamloch won.

Túathal stepped to the forward edge of the platform. It was forty feet tall and built on top of a modest hill that made its total elevation nearly a hundred feet above the level of the river. He could see his own troops arrayed before him, like green blocks on his sand table. Heavy cavalry, heavy infantry, archers, and peasant levies were in their predetermined positions.

Reserves were in the rear, but ready to deploy to either flank as necessary. Individual scout-wizards circled above the army, keeping watch from high above, while tight groups of wizards closer to the ground tossed small fireballs or tiny spheres of lightning from hand to hand like beginning jugglers.

Beyond the warriors of the royal army of Tamloch was a wide patch of unoccupied ground—the site of the battle to come. In the distance, past the open field, were the ranked units of blue-clad soldiers in Dâron's army. Túathal was pleased to see that his army was larger, though not by as much as he'd hoped. Dâron must have been able to assemble more of its levies from the southern reaches and west to the borderlands than his spies had reported.

Speaking of reports, thought Túathal, *where's that report Verro owes me on the status of the Bifurlanders?* He rubbed his chin. *It's probably nothing. That fireball just before dawn was disconcerting, however. The scout wizards had insisted it was a young wizard heading east, probably trying to get away before the armies engaged.*

Túathal leaned against the railing. Heights didn't bother him. He knew the Dâron encampment wasn't far behind Dâron's army, and behind the encampment was the wide gate linked to Verro's surprise.

Gwýnnett interrupted his contemplation of the field and joined Túathal at the rail. She didn't speak at first, which pleased Túathal. He wanted another moment to savor his preparations.

"Why are you being so mean to me?" she asked.

Why is it always about you, princess? Túathal wondered. *Don't you know it's always about me?* He laughed. The two of them *were* well-matched.

"My apologies, my dear," said the king. His tone held only a hint of patronizing mockery. He didn't think Gwýnnett would notice. "I've been preoccupied." He waved his hand at the scene below. "And you are, technically my captive, not yet my queen. We have to keep up appearances."

Gwýnnett snorted. Túathal was surprised. He'd never heard her make that sound before and didn't like it. Gwýnnett changed her tack.

"I want to be married in Brendinas," she said, surprising Túathal. "On midsummer day, in the palace gardens—or the grand hall if it rains. I'll wear a beautiful green and blue gown and Dârio will walk me down the aisle."

"Excuse me?" said the king. "I never thought you were the type to focus on frivolities." He faced Gwýnnett and saw she was smiling. He wondered what subtext of hers he was missing.

"Of course not," said Gwýnnett, "but while you've been concerned with battles, alliances and armies, *someone* has to think about how to get the people of Dâron to love you as much as I do."

"More than that, I hope," said Túathal. He relaxed, glad he hadn't been completely wrong about Gwýnnett. He'd need her for the next few years, at least. *Then, perhaps, a convenient accident...*

"We'll restage the ceremony in Riyas, so your nobles and subjects will see you can be changed through the love of a good woman," said the princess.

"Perhaps my subjects," said Túathal. "My nobles will know better."

"Whatever," said Gwýnnett. "We can save the details for later."

"There is the small matter of winning the battle first," said the king. He left Gwýnnett at the rail and returned to Duke Néillen at the middle of the platform.

"Where's your wizard?" he asked. "I want an update on the Bifurland fleet."

"I sent Tairí down to the keepers of the Blue Whale," said Duke Néillen. "I thought you might want to share a bottle of wine while we watch the defeat of Dâron's army."

"I might," said Túathal, "but I expect it will be too early for wine when we win. The battle should be over before noon."

"I expect a swift victory as well," said Néillen, "but will be glad to have a glass of red from the Isle of Vines no matter what the hour."

Túathal nodded, acknowledging his most senior commander's plan if not sharing it. The king stretched his shoulders and admired the construction of the viewing platform. It was built from logs and rope and had been erected before sundown the previous day. Verro had suggested a physical platform, since it would free-up six or eight wizards who would otherwise have to lift an extra-large observation disk with their magic. The king expected his brother was using those additional wizards to implement his surprise.

Gwýnnett called to Túathal. "Is that one of *your* projects?"

"What?" asked the king.

"All that ice on the river," Gwýnnett answered.

Túathal and Duke Néillen rushed to her side and followed her pointing arm. The Brenavon was frozen from shore to shore.

"Blast!" said the king.

"Now we'll have to worry about the Roma," said the Duke.

"It must be Ealdamon returned," said Gwýnnett. "This is just like the Master Mage freezing the Abbenoth when you and Dâri fought at the gates of Nova Eboracum. I thought he was dead."

"Blast!" Túathal repeated, tugging off one of his rings. "I have to talk to Verro. Why didn't he warn me something like this might happen?"

Chapter 67

Melyncárreg

It was still dark beside the wide gate in the valley. The only illumination came from glowing balls above the heads of the Merry, Nûd, and the four wizards sent by Inthíra to protect the gate's integrity. Nûd's sphere of light had been created by Eynon and was still tracking his movements, floating a yard up from his forehead.

Rocky was resting on a patch of dried grass with Chee on the padded saddle strapped to the wyvern's broad back. The raconette was weaving long strands of straw-colored grass into a circle. Chee hopped down from Rocky's back to Nûd's nearby shoulders and gently placed the woven circle on Nûd's head. The big man rubbed the fur on Chee's back and a higher-pitched sound of contentment came from the raconette to join Rocky's deep *basso* hum. Nûd didn't seem to notice Chee's gift.

Merry wondered if all raconettes wove grass, maybe as part of lining their nests. She wasn't sure, though. Chee seemed brighter than any animal she'd encountered who *wasn't* a wizard's familiar. Rowsch, Doethan's large hound, was able to communicate with him in complex ways she couldn't follow. Tutu, Fercha's owl familiar, had a particularly prickly disposition and obeyed Fercha's instructions, up to a point. Three examples weren't enough to generalize, but she wouldn't be surprised if Chee found a piece of chalk and started drawing geometric figures from Euclid's *Elements* on a piece of slate.

Was Rocky really Eynon's familiar, too? Merry wondered. *It wasn't fair that Eynon had two familiars when she didn't have any.*

Merry watched Rocky for a few moments. The wyvern's long body was only partially lit by the glowing ball above Nûd, who was leaning into Rocky's shoulder, inside the protective curve of the wyvern's long neck.

Rocky is as comfortable with Nûd as he is with Eynon, Merry realized. *Could non-wizards have familiars, too? That really wouldn't be fair.*

It felt odd for it to be close to dawn in Dâron, while still in the middle of the night in Melyncárreg. Merry was tired and the lows and grunts of the herds farther up the valley were soothing. She'd had to rub her eyes more than once while waiting for word from the other side of the gate. She wanted to step through to the Dâron side herself to look for Eynon, but knew her role was here. Someone had to get things started.

Nûd looked relaxed on the outside, but inside his mind was in turmoil. He'd known Fercha was his mother and Princess Seren was his grandmother all his life. He was well aware that he was first in line to be king of Dâron, but was quite happy to have Dârio fill that role as next in line. The biggest shock of the day was learning the identify of his *father* and finding out he was second in the Tamloch succession.

King Dârio, the swordsman who'd tricked Skavendr on the Bifurlander flagship the previous afternoon, was the rightful heir to the throne of Tamloch. *And my cousin,* Nûd realized, once he'd given it thought. *Our fathers are brothers.*

Was there a chance Fercha had lied to him? Nûd wondered. *Would Queen Carys consent to a test of their relationship made by a neutral wizard—not Fercha or Doethan or Damon? I could find a hedge wizard at random in Brendinas to see if Fercha's assertions were true if I had a hair from the Old Queen's head, and maybe one from Dârio.*

He scratched his head and felt the circlet of golden grass Chee had placed there. Then Nûd remembered the embroidered pillowcases Damon had said were a gift from his great-grandmother. Gold crowns and royal Dâron blue dragons. It seemed more and more likely that the Old Queen not only knew of Nûd's existence, but of his status as the Old King's true heir. Fercha wasn't lying—unless Damon was. The old wizard could have commissioned embroidered pillowcases from anyone and told Nûd a story to play games with Nûd's head.

Nûd felt like a pawn in a particularly vicious and complicated game of *shah-mat.* With a Master Mage for a grandfather *and* a father, as well as Fercha for a mother, he was glad learning wizardry had never appealed to him.

How could I ever live up to their expectations? Nûd considered. *The only good thing about being a wizard would be that they couldn't force him into being king.*

Kings never have time to themselves. They can't tramp around the countryside on their own, repairing fences or finding wild tubers for dinner. They're surrounded by palace intrigue and have to worry about invasions, the loyalty of their barons and raising money for the treasury. They can never know if potential mates love them, or love their crowns. Worst of all, thought Nûd, *kings don't have time to read—at least I don't expect they do. Maybe Dârio can tell me?*

Nûd unconsciously brought a hand up to stroke his chin. He couldn't see Chee, now back on Rocky's back, imitating his motion with comic precision.

Merry noticed, but didn't smile. She recognized Nûd's expression and could tell he was deep in thought. She got the same way from time to time, usually on her solo trips down the Rhuthro. The larger part of her brain would be thinking while a smaller part watched for rocks and steered around them. She hoped Nûd could steer around his own rocks as easily.

Why couldn't real life be like the stories in the Academy's library? Nûd wondered. *Kings in stories could make a difference for yeomen and tradesmen, lowering taxes and weeding out bad barons. They'd marry dairy farmers' daughters with freckles who didn't know they were kings and lived happily ever after.*

Unfortunately, Nûd had read the history books, not just the made-up stories on the library's shelves. He appreciated how hard it must be to be a king at all, let alone a *good* king like old king Dâroth XXIV.

Nûd's reverie was interrupted when Chee used his shoulder as an intermediate point on his way to the ground. The raconette scampered past Merry and the four other wizards who'd been talking quietly amongst themselves.

Chee! said the raconette, standing by the near corner of the wide gate.

Merry and Nûd moved to join Chee as he pointed at the disk of the sun on the other side. It had been light for close to an hour back in Dâron, but they were waiting for word that the Tamloch army had assembled.

A woman in the eclectic robes of one of Dâron's free wizards stepped across to the Melyncárreg side of the gate. Nûd, Merry, and the other four wizards gathered around her. Chee hopped to Nûd's shoulder for a better view. Rocky rose and came forward to join them, his massive black head looking down on the new arrival. The free wizard's eyes went wide when she saw Rocky, but then she noticed none of the others seemed worried, so she shared her message.

"Tamloch's forces are in place," said the free wizard. "At least most of them are. It shouldn't be more than ten minutes before they sound their attack."

"Thank you," said Merry.

"What's all this about?" asked the free wizard. "Inthíra didn't tell us."

"It's a surprise," said Nûd. "A *big* surprise—for Tamloch."

The free wizard looked puzzled.

"Did Inthíra tell you and the others on your side to stay on your flying disks and protect the sides of the gate with shields?" asked Merry.

"She did," confirmed the free wizard. "But what *is* the surprise?"

"You'll soon see for yourself," said Merry. "Just be sure to fly at least twenty feet up."

The free wizard walked back through the gate, pulling her flying disk off her back as she went. Merry thought she heard her mutter something uncomplimentary about *letting children be wizards*. She wished she could be on the other side of the gate to see the woman's expression in a few minutes.

"Ready?" Merry asked the other four wizards.

They nodded, stepped onto their flying disks, and ascended. They'd protect the integrity of this side of the wide gate.

"Come on," said Nûd. He was already on Rocky's back with Chee on the wyvern's neck in front of him. "I want to watch you make bolts of lightning."

"You and Rocky will add your own contribution," said Merry.

Rocky lifted his head and bellowed. Chee waved both front hand-paws above his head and said, "CHEE!"

The four of them flew to the far end of the valley where the largest of Melyncárreg's seven herds of wisents was grazing. Over a hundred thousand of the great beasts were peacefully sleeping or chewing cud, but not for long.

It was time to start a stampede.

Chapter 68

Eynon

It was bright enough to see now and the fog was lifting, at least as Eynon flew south. He wasn't sure where to find Fercha and Doethan, but expected his magically augmented ears would hear them before he saw them. Finding the Dâron army's encampment was easy. Most of the soldiers in blue were already on the mustering field immediately north of the small city of tents, opposite Tamloch's gathering forces.

Eynon had been wrong. He saw the battle to the south before he heard it. Green and blue fireballs lit up the ground, splashing off wizards' shields. Lightning blasts tracked jagged arcs, then thunder boomed, hurting Eynon's ears. He canceled his listening spell. Two blue wizards—one with auburn hair that looked like a dandelion in seed—were trying to hold off six wizards in green.

Imitating a hunting gryffon, Eynon hurtled down into the battle near Doethan and Fercha. He shouted for them to close their eyes, then released a tiny fraction of the energy stored in his red magestone as light. A bright red ball appeared in the middle of the opposing wizards, a thousand times brighter than stepping out into noon sunlight from a dark cave. The ten green wizards paused their attack to recover, giving Eynon a moment to talk to Doethan and Fercha.

"Is that Verro's surprise?" asked Eynon, pointing to a wide gate between two trees ahead of them. "Is he going to send a herd of his own wisents through to attack us?"

"No," said Doethan, "but just as bad, if not worse. Thousands of southern Clan Landers are on the other side of that gate, about to come through."

"We have to destroy the gate from this side," said Fercha. "It's the only way to stop them."

Eynon nodded. He looked at the gate closely. Only six of the ten wizards nearby had been attacking—the other four were holding shields over the top, bottom, and sides of the gate, protecting the circuit of powdered magestone from damage. The center of the gate itself was unguarded. He pointed to his pulsing red magestone.

"I'm going through," said Eynon. "Maybe I can stop them *before* they cross over?"

"Don't destroy their side of the gate before you return," said Doethan. "We need you here."

The six wizards in green were recovering from almost being blinded.

"Time to go," said Eynon. He sped off toward the gate.

"Wait!" shouted Fercha. "Verro..."

Eynon didn't hear the rest of Fercha's warning. He transitioned through the interface, flying near the top of the rectangle. Once across, he initially saw tens of thousands of barbaric Clan Landers wearing tartan blankets wrapped around their waists and not much else. Most carried spears and swords of varying lengths. Many held wicker shields.

The braying sound of a hundred sets of bagpipes filled the valley where the Clan Landers were gathered, sounding like packs of wolves being tortured under a full moon. Eynon thought the barbarians looked like the opposite of the pictures of the Roma legions he'd seen in Robin Goodfellow's *Peregrinations*. The legionnaires looked exactly alike in standardized armor, shields and weapons while no two of the Clan Landers looked alike. Most of the warriors below Eynon were covered in fiercely swirling blue tattoos. Eynon was glad his cousins who'd fought off southern Clan Landers hadn't shared their experiences with him when he was small. He would have had nightmares for months.

Near this side of the gate Eynon spotted four figures in more familiar Dâron-style leather armor. It was Fox, Oaf, Dolt, and Fool—the men from Mastlands he'd encountered going down the Rhuthro with Merry. They were standing on a small hill to the left of the gate. A crossbow bolt from Fool buzzed past Eynon's ear like an angry wolfhornet. Eynon triggered his shields.

I'm an idiot, he thought. *I should have put my shields up before I went through the gate.*

Below, he saw Fool cocking his crossbow and loading another bolt. Eynon ascended and moved away from the gate. Presiding over the far end of the valley was a tall mountain that reminded Eynon of a great seated bear, with its arms the hills that defined the valley's wide floor. The mountain was rocky and covered with talus, the slippery fragments of rock Eynon had found a challenge to cross when he'd first left home to start his wander year. The top third of the mountain was still blanketed with snow. This mountain wasn't anything like the massive purple peaks around Melyncárreg, but by the standards of a young man from the Coombe it was big enough.

More crossbow bolts and an orange fireball hit Eynon's shield as he reconnoitered. He flew higher as the bagpipes' cries grew louder. The Clan Landers were ready to go through the gate. Eynon's red magestone pulsed hot and fast, strobing crimson light across the snow near the top of the mountain. Lightning struck his shield and sent small, tingling jolts of electricity inside it, making the hairs on his arms stand up. The Clan Land wizards' attacks made Eynon's red magestone even more eager to release its energy.

He didn't turn around to see how many pursued him until he made it to a spot a hundred feet above the mountain's white summit. Five Clan Land wizards were closing on his position. Each had a strong protective shield.

Eynon bled off a tiny portion of the energy from his red magestone to make his own spherical shield as thick and strong as possible. He sent an anchoring spear of solidified sound from the base of his shield and sank it twenty feet into the stone of the peak. Then he leaned back and gave his red magestone permission to release the energy it had stored when it helped him freeze the river. At the last second, Eynon called on his blue magestone to moderate the blast, so the top of the mountain was only struck a hammer blow, not disintegrated.

He was lucky his blue magestone could act fast enough. Eynon bounced around the interior of his shield like he was rolling down a steep hill inside a barrel. The blast above his head had driven the spike so deep into the rock at the peak that the bottom third of his shield was embedded there. Eynon shook his head to clear it and looked up. A sphere of crimson energy was only now contracting. It still illuminated the land like the light of a dozen suns.

Down into the valley, Eynon saw the true damage he'd done. His fireball had melted the snow on the mountain all it once. It cascaded down, turning the talus slope into a wave of churning fragments of stone that washed over the southern Clan Land barbarians like a flood made of knives. The lucky ones nearest the gate ran through it ahead of the slurry of talus, but most of the Clan Landers had been knocked off their feet by the blast and caught in the deadly wave coming down the mountain.

Eynon swooped down the mountain behind the melted snow and talus and examined the gate. It was still functioning. Demoralized Clan Landers were still crossing over, wet and covered with cuts and bruises from sharp rocks. The Mastlanders stood defiantly atop their small hill. The initial blast had clearly knocked them over, but now they were back on their feet. Oaf and Dolt screamed at Eynon as he flew over their heads. Eynon stopped for a moment.

"Why are you fighting with barbarians?" he asked. "You're men of Dâron."

"Are you really that stupid?" asked Fool.

"What do you mean?" asked Eynon. He didn't like being called stupid, especially by Fool.

"You and Derry's daughter are the reasons we're with the clans now," said Fox. "Derry's daughter wouldn't go along with our fun and said she'd tell the earl."

"We didn't wait around to be banished," said Fool.

"Seems like you made your own trouble," said Eynon.

"And you've made plenty of trouble for yourself," said Fox. "Enough Clan Landers made it through to attack Dâron's royal army from the rear."

"I'll have to do something about that," said Eynon.

He crossed the barrier at twenty feet above the ground and saw the result of the floodwaters that had shifted through the gate to Dâron.

The four green wizards closest to the gate had been caught in the deluge and washed away. Doethan and Fercha used planes of solidified sound to push the remaining six surprised Tamloch wizards through the wide gate's interface before they recovered from the shock. Fercha stared at Eynon and raised an eyebrow. Doethan nodded at Eynon and the young wizard used a fraction of the remaining power in his red magestone to burn up the sparkling rope covered with magestone fragments that formed the upper side of the gate. Tiny bits of magestones fell like glittering rain.

"Well done!" said Doethan as he circled Eynon on his flying disk. "I don't know *what* you did exactly, but it's hard to argue with your results."

"It might have been better if you'd stopped *all* the Clan Landers, not just most of them," noted Fercha. They saw perhaps two thousand warriors wearing tartans digging themselves out of piles of talus and searching for shields and weapons. The Clan Landers didn't look happy. They eyed the Dâron army's encampment not far to the north.

Two blonde girls with long braids circled Eynon, Doethan and Fercha on small gold dragons.

"Hello, Eynon," said Sigrun.

"This is awesome!" said Rannveigr, staring down at the aftermath of the flood. "Are those southern Clan Landers? I've never seen any of them before."

"Yes, they're southern Clan Landers," said Eynon. "There are eight or ten thousand of them on the other side of the gate I just closed."

"Wow!" said Rannveigr. She moved her head and her braids swung back and forth, emphasizing her excitement.

"Could you take a message back to your parents?" asked Eynon.

"I see where this is going," said Rannveigr.

"I'd be glad to," said Sigrun. "Bifurlanders haven't tested their warriors against southern Clan Landers yet either. They look like they'd be more fun to fight than legionnaires."

"See if Bjarni can land troops north of here soon enough to prevent the Clan Landers from sacking our encampment," said Fercha.

"We'd really appreciate it," said Doethan.

"We'll hurry," said Rannveigr.

"Please warn your mother and father about the ice across the river to the north," said Eynon.

"We know about that," said Sigrun. "We watched you do it."

"You were *awesome,*" said Rannveigr.

Eynon smiled. "Thank you," he said, giving a small bow to both girls.

"You might also tell him to send enough ships up to the ice to form a broadside wall along it," Eynon suggested.

"Why should they do that?" asked Rannveigr.

"Odds are good you'll be able to collect a lot of Tamloch soldiers to ransom back to King Túathal," said Eynon.

"That's not *fun,*" said Rannveigr.

"I'll pass the word," said Sigrun. She turned her dragon to the east, ready to leave.

"Thank you," said Eynon. "You should find plenty of meat on the hoof to roast for tonight's dinner, too."

"Wow!" said Rannveigr. "We're going to have a feast!"

"Come along, cousin," said Sigrun.

The two girls leaned forward on their gold-scaled mounts and soon were just dots against the eastern horizon.

"If you hurry, you can get back to Tamloch's army in time to see your surprise pay off," said Fercha.

"Aren't you coming?" asked Eynon.

"No," said Doethan. He glanced over at Fercha. She seemed deep in thought. "We still have to worry about Verro."

Chapter 69

On Túathal's Platform

A bald scout-wizard with a fringe of gray hair landed on the observation platform near the king, Duke Néillen, and Princess Gwýnnett. Uirsé, the dark-haired and earnest young wizard Verro had assigned to King Túathal, stood unobtrusively in a back corner.

"Report," barked Túathal. "What did you learn?"

Uirsé felt a flash of resentment inside at the king's tone. Verro's voice was honey; Túathal's sour wine. She'd heard the king speak to her that way often enough and felt sorry for the bald scout-wizard. She thought his name was Calvi.

"The ice is more than two feet thick, Sire. Your Grace," said the scout-wizard. "It's clearly a product of wizardry and looks strong enough to support an army, should the Roma choose to cross the river."

"They're not crossing already?" asked the duke.

"No, Your Grace," said Calvi. "They've locked their shields into a wall on the far bank, but they're not advancing."

"What are they up to?" Túathal asked Néillen.

"My guess would be hedging their bets," said the duke. "Perhaps they're double-crossing Dâron and intend to wait and see who's winning before choosing sides?"

Uirsé shook her head, confident none of the others except Calvi could see her. Twisted minds always looked for devious answers.

"Send wizards to break up the ice with fireballs," said the king to Tairí, the wizard Verro had assigned to Duke Néillen. "I don't care *what* Quintillius has in mind, I don't want him on this side of the river."

"We don't have wizards to spare for that, Sire," said Tairí. "They're all to the south."

"Just do it," Túathal commanded.

"Yes, Your Majesty," said Tairí. The wizard jumped over the railing in a rush to get away from the king.

Uirsé was pleased Tairí was holding his flying disk when he leapt.

"Who froze the river?" the king asked the scout-wizard. "Has Ealdamon returned from the dead?"

"Other flying scout-wizards saw an old man fitting Ealdamon's description landing near the river," said Calvi. "Of course, I fit that description as well. There's no guarantee it was Ealdamon."

"What about the young one who threw that fireball?" asked the duke.

"It could be him as well," said the bald wizard, "but it's unlikely."

"Why so?" asked Princess Gwýnnett. "Don't underestimate the young. Look at Dârio."

Túathal didn't comment. He was thinking about soon being able to educate his son and turn him into a worthy heir, the sort of monarch who would never be underestimated.

"Ealdamon was in his forties when he froze the Abbenoth, princess," said Calvi. "It's hard to believe a young wizard would have the knowledge needed to perform such a feat."

Unless Ealdamon taught him, thought Uirsé. *Túathal considers himself astute, but Verro is the wiser brother.*

Tairí floated back up to the platform and nodded to King Túathal to indicate his orders were being followed. A pair of less than powerful wizards who enjoyed Verro's liberal hand with beer and hard cider had been dispatched to try their hand at melting ice. Verro had thought them only fit to run messages, and didn't have faith in them doing even that well. "Your Magesty," he said.

The king glared at Tairí. He didn't like being interrupted during interrogations.

"Wizards have been sent, Sire," said Tairí. He tried, but failed to disguise a tremor in his voice.

"Hrrumph," said Túathal. He returned to his previous train of thought, answering Calvi. "I can think of another wizard in Dâron who could do it."

"Who might that be?" asked Duke Néillen.

"Fercha," said Princess Gwýnnett, making it sound like a curse.

"Correct," said the king. "But it doesn't matter now *who* did it. The legions aren't crossing the river..."

For now, said Uirsé silently.

"...and everything is ready for us to crush Dâron on the field." Túathal turned to Duke Néillen. "Give the order to advance."

"With pleasure, Your Majesty," said the duke. He nodded to Tairí, who triggered prearranged signals notifying the other commanders that it was time.

Pipes began to wail, except in the cavalry units. The horses didn't like them. Drums echoed across the mustering field, calling all units to make ready. Túathal watched with pride as the lances of his heavy armored cavalry snapped up, the green pennants near their tips waving in the early morning breeze.

Beside the king, Princess Gwýnnett heard the drumming grow louder. It came from the west and sounded more like thunder than sticks hitting stretched skins. She looked in that direction, expecting storm clouds, but the sky was clear. The fog had vanished. *It was one of those crystal-clear spring days that made you glad to be alive,* she thought. Gwýnnett was still puzzled by the thunder and its increasing volume.

Unbidden, Uirsé stepped on her flying disk and rose up to scan the western horizon. If her king wasn't fast enough to command her, she could take the initiative to report on the phenomenon herself. All she could see to the west was a dark black line and a slowly rising cloud of dust. *Could it be a tornado? No, the dust would be higher—a spinning funnel, not close to the ground.* Uirsé crafted lenses to help her see better at a distance. It took her a few seconds to focus. When she did, all she saw were churning legs and thick-furred brown bodies splotched with curly black hair—and horns. Large, sharp horns.

Uirsé descended slowly. The king was staring west, along with Tairí, the duke, and the princess. The king noticed her out of the corner of his eye and summoned Uirsé to the front of the platform near the others.

"Report," barked Túathal. "What did you see?"

Uirsé was uncertain. She wasn't sure *what* she'd seen. The only animal remotely like these was one she'd seen in Tamloch's royal zoo on the palace grounds in Riyas. It was old and mangy, its fur falling out in places, and one of its horns had been sawed off—probably as a trophy, she supposed. She did remember the name of the beast on the side of its enclosure, though.

"Spit it out, you foolish child," the king insisted. "Don't keep me waiting."

Uirsé's stomach knotted and her throat grew tight, but she managed to squeeze out an answer.

"I'm not sure, Your Majesty. Your Highness. Your Grace," she said, "but I think it's wisents. Thousands and thousands of wisents."

Túathal turned to Tairí. "Get me Verro! I don't care what you have to do, but tell him to come here immediately. Tell him it's an emergency."

"Yes, Your Majesty," said Tairí. Standing behind the king, he looked like a frightened rabbit.

"Where's my head?" said Túathal. He reached for a plain gold ring on his right hand and removed it. With a word he commanded it to expand. "Come on, come on," said the king. "Answer me!"

Túathal glanced up and noticed the others still standing nearby.

"Get away," he ordered. "I need to talk to my brother in private."

Everyone gave the king room. Uirsé created a ten-minute privacy bubble around Túathal and shifted her feet to look west again. The front edge of the stampeding herd was colliding with the right flank of the Tamloch army. Like a hand shoving unit markers across a sand table, the soldiers on the right flank pushed against the troops in the center and those in turn ran east, colliding with the left flank. Everywhere, soldiers were dropping their weapons and shields to move faster. The calvary units made the best time. They tossed their lances to the ground and rode east toward the river with tens of thousands of wisents on their heels and hooves.

Tamloch's knights might have stood to fight, but their steeds would not. The caught the wisents' panic and sped toward the rising sun. When they reached the frozen river, they couldn't stop. Horses slid and skidded on the ice, tossing their armored riders and sending them out toward the island in the middle of the river like stones flung by children for their amusement. They were joined by more soldiers and more wisents as the majority of Tamloch's army moved out onto the ice.

Uirsé adjusted the lenses that let her see farther. She saw wisents smash into soldiers and go down. Some of the big beasts hit the ice and just slid, tossing fighters into the air as they passed. Those fighters landed on other fighters who bounced off wisents until the entire frozen river was a confused, writhing mass of humans, horses, and wisents. The luckiest soldiers had reached the island and climbed trees. A few wisents calmly grazed on new leaves in the undergrowth below them, no longer driven by the urge to stampede.

Looking to the right, at the south edge of the ice, Uirsé noticed that Bifurlander dragonships had anchored their lengths flush against the frozen surface. *There's no escape into the water in that direction,* she realized. She shook her head sadly. *So many soldiers. So many dead and wounded. So many frightened and injured beasts.*

Someone grabbed Uirsé's arm and slapped her face. It was Túathal. His privacy sphere had ended and he was screaming at her.

"I have to see what's happening," said the king. "Make me lenses!"

Uirsé rubbed her cheek and generated a pair of distance lenses for Túathal. She resolved to talk to Verro about a new assignment as soon as possible and stepped away from the king.

Túathal was angry. No, he was furious. Verro hadn't answered him, so he'd collapsed the golden hoop back into a small ring and returned it to his finger. *Where was his brother, blast it?*

The king's temper grew hotter as he watched what was happening on the ice. The Roma were opening gaps in their shield wall and allowing Tamloch soldiers through to safety if they removed their weapons and armor. Hundreds upon hundreds of troops were taking that option. What looked like golden hummingbirds—*no, small gold dragons*— were plucking men and women out of the chaos on the frozen river and dropping them on the decks of Bifurland dragonships. *More fighters lost,* thought Túathal. *Along with the battle. At least the southern Clan Landers will do the Dâron army damage.*

Túathal pushed down his anger and controlled his frustration.

This was a setback. He could still win the war by surrendering and naming his son as his heir.

Uirsé ignored the king for a few minutes. He would be focused on watching what transpired on the ice for some time. Instead, the young dark-haired wizard turned her gaze back to the west. She could see the last of the wisent herd thundering this way. Odd motions above the wisents attracted her. She saw a wizard—a young one, almost a girl—on a flying disk shooting lightning bolts above the herd. Force-beams of tight light from her fingertips kept the beasts moving straight toward where the Tamloch army had been instead of spreading out.

A huge black wyvern flew near the young wizard. It was encouraging the wisents to rush forward by snapping at them. The wyvern's mouth was wide. Uirsé assumed it was roaring. *I'd run away from that if I were a wisent,* she thought. Then she realized something was on the wyvern's back. She increased her magnification and saw a tall young man and a tiny animal resembling a raccoon were riding the wyvern. *Could today get any stranger?* Uirsé wondered. She laughed to herself. *She might not need to ask Verro for a reassignment in the morning. She and the king might both be locked in Dâron prison cells.*

Uirsé didn't notice four creatures with the heads of eagles and the bodies of lions flying behind the wizard and the wyvern. Princess Gwýnnett was pulling on her shoulder, demanding far-seeing lenses of her own.

Chapter 70

Fercha and Doethan

"What is Verro up to?" asked Doethan. "You know his mind as well or better than anyone."

"I know his body better than anyone," said Fercha.

Doethan rolled his eyes at hearing more than he wanted to hear.

"Túathal knows Verro's mind better than anyone," she continued. "I wish some of Verro would rub off on his brother."

"Not much chance of that after all these years, I expect," said Doethan.

"You're probably right," said Fercha.

The two of them were side by side on their flying disks heading north toward the Dâron army's encampment and Dâron's army itself. They were flying slowly to give Fercha time to think.

"Would it help if I asked questions?" Doethan offered.

"Maybe," said Fercha. "I'll let you know if it doesn't."

"Very good," said Doethan. "Let's go back to the differences between the way the two brothers think. Túathal is as twisted as the Rhuthro winding its way through the marshlands, while Verro is fast and straight, like the river cutting through the gap at Rhuthro Keep."

"Granted," said Fercha. "Túathal's a snake, Verro an arrow."

"The attack by the southern Clan Landers was straightforward," said Doethan. "So was the raid on the quarry near the Coombe. Nothing particularly devious about either one, except planning the quarry raid for dawn, and that's just good strategy."

"Right," said Fercha.

"That means we're looking for something else from Verro that's equally straightforward. It may be audacious, but it won't be devious."

"Keep going," said Fercha. "You're helping me think."

"Where is Dâron most vulnerable?" asked Doethan. "What one thing could Verro do to hurt the kingdom the most?"

"He wouldn't," said Fercha.

"Wouldn't what?" asked Doethan.

"Kidnap Dârio," said Fercha.

"Hah," laughed Doethan. "How *can* he kidnap the king? Dârio's in armor, in the middle of Dâron's army, surrounded by soldiers and protected by wizards."

"Like Hibblig?" asked Fercha.

"We're in trouble," said Doethan.

"With luck, Eynon will be with Dârio by now," said Fercha. "That should help."

"How do you think Eynon would fare against Verro?" asked Doethan. They'd already begun to accelerate the northward movement of their flying disks.

"If Eynon manages to pull off some naive and creative piece of unexpected magic, he might stand a chance," said Fercha, "but I'd feel a lot better if I was there, too."

"I'm not sure if you'd kill Verro or kiss him," said Doethan.

"Neither am I," said Fercha, smiling and shaking her head.

"I'm going to summon Damon," said Doethan. "He can make a direct gate and jump from the Roma camp to Dârio's side in seconds."

"I don't want to run to my father with all my problems," said Fercha.

Doethan stared at her.

"Summon him," she said. "This is too big to let my issues with Damon get in the way of the good of the kingdom."

"I will," said Doethan. "Lock us together and keep me on course while I do."

The two wizards sped north, a shared shield keeping them safe from attacks by Tamloch scout-wizards.

"Uh oh," said Fercha. "We're too late."

"No we're not," said Doethan. "Damon just said he'll be on his way."

"Look up," said Fercha.

Doethan did. Red streamers were ascending in the sky above the center of Dâron's army.

"That's Eynon," he said. "It has to be. Verro's already taken Dârio."

"Maybe not," said Fercha.

Doethan felt a buzzing from one of his rings.

"You go ahead," he said. "You can make better time without me. If you and Eynon and Damon can't handle Verro, nobody can."

"See you soon," said Fercha.

Doethan reset his shield for self-guided flight, removed the buzzing ring, and made it grow.

Chapter 71

With Dâron's Army

"What do you see, Inthíra?" shouted Dârio. "There's too much dust for me to make anything out."

Inthíra descended to stand beside Duke Háiddon and the king. Both men wore coats of plates over their gambesons, but hadn't donned their helms.

"Eynon's surprise is working perfectly," Inthíra said as she shifted her flying disk to hang on her shoulders.

Three Tamloch soldiers and a confused wisent strayed close to the front ranks of the Dâron army. The soldiers were taken prisoner and placed under guard, while the wisent was directed at spear point toward a makeshift pen made from confiscated enemy shields reinforced by solidified sound. Wizards enjoyed roasted meat as much as warriors.

A few minutes later a strange-looking giant deer with wide flat antlers trotted by. It stayed far enough away from the soldiers to avoid capture but prompted speculation about its nature up and down the Dâron lines as it passed in review. Some were curious about whether or not it would be good to eat, while others remarked that its sharp front hooves looked dangerous and could probably do a lot of damage to any pack of wolves or squad of fighters who tried to attack it. One archer wondered if the unusual animal could be ridden. Her mates joked that they'd like to see her try. In the end, the great beast turned back west and headed for the forested uplands located in that direction. Young soldiers asked gray-haired veterans if they'd seen anything like the unusual beast before, but none of them had.

Eleven wizards were arrayed around the king and duke in addition to Inthíra. They had multiple roles, from observing the enemy and delivering messages to defending Dârio, Duke Háiddon, and the duke's senior officers. At present, there wasn't much need for the wizards' defensive role. By Princess Gwýnnett's prior arrangement, Hibblig was one of the wizards attending the king. The belligerent and overbearing mage stared impatiently across the field toward where Tamloch's army had been before the wisents arrived, looking for someone or something he couldn't find. Hibblig nervously smoothed his blue-striped robes and shifted unhappily from foot to foot.

Duke Háiddon noticed Hibblig's odd movements.

"There's a privy past the king's heavy cavalry and twenty yards to the rear," said the duke. "Don't be gone too long and watch your step, especially near the horses."

"Thank you, Your Grace," said Hibblig. He spared a moment to scan the northern horizon again and lingered at some sort of thrown-together log platform before moving off in the direction the duke had indicated. He forgot to look down until it was too late and grimaced as he wiped the sole of his boot on a rock.

"No great loss," whispered Dârio to Háiddon as his mother's favorite wizard walked away.

"Isn't it wonderful," the Duke replied. "No losses at all, and no injuries except for the odd sprained ankle or broken arm soldiers get on every campaign."

"I meant it was no great loss to have Hibblig leave," said Dârio. "The man's lip prints are all over my mother's..."

"Behind you, Your Majesty," said Inthíra. "Turn around, please. You've got a visitor."

Dârio turned and flashed a broad smile.

"Eynon! Welcome!" said the king. "This is no visitor, Inthíra. This is Eynon, from the Coombe, the architect of our victory. He's an honored guest. Hail Eynon!"

Several nearby soldiers who'd been listening to Dârio sent up a ragged cheer of "Hail Eynon!" but it faded fast, since they had no idea what someone named Eynon had done to deserve praise.

Eynon's cheeks turned red. He wasn't used to compliments from royalty.

"No need for that, Your Majesty," said Eynon after a deep breath. "I came to report—and to see the wisents rout Tamloch's army."

"I can understand that," said Dârio. "Every genius likes to see his plans realized—but you're too late. Inthíra says her scout-wizards tell her Tamloch's army is demoralized and neutralized, skating around on the frozen Brenavon with enough wisents to feed the kingdom for half a year. I'll have to come up with a suitable reward for your service, Eynon of the Coombe."

"Thank you, Your Majesty," said Eynon. He could feel blood rushing to his cheeks again and blurted out something he knew he shouldn't say. "I live in the Coombe, Sire, but that's not where I consider I'm *from*. I'm Eynon of Haywall. You've probably never heard of it."

"Of course I have," said Dârio. "From maps, anyway. A king must know the land he rules. Haywall is east of Wherrel, in the central Coombe. You're part of the barony of Cadelluin. How is old Whats-His-Name?"

"The baron?" asked Eynon. "I've never met him."

"His loss," said Dârio.

Eynon was confused and pleased. He never expected King Dârio to have heard of Haywall and was happy the wisent stampede had worked so well.

"Nûd gave me the idea," said Eynon. "He showed me the wisent herd back in Melyncárreg and said we needed to come up with a few surprises of our own. I just put the pieces together."

"I'll have to come up with a suitable reward for Nûd, too," said the king. "Where is he? And where's that wyvern of yours? And Merry, for that matter? I expected her to be standing hip to hip with you."

"There they are," said Eynon, pointing over Dârio's head.

The king, Duke Háiddon, and most of the people nearby followed Eynon's outstretched arm to see a black wyvern and a single wizard on a flying disk gliding toward the army. Archers near the king cocked their bows and nocked quarrels.

"Stand down," said Dario, adding a gesture with both hands pushing toward the ground. "Inthíra, signal to them that it's safe to land."

Eynon laughed when he saw Inthíra's signal. The curly-haired wizard created a blue-tinted solidified sound construct in the shape of a giant hand and used it to beckon his friends down. He waved to Merry and she waved back. As Rocky and Nûd got closer, Eynon spotted his raconette familiar waving, too.

"Chee's here, too, Sire," he told the king.

"Fetch my arming cap, please," said Dârio. "Better keep my helm nearby, too." A pair of royal attendants rushed off to fulfill their king's request.

Eynon could understand why Dârio, with his shaved head, especially needed a padded arming cap under his helm, then he made the connection to his announcement of Chee's impending arrival.

"Don't want your head polished today?" he asked the king.

"Precisely," said Dârio.

There was plenty of space in front of them for Rocky to land. Merry touched down gently beside the wyvern, put her flying disk on her back, and ran to meet Eynon. He'd stepped out from the royal entourage to greet her and they embraced.

"It worked beautifully," said Merry. "The whole herd ran straight down the valley toward the gate. Nûd said that was their usual migration path to their other grazing grounds."

"Wonderful," said Eynon.

"Me, or your plan?" teased Merry.

"Both," said Eynon.

Nûd joined them and Eynon gave him a hug as well.

"Thanks for your help," he told his friend. "I hope Rocky followed instructions."

"He's a good wyvern," said Nûd.

Rocky stretched out his head close enough for Nûd to rub one side of his jaw, then nudged Eynon.

"Who's a good boy," said Eynon, rubbing the other side.

The wyvern let out a satisfied rumble from his chest, then turned and took to the air again. He'd spotted another stray wisent and set off for an early feast of his own that didn't require hours of roasting.

Chee had jumped from Rocky's back to Nûd's shoulder moments earlier. Now he shifted to his usual spot on Eynon's shoulder and eyed the king's shaved head as Eynon, Nûd and Merry walked across the trampled grass to join the king and the others around him. When Eynon was close enough to Dârio, Chee pushed off and landed on the king's shoulder.

Before Chee could start polishing Dârio's head, a nearby retainer handed the king a small cloth bag. Dârio dangled it in front of Chee.

"Want some dried cherries, little fellow?" asked the king, who knew it was a rhetorical question. Chee grabbed the bag, kissed the top of Dârio's head, and jumped back to Eynon. The raconette hid himself in the space on top of Eynon's pack, partially enclosed by the upper section of his flying disk. From time to time, Eynon could hear contented sounds of *chee-chee-chee* behind him.

Eynon had another chance to see Nûd and Dârio together, standing just a few feet apart. The resemblance between the two men was striking. Eynon told himself he'd ask Nûd about it later, in private. The old made-up stories he'd heard and read were full of illegitimate royal children and he didn't want to embarrass his friend by asking about it in public.

Merry didn't seem concerned by how much the two men looked alike. She was talking to the king.

"Hi Dârio," said Merry. "You look good in armor."

Eynon saw Duke Háiddon hide a smile, then a smiled himself when he watched a young woman with brown hair step out from behind the duke to stand beside Dârio. She was poised in a way the girls back in the Coombe could never be, and wore a sky-blue leather jacket over a wine-colored shirt and practical black pants tucked into high black boots. He was surprised to see someone who clearly wasn't a soldier or a wizard here with the king on the battlefield, but assumed it was as safe to be here as anywhere, given that Tamloch's army was skating on not-so-thin ice to the east.

"Who's this?" asked the young woman, indicating Merry.

"Jenet, meet Merry, Merry—Jenet," said Dârio. "She's with Eynon."

Eynon put his arm around Merry's shoulders and smiled at Jenet. Merry looked up at Eynon with a different kind of smile, pleased he was more interested in her than Jenet.

"Any friend of Dârio's is a friend of mine," said Merry.

"I look forward to getting to know you," said Jenet.

The king put his arm around the newcomer. "Jenet is my favorite *shah-mat* partner," he said.

Duke Háiddon cleared his throat.

"Since we're all friends here," said Dârio, "didn't you say something about coming here to make a report, Eynon?"

"Of course. I forgot," Eynon replied. "I'm here to tell you we dealt with Verro's surprise—an attack from the rear by barbarians from the southern Clan Lands."

"Dealt with?" asked Duke Háiddon. "The southern clans could raise a large force. Did Verro build a wide gate like Fercha did for the legions?"

"Exactly," said Eynon. "I had a lot of energy stored in my magestone from freezing the river."

He looked at Dârio, who nodded, remembering how much Eynon's unusual magestone had been pulsing.

"So I went through the gate and released it all at once," Eynon continued. "A couple of thousand Clan Landers got through, but some friends are taking care of them before they can reach our encampment."

"Let me guess," said the king. "You offered Bjarni and Signý's warriors a bit of sport?"

"I told Sigrun and Rannveigr," Eynon replied.

Dârio laughed. "I can figure out the rest," he said.

Duke Háiddon stepped in front of Eynon and offered his hand. The two men shook.

"Congratulations, lad," said the duke. "Not many men can defeat two armies on a single day. Verro is reputed to be a powerful wizard, but you ruined *his* surprise."

"I wouldn't say that," came a new voice from the spot where Rocky had landed. A tall green-robed wizard with dark hair who looked a lot like Nûd *and* Dârio was speaking. He'd been the leader of the attack at the quarry the previous morning. A dozen experienced wizards, also in green robes, surrounded him. The interface of a gate the size of the double doors of the Blue Spiral Tower back in Melyncárreg shimmered behind them.

As if imitating Inthíra, Verro created a green-tinted hand of solidified sound that he used to grab Dârio, lift him over his guards, and firmly hold the young king in place beside him. A thick tendril of force extruded itself from the green hand's wrist, encircled Dârio's neck, and tightened until the young king could barely breathe.

"Verro," said Merry softly. It was quiet enough that everyone heard her.

Eynon reached for his setting and raised his magestone. He launched seven streamers of red fire high into the air.

Chapter 72

Doethan and Salder

Doethan was surprised it hadn't been Eynon's ring vibrating. Instead, it was the counterpart of the ring he'd given Salder, Merry's brother. His old friend Derry was Salder's father and Doethan had advised and assisted the young man as he spied on the court in Riyas.

I hope it's not something serious, thought Doethan. *Salder's true profession couldn't have been discovered. They'd never let him keep his rings if it had.* Doethan knew Salder carried rings linked to Damon and Astrí as well, and was pleased the lad had chosen to contact him.

"Hello, young man," said Doethan as the image on the other side of the expanded ring's connection grew clearer. "How are things in Riyas?"

"I'm not *in* Riyas, Uncle Doethan," said Salder. "I'm in Dâron, south of Brendinas along the Brenavon. Were those stampeding wisents *your* doing or Damon's?"

"I'm there, too," said Doethan. "Just south of the Dâron army's encampment. Unfortunately, the wisents weren't my idea."

"Damon, then," said Salder. "What a brilliant idea. I'd compliment the old man if his head wasn't big enough already."

"It wasn't Damon either," said Doethan. "It was Merry's new friend, Eynon."

"Wonderful," said Salder. "I'd be glad to give *him* a compliment. Her friend's plan with the wisents was more successful than you might realize."

"What do you mean?" asked Doethan.

"Tibbo, Tannis and I are standing at the base of a wooden tower," said Salder. "There's a royal observation platform at the top. We gave cider laced with sleeping drugs to the guards at the base. King Túathal, Princess Gwýnnett, and Duke Néillen are above, with only a pair of wizards to protect them. A small force should be able to capture them."

"Then *shah-mat*," said Doethan. "Checkmate."

"Exactly," said Salder. "Hurry."

"On my way," said Doethan.

He closed the connection and found the ring that paired with one he'd given Inthíra. She'd be closest and would have the most resources. He tried three times, but she didn't answer.

Doethan changed his course from north to northwest. He knew where he could find eight wizards who weren't busy with other assignments.

* * * * *

The eight mages protecting both sides of the gate to Melyncárreg had been happy to hear the rampaging wisents had totally disrupted Tamloch's army. They hadn't been given additional instruction after the last beasts had crossed over and had been taking turns passing through the gate themselves to admire the mountains of Melyncárreg as the first rays of dawn caught their snow-capped peaks. They were all pleased to accompany Doethan to the temporary Tamloch observation tower, once Doethan had told them who was on top.

They circled in quietly from the north, since Doethan assumed Túathal and the rest would be looking south at their enemy or east at their lost army on the ice. He warned them to take particular care with Princess Gwýnnett, since Salder's previous reports had confirmed her loyalty was to herself, not Dâron.

Salder, Tibbo and Tannis met Doethan and the eight blue-robed wizards at the base of the tower. Sleeping guards in green livery were propped up against log uprights. Some were snoring. Salder explained his plan in whispers. Doethan and the eight wizards nodded. They all moved out of sight below the observation tower.

A few moments later, Salder started up the stairs to the platform at the top. He carried an opened bottle of wine, but didn't need to bring goblets. Tairí had delivered them earlier, at Duke Néillen's command. On an earlier trip, he'd seen the goblets and the unopened bottle of red from the Isle of Vines, meant to mark

Tamloch's victory, remained untouched on an empty wooden crate serving as a table at the back of the platform. Several other crates had been carried to the top of the platform to provide makeshift chairs as well.

Uirsé was the only person on the platform to note Salder's arrival. King Túathal was next to Duke Néillen looking out to the southeast at the last of the wisent herd. Their panic had ended and several hundred of the massive beasts were calmly eating grass on the would-be battlefield.

The king was anything but calm, however. He was yelling insults at Duke Néillen with occasional digressions to note the shortcomings of Tamloch's Master Mage and his lack of foresight.

Duke Néillen stood stoically, letting King Túathal's insults bounce off him like pellets of hail. Uirsé didn't like hearing the king berate Verro, especially when his brother wasn't present to defend himself. She wondered if the duke had thoughts of throwing King Túathal over the edge of the platform. Uirsé knew she shouldn't have similar thoughts, but she did.

Tairí stood a few steps behind the king and duke, trying—like Uirsé—to be invisible.

Princess Gwýnnett stood apart from the others. She looked south, toward Dâron's army, and fingered one of the oversized rings on her left hand.

She must be thinking about her son, thought Uirsé. *I wonder if he's more like my Salder—or Túathal?*

Had Uirsé truly been privy to Gwýnnett's thoughts, she would have known the princess was thinking more about Túathal than Dârio. Gwýnnett had come to a decision. She didn't need to be a queen. Being the mother of the king of two kingdoms would be enough.

"Hello, my love," said Salder quietly. Uirsé leaned against Salder's side for a moment, enjoying his solid presence. Her feelings for Salder were one of the things that centered her and helped her cope with Túathal's peremptory commands and tirades.

"It's been awful here," whispered Uirsé. "The king blames everyone but himself for his losses."

Salder put his mouth close to Uirsé's ear. "I'm glad Túathal isn't my king," he said.

"What do you mean?" asked Uirsé.

"I'll explain it later," said Salder. "Have a sip of wine straight from the bottle before I serve the others."

Uirsé looked at Salder, wide-eyed, like he was asking her to commit a crime—against proper manners, at least.

"Let it be a small act of rebellion, my love," said Salder.

Uirsé took the bottle Salder offered. He'd removed the cork. She didn't check the bottle for potions or poisons. Her beloved had shared it with her. She drank.

Salder supported Uirsé with one arm as she slumped. He took the bottle from her hands with the other and eased Uirsé onto one of the empty crates with her back against the rear railing of the platform. Her features were relaxed. It looked like she'd simply fallen asleep. Salder hoped she'd forgive him when she woke.

He kissed her forehead, squared his shoulders and crossed to the opposite side of the back of the platform to collect the goblets. They were still on the silver tray Tannis had given Tairí earlier. Salder hid the original unopened bottle of red behind the crate and filled three goblets with the wine he'd given Uirsé. He cleared his throat.

"Your Majesty. Your Highness. Your Excellency. I've brought you wine," said Salder in a loud voice that carried to the others below.

"Wine would be good," said Princess Gwýnnett. She turned toward Salder and he brought the tray of goblets full of wine toward her.

"I'm your king. Serve *me* first," said Túathal, summoning Salder to him with a wave of his hand. "I'm thirsty."

"Let the princess have her wine," said Duke Néillen. "You can tell me more about my failings as a military commander while you wait."

"How would you like to lose your lands and title," said the king as he turned away from Salder and Gwýnnett to reply to the duke.

"I'll take *this* goblet," said the princess. "It's best to save the one with the most wine for the king."

Gwýnnett took the goblet closest to her then abruptly looked over Salder's head.

"Is that a wizard or a buzzard?" she asked softly.

"Where?" asked Salder. He turned and looked up, but saw nothing.

"Never mind," said the princess. "It's gone now, and good riddance."

"Yes, Your Highness," said Salder. He carried the tray with the remaining two goblets to the king and duke.

"Noble gentles, your wine," he said.

Túathal snatched up the goblet with half an inch more wine, leaving the last one for Duke Néillen.

"To better days than this one," said the duke. He raised his goblet and drank it down. The king grimaced and took several swallows.

Salder was able to take Túathal's partially full goblet from his limp fingers so none of its contents spilled. He put the rescued goblet on the floor of the observation platform next to the sleeping bodies of Duke Néillen and the king and whistled three times. A pool of red wine was slowly working its way over the edge of the platform from the goblet Princess Gwýnnett had dropped when she fell.

Doethan and eight blue wizards on flying disks rose up to the level of the platform. Tibbo had one foot on each of two disks, to better manage his size and bulk. Tannis waved at Salder and smiled from her position behind one of the eight blue-clad wizards.

Tairí stared at the new arrivals for a few seconds, looking like a field mouse surrounded by cats. Then he took his flying disk off his back and jumped over the rail.

Chapter 73

And the Emperor of the Roma

"Let him go," said Duke Háiddon. "Don't you see that you've lost?"

"I haven't lost," said Verro. "Your king is in check."

Dârio brought his hands up to tug at the green tendril around his neck, but it didn't loosen.

Nûd moved forward to get a better look at Verro. Eynon realized why Nûd was interested in Tamloch's Master Mage. The two of were very much alike. They could be older and younger editions of the same man. Both were tall and muscular, with dark hair and eyes. Verro's voice was mellow, while Nûd's was raspy, but that could be due to something as simple as Nûd growing up in the thinner air of Melyncárreg. *Or a cold,* Eynon realized.

Verro saw Nûd near Duke Háiddon and the tendril's tension reduced. Dârio's neck was still trapped, but at least he could draw a full breath.

"Excuse me, sir," said Eynon. "Several other powerful mages are on their way here. You won't want to fight them."

"I don't *need* to fight them," said Verro. "And I'm not here to harm Dârio. I'm here to ensure he doesn't leave until my brother can arrive to surrender."

"You're holding the king of Dâron to make sure he's here so the king of Tamloch can surrender to him?" asked Merry. "That doesn't make any sense. Why would Dârio go anywhere if Túathal is coming to admit his defeat?"

"Because I'll be taking Dârio to Tamloch immediately afterward," said Verro. "Túathal will be naming Dârio his heir."

A small gate opened between Verro's party and the royal guards. Damon stepped out with Quintillius ducking his head to fit through behind him. A *contubernium* of eight legionnaires along with two purple-robed wizards crossed the gate's interface to join them.

Verro and his wizards stood their ground. The newcomers' gate stabilized, and Damon and his Roma companions circled to stand near Inthíra, Merry, Eynon, Nûd and Duke Háiddon.

Eynon was surprised by Quintillius. He was the tallest man Eynon had ever seen and had dark black skin. Previously, Eynon had only come across black-skinned people in illustrations from Robin Goodfellow's *Peregrinations*. The world was full of marvels. Both the wizards with Damon had the same sort of skin. One was a short, well-padded older woman with hair like a black sheep's fleece. The other was a tall, skinny young man not much older than Eynon. The purple of their robes made a striking contrast with their faces. Eynon wondered if any people across the Ocean had striped or splotched skins. He hadn't read of any like that, but there were still so many more books to read.

Damon stepped forward to confront Verro. "Going after young men instead of young women now?" he asked.

Eynon thought the master mages looked like two hungry hounds ready to fight for a bone. He'd never seen as much hatred in Damon's eyes before. These two had history together. *What had Verro done to anger Damon?* Eynon wondered. *It couldn't just be holding Dârio.*

"No," said Verro. "As I'd said before you arrived, when Túathal joins us, he will name Dârio as his heir and unite Dâron and Tamloch."

A gust of wind blew dust around the field where they were standing. Twelve small gold dragons landed two by two. Each pair held nets supporting passengers. King Bjarni, Queen Signý, Astrí and three women in gold-colored robes who were clearly wizards pushed their way out of the netting and got to their feet. The Bifurlanders joined Quintillius and his legionnaires, with Bjarni clasping hands with the tall Governor-General. Astrí moved to stand by Damon's side and put her hand on his arm. Damon smiled.

Sigrun, Rannveigr, and the other blonde and mostly-braided dragon riders swarmed toward Nûd and Eynon, chattering in rapid, high-pitched voices.

"Why is the Tamloch wizard holding the strawberry merchant?" asked Rannveigr.

"It's complicated," said Nûd. He stepped away from the girls and stood on Damon's other side, opposite Astrí.

Nûd spoke to Verro.

"I know who you are," he said.

"Wait," said Merry, looking south. "Someone *else* is coming."

It was Fercha. She brought her flying disk in for a hard, fast landing beside Nûd, kicking up still more dust to join what the gold dragons' wings had raised.

"This wasn't how I wanted the two of you to meet," she said, taking Nûd's hand and locking eyes with Verro.

The tall wizard in green looked at Nûd while everything went silent around him. The dragon riders stopped their conversations to stare. A huge smile filled Verro's face as he realized who Nûd must be. Then the smile was replaced by storm clouds ready to shoot metaphorical, if not actual lightning bolts at Fercha.

Verro released his grip on Dârio and took four quick strides forward to put his hands on Fercha's shoulders.

"You never told me," he said. "Why didn't you tell me?"

"I didn't want my son to be caught up in Túathal's machinations," said Fercha. "Even before he was king he was plotting, turning you into someone more like him and less like the man I married. I didn't want the same thing to happen to Dârianûd."

"Dârianûd?" asked Nûd.

Fercha didn't answer.

"Now what," said Merry, pointing to the north at nine wizards on flying disks approaching the field.

"Who else will show up?" asked Duke Háiddon. "Will the emperor of the Roma with a thousand ships from across the Ocean sail up the Brenavon?"

"If he does, we'll stop him," said King Bjarni.

Quintillius caught Bjarni's eye and nodded his approval. The young dragon riders laughed, sounding like small golden bells.

Eynon saw some of the legionnaires smile as well. He crafted a set of far-seeing lenses from solidified sound and looked north.

"It's Doethan," he said. "And the wizards from the wisents' gate. They've got passengers."

Dârio rubbed his throat for a moment then walked around Fercha and Verro to join Duke Háiddon, Eynon, and Merry. The wizards who'd gated in with Verro didn't try to stop Dârio. When the young king saw the looks on their faces after he turned around, it was clear they were shocked and puzzled by Verro's words and actions. The seven women and five men in green robes crossed their arms and waited for instructions from their leader.

The nine blue-robed wizards landed in the only remaining open spot near where Verro and his companions had appeared. Dârio saw his mother, Princess Gwýnnett, sitting on the back of one of the flying disks. He left Jenet's side and rushed to help Gwýnnett. Jenet was glad to stay as far away from Dârio's mother as possible. Gwýnnett seemed sleepy, but was waking up and able to stand with help from Dârio.

"Thank you, son," she said, smoothing back her hair from the wind of her flight. "You'll be twice the king your father ever was." Dârio escorted his mother to the others.

Salder jumped off Doethan's flying disk and ran to the disk where a wizard, a pretty young woman with dark hair, was beginning to wake. Merry considered joining him to help, but Salder's focus was on the woman he was holding in his arms.

A short man with scarred and tattooed forearms was sleeping on another of the blue-robed wizard's flying disks. Merry watched Tibbo toss the man over his shoulder like a rag doll and put him down gently on a patch of thick grass. Tannis, wearing a white apron, closely followed Tibbo's actions.

She glanced over at the others and realized the tall man who looked like Verro must be King Túathal. If the resemblance alone wasn't enough, he was wearing an impressive green robe trimmed in gold and covered with hundreds of royal Tamloch quatrefoils outlined with gold thread. Túathal was standing, but still a bit unsteady on his feet. Despite that, he looked ready to shout at any-and-everyone within earshot. Then he saw Dârio.

Túathal rushed to stand before Dârio. He fell to his knees, then pulled Dârio's arms down and away from Princess Gwýnnett. Bowing his head, he placed his hands between Dârio's.

"I pledge you my fealty," said Túathal. "You shall be my heir and rule my kingdom after me. Thus shall we end the enmity between our realms."

"He talks a good game," said Eynon.

"Shush," said Merry. "Listen."

Dârio looked down and spoke sternly.

"You've lost, Túathal. You're defeated. Your forces are routed. You will no longer rule in Tamloch."

Princess Gwýnnett smiled at her son. She didn't know how easy it would be to get him back under her thumb, but she was quite glad to see him give Túathal a taste of his own medicine.

"By all rights I should have you executed," said King Dârio. From the corner of his eye, he saw a sly smile cross his mother's lips.

Verro faced away from Fercha when he heard Dârio's words. He and Fercha had been talking quietly while the chaos of all the new arrivals had gone on around them. Now he stared at the young king, his eyes flashing a warning. *Take care what you say next.*

"But I will show mercy," Dârio continued. "I'll send you into exile in a tower somewhere inaccessible, like a pile of rocks off the Isle of Vines. You can plot all you want with the spiders and lizards."

Verro nodded. Fercha moved up to stand beside him. Without Túathal's influence, she'd help him make himself back into the better man he'd been when she first met him.

Túathal stood and glared at Dârio. He took a step back and regarded everyone around him with distaste, then brought his gaze back to Dârio.

"We could have done so much together," said Túathal. "I would have taught you how to be a king who inspires fear and obedience, one truly worthy to rule."

Dârio looked away, then turned back. "Don't make me reconsider my decision," he said.

"You would exile your own father?" asked Túathal.

"You're not my father. Prince Dâri was my father. Tell him, mother," said Dârio.

Princess Gwýnnett hesitated before speaking. "He's right," she said. "Túathal *is* your father."

"That can't be true," said Dârio.

"Unfortunately it is, Sire," said Doethan. "Baron Derry and I saw Túathal enter your mother's chambers the requisite number of months prior to your birth. I performed a consanguinity test using one of Túathal's hairs and confirmed you were his son on the day you were born."

"It's true," said Verro. "My brother bragged about it, saying he'd put a cuckoo's egg in Dâron's royal nest."

"So I'm not the rightful king of Dâron?" asked Dârio.

"With my brother banished to exile, you're the rightful king of Tamloch," said Verro. "You're also my nephew. I'm glad to help you any way I can."

"Let me take that under advisement," said Dârio.

"Spoken like a true king," whispered Eynon.

"Shush," said Merry. She was watching her brother and the young dark-haired wizard. The two were arguing, but they were talking too softly for her to hear. Merry considered using her listening spell, but decided that wouldn't be the best way for her to be a good sister to her brother who'd so recently come back from the dead.

Duke Háiddon stepped close to Dârio and put his hand on the young man's shoulder.

"You'll make a good king, lad, whatever crown you wear," said the duke. "But if you're not the rightful king of Dâron, who is?"

"I can answer that," said Astrí.

Damon tugged at her dark-blue robes as she came forward, but he only managed to slow her down, not stop her.

"Please do," said the duke.

Astrí lowered her hood. "Do you recognize me, Your Grace?"

Duke Háiddon looked at her closely. "We've met many times, but I've never seen your face, good wizard. You do look familiar, but I can't say from where."

"How many times have you walked through the palace gardens?" asked Astrí.

"Dozens of times. Hundreds," said the duke. His eyes unfocused for a moment as he thought about his path through the gardens and what he'd seen there. Thousands of images spun through his brain.

"Subtract more than forty years," said Astrí.

The duke looked back at her, then turned his head toward Fercha.

"You look like *her,*" he said. "Like Fercha."

"Why shouldn't I look like my mother?" asked Fercha.

"I think I've figured it out," said Eynon softly.

"What took you so long?" asked Merry.

Eynon watched Nûd, not the duke and Astrí. His friend was slowly easing away from the crowd, scanning the skies. Eynon took Merry's hand and guided them both closer to Nûd.

"Astrí is your mother," said Duke Háiddon. He looked from Astrí to Fercha to Damon. "And *Ealdamon* is your father?"

"Guilty as charged," said Damon.

"Wait!" said the duke to Astrí. "Now I remember who you remind me of. You look like the statue of Princess Seren near the roses."

Even the Bifurlanders and Roma had heard about Princess Seren. So had the wizards from Tamloch. Everyone was staring at Astrí and talking, wondering if Duke Háiddon's speculation was true.

"My mother is Queen Carys," said Astrí. "Fercha is my daughter. And her son—my grandson—is the rightful king of Dâron."

The crowd began to buzz with excited conversations. Astrí, or Princess Seren, if she was to be believed, scanned the crowd for her grandson, but couldn't find him.

Túathal looked daggers at Verro. His brother's son would be king of Dâron while he couldn't be by *his* son's side ruling Tamloch. It was intolerable. Then waves of intense pain hit him, like sharp rocks in his gut. He fell to the grass, moaning.

Uirsé rushed to her king, with Salder behind her. She put her hands on Túathal's abdomen and sensed the glow of poison inside him. Uirsé looked back at Salder. She was angry, but she needed him.

"Get me milk, or cream, as much as you can find," she ordered. "And eggs. Raw eggs. I need to make him vomit."

Salder nodded and ran toward the Dâron encampment, looking for the closest mess tent. *They might have clotted cheese if they didn't have milk,* he thought.

Dârio turned to his mother, as if expecting some sort of confession from her. Gwýnnett slipped an *I-have-no-idea-what-happened* mask on her face and gleefully contemplated two lovely little words beneath its surface. *Slow acting.*

Unfortunately, wizardry was better at detecting poisons than dealing with their effects. Astrí, Doethan and Verro offered to assist Uirsé. Mafuta, who'd overheard the young Tamloch wizard's instructions to Salder, sent Felix through the gate to the Roma legions to see if he could find something to counteract the poison faster in *their* supplies.

Túathal's face was pale and his skin was clammy. He pulled his knees against his chest and panted against the waves of agony racking his body. It was clear he was dying.

Chapter 74

The Reluctant King

Eynon and Merry missed Túathal's collapse. They were following Nûd west, away from the center of the army. Nûd had moved toward the middle of the field, still dodging the occasional wisent cow or flathorn. Once he was far enough from the gathered dignitaries near Dârio, he started running and calling for Rocky. Eynon and Merry had expected Nûd to stay close to the Dâron lines so he could avoid detection, but he'd outsmarted his friends by shifting direction. By the time they'd figured it out, Nûd was on Rocky's back flying west as fast as the wyvern's wings could take him. To their surprise, he flew over the gate the wisents had used.

Merry spun her flying disk in front of Eynon's to stop him from zooming off in pursuit.

"Wait," she said. "We have to be smart about this. Flying disks aren't much faster than wyverns, if they are at all. Where do you think Nûd's headed? It can't be Melyncárreg."

"It can," said Eynon. "It's his home. He just needs to lose us first."

"I'll bet he won't be *staying* in Melyncárreg if he goes there," said Merry. "It's the first place he'd think we'd look."

"What do you think he's planning then?" asked Eynon.

"I think he'll go to Melyncárreg for supplies, then head off to find a place to hide in the western mountains," said Merry. "I don't know enough to be sure. I've only been to Melyncárreg twice, and didn't see much in daylight, but it looked like there'd be lots of places for a man and wyvern to hide out there and not be found."

"Damon might have some ideas," said Eynon. "My guess is Nûd is flying to the Blue Spiral Tower on the Rhuthro. He wants to take the gate from there to Melyncárreg, skipping all the miles in between."

"We can beat him to the Blue Spiral Tower by taking a gate from Brendinas," said Merry. "I'm sure Fercha has a gate that goes from the capital to her tower."

"I agree," said Eynon, "But I have an idea about where he might stop before he goes all the way to Melyncárreg. He's sweet on my sister."

Chee finished the bag of dried cherries from Dârio and climbed back on Eynon's shoulder. The three of them watched Nûd and Rocky dwindle into a dot on the horizon. The little raconette let out a soft, mournful *chee* as he watched the wyvern disappear.

Merry and Eynon swung back to the gathering on the field and spoke with Fercha. They got directions to her townhouse and the phrase that opened the gate to the Blue Spiral Tower, then flew north, and went through it.

At the tower, Tuto, Fercha's owl familiar, reported a man on a wyvern had come through a supply gate from the Serendipity Supply warehouse in Brendinas and arrived at the tower an hour or so earlier.

Merry thanked Tuto and the two young wizards left the tower flying toward Haywall in the Coombe. Applegarth was nearby to the south, and she missed her mother and father, but she still wasn't sure how she felt about them keeping the fact that Salder was alive from her. It might be a good idea to wait awhile—perhaps a few months—before she came home.

The smile on Eynon's face got bigger the closer they got to his home village. He got along well with his parents and little sister, mostly, and Merry envied him all the aunts, uncles and cousins— real and honorary—he had nearby. It was just past lunch time when they landed in the slate-covered courtyard shared by several cottages. They could tell that Nûd and Rocky had been there recently. Neighbors were out in the courtyard gossiping and three of the middle-sized children from cottages near Eynon's were shoving sticks into a huge pile of cooling wyvern dung.

Chee jumped down from Eynon's shoulder and found a stick of his own. He pried bits of dung from the pile and flung them about randomly. Some hit the children and the other onlookers.

"Stop that," said Eynon. Chee returned to stand near Eynon and Merry, but he didn't return to Eynon's shoulder. *Just as well,* thought Eynon. *He probably smells like wyvern dung.*

Braith came out in the courtyard when she heard the additional commotion caused by Eynon and Merry's appearance. Chee immediately tried to jump on *her* shoulder, but Braith sniffed and fended him off with her apron. The raconette contented himself to sit on one of her boots.

"If you're looking for Nûd you just missed him," said Braith. "He told me you would probably be following him. Nûd said he just wants to be alone to think. What is he worried about?"

"It's a long story," said Eynon.

"You can tell me later then," said Braith. "Who's your friend?"

"This is Merry," said Eynon. "Merry, this is my little sister, Braith."

"Eynon's told me a lot about you," said Merry. "You've got a lovely smile."

"Thank you," said Braith. "I've also got too many freckles. You're very pretty."

"Thank *you*," Merry replied. "So are you. I think you've got exactly the right number of freckles."

"She's nice," Braith informed her brother. "Are you going to marry her?"

Eynon smiled at Merry and she smiled back.

"Probably," he said.

"Probably?" asked Merry.

"Make that, 'Yes, if she'll have me,'" said Eynon.

"Good," said Braith.

"*Very* good," said Merry. She licked her upper lip suggestively and Braith giggled.

Eynon's cheeks started to turn red and he changed the subject.

"Where are Mom and Dad?" he asked.

"Dad's at the milking barn helping to dig out the cold storage pit," said Braith. "Some of the stones fell in and they decided to enlarge it when they repaired it."

"I'm glad I'm not with him hauling rocks then," said Eynon. "And Mom?"

"She's visiting in Brynhill, trading a wheel of cheese for flower bulbs for the garden," said Braith. "She said they'll be really lovely when they bloom."

"That should take the rest of the day," said Eynon. "Tell them I'm sorry I missed them."

"Which way did Nûd go when he left?" asked Merry.

"He asked me to tell you he was going to look for a gate in the baron's castle in Caercadel," said Braith, "but he's really going to the quarry."

"Why would he go back there?" asked Merry. "The last time we went there we were attacked."

"He said he felt like something was drawing him there," said Braith. "Nûd thought it would be a good place to think. The quarry workers are helping to build a new storehouse off the square in Wherrel, so I told him the quarry should be quiet and deserted."

"Thanks for the details," said Eynon. "Did he try to kiss you?"

"No," said Braith. She smiled at Eynon and Merry. "But I kissed him."

"Don't grow up too fast, little sister," said Eynon as he gave Braith a hug.

"It was just on the cheek," said Braith.

"Good," said Eynon.

Merry winked at Braith behind Eynon's back.

"Wait just a second," said Braith.

She smiled at her nosy neighbors and the small children with sticks, then stepped back into her family's cottage. Chee went for a ride on Braith's boot and returned with clean paw-hands a couple of minutes later.

"I washed him off," said Eynon's sister. "He pumped the sink and I made him use soap."

"Thank you," said Eynon.

"This is for you," said Braith. She was holding a napkin knotted around something bulky. "I made lunch for Nûd, but he didn't stay for me to give it to him. I think he was worried about all the attention Rocky was getting."

Braith handed the knotted napkin to Eynon and accepted hugs from Eynon, Chee, and Merry. Chee moved back up to Eynon's shoulder. The two young wizards and the raconette waved goodbye to Braith and Eynon's neighbors and flew northwest toward Wherrel.

It wasn't long before they were circling the quarry. Rocky was easy to see—his black bulk stood out against the quarry's green-tinted floor. It looked quite a bit different at midday.

Nûd was sitting on a boulder with his elbow on his knee and his chin in his palm. It was clear he was thinking. He waved and didn't seem too unhappy to see them.

Eynon and Merry landed a dozen yards away and didn't address Nûd immediately. Their friend's mind seemed preoccupied. They assumed he was concerned about recent revelations.

An odd-looking green triangle of some strange material poked out from the floor of the quarry close to Eynon's flying disk. It was big, nearly four inches thick, and almost as tall as Eynon's outstretched arm. He waved Merry and Nûd over, but only Merry joined him.

"It looks like some kind of sail," said Merry.

"Leave it alone," said Nûd from his boulder. "Something tells me it will be nothing but trouble."

"Don't tell Eynon to leave it alone," said Merry. "Now he'll have to find out what it is."

"You won't change my mind," said Nûd.

"Change your mind about what?" asked Eynon.

"About being king," said Nûd.

"You'd be a good king," said Eynon.

"Not wanting to be king will probably make you a better king," said Merry. "At least from the stories I've read. I've only met two kings and Túathal is definitely a *bad* king. I'm not sure about Dârio yet."

"I like him," said Nûd.

"You look like him," said Eynon. He paced around the strange green triangle and his red magestone began to pulse rapidly.

"I asked you to leave that thing alone, whatever it is," said Nûd. "I've got a bad feeling about it."

Merry teased Nûd and distracted Eynon simultaneously.

"If you don't want to be king, we're fine with that, aren't we, my love?"

"What?" said Eynon. He was on his knees now, scraping pebbles away from the base of the triangle with his fingers.

Nûd stood and found one of the lengths of wood the quarry workers used as levers. He held it up in his right hand.

"If I were king," he said. "I'd make it a royal command."

"Yes, Your Majesty," said Eynon. He got to his feet and stared at the triangle.

"Do you like the sound of that title?" asked Merry. "Your Majesty," she said, giving Nûd a deep bow.

"Not really," said Nûd. He glanced at the knotted napkin on Eynon's flying disk and dropped his wooden sceptre. "Is that my lunch?"

"It's our lunch," said Merry.

"I want to eat it back at your cottage," said Nûd. "Let's go."

"You want another chance to kiss my sister," teased Eynon.

"She kissed *me*," Nûd protested.

Merry stepped on her flying disk and Nûd climbed aboard Rocky's back. Chee ran over to the green triangle, jumped up to stand on its edge, and wiggled its tip back and forth.

Eynon was surprised the triangle moved. He'd thought it was like a sheet of green slate used to cover the roofs of stone houses in Wherrel. He stepped over to the triangle to retrieve Chee and leaned against what Merry had called a *sail* to see if the whole thing was flexible, not just the tip. It was. The triangle bent over under Eynon's weight, then sprang back, tossing him—and Chee—onto the scree on the quarry floor.

Getting back up slowly, Eynon collected Chee and got on his flying disk. The two wizards and the wyvern rose above the quarry and looked down to see the green triangle continue to move and free itself from the stone around it. The sail was revealed to be the end of a tail as big around as a wisent. They saw the ground shake and rocks fall from the quarry wall as the spiked and scaled back of a great green monster as large as Fercha's tower began to free itself from its prison of stone.

To be continued in the third book of the Congruent Mage series:

The Congruent Dragon

Please visit

www.CongruentMage.com

for more information about
Eynon, Merry and their friends

Sign up for the Congruent Mage mailing list
on the web site to get advance notice of publication
and receive a free short story set in the author's
Xenotech Support universe.

XenotechSupport.com/mailing-list

Additional Material

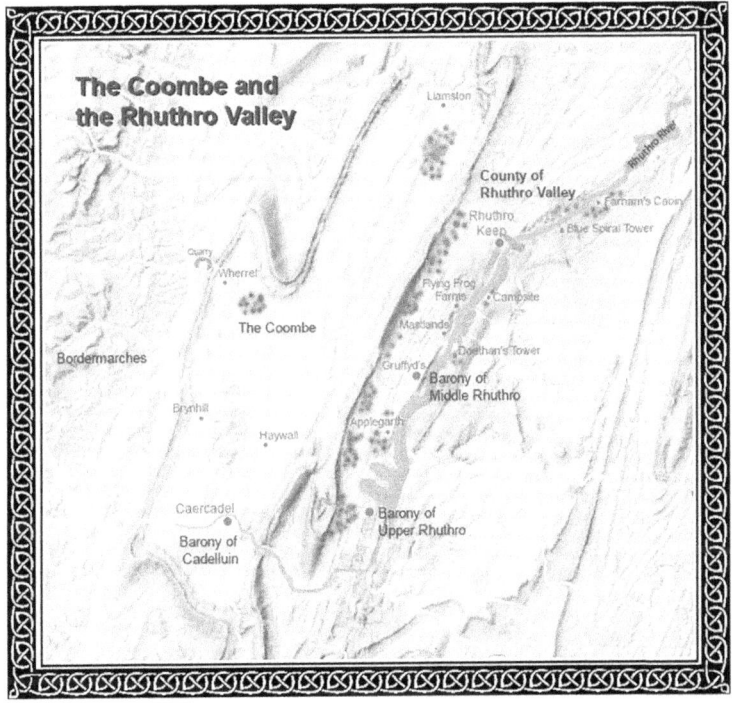

A larger color version of this map is available at:

CongruentMage.com/maps.html

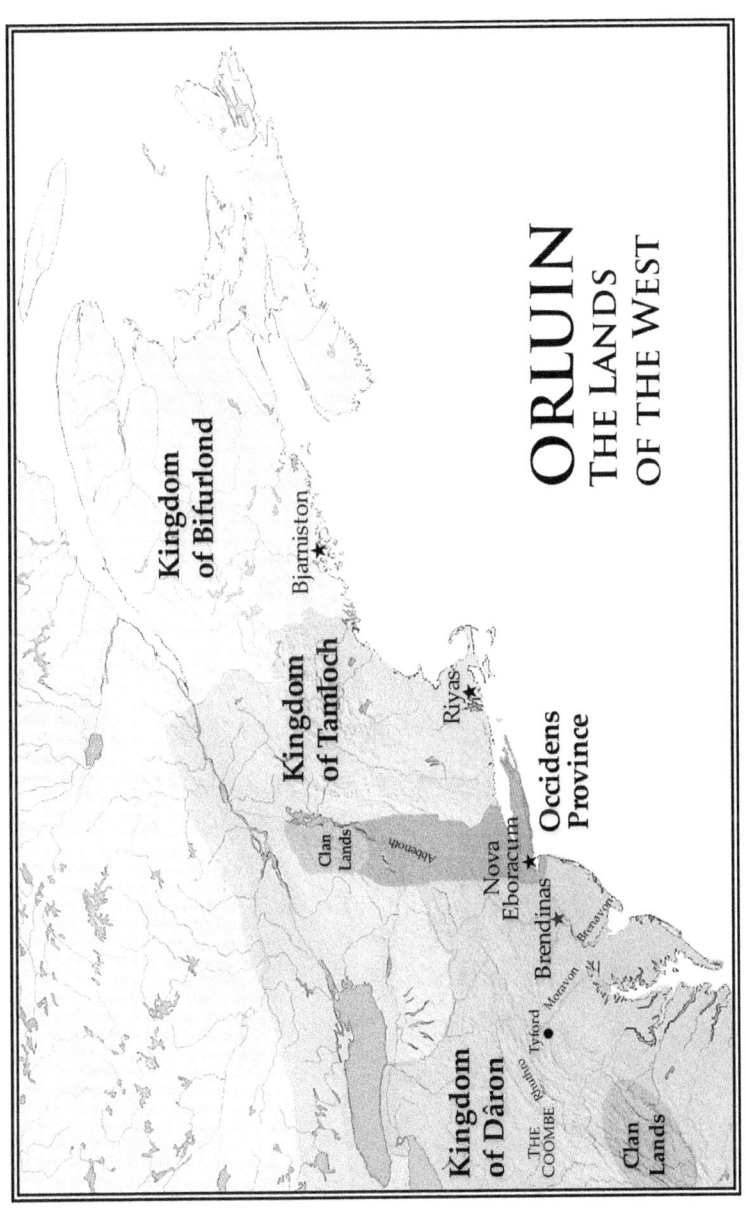

A larger color version of this map is available at:

CongruentMage.com/maps.html

THE BATTLE
OF THE BRENAVON

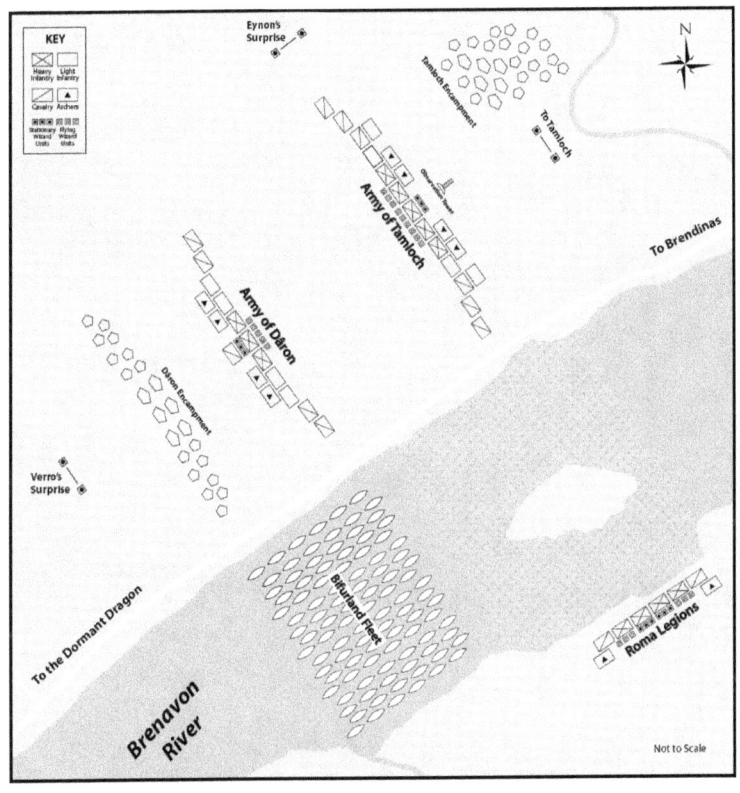

A larger color version of this map is available at:

CongruentMage.com/maps.html

Royal Dâron Family Tree
Dates are recorded from the year the First Ships landed

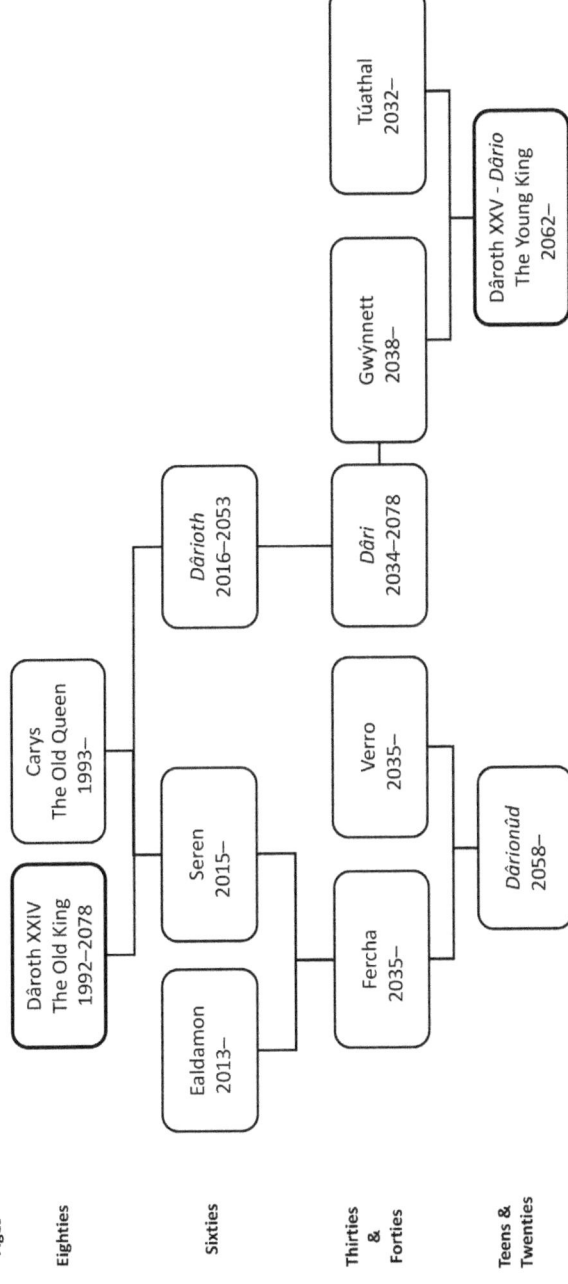

Character Ages

Eighties

Sixties

Thirties & Forties

Teens & Twenties

Dâroth XXIV
The Old King
1992–2078

Carys
The Old Queen
1993–

Dârioth
2016–2053

Ealdamon
2013–

Seren
2015–

Dâri
2034–2078

Gwýnnett
2038–

Túathal
2032–

Fercha
2035–

Verro
2035–

Dâroth XXV - *Dârio*
The Young King
2062–

Dârionûd
2058–

Royal Tamloch Family Tree

Dates are recorded from the year the First Ships landed

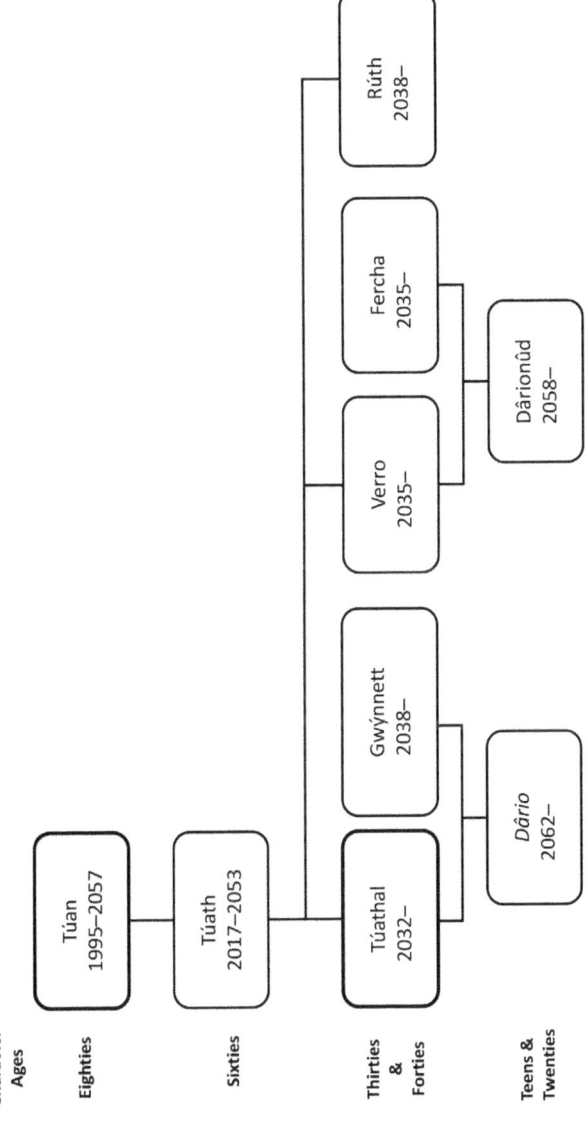

Character Ages		
Eighties	Túan 1995–2057	
Sixties	Túath 2017–2053	
Thirties & Forties	Túathal 2032–	Gwýnnett 2038–
	Verro 2035–	Fercha 2035–
		Rúth 2038–
Teens & Twenties	Dário 2062–	Dârionûd 2058–

www.ingramcontent.com/pod-product-compliance
Lightning Source LLC
Chambersburg PA
CBHW050022030726
47506CB00001B/70